A Seaside Story

A NOVEL

C. J. Foster

Foundations Book Publishing
Brandon, MS 39047
www.FoundationsBooks.net

A Seaside Story
By C.J. Foster

ISBN: 978-1-64583-027-6

Cover by Dawné Dominique Copyright © 2020
Edited and formatted by: Steve Soderquist

Published in the United States of America
Worldwide Electronic & Digital Rights
Worldwide English Language Print Rights

To my beloved mother...

Table of Contents

Chapter One

"The Strip is no place to take the boy," Lydia Toscano declared, and not for the first time since Kate had originally announced her intentions.

The latter, accustomed to her mother's annoying affinity for beating even the most inconsequential issues to death, looked up from the last of her packing. "Vegas isn't just The Strip, Mom," Kate reminded her, amused by the older woman's perceptions that the entire city was comprised of mob-run casinos, superficial celebrities, and quickie wedding chapels that featured serenades by Elvis impersonators.

"How should I know?" Lydia retorted. "It's all that boss of yours ever lets you write about."

Kate sighed, mindful of the reality that Lydia rarely read anything past *Vegas Essential*'s table of contents because it was a glamorous world that she simply couldn't relate to. She was mindful as well the unsettling events of the past week had made her mother even edgier and more contrary than usual. Kate absently tucked her black pumps into the space between her bathrobe and quilted lingerie bag. "I think a little change of scenery might do him a world of good," she said. Unspoken between them hovered the painful words neither one was quite ready to accept.

Cassy isn't coming back. Cassy is dead.

Lydia was now clucking her tongue as she paced the length of Kate's former bedroom. "You have no idea what you're getting yourself into," she warned. "A boy like that—"

"His name's Jimmy, Mom."

Lydia glared at her. "Are you saying I don't know my own grandson's name?"

"Well, as infrequently as you use it..." Kate let the sentence go unfinished, opting instead for a diversion that would allow her to finish her packing in peace. "I'll need you to get me the doctor's phone number in case there's any problem filling prescriptions."

Lydia put both hands on the armrests to push herself out of the comfy depths of an overstuffed—and much-circulated—chair that had seen better days. It had begun its service in the living room when Kate's parents were newlyweds, gravitated to the master bedroom as the bedtime-story chair when Kate and Cassy were little, then finally found its current niche when Kate left home to go to college. At this moment, though, the only thing Kate could see was how fatigued and fragile her mother suddenly looked to her as she crossed the room and stepped out into the hallway.

The Toscano women had always shared a lean physique and varying degrees of sun-kissed blonde hair. From her late father, Kate had also inherited deep green eyes and a defiant chin. On what had become too infrequent visits lately to the Jersey shore of her birth, she'd catch herself looking at the now silver-haired Lydia and wondering how much of what she saw was a glimpse into the future. Was it just the hardships of life in general that had taken such a perceptible toll on a woman who had yet to turn sixty, Kate wondered? Or had whatever enthusiasm Lydia once embraced for getting up every morning fallen by the wayside when she became a widow?

As she folded the silk jacket of the suit she had worn to Cassy's funeral, her gaze wandered to the open window.

To the east and across Ocean Avenue lay a broad strip of beach that flirted with a glistening Atlantic. In the early 1900s, Avalon Bay had been a booming seaside resort that brought stylish tourists from New York, Pennsylvania and as far away as Boston. Even its brief resurgence in the late '70s and '80s, as many of the surrounding shore towns began to decline, had introduced new generations to the tempo of the Jersey shore and invited pushcart entrepreneurs and street performers to respectively hawk their wares and talents to the fun-loving crowds.

Even its reputation as a playground for mobsters hadn't suffered from the popularity of shows on TV, though Kate was fairly certain that any wannabe thugs she may have encountered during her upbringing weren't exactly bright enough to be classified as Mafia kingpins. She caught herself smiling in reminiscence of the neighborhood pizza parlor she and her friends liked to frequent after football games.

Come next weekend, Memorial Day, a predictable trickle of sun-worshippers in all manner of swimsuits and large-brimmed hats will converge on what had been the old Boardwalk, though never in the profitable numbers of an earlier era. A part of Kate half-wished she could extend her stay an extra week and introduce her nephew to some of the sillier rituals associated with the advent of summer by the sea: Noisy arcades, games of chance, and a neon Ferris wheel harkened back to simpler times when kids and adults didn't rely on iPods, cell phones, or text messaging to keep them entertained. That Cassy had fashioned no shortage of excuses the past five years not to bring her son to the old stomping grounds only fueled the irony that his first time in his grandmother's seaside house should be under such unhappy circumstances.

To the west and dismally visible above the treetops were the smokestacks of the plastics factory where many a local had earned his or her first paycheck working an assembly line. For some inexplicable reason, advances in technology and foreign outsourcing had yet to breach Avalon Bay and thus, nudge this fire-belching, rusted dragon into a long-overdue state of retirement. Until that day came, however, it remained a dreary environment of regimentation, low pay, long hours, and minimal advancement that fostered two kinds of individuals in Kate's view: those who welcomed the daily monotony as an excuse not to think about the past, and those who regarded factory tenure of any length as a rapidly closing door to the future.

Her father had fallen somewhere in-between. He was a hard worker whose company loyalty was a mix of not wanting to stray too far from his hometown roots and being aware that he hadn't been able to get the education required for a desk job. It was either the factory or become a security guard like his friends Sean Neal and Rob Lorenzi. Jim Toscano chose the former so he could be home in the evenings with his family.

"Make me proud, Katie," he had always told her, lamenting his blue-collar prison. A lump came to her throat whenever she remembered his request, bringing with it the regret that he hadn't lived long enough to see her rise to the challenge and become a well-paid featured writer.

The silence of her nostalgia was suddenly broken by the sound of a loud shriek coming from the direction of her mother's bedroom. As Kate ran into the hall in response, an exasperated Lydia had already emerged and was gesticulating that a crisis of unspeakable proportion had just transpired. It was a look, of course, that Kate had come to know well throughout her childhood, and which covered anything from running out of sugar for a cookie recipe to discovering that moths had made a sumptuous snack of a favorite wool sweater.

The source of her current vexation was readily apparent from the clue of only one pronoun. "Just look at what *he's* gone and done now!" she snapped as Kate reached the open door and, brushing past her, stepped inside.

She suppressed a smile at the sight of all her mother's shoes and slippers placed toe-to-heel in a colorful serpentine across the carpet.

Just over her shoulder, she heard Lydia mutter that she had absolutely no idea what had gotten into him to make such a mess of her footwear. That the young perpetrator was nowhere in sight filled Kate with more concern than her mother's assessment that it would probably take at least a month of Sundays to restore order to her closet. "Jimmy?" she gently called out. "Jimmy, honey, where are you?"

A giggle from behind the wicker clothes hamper rewarded Kate's patience. Grape jam from his morning's toast still creased the corners of his mouth as he burst out of his hiding place like a miniature cannonball heading for the hallway. Kate intercepted him and held him in her arms as he struggled to get free. The dark blond hair she had so meticulously combed after breakfast was already unruly and one of his shoes, she noticed, was missing. "Parade!" he squealed, pointing to his pint-sized contribution to the colorful line-up as he broke free from his aunt and returned to the shoes. "Parade!"

"It's a beautiful parade," Kate praised him. "But we need to put all of these back in Nana's closet now, okay?"

"Parade!" Jimmy shouted again, this time louder.

From the corner of her eye, Kate could see her mother folding her arms and shaking her head. Truth be told, she could also read exactly what was running through Lydia's mind; specifically, the same script she'd been playing over and over ever since Jimmy's condition had first been diagnosed. It was Cassy's deadbeat ex—and not a twist of fate—whom Lydia would steadfastly blame throughout all eternity for providing the genes that made her first grandchild defective.

Jimmy had now grabbed a fuzzy pink slipper and a tennis shoe and was twirling around in a headache-inducing circle with them.

"It's not like he comes equipped with an 'off' button, Mom. We just have to be patient."

Even as the words left her mouth, Kate knew that Jimmy's autism wasn't a phase he'd simply grow out of on his own. Cassy's income since his birth had been sporadic at best, making it hard to acquire, and maintain, medical insurance to cover the myriad of therapy

Jimmy needed. Her periodic reliance on subsistence from the state had helped a few of his medications, but even Cassy seemed to recognize that government handouts weren't a long-term solution.

"Maybe I can find a special-ed school for him or something," she had mentioned to Kate in what turned out to be one of their last phone conversations. With or without their mother's help Kate had promised her that she'd look into some options, she realized figuring out where Jimmy was going to live would soon become a more significant priority.

Her attempts to currently restore some semblance of order to Lydia's closet weren't getting anywhere fast, largely owing to her boisterous nephew's, *help*.

"Oh, just let me do it," a vexed Lydia said. "Your cab's going to be here in another twenty minutes."

Kate sighed as she got to her feet and reached for Jimmy's hand. Their transportation to the airport had been another bone of contention, with Lydia insisting it was easier for the two of them to take a taxi than it was for her to take them herself and then spend an hour orbiting the parking lot. Kate's observation that the drive would give them that much more time together fell on deaf ears. Unspoken was the reality that any amount of time in a confined space with Jimmy was a level of torture Lydia would just as soon not endure.

As they reached the bedroom doorway, Jimmy suddenly pulled his hand out of Kate's and hurled himself straight at Lydia's knees with a force that nearly caused the older woman to lose her balance.

"Parade!" he hollered.

Lydia's eyes met those of her daughter as the latter crossed the room to collect him. "You have no idea what you're getting yourself into with the boy," she warned. "No idea, whatsoever."

The cab pulled into the driveway of the two-story clapboard house a few minutes earlier than expected. Not surprisingly, the strident tooting of a horn to announce its arrival gave Jimmy a new sound to imitate.

As Kate hurriedly tucked in the hem of the Curious George t-shirt he had already managed to spill juice on, she offered to give him a special prize if he could play 'The Quiet Game' with her. She pretended to zip her lip and put the imaginary key deep in her pocket. Jimmy giggled and imitated her, dramatically flailing his own imaginary key with both hands.

"I really don't know where you get some of your ridiculous ideas on parenting," Lydia chided her.

Kate shrugged. "Pretty much making 'em up as I go along, Mom."

"Well, you can't bribe the boy like that forever. For heaven's sake, Kate, what are you going to do when he's a teenager?"

The thought of her trying to coax a grown-up Jimmy with a plastic baggie of Fruit Loops struck Kate as funny and it was all she could do to keep from chuckling at the imagery. She had never met Cassy's ex, only seen pictures of him, but at moments like this, she'd catch herself wondering how much Jimmy might one day emulate Luke's edgy arrogance, shaggy hair and total disdain for neatness. If the latter ever made the ranks of rock stardom he seemed to so covet, Kate predicted that his picture would be regularly splashed across tabloid covers for trashing hotel rooms.

The sound of the cab honking a second time precluded her from further musing on the subject. "Could you run Jimmy downstairs for me, Mom? I just want to take one last look and make sure we haven't forgotten anything."

Lydia pursed her lips but, to Kate's relief, offered no protest.

Their bags, including Jimmy's much-worn Mickey Mouse backpack, had already been loaded into the trunk of the cab when Kate stepped out the front door and onto the porch. Jimmy, she noticed, was already in the backseat, his pudgy fingers splayed on either side of his face in the window as he flattened his nose against the cool glass.

"Are you sure you've got enough cash?" Lydia asked her.

Some things never change, Kate reflected in amusement. Her mother had been using the same sign-off line ever since Kate had been old enough to go anywhere on her own. That she had just flown out from Las Vegas on her own dime and that many of her clothes were designer labels, a tangible testament to her doing well apparently hadn't registered with Lydia one iota. *Maybe she thinks it's what keeps us connected*, she thought, tempted to ask her for a couple of dollars of snack money just to validate their fragile mother-daughter bond.

"I'll call you when we get in," Kate promised as she leaned in for a hug.

"Are you sure it's not too much?" Lydia murmured, tilting her head in the direction of the cab.

For a second, Kate wasn't sure whether she was referring to the cost of the cab fare or to the pint-size occupant who was now doing his best impression of a goldfish. "We're going to be just fine, Mom," she assured her, an answer that conveniently fit the parameters of either question.

Goodbyes had always been awkward between them, this one being no exception. As both women hovered in the awkward limbo of who should pull away first, neither of them heard the driver's approach until he spoke. "Excuse me, ma'am, but if you want to make your flight..."

Her sidelong glance of acknowledgment of his presence was enough to render them both suddenly speechless. In the space of Kate's quick breath of astonishment as he removed his dark glasses, she felt her heart jump into a somersault.

The beginning of a smile tipped the corners of John Neal's mouth as his eyes of sapphire blue regarded her with speculative curiosity.

"If I knew you were coming," he said, "I'd have baked a cake."

Chapter Two

K ate had often heard the saying that time was rarely kind to high school quarterbacks once they got past the regimen of daily drills and high school exercises. As she composed herself from the shock of seeing one of them standing at that very moment on her mother's porch, she resisted the urge of blurting out a "Wow." The passage of fourteen years had made John Neal even more rugged looking and tan than she last remembered him. His dimples likewise reminding her of all those wistful times she had mentally compared him to Robert Redford.

It was his offhand comment about cake though, that made her hesitate between the spontaneity of throwing her arms around his neck or simply smiling politely and asking him how he had been. Within the space of a nanosecond, the memories of their last bittersweet encounter on this very porch came hurtling back and she could feel an unbidden heat start to steal into her fair complexion.

"So, how have you been?" she heard herself ask in a voice that mistakenly suggested she had just whiffed a shot of helium.

If he noticed the definitive octave spike at all, he was too much of a gentleman to comment on it. "Doing great," he said. "How 'bout yourself?"

You haven't seen me in fourteen years, she thought in dismay, *and that's the best you can come up with?*

"Uh, fine," she replied, annoyed even as she said it that her reply was no more scintillating or inspired than his question. A sudden sense of inadequacy swept over her and she realized she needed a prop to deflect his attention. "You remember my mom," she blurted out, physically pulling Lydia into his immediate radar screen.

The warmth of John's smile echoed in his voice. "Nice to see you again, Mrs. Toscano," he said.

Lydia turned to Kate, her thin face registering total cluelessness.

Oh great, said the little voice in Kate's head. *How do you work 'John Neal' into a sentence without making it obvious?* She tried to force her confused emotions into some semblance of order, but the result was less than stellar. "You know, Mom, I was just saying to myself the other day, 'I wonder whatever happened to John Neal' and, lo-and-behold, here he is." *Lo-and-behold? Where did that come from?*

She felt Lydia perceptibly stiffen as the older woman quickly returned her attention to him.

"Sean's younger boy?" she asked with an underscore of disapproval.

"Actually, the middle one," he politely corrected her. He tilted his head in Kate's direction. "Jeremy was still in eighth grade when the two of us were graduating."

Kate flashed briefly on the memory of a tow-headed kid—a smaller version of John except for the hair color—who clearly adored both of his older siblings but especially always tried to tag along with John whenever he went with friends to the Boardwalk.

Funny, she thought, *that Mom doesn't remember that.*

She opened her mouth to ask whether Jeremy had grown up to be the heartbreaker she always predicted he'd be but was cut short by a surprising suggestion from her mother.

"You know, it's really much too expensive for the two of you to be taking a cab. I'll just run upstairs and grab my purse."

Kate's mouth dropped open. "What?"

"It won't take me but a second." Lydia turned to John, lifting her chin in a somewhat defiant manner that wordlessly communicated he was being dismissed from her presence.

"Don't be ridiculous, Mom. The cab's already here." Kate hoped her face wasn't turning as red as it felt in reaction to her mother picking this particular moment to provoke an unfathomable scene of contention.

Lydia's back had now gone ramrod straight. "Well, are you sure you haven't left anything behind?" she pressed. "You know how many times I had to keep picking up after the boy."

Unsubtle a ploy as it was to get Kate back inside the house and tell her goodness-knows-what, Kate opted to ignore it. "If you find anything, just mail it to me in Vegas," she said. She turned back her cuff to make a point of checking her watch, even though she knew she had allowed plenty of time to get to the airport. "Wow, how did it get to be so late?"

If she had been hoping for John to rescue her with a convenient comment about traffic being bad at that hour of the morning or that his meter was running, it was soon apparent that he wasn't going to accommodate her. Apparently, misinterpreting Lydia's discomfiture as a message she simply didn't want him to witness a mushy motherly goodbye, he amicably volunteered that he wasn't in that big a hurry. "I'll just go wait in the cab with your son," he told Kate.

My son? How could he think that I was—

Dumbfounded by such a casual assumption, she couldn't rally fast enough to correct his mistake before he returned to his seat behind the wheel of the cab. *My son?* All right, so maybe they hadn't seen each other for fourteen years, but Avalon Bay wasn't that big a community. Hadn't any of the resident gossipmongers dropped her name into a conversation at least once in a while? Wouldn't he already have known that she was doing well for herself in Vegas and that she hadn't married?

She suddenly realized that Lydia hadn't spoken up on her behalf either. The fact that her mother relished any opportunity to set other people straight, including total strangers, made the omission even more glaring.

"You know I don't think I like the idea of you getting in a car with him," Lydia was now murmuring to her in a dark whisper. "Maybe we should call someone else."

The corner of Kate's mouth twisted with exasperation as she turned to look at her. "What am I? Thirteen? Honestly, Mom, you're going completely nuts on me. What's wrong with John driving us to the airport?"

Lydia shrugged. "I'm just saying that you know how people in this town like to talk about things."

"Yes, I'm sure they've got their high-powered binoculars trained on us even as we speak. Listen, I have no idea what this is about, but I've really got to get going." She moved in for one last hug but extricating herself from her mother's clinging grasp proved to be not as easy or graceful a maneuver.

"He is just a cab driver," Lydia remarked as if her daughter were on the verge of abandoning all sense of modesty and passionately throw herself at the waiting feet of her former high school swain.

Kate reiterated that she'd call from the Las Vegas airport as soon as their plane landed. Still baffled by the concerned look on her mother's face, she asked, "Are you going to be okay?"

"Well, there is one more thing..." Lydia cryptically replied. She cast a fleeting but wary look at the cab before continuing. "If I were you, I wouldn't go asking any questions about his brother."

"Sorry to hold you up," Kate apologized as she slid into the back seat. "Mom has a hard time with goodbyes."

John's eyes briefly met hers in the rear-view mirror. "No problem. Big Man here and I had fun talking."

Big Man? Talking? She glanced over at Jimmy who was now in a studied concentration of the mechanics of powered windows.

"Actually, I was doing most of the talking. He was just listening." John turned the key in the ignition. "He's kind of a quiet little guy, isn't he?"

Kate hesitated a moment between whether she should tell him that Jimmy was autistic or that he was just playing The Quiet Game for a handful of the promised Fruit Loops. First things first, of course, and that was to explain the relationship.

"Jimmy's my sister's little boy," she said. "Cassy. She was a couple of years behind us in school." As the words left her mouth, Kate remembered that her sister had skipped a grade when she was in elementary school and thus, been in the same class as John's brother, Jeremy. All of which made her mother's mind-slip about the Neal brothers' hierarchy that much more peculiar.

John nodded in recognition. "Oh yeah, right. So, how's she doing these days? You guys just back to the ol' stomping grounds for a visit, or what?"

Whether it was her uneasiness at speaking the truth out loud or Jimmy being in close enough proximity to hear it, Kate stalled with a reply by pretending to clear her throat.

"You okay back there?" he asked in concern. "I've got a water bottle if you need it."

"No, no," she declined. "It comes and goes. Just allergies." She hoped a change of subject would make him forget his question. It didn't.

"So, I heard she hooked up with a musician or something," he continued. "How's that working out?"

Safe enough ground for the time being, she thought, though it was disconcerting he hadn't heard anything about her sister's memorial service when it was so recent. "Oh, you know Cassy," she forced herself to cheerfully reply. "Always living for the moment." She paused. "They broke up when Jimmy was only two."

"When was that?"

"A little over three years ago." Inwardly, she still seethed whenever she recalled the ugly reason that Luke had given as justification for his bailing on his marriage to Cassy and his responsibilities as a father.

C.J. Foster

John nodded sympathetically at Kate's disclosure that the break-up had left her little sister a single mom. "Always rough when you've got kids in the picture. I don't know how they do it."

Was he speaking from personal experience? She tried to remember if she had seen a flash of gold on his left ring finger, but everything had happened on the porch too quickly for her to even notice. *Not that you should notice*, the little voice in her head chided. *If he had cared where you've been for the past decade, he could easily have—*

"So, you like being an aunt?" he said, cutting into her thoughts.

"Huh?"

"An aunt," he repeated. "I bet that's a lot of fun."

"It...uh...has its moments."

At that moment, of course, she was too distracted by her self-initiated charade of verbal dodge ball about Cassy to come up with any examples if he asked her. She glanced over at her young nephew, his head animatedly bobbing along to the rhythm of a happy song that only he could hear. *Maybe it's a blessing he's the way he is*, she thought, trying to equate her bewildering feelings of parental loss as a teenager and feeling grateful that Jimmy was much too young, and much too detached, to fully comprehend that his life was never going to be quite the same again.

John was now chuckling as if enjoying a private joke. "I remember how my Aunt Patty used to say that being an aunt beat motherhood any day of the week, probably because she'd load us up with sugar, spoil us rotten, and then drop us off and go home to a Whiskey Sour on the rocks."

Kate smiled, wistfully reminded of what a close-knit family the Neal's were. "Maybe I should ask her for some pointers next time I'm out," she said.

"Only if it's by séance."

It took a second for the meaning of his response to register. "Oh, John, I'm so sorry. I didn't realize—"

"It's okay," he assured her. "She went pretty fast and without much pain. Just the way she would have wanted it." He shrugged nonchalantly. "I guess we should all be so lucky when our number's up."

Okay, so if you were waiting for an opportune segue, she told herself. Still, the words couldn't come. Maybe they don't have to. What were the odds of their paths crossing again, anyway? Whatever was going on with her family wasn't really any of his concern. She could just play along, get on a plane home, and that would be the end of it.

John said, "So that's nice of you to be giving your sis a break. How long do you get to keep him?"

The cold knot that had formed in her stomach ever since this conversation began refused to untie itself. She measured her words carefully, trying to discipline her voice to maintain control. "Cassy was…in an accident," she murmured. Even without looking, she knew that John's attention had instantly shot up to the rear-view mirror. "She…uh…didn't…"

The sentence went unfinished, but its tragic significance had not been lost on him.

He was suddenly pulling the cab over to the shoulder, getting out and opening the back door. A muscle quivered at his jaw as he extended his hand to her, his blue eyes gently imploring her to step out. He started to say something as she emerged from the back seat but as if propelled by an unseen force, she gave him no chance to, burying her burning face against his broad chest and surrendering to the feelings of helplessness she had held inside ever since she first heard the news of Cassy's death.

Within the safe but transitory refuge of his muscular arms, she allowed herself to be tenderly rocked back and forth, only vaguely aware that he was whispering her name over and over as one hand compassionately stroked the nape of her neck.

And in that fragile moment by the side of the road, Kate was overcome with a wave of déjà vu remembrance that it was not the first time in her life John Neal had tried his valiant best to hold her world together as it slipped away.

C.J. Foster

Chapter Three

E mbarrassed by the ease with which she had let down her defenses, she hastily tried to compose herself with a mental reminder that Jimmy was depending on her to be a strong and steadfast adult; not one who fell apart at the drop of a hat. This was no time to give in to the temptation of emotional resonance that lingered as hauntingly as the scent of John's sandalwood aftershave. A sense of having to hold close to herself, to not let anything distract her, had to be her mantra if she was going to get through her newly acquired yet unexpected responsibility.

"I'm okay, really," she lied, as she clumsily withdrew from the reassuring comfort of his protective embrace. "We should get going."

She could almost feel his thoughts as his hands reluctantly relinquished their hold on her upper arms. *This is too familiar,* she realized, recalling the last time she saw John all those years ago. Ironically, it had ended the same way this was starting.

Whatever *this* is, she thought to herself, her emotions bouncing from one extreme to the other. That it had taken all these years to bring her to this precarious juncture only made her former boyfriend's presence that much more bittersweet.

John's brows were now lifting a question in response to the humming sound coming from the back seat. Jimmy, oblivious to what was transpiring between them, continued to roll the window up and down, meticulously studying the mechanics of the electronic switch as he did so. To the casual observer, Kate knew that he probably looked no different from any other fidgety five-year-old. Even those who tried to coax a conversation out of him, especially older ladies, were inclined to misinterpret his apparent inattentiveness and short attention span as nothing more than childhood shyness.

"I never know what's going on in that little head of his," Cassy used to tell her, always punctuating her observation with a deep sigh of resignation. "It's like he's living on another planet or something."

Ironically, her own death had proved no exception when it came to deciphering Jimmy's emotions or cognitive abilities. That he had just lost the most important person in his life, Kate realized, would certainly not be concluded by anyone witnessing the distractive, seemingly random behaviors he was currently exhibiting. But Kate knew his mother's death must have affected Jimmy deeply. As they eulogized Cassy only a few hours ago, her eyes remained on the small boy sitting quietly beside her. She could see the emptiness in his eyes. Perhaps it was just wishful thinking on her part to believe that his world had somehow connected with hers, a difficult feat for any autistic child.

In a lowered voice and with her back discreetly turned toward the open door, Kate recounted how she and Lydia cautiously broached the subject with the story that his mommy had been hurt and had to go away. "The experts say you're not supposed to use the 'D' word with kids," she reflected. "But how do you know they're not going to think they were deserted? That's a 'D' word, too."

More than anything, she explained, she had tried to convey to him through words and gestures that Cassy's being gone had nothing to do with anything he had said or done and that they loved him and that he was the best little boy in the world. Her throat still ached from the deflating awareness that none of her earnest attempts seemed to register and that he had been more transfixed with rotating her jade bracelet over and over on her wrist than acknowledging anything she had to say. An anguished Lydia had left the room shortly thereafter, too consumed by the devastation of losing a daughter to even begin to give comfort to a child whose responses to personal tragedy weren't "normal". Not on the surface, anyway.

"I sat up with him that entire first night just in case he woke up and was afraid," Kate confessed with a sad smile.

Her nephew, it turned out, had slept more soundly than either of the women beneath the same roof, quietly absorbed in a strange world of his own making that defied easy translation.

John glanced at Jimmy, then back to Kate, the warmth of his smile echoed in his voice. "I'm sure you and your mother have got plenty of love to make him feel secure until he's old enough to understand what happened."

Me, yes. Mom, the vote's not in yet.

Out loud, she remarked that the symptoms of autism varied from child to child. "Even the doctors we've talked to – and Cassy talked to quite a few of 'em herself – they told us it's hard to know for sure how much gets through to him and how he processes what he sees and hears. For now, I guess we just have to take it a day at a time."

John nodded thoughtfully as he reached out to caress her cheek with the knuckle of his forehand. "Sometimes, a day at a time is all you *can* do."

Kate reflected on his last words as the Jersey landscape, an alternating mixture of shoreline, factories and blue-collar suburbia, glided past the backseat windows. She wasn't sure how she was going to take care of Jimmy by herself and maintain her career at the magazine. Take it day by day. That's how she thought she would be able to keep her relationship with John alive while away at Amherst.

Was it purely a defensive mechanism on his part, she wondered, to keep either of them from clumsily sliding into an abyss of "what-if'" fairy tales that had no bearing on the here and now? Or was it just that his life, like countless others she knew who never left their hometown borders, had simply become a palette comprised of neutral colors and, accordingly, detached emotions? That the mere touch of his hand on the side of her face had sent a warming shiver through her entire body made the latter speculation a disturbing one, especially since her mother had cautioned her fourteen years ago against falling for someone whose ambitions weren't comparable to hers.

"You can do a lot better than a Neal," she could still hear Lydia disdainfully mutter. "Boys like *that* never make anything of themselves." She caught herself half-wondering whether her beloved father, if he had lived, would have felt the same way and contested Lydia's prejudicial views, especially since he himself had come from a similar blue-collar background.

Uneasiness spiced with modest irritation at this particular reminiscence managed to underscore Kate's half of the conversation after they had both gotten back into the cab to continue the trip to the airport. In deference to her distress about Cassy and the ambiguity surrounding how much Jimmy was absorbing of their dialogue, John was doing his level best to keep the chatter focused on bringing her up to date about local happenings on the shore, some of which by his own admission was already at least a couple of years old in their newsworthiness.

There was Cliff Harwood, for instance, the local publisher who fancied his weekly gazette a serious challenger to the likes of The New York Times. Did she hear about Eddie, the town barber who had taken a third bride young enough to be his granddaughter? Well, she was already talking divorce, or so he had heard the last time he dropped into Carboni's for a haircut. Or what about that quaint little diner on the corner of Main that served the best cheeseburgers with steak fries, the one the two of them used to hang out at after school? He tossed the question over his shoulder of whether Kate still remembered it.

"*Ruth's?*" she asked.

Two summers ago, John sadly reported, *Ruth's* had accidentally burned to the ground and there were no plans to rebuild. Its namesake, Ruth Miller, claimed that she no longer had the energy to run a diner after her hip replacement, but still bakes for some local eateries. "Can't blame her, I guess," John candidly opined. "She's got to be older than dirt by now. Oh hey, and you remember that guy from Chem who was always—"

What about you? she felt like blurting out. *Why are you telling me about all these people who don't even matter?*

Her spontaneity was tempered only by the dismal possibility that maybe she didn't want to hear the answer. The answer, perhaps, that he was happily married to one of her rivals, that they had four perfect and well-mannered children, and that driving a cab was only a hobby he dabbled in just to occasionally freak people out.

"So, uh, how long have you been driving a cab?" she casually inquired when, for lack of further material on his part or perhaps her lack of encouragement for him to continue, his discourse unexpectedly slowed to a pause.

He shrugged. "If you count Wednesday, I'd say about thirty-three hours."

In response to her puzzled look, he explained that a friend of his had just become the proud father of a newborn and was stressing out about his schedule. "So, I told him I'd take a few shifts for him so he can spend some time with his wife and baby girl. I used to drive for Shore Cab awhile back and still have my license.'"

"What do you do the rest of the time?" she asked.

"Trees."

"Huh?"

"Trees? You know, those tall things with branches and leaves." He pointed with great exaggeration toward the side of the road. "Wow! There's one now! Who'd have thought."

"You are such a smart ass," she retorted with a smirk. If there was one thing that the years hadn't toyed with, besides, of course, his looks, it was his sense of humor.

"I save them," he continued.

"From what?"

"Mostly from their owners. You'd be amazed at how many stupid things people do just because they don't know any better."

Doesn't just apply to trees, Kate thought, momentarily saddened by all the lost opportunities that were the pattern of her sister's short life. Cassy should have known that foregoing a college education in order to "search" for herself was a mistake. Hadn't everybody tried to tell her so? She should also have at least suspected that going all hot and heavy with a loser like Luke wouldn't end well.

John had now changed the subject and was asking about her writing. "I heard it's for a magazine or something?"

A secretive smile softened her lips. *So, they have been talking about me*, she thought, wondering who it might have been. Wondering, too, how often he asked around or if it was just thrust on him out of habit, like a refill of coffee.

"It's all about Las Vegas," she explained. "Glamour stuff, shopping, shows, that kind of thing." She didn't realize until it came out of her mouth just how fluffy and superficial it sounded. In hasty postscript, she added that sometimes she even interviewed politicos like the mayor and city council members. "Never a dull moment."

John nodded. "It's nice you got your dream," he said. "I remember how important writing was to you."

He seemed pensive, not disturbed or angry. *Is he baiting me, testing me to see if I'm going to say that maybe I was wrong?* He had brought her yet again to a haunting but familiar place. Like a hidden current, the memories came crowding back to rob her of an answer. It was an overcast day on the Boardwalk, the smell of impending rain in the air.

She recalled insisting to him that it really wasn't that far away, even though every map in print indicated the contrary. She knew that for all intents and purposes, the prestigious Amherst was in a galaxy far removed from the monotony of Avalon Bay. She had told him that maybe they could get together on her school break, or even meet somewhere halfway. But, even all those years ago, they both knew it wouldn't work out that way.

"So how's he doing?" John interrupted her contemplation.

"Huh?"

"Jimmy," he said. "Is he doing okay back there?"

She glanced over and was surprised to see that, unbeknownst to either of them, he contentedly had fallen asleep. Was he bored by the ramblings about the Jersey Shore? Or was he just – why couldn't she get the word "content" out of her head? It certainly wasn't a word she typically associated with autistic children. From her limited research on the condition, she had learned that being moved around from one strange setting into another often fostered agitation. Then again, she remembered, Cassy had been somewhat of a nomad and was constantly uprooting him as a result of job changes, new romances or dwindling resources. Maybe staying in one place for too long had resulted in exactly the opposite effect on him.

"Sleeping like a baby," she reported.

She raised her eyes to find John watching her in the rear-view mirror, his voice pleasantly soft and infinitely compassionate.

"Then we shouldn't wake him," he said. "He's got a big adventure ahead of him."

They continued the rest of the drive in awkward silence.

"I'd help you take these inside," John offered as he unloaded their bags from the trunk, "but with the cab 'n' all..."

A strident police whistle a few cars back at the curb was reminding drivers that anyone lingering in the loading zone was subject to citation.

"It's okay, we can manage," she assured him. She fumbled inside her purse for her wallet. "What's the damage?"

He made a dismissing gesture. "On the house."

"No, really, I can't."

"Hey, it's the least I can do for an old—" He bit back the word but Kate already knew what he was going to say.

"It was great seeing you, too," she said, turning her attention to a yawning Jimmy, lest he sees too much in her telling eyes. "Can you say goodbye to John, honey?"

The yawn immediately dissolved into a stony pout.

"He was nice enough to bring us to the airport," Kate said, hoping that if she gave him a tummy tickle she could at least coax a giggle out of him. Jimmy stubbornly focused his attention on the ground.

"Maybe next time," John suggested when her efforts proved fruitless.

They stood facing each other for a moment. *Do I hug him? Do I shake his hand? Do I just wave and say, "See yah?"*

"Well, uh, have a safe trip," he said and impulsively stepped forward.

"Parade!" Jimmy suddenly squealed, causing John to take a step back.

"Why's he pointing at my shoes?" John asked.

"It's his word du jour," she explained with a blush of embarrassment. "Things just, I don't know, he can go for two entire days without saying anything at all and then he goes and starts saying the same word over and over."

This one, she went on, seemed to have stuck in his head from when he was three. "Cassy and a friend camped out with him to watch the Macy's Day Parade a few years back." It had, of course, drawn no shortage of censure from Lydia who thought it was irresponsible to expose a toddler to a cold night of sleeping on the sidewalk just to watch floats and marching bands. "Whenever he sees shoes he likes, I guess it reminds him of all those feet marching by."

John's smile was disarmingly generous. "Then I guess I'll take that as a compliment."

"Taxi!" a male voice bellowed in preface to a red-faced, portly man with multiple bags angrily shlepping his way toward the open trunk of the cab.

Goodbyes, whatever form they might have taken, were swiftly preempted.

"We'd better go. Take care, John," said Kate, happy for the escape but, at the same time, she yearned for resolution from her past. *Resolution or atonement,* she asked herself as she scurried from the cab, not wanting to look back.

C.J. Foster

"Goodbye, Kate," was all she heard, the words resonating in her ears, bringing her back to that warm summer night. How long would it be before she saw him again, she wondered. If ever?

- 30 -

Chapter Four

"**B**ig appetite tonight?" Sandy Miller teased John as she loaded two subs and a bag of chips into a paper sack for him and rang up the order. Until the fire at her grandmother's dinner, she had been a plump, pleasant and permanent fixture behind the counter at Ruth's. Transferable skills, as she liked to call them, had not only landed her the same kind of job at Gull's Galley down the street but also, if the rumors John had heard were true, had brought her the smitten attention of the cook's second cousin, Sam.

John grinned in response to her question as he reached into the hip pocket of his jeans for his wallet. "Mom's playing Bridge tonight with her friends so Dad 'n' I are fending for ourselves tonight."

"How's he doing?" she thoughtfully inquired.

There had been no shortage of community concern and outpouring of get well wishes when the senior Neal had suffered a stroke the previous year that paralyzed the left side of his body. That there was always someone asking after him or wanting to know how Abby was holding up was just another one of the hometown constants that made John appreciate why his family had never wanted to live anywhere else.

"'Bout the same," he confessed. "Good days 'n' bad. Doc keeps telling him that he's trying to do too much too soon but you can guess how successful that is." Sean Neal, just like his father before him, had a reputation for being one of the more stubborn denizens of Avalon Bay.

Sandy playfully poked the side of the bag. "Sure I can't throw in some pie for you growin' boys? Certified cure-all for whatever ails you." She proceeded to tick off on her fingers the assortment she had available. "Oh, and I've got carrot cake, too," she added, comically smacking herself in the forehead for having previously omitted it. "Your Dad love's Nana's carrot cake."

"Sure," he replied. "Mom's won't be back for a couple of hours. It'll give me plenty of time to get rid of the evidence." Ever since his stroke left the senior Neal in a wheelchair, his lack of exercise had caused him to put on a few pounds. Abby had put him on a strict, and successful diet to keep her husband as fit as possible to help his rehabilitation.

"No charge for the pie. Tell your Mom it's from Nana. She wouldn't dare get mad at her."

"Will do. Thanks, Sandy. Say hi to Sam for me."

The blast of a Quad cab truck horn as he stepped off the curb prefaced a yell from the passing Lenny Molino, one of several friends he still hung out with since his football-playing days. Unlike John, however, who had a successful business, Lenny was irresponsibly content to keep living his life as if he were on an endless summer break. A low-rung job at the factory kept him in just enough green to pay his rent and buy kegs but not so much that any of Avalon Bay bachelorettes would ever have considered him to be suitable husband material.

With muscular, tattooed arms wedged into a white T-shirt and a shock of woolly dark hair that perpetually needed a good trim, Lenny's perceptions of himself as a babe magnet paled in comparison to the natural charm that John exuded just by cracking a smile.

"Wanna go to Kelley's 'n' shoot some stick for beers?" Lenny called out.

"Don't want to take your money," John shot back. "Besides, I already promised Dad I'd spring for dinner."

Lenny snorted as he pointed at the Gull's Galley sack in his friend's hand. "Cheap date."

"Yeah? Takes one to know one."

With another juvenile blast of his horn, Lenny took off down the street, reminding John for a brief moment of the funny truism that life in a small town moved at a different pace from the rest of the outside world. If he counted today, in fact, sometimes it felt as if it hadn't budged in fourteen years.

As he pulled into the driveway, John could see that the curtains were open in the front room. Furthermore, that his dad was waving at him from the comfort of the sofa, not his wheelchair. The latter, he noticed once he stepped inside, was parked over by the television where his dad's favorite game show was in progress.

Shelby, the female German Shepherd that John had bought as a puppy after he moved back from NYC, came bounding out in a black and tan blur from around the corner with a moist chew toy in her mouth that she promptly deposited on her master's work boot.

"Not now, girl," he apologized, dutifully scratching her head and tossing her toy a few feet away. Happy for only this fleeting moment of acknowledgment, Shelby went pouncing after it, vigorously shaking it back and forth before hunkering down and proudly trapping it between her paws.

"Mom come home early and help you out of the chair?" he asked his dad, this being a task that normally fell on his own broad shoulders.

Sean shook his head, dislodging a lock of grey hair into an unruly dip over his left brow. "Did it...myself," he answered. Though he formed his words slowly and delivered them with a slur, there was no mistaking the sense of satisfaction that underscored the senior Neal's announcement. "Even...cleaned up...too," he added.

John scowled. "You know you're not supposed to be doing stuff like that when we're not here," he reminded him. "What if you fell and hit your noggin?"

"Might be...an improve...ment," Sean said. He lifted his right hand off his lap and pointed a shaky finger at the sack John was holding. "Good...eats?"

"Just a couple of sub's from the Galley. Sandy threw in some carrot cake for you."

A look of confusion came to Sean's weathered face. "I...like carrot cake?" This seemed to be news to him. Along with his left-sided weakness, Sean's memory also took a hit from the stroke.

"Last time I checked. But hey, if I'm wrong, it's all the more for me."

Sean nodded and, in returning his attention to the television, missed the melancholy frown that flitted across his son's chiseled features.

Bored with her toy, Shelby came padding back into the room and now leaned dead-weight against John's thigh, looking up at him with loving eyes of liquid amber.

"So how are these guys doing?" John asked, indicating the three contestants who were eagerly hanging on the host's every word about how much money they could wager in the final round. "Do they know as many answers as you?"

"Not...so good...today," Sean answered, although it was unclear to John whether he was referring to himself or to Donald, Susan and the bespectacled Carl with an ugly orange tie. In a halting speech punctuated by choked chuckles, he alluded to Donald having an eye for Susan. "He...smiles...at her," he said.

"Smart dude," John remarked, seeing as how Susan was currently besting both of her male opponents by the happy tune of $2,500. "Why don't you keep watching and I'll go grab us a couple of plates."

As he crossed toward the kitchen, Shelby enthusiastically following, John's glance absently fell on the day's modest stack of mail on the mahogany end table.

"So who brought the mail in?" he inquired but his father was currently too absorbed in Susan's next answer about heroes of the

American Revolution to give a reply. Granted, the task of collecting letters and bills only involved retrieving them from where they landed on the carpet once they were shoved through the brass slot in the front door but it still bothered him that his dad may have exerted himself in that fashion.

Sifting through the pile, he was surprised to see a pair of large envelopes respectively bearing the names of two local colleges.

"Thinking about going back to school, are you?" he asked his dad. He repeated the question a second time, this time a little louder.

"What?" a distracted Sean murmured.

"Looks like you got some college brochures here," John replied. "What's up?"

"For...you."

"Come again?"

Sean coughed and cleared his throat of some stubborn phlegm. "For...you," he said again. "You could...go."

John's mouth quirked with humor. "Now why would I want to go back to college at my age?"

"Not...so...old."

"Not so young, either," he facetiously countered, wondering what, exactly, was behind all of this. "Besides, you've gotta admit I'm not doing that bad with the business." He tossed out the reminder that he was even hiring a new helper for the summer.

"Carl...went to...Pur...due."

John scratched his head. "Carl who?"

"Him," Sean said, waving his good arm at the TV. "Pur...due."

"You mean the guy who's in third place? Yeah, uh-huh, I can see how all that learning's really paid off for him." He tossed the two envelopes on the coffee table. "Want me to set up some TV trays out here or shall we eat our feast in the dining room?"

Sean, however, refused to be deterred from what he had struggled to start. "We can...pay," he said.

It was impossible for John not to return his dad's lopsided but earnest smile or to walk back to the sofa, lean over and squeeze his good hand. "You guys really don't have to do anything for me, Dad. I'm doing just fine." In fact, he went on to explain, he'd gotten a couple of calls only the other day from a contractor who wanted to talk about trees for the new exclusive subdivision being built along the beachfront.

Sean blinked his eyes a couple of times as if trying to re-catch a fleeting train of thought. "There's...mon...ey," he said. "Still...is. All of...it."

He bowed his head and drew a deep breath. "That money's for you and Mom," he quietly replied. "End of subject."

"So, how'd I do on the sub?" John asked ten minutes later as he wheeled Sean to the head of the dining room table. Shelby, as was her canine tradition, had already taken up her post under John's chair and was awaiting her usual slip of forbidden treats.

To a sub purist, the sight of the neatly dismantled cold cuts, cheeses, and two halves of bread splayed on either side of the plate would not only have been alarming but also seeming to defeat the purpose of its being artfully stacked high to begin with. That Sean functionally possessed the equivalent of just one hand to work with and had difficulty chewing, however, had called upon John to be creative.

"Good," he replied, a bit sadly. Sean tentatively grabbed one end of the sandwich and dragged it over to the side. John could see the sorrow in his father's worn eyes. Subs were one of his favorite foods. John knew it pained him to not be able to enjoy them as he used to.

John put the matter aside with casual humor, cognizant of the reality that there was no one-size-fits-all pattern to a stroke victim's recovery process. Like he'd told Sandy, there were good days and bad and no predicting the order, or frequency, of either one.

"So, you'll never guess who I gave a ride to today," he said between noshes on his sandwich. "Remember Kate Toscano? We used to go out in high school?"

"Tos...Tos..."

"Toscano," John repeated, trying not to appear too anxious for a glimmer of memory on his father's part.

"Lid...die's...girl?"

John grinned. "Right. Lydia's girl. Do you remember her?" He proceeded to offer a brief description that ended with the observation she was even prettier than she was as a teenager.

Sean, however, was absorbed at the moment in trying to jiggle a slice of Provolone cheese out from under the piece of Salami that partially covered it. Shelby's twitching black snout poked out from beneath the tablecloth in anticipation of a mishap.

"Anyway," John continued, "she was out visiting her mom for a while." He hesitated, wondering whether he should tell him the reason why or just leave it at that. "Did I mention she lives out in Vegas?" He went on to relate that she'd become a writer just like she had always said she would and that she worked for a magazine that was all about shows and shopping and celebrities. "She's got a nephew, too," he said, deeming Jimmy a safe enough topic to yak about. "His name's Jimmy and he's five or so. Sweet kid. He likes parades."

John allowed his mind to wander for a moment, savoring the memory of what it had felt like, even briefly, to hold Kate in his arms again and pretend he was her knight in shining armor. Wishful thinking, of course. Someone as special as Kate deserved a real one, not some blue-collar guy who saved trees for a living and had moved back home to look after his parents. It seemed, sadly, that the chasm between them had widened even farther since the last time they parted.

Purposely, he reflected, he hadn't asked her too much about her personal life during the ride to the airport. Certainly, though, it had to be a secure one that included a husband or a boyfriend or else she wouldn't have taken on the enormous responsibility of bringing a special needs child into it. Good for her, he thought, trying to tuck away any lingering feelings of regret about the past and simply label the unexpected crossing of their paths that morning as just a freaky coincidence that didn't merit any further speculation.

He reached for a handful of chips. "So, did you catch any good games today on TV?" he asked, trying to change the conversation to anything rather than talk about the girl who got away.

Sean gazed upon his son knowingly. The damage from the stroke had affected the motor cortex and perhaps a part of the deeper hippocampal formation on the right side of his brain. Despite these deficits, his mind was still as sharp as ever. He noticed the dull ache in his son's eyes, a pain he hadn't perceived in some time. As a matter of fact, it had been well over twenty-five years since he had seen a similar look in the mirror. He decided to let it pass, not wanted to resuscitate such sadness in either himself or his son.

"No," Sean answered quietly. His appetite suddenly gone, he pushed his plate aside. I think... I'll go lie down."

"You feeling alright, Pop?" John asked. "I told you before you need to wait for us to help you out of your chair. I know therapy's going well, but I think you're doing too much, too fast."

"Not... enough."

John regarded his father. He had become so frail since the stroke. His mind and will was strong, but his body was failing. "Let me help you upstairs, at least."

The Neal's old two-story house had no downstairs bedroom. John had moved in after the stroke to help his parents. He was putting money aside to help get them a one-story, wheelchair compatible house, but real estate on the shore was getting so expensive. In the meantime, he would do what he could to ensure his father had some quality of life and normalcy.

"Look at...brochures," Sean told his son, enunciating carefully to ensure he was understood.

"I will. We'll talk about it another day," he replied as his father stood up from the chair. The lack of strength and tone of his left arm and leg had prevented him from being able to use a walker, but he could walk while holding on to John. One step and a time, John carefully helped lift his father's heavy, weighted left leg as they slowly climbed the steep stairs. Finally, Sean breathing a bit heavily, they reached the top.

"Take a rest, Dad."

"I'm okay," replied Sean as he started out again, carefully making his way down the short hall to his bedroom.

Sean's tenacity was legendary, but John feared he was pushing too hard. He let it pass, knowing his father's self-esteem and pride were being chipped away every time he needed someone to cut up his food or help him get up from a chair. Hope, determination and the love of his family was all that kept Sean alive. John would ensure his father kept all three.

After John helped Sean into his room, he closed the door and returned downstairs. He walked by the unopened college brochures on the coffee table.

"Another day," he said aloud and continued into the kitchen to clear the table.

Chapter Five

There were twenty-three messages waiting on Kate's machine when she got home, half of them from an anxious Dee who had apparently forgotten until her penultimate one that Kate wasn't even in town. Kate was glad she had left her cell phone turned off since the funeral.

"Geez, I'm such a jerk," the recording began with an effusive apology. "It was the funeral thingy, wasn't it? Your sister? My God, you must be feeling terrible and here I'm harping on and on about work. Well, listen, never mind. You just hang in there and we'll talk when we talk."

Five minutes later, she had left another one breathlessly asking whether it was at all humanly possible to wrap up the new Cirque du Soleil piece the very second she got home. "No pressure," Dee added, "but I really, really, really need it."

Kate smiled in amusement. Dee's emergencies, she had come to realize over their years of working together, could be always be prioritized by the number of "really's" she used in any given sentence.

As she played the rest of her messages back, scribbling their essence on Post-It Notes, she watched a perplexed Jimmy take in the strangeness of his new surroundings. If he had moved a single inch except to scratch his nose since the last time she looked at him, it was microscopically imperceptible. *Welcome to Oz, little one*, she wanted to tell him. Except for the fact that neither the name nor the correlating view of an Emerald City that would be magically glittering all around them as soon as the sun went down would likely have registered with him a single iota.

That Vegas' grandeur from the forty-fifth floor of her condo—Dee's condo, actually, since she was informally subleasing—routinely took the breath away of her visiting *adult* friends made it hard for Kate to conceptually put herself inside the head of a youngster who had always lived in ground floor apartments and a succession of motel rooms. The Art Nouveau furnishings alone, with a tasteful mix of black, white and splashes of hunter green, were certainly a far cry from what he had spent the past five years growing up with.

Likewise, the expansive open floor plan that included two-bedroom suites and a custom kitchen that spilled into a step-down dining and entertainment room even made Kate sometimes feel as if she were visiting a lavish movie set.

When she and Jimmy first arrived, she had made a point of taking his hand and giving him the full tour, chattering the whole time about Dee and her job, and about how Dee's oil baron daddy in Texas had bought this place for his only daughter but that she was never there anymore since she was either always working long hours at the magazine or being seen at the clubs or hanging out with her new boyfriend, Anton.

I may as well be reciting the Vegas phone directory, she realized with a wry pang. "I'll tell you one thing, you'd make a great little poker player with that face," she praised him, kneeling to his level and affectionately ruffling his hair. Her expectation of a smile, a laugh, even the most minimal of eye contact, went unrewarded.

"I need to check my messages before we start putting our things away," she told him, squeezing his hands and kissing him on the nose. A part of her expected him to happily follow her across the room to see what she was doing but he didn't. For whatever reason, the patch of carpet he was standing on now held his undivided attention.

Who could have seen any of this coming, she thought, suddenly conscious of the fact that the last time she'd sat at her desk on the perimeter of the living room was when she'd gotten the phone call about her sister's accident. Up until that moment, her life had been entirely her own and she had gone to sleep every night with only the sound of her breathing to keep her company. She had eaten when she felt like it, partied with friends whenever invitations were extended, indulged in long bubble baths for stress reduction, and, when her workload at the magazine accommodated it, even taken extended vacations.

Yet none of those freedoms she so casually took for granted as a single career woman ever entered into her mind when she offered to bring Jimmy back home with her after Cassy's funeral. Nor, until now, had she pictured the condo as such an incongruous place to take in a child she had previously only seen for short stretches at a time.

Why, then, was she guiltily starting to question whether she had really allowed herself enough time to make such a profound and life-altering decision for the both of them? With a mild shudder, she caught herself wondering whether Lydia's cynical remarks that maybe she'd bitten off more than she could chew held more truth than she dared to admit. What did she really know about the demands of motherhood anyway except, perhaps, not to emulate the traits that vexed her so much about her mom.

For one thing, she couldn't begin to imagine what the world looked like through Jimmy's eyes, especially since none of his reactions followed any sort of predictable pattern. There had been her initial apprehensions, for instance, of how he'd feel about riding on an airplane for such a long flight. She knew he had been on one at least once before with his mother and, by Cassy's account, had screamed from takeoff until landing.

To that end, Kate had encouraged him to run around and play as much as possible beforehand to tire him out a bit. That it worked so well he had conked out prematurely in the taxi before they even got to the airport made her worry that his second wind of hyperactivity could threaten to make her one of those passengers everyone else glared at with venom.

To her surprise, however, he'd been completely unperturbed by the noise of the engines, mesmerized by the clouds out the window, and, unless she was mistaken, even grinned at a little girl about his same age and tried to crane his neck to see where she went. She even prided herself on discretely slipping the flight attendant a single-serving box of Fruit Loops and asking her if she'd mind presenting it to him half an hour after takeoff as if it were part of the airline's regular meal service. Jimmy had looked pleased with this even if he subsequently managed to disperse half the contents into his lap and on the floor.

At least he'd been neater in John's cab, she thought. Or rather, John's *friend's* cab. *Typical John*, she thought with a smile, *always there to help others out*. If memory served, the caption under his yearbook picture said pretty much the same thing. Kate shifted uneasily in her chair, disturbed by the effortlessness with which she was able to conjure such snapshots from a past she no longer belonged to.

She glanced at her watch and, in doing so, discovered that she hadn't reset it to the right time when they'd landed at McCarran. Her mother would be watching the news about now, she imagined and then trying to decide what to fix herself for dinner, an exercise that, by Lydia's own admission, she found to be tedious if there was no one around to share it with.

John was probably sitting down to dinner, too, she thought. His wife, if he had one, was no doubt a good cook. At least a way better cook than *she* was, having inherited her mother's lack of culinary imagination and patience. Were there children at the dining table as well or were they young enough to have already eaten before he got home? Behind closed eyelids, she tried to envision the scene. Were they laughing and passing the mashed potatoes and talking about their day as if they didn't have a care in the world? Did John and his spouse sit at opposite ends of the table or right next to one another so that he could occasionally touch her hand?

Why are you beating yourself up like this? the little voice in her head screamed. *Let it go already!*

Opening her eyes, she came back to the reality of not only having to fix dinner for Jimmy and herself but also not having any real clue of what his favorite meals were. She looked up to ask him if he was getting hungry and discovered he had moved over to the floor-to-ceiling windows and was pressing his hands and nose against the glass. *What is it about kids and leaving their mark on glass*, she wondered, trying to remember if she and Cassy had shared that particular fascination when they were little girls growing up in Avalon Bay. She made a mental note to pick up a healthy supply of Windex wipes.

"It's a pretty view, isn't it?" she said as she stood next to him. "Did I tell you we're forty-five stories high? That means there are forty-four floors below us." She quickly recalculated. "Actually, forty-nine if you count the garage that's underground. That's where all the cars live."

Jimmy was completely nonplussed by this revelation even though she knew for a fact that some of his favorite toys were cars.

Toys. *Yikes.* With the exception of a fleecy stuffed bear named Mr. Ollie that he'd brought along in his backpack, everything else was being packed up in boxes by a neighbor of Cassy's who had offered to keep them until she got instructions on where they should be shipped. Having no idea when that would be, Kate made a second mental note to take him toy-shopping the next day.

Vegas. Toy-shopping. Okay, not exactly the words she'd expect to find in the same sentence unless the latter was of the adult variety. Maybe instead she could just go online after he went to bed and find some playthings that could be FedExed overnight.

"Do you think Mr. Ollie would like to look at the view?" she suggested. "I bet he's never been up this high before."

When Jimmy made no move to go get him, Kate went into the spare bedroom herself to retrieve the bear from his backpack. In her best falsetto voice, she squealed Mr. Ollie's excitement at being in a new place and flapped his tiny arms up and down.

Jimmy looked at her, his mouth dipped into a frown, and then resumed his vigil at the window.

What? She thought. *Didn't I get the voice right?* Clearly, there was quite a lot about doing anthropomorphic impressions that she didn't know. With a sigh, she set the bear down on the carpet facing the window. *Patience*, she reminded herself. *He'll come around when he's ready to.*

"I'm going to call and order us some groceries," she continued. "What do you think we should have for our dinner? Spaghetti? Mac and cheese? Fish and chips?" She paused. "Squiggle bugs and ants?"

No response.

"All righty then," she said. "Let's make it a surprise."

She crossed back to the desk and flipped her Rolodex to the entry that was every career woman's Godsend—home-delivered groceries. "Comes free with the condo twenty-four-seven," Dee had informed her when she first moved in. Kate tried to remember the last time she'd set foot in an actual supermarket and cruised the aisles. Rarely had she ever exceeded the $500 monthly cap. The responsibility of feeding a growing child three squares and snacks, of course, would probably change that fairly fast.

She had barely hung up the phone after placing her order when it rang again.

"Hello?"

"You were supposed to call me from the airport," Lydia sharply chided. "How do I know your plane didn't crash?"

It would probably have been on the news, an exhausted Kate was tempted to reply. "Sorry, Mom," she apologized, "but things got a little crazy."

"Problems with the boy already, hmm?"

Lydia Toscano, the queen of gloating, was already seeking confirmation of her predictions.

"No, just getting our bags, getting a cab, that kind of thing." Jimmy, she noticed with a smile, had picked Mr. Ollie up by his hind leg and was casually swinging him back and forth at his side.

"Speaking of cabs..."

"Yes?' Kate asked.

"Did he say anything to you?" Lydia wanted to know.

"Who are we talking about, Mom?"

"Don't be smart with me, young lady. You know exactly who I'm talking about."

"Oh, you mean John Neal? Yeah, I suppose we caught up on some news and stuff. Why?"

"You're not going to get back in touch with him, are you? Because if you are, I don't think it's a good idea."

"I kinda gathered that," Kate remarked. "Besides John and I moved on a long time ago. Why are you so wrapped around the axel about him?"

Lydia ignored her question, inquiring instead as to how the boy was liking Las Vegas.

"Too early to tell, I think." Vegas at any age, she added, was an acquired taste that took a little getting used to.

From the corner of her eye, she saw a sudden movement at the window followed by an unintelligible grunt. Inexplicably, a red-faced Jimmy was now repeatedly pelting Mr. Ollie against the glass.

Kate cut her mother off in mid-sentence. "Gotta go, Mom! I'll call you back!"

Dropping her handheld phone on the desktop, she hurried over to subdue him. "Hey, hey, hey," she cooed as she tried to calm him down and grab hold of his flailing arms. "What's this all about, huh?" She repeated his name over and over but he only responded with grunts and whimpers and tried to extricate himself from her firm grasp. After what seemed an eternity, he finally gave up and plopped down on the carpet with a thud.

As casually as she could manage, Kate brushed the hair off his forehead and asked him again what was going on. "It's okay," she said. "It really is. I'm going to make everything all right. I know it's all new right now and kinda scary, but we've got each other, okay? Okay, honey? Do you understand what I'm saying?"

He sullenly turned away from her to look at the window and for a moment she wondered whether he was going to pick up where he left off just as soon as she let him go. *Thank goodness it was only a bear,* she thought in relief. She took a glance around the room, reminding herself that the phrase "childproofing a house" had suddenly taken on a dark and significant meaning that she'd have to attend to as soon as possible.

The phone rang.

"Ooooooh," she said, feigning giddy astonishment in an attempt to distract him. "Shall we go see who that is?" She gently hoisted him to his feet, took his small hand in hers, and pointed toward the desk. "Let's go answer the telephone, okaaaaaay?"

To her surprise, he didn't try to pull away from her or hold his ground but, to the contrary, actually looked a little curious about where she was taking him. "He likes to go for walks," she remembered Cassy telling her when Jimmy was around three. "I think he thinks it's an adventure."

Either that, Kate now mused, *or something in his head is connecting the touch to feeling safe.*

She picked up the phone with her free hand.

"Oh cool, you're back," she heard Dee say. "Have you had a chance to work up the Cirque piece yet?"

Chapter Six

A bby Neal was all smiles as she let herself in through the back screen door and saw John reading the sports section at the kitchen counter. A sleepy Shelby lifted her head only briefly off of John's foot, thumped her tail twice, and proceeded to go back to sleep on the cool linoleum.

"Win big tonight?" he asked.

"Three dollars and Helen's recipe for rum cake," she proudly proclaimed. "I should make some of it for us over the weekend."

John whistled. "Three dollars, hmm? I should put you on a plane for Vegas and you could parlay it into enough to buy a Winnebago..."

"Oh honestly! Can you picture me squandering my life's savings away in Sin City?"

No, he reflected, but then again it was just as hard for him to picture a girl like Kate Toscano there, either. He glanced over at the kitchen clock. She and Jimmy and whoever were probably eating their dinner by now.

"How'd it go with your dad?" she asked. "And do you want some coffee?"

"Stubborn as ever and coffee sounds great." He debated a second about ratting his dad out but decided that she may as well know. "He was out of his wheelchair again when I got home."

Abby ran a hand through her short salt and pepper hair. "That man!" she groaned in mild exasperation as she pulled open the silverware drawer for a spoon. "I swear we're going to have to put a *bell* on him!"

"Yeah, like it'd help any."

"Still..."

On the one hand, they both knew it was good that he had the willpower, and obstinate pride, to want to get back to living a normal life quickly instead of having to rely so heavily on his wife and son to take care of him. Too many times, the doctor had told them, he had seen stroke victims who ignored their therapy, wallowed in self-pity, and settled into a lethargic half-life that made it even harder on their loved ones. On the other hand, however, was their mutual, unspoken worry that he'd end up doing himself a lot more harm by falling if he rushed things.

"He didn't try to get the mail, too, did he?" Abby asked, remarking that the new carrier on the route couldn't seem to get his deliveries done while it was still daylight and that she'd had to leave that afternoon before it arrived.

"Afraid so." John gently dislodged his bare foot from under Shelby's head and got up to go pull two coffee mugs out of the cupboard. "By the way,"

"Hmm?"

"I understand you and dad think I need to better myself."

"Come again?"

"Nice try, Mom, but he told me the brochures were *your* idea."

"Oh that," Abby nonchalantly replied. "So, they came already?"

John folded his arms and cast her a stern look.

"Well, it wouldn't hurt you to at least think about it," she said, defending her decision to take the initiative and send away for them for his own good. "People go back to college all the time, you know."

"People who want to do something different from what they're already doing."

"Or make more money at it," she pointed out. "There's certainly nothing wrong with that."

"Look, we've talked about it before. Until Dad's back on his feet again and you're able to quit your job," explained John.

"I happen to like working," she archly insisted. "It gives me something to do during the day."

All right, so maybe he couldn't argue with her on that score. When she'd retired from the factory as a bookkeeper after 25 years, it had taken her only a scant four months to ask her former boss if she could please have her old job back. John always wondered if the coincidence of his father retiring around the same time from his job as a security guard had anything to do with her sudden renewed interest in wanting to get out of the house.

By and large, of course, there was an old-shoe sort of comfort level between his parents that John not only admired but also deemed a rarity in a country where half of all marriages ended in divorce. Since his dad's stroke, they seemed to have grown even closer as a couple despite the emotional and physical toll he knew that the extra workload had to be taking on his mother.

In the earlier years, just before Jeremy came along, it had been an entirely different story punctuated by late-night fights and stony silences which invariably lasted for a few days thereafter. John recalled many a time that he had anxiously gone to his older brother Mitch's bedroom to ask if the latter thought their parents were going to break up.

"If they do," Mitch always told him, "I'm gonna stay here with Mom and you have to go live with Dad."

"How come you get Mom?" John wanted to know, even if he fervently hoped the fighting downstairs never actually came to that.

"'Cause she's a better cook and I'm staying where the food is!"

Though it was hard to fault his older sibling's logic, it bothered him that, as brothers, they didn't seem to share the same level of concern about the future of their family. Not until he got older was he finally able to understand the reason why.

Mitch, plain and simple, was a self-centered jerk.

Abby had finished pouring the coffee and handed him a mug across the counter. "Did I tell you Mitch called us this morning?" she said.

"Wow," John replied sarcastically, "has it been a year already?"

Abby swatted him with a napkin. "Be nice. You know he's got a busy life."

Too busy, John remembered, to come home and stay for more than an afternoon when their dad was first hospitalized. "So, what did he want?" Calling out of the blue to say "hi" and chat was far from Mitch's style.

"Well," she mischievously drew out the suspense of what had prompted her lobbyist son to call them from Washington, D.C. "It seems that he and Mindy have been talking lately about settling down."

John lifted a brow. "And this differs from living together *how*, exactly?" If his memory served, the pair had been casually cohabiting in a Georgetown rowhouse for four years already, maybe even five.

Abby scoffed at his flip remark. "He meant legally," she said. "Although I think maybe a fall wedding is more Mindy's idea than his. She's a nice girl, don't you think?"

"Well, having only seen her picture on Christmas cards," John replied.

"You think your father might be well enough to travel by then?"

"Travel where?"

Mindy's family, she explained, all lived in Silver Spring, Maryland so it only made sense to have the wedding and reception there.

"Why can't they have the wedding here?" John retorted. "It'll be much easier for Dad."

Abby rolled her eyes. "Can't you just be happy that your brother's finally doing this?" she said.

"Let me finish my coffee and I'll go do cartwheels down the Boardwalk."

"The funny thing is, though," she mused aloud, ignoring her son's remark. "I always thought you'd be the first one to give me a daughter-in-law."

"Translation; give you grandchildren."

"That, too," she said, brightening at the prospect that Mitch and Mindy might already be thinking about accommodating her not-so-secret wish. "Just think," she continued as she sipped her coffee, "that would make you an uncle."

In spite of his resolve not to give Kate Toscano any more thought than he already had his mother's comment triggered the image of her once again.

"So, guess who I drove to the airport today?" he said.

"I don't know, dear. Who?"

"Remember Kate Toscano?"

A puzzled look flitted across Abby's face. "Kate Toscano was here in town?"

"Uh-huh."

"Well now, isn't that the strangest thing," she absently murmured.

"What's strange?"

Abby set down her cup. "When I was driving through town yesterday, I could have sworn I saw a girl who looked just like her."

John shrugged. "Probably because it was."

She shook her head. "The thing about it was that I thought it couldn't be her, because there was a little boy with her."

"Her nephew, Jimmy," he said in the preface to relating the tragedy that had brought Kate back to Avalon Bay.

"Funny we didn't hear anything about it," she pondered for a moment. "Then again, Lydia's always been kind of close-mouthed." She turned her attention back to the topic of the little boy. "You said he has some kind of learning problems?"

"Autism," he replied, admitting that he didn't really know that much about it, but that Kate told him she had already phoned a couple of experts back home that she was going to take him to.

"And home is?"

"Las Vegas."

Abby scowled. "That's kind of a strange place to be raising a child, don't you think? All that hustle and noise and goodness knows what else?" That she had never actually been within the Vegas city limits herself was no obstacle to repeating what she'd heard from various friends who had.

John pointed out that there were probably a lot of places that were much stranger, discreetly omitting any mention of Kate's reference to her sister's nomad lifestyle and the instability it must have imposed on an already confused little boy. "I'm sure they'll do just fine," he said. "Kate's always had a good head on her shoulders."

"Well, it's too bad she couldn't have talked to Gabrielle while she was here."

"Gabrielle?"

"Helen's daughter?" Abby went on to explain that the girl had worked at a school for autistic children in South Carolina and was now back in Avalon Bay with the idea of starting a similar facility of her own. "She's very smart, very pretty...did I happen to mention that she's also newly divorced?"

Evening had fallen on the West coast but the sparkling city light show Kate had hoped to show her nephew would need to wait. After only three bites of spaghetti, a couple of spoonfuls of instant chocolate pudding and a partial glass of milk, the little lad was yawning wide enough to turn himself inside out.

"Maybe we've done enough for one day," she announced, scooting back her chair and standing up, held out her hand to him.

He yawned again and reached for Mr. Ollie who had been invited to join them at the dining table. With a squeak of spontaneity, he now plopped the bear on top of his head like a funny-looking four-legged beret and proceeded to follow her into the spare bedroom without it once falling off.

"Sweet dreams, angel," she whispered a few minutes later as she tucked him in and kissed his forehead. Nearly asleep, he really did look like a contented little cherub and she found herself wistfully thinking that maybe this wasn't going to be so difficult after all, especially once she talked to someone who knew the ropes and could give her advice.

As she started toward the kitchen to clean up, her glance fell on the phone and she realized she hadn't called her mother back as she'd promised. Considering it was almost 10:30 on the East coast, of course, it was unlikely the older woman would still be up and puttering around. She'd call her in the morning.

She had just finished rinsing off the first plate to put in the dishwasher when there was a sharp rap on the front door. Puzzled, she crossed to answer, safe in the knowledge that the combination of coded key cards and judicious doormen at the luxury high-rise permitted access only to residents and their invited guests.

"Hey, gorgeous," her visitor said as he winked and gallantly offered her a single long-stemmed red rose. "Ready to do the town?"

A Seaside Story

Chapter Seven

T hat Derek Jones, or "DJ" as he preferred, was often
mistaken for Keanu Reeves by Las Vegas celebrity-
seekers brought him a head-turning level of attention
that some might say he enjoyed with great amusement. Witty,
urbane, well-traveled and possessed of a phenomenal business
sense when it came to media relations and product placement, there
was no shortage of speculation among the staff at *Vegas Essential,*
including Dee herself, as to why this oh-so-eligible bachelor hadn't
been grabbed up long before now.

The immediate mystery in Kate's mind, however, was what,
exactly, he was doing standing outside her front door with a single
red rose.

"Uh—hi," she mumbled with a forced show of cheerfulness that
belied her complete confusion.

Reflected light from the corridor's chandeliers glimmered over his
tanned face like beams of star-quality radiance. "Just get home from
work?" he asked, doing a quick once-over of her casual ensemble

and, though subtle in his reaction, apparently not finding it a particularly suitable complement to his *GQ* attire.

"Actually,"

"Hey, no problem," he assured her with a suave smile as he stepped inside the marble-floored foyer. "Our dinner reservations aren't 'til 8:30." He cast an appreciative eye around the stylish décor of the condo. "Nice place. I like your style."

Kate's mind was racing. *What's he doing here?*

"I thought that maybe we could go catch some drinks first," he suggested, sensuously trailing the fingers of one hand down the full length of her bare arm. "Unless you've already got something on ice for us?" There was a maddening hint of arrogance and expectation about his demeanor that suddenly seemed magnified to her out of the usual context of their chats at the office and media events with the magazine's advertisers.

"Uh,"

He flashed her a charismatic and blindingly perfect grin that she suspected had to have been chemically induced to be that dazzling of a shade of white. "You didn't forget it was tonight, did you?" he teased.

Distraction had to be evident in her every move as he followed her into the kitchen and yet her visitor seemed to be totally oblivious to it.

"Okay, I'm going to feel like a complete idiot here," she confessed, "but did the two of us have something planned for this evening?"

His smile deepened into laughter. "You're kidding me, right?"

Kate shook her head. "Sorry."

He tilted his head in puzzlement. "Three weeks ago at Ivan's bash?" he said, hoping to jog her memory. "We talked about maybe getting together."

Their conversation suddenly came crashing back to her. The champagne. The flirtation. An invitation to go clubbing and dancing that had come well before she got the news about Cassy. "Lucky duck," Dee had said in envious admiration when she told her that DJ had asked her if she'd like to go out to dinner with him sometime.

There had ensued at Ivan's, she recalled, a simultaneous and moderately humorous reach for their respective smartphones to scroll through their calendars and lock down a night in the coming weeks that neither one of them had any prior commitments.

Tonight, it seemed, was apparently it.

"The truth of it is," Kate now awkwardly admitted, "I've been out of town and just got back. My younger sister, Cassy, was, uh..." *Will it ever get easier to say it out loud?* she wondered. "She was killed in an accident."

DJ exhaled a mild expletive in response. "Whoa, you must be, like, totally bummed," he remarked, his dark brows slanting into a frown.

Though 'bummed' certainly wasn't the word she would have chosen herself, Kate nonetheless nodded in acknowledgment of his concern for her recent loss. "It hit my mother and me pretty hard," she said. "Mom especially." Lydia, she went on, felt there was something wrong with a universe that allowed parents to outlive their children.

"So, I guess our going out tonight's probably the best medicine, huh?" he opined with a cavalier wink.

Did I just hear that right? "Excuse me?"

He shrugged. "Death 'n' stuff. Nothing you can really do about it," he said. "May as well go catch some fun, have a few laughs, move on with your life."

Move on? Kate couldn't believe what she was hearing. "I'm afraid it's not that simple," she replied, explaining that she had brought her five-year-old nephew back with her from New Jersey and that she had just put him to bed.

"Five, huh? Whoa." His face spoke volumes. Children, it seemed, weren't a part of his operating vocabulary or personal interest.

"It's been a rough week," she continued, "and a pretty long day for both of us, flying back from Jersey 'n' all."

"So, like, what's the big deal if he's crashed out for a couple of hours without you here?" DJ replied after a contemplative pause that Kate mistook for a show of compassion. "We'll probably be back before the little squirt even knows it."

"Are you crazy?" she snapped at him in response, astonished that he'd even suggest such a stupid idea. "You can't just leave a child home alone like that! What if he got hurt? What if he gets scared? What if—"

He playfully put up his hands in mock surrender. "Hey, hey, relax," he interrupted her with an accompanying chuckle that she assumed was supposed to suggest he was only pulling her leg. "There's no reason we can't just hang here for the evening…"

I can think of one, Kate thought. *I'm really starting to not like you all that much.* Out loud, she mustered the diplomacy to tell him that she didn't think she'd be very good company. "Maybe some other time."

His left brow rose a fraction in response, an intimation to Kate that he clearly wasn't accustomed to his dates dismissing him before they even got out the front door. He was now unbuttoning his double-breasted jacket to retrieve his ever-present smartphone from the inside pocket. "Let me see what I've got cookin' after Cannes," he started to say but Kate reached over to put a light hand on his wrist.

"Why don't we just play it by ear instead?" she recommended, surprising herself by how breezy and lackadaisical she sounded, in spite of the fact she couldn't wait to get rid of him.

DJ shrugged. "Whatever," he replied, hanging back a moment for one last try and pressing his moist lips to the back of her hand as he weighed her with a critical squint. "Sure I can't twist your arm for a glass of wine or something?"

"I'm pretty untwistable," she declined, "But, thanks for asking."

Sleep, when it finally arrived, was fitful at best. Kate had purposely stayed awake for as long as she could, straining for any sounds of fears, tears or anxiety that might emanate from the spare bedroom. Several times, in fact, she had tiptoed in to check on him and was greeted by the same sight. Jimmy, wherever his dreams were taking him that night, was truly in no hurry to return to the waking world.

How do new mothers ever manage to get through their first night with a newborn in the house, she asked herself while she was getting ready for bed. Was the obvious answer that they had nine months to prepare for a change in the status quo and had filled that time going to every class and reading every baby and parenting how-to book they could get their hands on? She tried to think back and remember how Cassy had handled it.

Cassy, of course, had been girlishly giddy about the entire prospect of being pregnant, a surprise development that she blissfully believed would not only encourage Luke to become a more mature human being but also keep him from straying into the arms of one of his groupies. In their sporadic conversations on the phone from San Francisco, she had eagerly recounted to Kate how she planned to decorate a nursery, fill it with cute toys, and devote every waking minute of her life to the joys of motherhood.

How she and Luke planned to pay for any of this, of course, was a topic that she'd quickly change whenever it came up.

Even after Jimmy's condition was diagnosed and Luke had extricated himself from any responsibility beyond occasional support checks whenever he had a good gig, Cassy continued to extol the value of her son's companionship. "He keeps me focused," she'd say, though neither Kate nor her mother saw it manifested in the hit-and-miss way she seemed to manage her affairs and her finances.

One thing for certain, though, she'd seemed to know more about being a nurturing mother than Kate had ever picked up from being a long-distance aunt. Even when they were younger, Cassy had always been the one who jumped at any opportunity to babysit for their neighbors' babies and toddlers while Kate excused herself to go study at the community library. It was Cassy who teased her that if Kate ever had children of her own, her woeful lack of experience would render her clueless about what to do with them and she'd probably have to hire her sister to come over just so the little tykes wouldn't starve. "And I'll charge you double for it, too!" she'd threaten.

So many things I wish I'd had the chance to ask you, Kate now reflected. *So much stuff I'm going to have to figure out all on my own.*

She wondered, for instance, whether she should close the bedroom door so Jimmy wouldn't wander out and hurt himself or keep it open so that she could hear him if he cried out. Should she throw a blanket on the leather chaise and stay in the room all night with him? Should she brew a pot of strong coffee, move a chair in front of the door and try to keep a vigil until morning? In the end, exhausted by all the worst-case scenarios and what-if's that her imagination was conjuring, Kate laid down atop the satin covers of her bed with the intention of napping only briefly.

Behind closed eyelids, the first image that flickered into focus was John Neal. He was intently staring at her and his lips were moving but no sound was coming forth. Instinctively, she put out a hand to touch him but his expression suddenly darkened to one of anger as he stepped just beyond her reach and turned his back. A wave of water ominously rose between them, drenching her as she struggled to catch up with him and washing her away from her high school sweetheart.

Giggles from a woman and a child assailed her ears and she could see the chocolate-smeared faces of her sister and Jimmy as the two of them pretended to walk a circus tightrope across the pier at Avalon Bay. "Look out!" she tried to shout in warning as the Boardwalk gave way with a crash but her cry was that of a screeching seagull.

"You didn't say goodbye," she heard John accuse her.

He was standing behind her, not as the man who had driven her to the airport that morning but as a muddied high school quarterback with black tears running down his face. "You didn't say goodbye," he repeated again but as she moved toward him a second time, his image was replaced by the towering appearance of Dee, her tanned arms full of loose paperwork. "I need all of this done by yesterday," she shrieked, summarily dropping the entire stack on Kate's head, knocking her off the boardwalk.

She awoke with a start and it took a blurry moment for her eyes to adjust to the familiar shadows of her bedroom. *Serves me right for eating spaghetti and pudding for dinner,* she chided herself in an attempt to rationalize the weirdness of her dream's content. It was Cassy, she recalled, who put great store in dreams having profound meaning and was always poking her nose in special dictionaries that purported to explain what the dreamer was secretly thinking about.

What a no-brainer, Kate thought. *I'm thinking that I'm overwhelmed. I'm thinking that I miss my sister. I'm thinking that I really miss*—She firmly pushed this last thought aside.

Reluctant to go back to sleep right away lest she pick up where she left off, she decided to check in on Jimmy again. Sometime since her last visit, Mr. Ollie had fallen to the carpet and she bent down to pick him up, gently setting him on top of the covers near Jimmy's hand. Jimmy didn't stir. Kate decided on closing the door to Jimmy's room as she walked into her living room to turn on the computer.

With the glow of the monitor the only illumination in the room, Kate scrolled through the online dream dictionary she had found via Google. *Am I that unique,* she wondered, *that I'm the only person who has ever dreamt this?* Falling in one's dreams, on the other hand, yielded no shortage of warnings that the dreamer might be experiencing a spiraling loss of control in his or her life.

"Duh," she murmured as she exited the screen.

She strolled over to the window and looked out on the jewel of Nevada, its proliferation of casino and hotel windows still feverishly glittering with bright lights in spite of the hour. A far cry from sleepy Avalon Bay, she reflected, where, for the lack of much pulse-pounding excitement, they may as well have rolled up the sidewalk every night except New Year's and the 4 of July. Only the breeze-jiggled string of amber lanterns along the harbor and now mostly closed Boardwalk defied any adherence to curfew.

Unexpectedly, a lump came to her throat.

Until tonight, she had never felt more alone.

C.J. Foster

Chapter Eight

Try as he might to keep the sweet remembrance of Kate at a safe remove, John Neal was fighting a losing battle. It was pointless to close his eyes again, he realized. He'd only fall asleep and see her in his dreams, dreams that had no bearing on the reality that she was two thousand miles away and, in all likelihood, in a committed relationship with someone who wore Armani suits, drove an expensive car and sported a tan direct from St. Tropez. The two of them probably turned heads wherever they went, he imagined, though a cynical part of him also wondered whether Kate's escort was the type who liked to repeatedly check his reflection in elevator mirrors and silverware.

On the other hand, he mused, the perfection of a GQ jet-setter image didn't seem entirely consistent with the companionship of a child who probably liked to leave grape jelly handprint smears on every surface he touched. He caught himself smiling in the dark at how Jimmy had pointed at his shoes and said "parade". Funny word to stick in a five-year old's head, he thought, trying to fathom how much he'd understood about the floats and the marching bands that Cassy had camped out overnight on a sidewalk to share with him.

That he couldn't articulate those memories to anyone was an irony John could personally relate to, especially in light of the daily struggles he saw his father go through to regain his ability to walk and talk. Certainly, there'd been no shortage of outbursts of seemingly unrelated words from Sean when he first came home from the hospital, a situation that often left Abby baffled.

"What do you suppose he means by 'Joof cat'?" she'd ask John, relating that this was something his father had been angrily repeating to her all afternoon. The next day, it would be completely forgotten and either replaced by a different string of strange words or complete silence. "Do you want some Joof cat?" Abby would ask him, hoping that her mimicking might lead them to invent a special interim language through which they could more easily communicate with one another. Sean, in response, would look at her as if she were some kind of an idiot who was trying to drive him crazy.

The doctors had explained to them in layman's terms that everything was still in Sean's head but that it would take time for his brain to learn how to retrieve it. They had also been honest in their assessment that some of the older man's memories were probably lost forever. John remembered his mother saying, "As long as they're only the unhappy ones, maybe that's not such a bad thing."

A black veil was now moving painfully at the back of John's mind, triggered by his father's mention the previous afternoon of the money that was available for him to go back to school. If he remembered the money, it was only a matter of time that he might also start remembering where it had come from.

Shelby was now stirring at the foot of the bed, her canine sixth sense perhaps telling her that her master was awake, restless, and in need of a wet nose in his ear.

"Bed hog," John said to her as she maneuvered herself into a comfy spot closer to the pillows. He glanced over at the alarm, dismayed to see that the time displayed was a tweener, too early to get up and start the day but too late to roll over and try to catch a few more zzz's. For a moment he was tempted to go downstairs and retrieve the college brochures just to give himself something to do until daybreak. "It wouldn't hurt to just look at them," Abby had tried to coax him.

To John's way of thinking, of course, even a casual perusal might suggest that he was admitting his parents were right, that his life could stand for a little improvement. Even worse – and unspoken – was the reminder of why he and Kate had gone their separate ways after high school. Seeing the trappings of success that her Amherst education had brought her, he reflected, only widened what was already an impossibly wide chasm between them.

"Well, aren't you the early bird?" Abby declared in surprise.

John, with his back to the entryway, was making a Cajun omelet for himself when his mother entered the room. Had he turned at that precise moment to acknowledge her presence, he might have dropped the frying pan at the alarming sight of her sporting a facial mask.

"Not a look for everyone," he remarked, mindful of the silly fact that his mother's penchant for trying out radical new beauty remedies had been a family joke for at least a decade. "What's this one supposed to do?"

"Anna swears that it takes twenty years off."

The image of Anna Loftig, wizened and not unlike an apple doll with clove eyes, made John chuckle. "Anna's older than dirt," he said. "You mean she'd look a lot worse if she didn't use it?"

His mother quickly rose to the retired librarian's defense. "She happens to be very well preserved for her age."

"Yeah, that's what they say about mummies, too. So, where did she get it?"

Abby poured herself a generous cup of coffee as she explained that the youth-rejuvenating mineral masque originally came from the Dead Sea and that her friend had recently purchased a jar from two lovely girls at a kiosk down in Cape May. "Anna had quite the chat with them and found out that they're from Israel. Isn't that interesting?"

"And they're selling the beauty products here in Jersey?" John replied with an arched brow of suspicion. "They're probably with the Mossad."

"Oh don't be silly! Why would spies be selling facials and body butter off a cart at a mall?"

"Sounds like a good enough cover to me," he opined.

Abby took an appreciative whiff of the spicy omelet he was now getting ready to transfer to a plate. "I'll have one of the same as long as you're up," she announced. "Smells good."

"Take this one and I'll make myself another," he offered, thankful for having learned when he was still in high school how to put a meal together without killing anyone. His interest in the culinary arts, of course, went back to Mitch's juvenile taunts that he'd starve if the Neal household was ever torn asunder. To everyone's surprise, he'd gotten quite good at finding his way around a kitchen, an asset that Abby frequently liked to remind him would be an attractive draw to any young lady he chose to woo. Mitch, on the other hand, subsisted wholly on take-out and corporate expense accounts. If anyone did the cooking at his Georgetown digs, it was obviously Mindy.

As he handed her the plate, he couldn't help but stare again at the coal-black concoction that camouflaged everything except her eyes. "So, has Dad seen you yet?" he asked.

"Heavens, no. He'd probably freak out, wouldn't he?"

"To say the least."

Sean, she explained, was sleeping soundly like a baby while she'd been in the bathroom applying her latest modern miracle. "Isn't it funny," she said, "how he can drive us to distraction all day long from worrying about him and yet every night he goes to bed like he doesn't have a care in the whole world?"

John gently reminded her that neither of them knew that for certain.

"I suppose," she agreed, wondering aloud that if he ever regained full control he might proceed to talk non-stop just to catch up on all of the time he'd been forced into silence. "Getting a word in edgewise with him could be like trying to thread a sewing machine while it's still running."

"I'd been wondering the same thing about Jimmy," he said.

"Jimmy?"

John refreshed her memory concerning Kate's nephew. "It's gotta be hard," he commented, "taking on a responsibility like that for a little kid who's not even your own."

Before his mother could contribute her two cents on the subject, the doorbell rang. Shelby was already barking to alert her household to an unexpected morning caller.

"I probably should get that," John offered, "seeing as how—"

Abby finished the sentence for him. "I wouldn't want to scare anyone off."

"Y'know, if we got ourselves a video phone," he mused. "Maybe you could scare off the telemarketers, too."

Shelby was impatiently pacing back and forth in front of the front door when he reached the living room. John snapped his fingers to command her to move out of the way so he could at least open it without 70 pounds of canine curiosity wedged in-between.

A petite young woman with long black hair swept into a high ponytail and wearing a rose pink jogging suit was standing on the porch and holding a pair of half-frame reading glasses.

"Oh hi," she said, enthusiastically extending her free hand in greeting. "You must be John?"

"Guilty," he replied. "And you're?"

"Gabrielle Davis—uh, I mean Delvaggio," she replied with a movie star smile. She indicated the glasses in her left hand. "I think that your mom left these at the bridge game last night."

"The challenge in dealing with autism," Muriel Moran reiterated, "is that there's no one-size-fits-all presentation or treatment."

She had been sitting on Kate's sofa and taking notes for nearly an hour and a half but so far the school caseworker had yet to divulge anything about Jimmy's condition that Kate didn't already know from her research on the Internet and experience with the boy. Despite the increase in and diversity of clinical therapies available to help autistic children and adults learn communication, social and life skills, the complexity of neurological factors that interfered made individual results a total crapshoot.

Nor, Muriel emphasized, was the expense of special education classes, speech, and occupational therapy as well as the ongoing tests easily affordable for most families. That she had commented several times on the condo's furnishings and fabulous view since her arrival underscored the woman's awareness that her potential client was not looking to effect change on the cheap.

The only flicker of a bright spot, or so Kate reassured herself, was that Jimmy's symptoms weren't as severe as they might be on the spectrum of developmental disorders. She had often wondered if his being seen by so many different pediatricians in such a short stretch of time might have contributed to some mistakes in his record. Certainly, from her viewpoint as an adult, the stress of having to recount her health history to someone new was never a task she looked forward to whenever an employer's health plan changed.

A short distance away, Jimmy had taken off both of his socks and was attempting to stuff Mr. Ollie's head into one of them.

"The important thing," she told Muriel, "is that I'd like to get my nephew enrolled in the right level program and be around kids his own age." Playing with other children, she explained, hadn't been part of his upbringing with Cassy since the latter was always worried about him being picked on for being different. Not to mention that Jimmy preferred being alone. There was an indefinable feeling of rightness, Kate thought, to be able to move him into an environment that would allow him to just be himself and explore his surroundings. "How soon do you think we could get him started?"

"Wanting to make up for lost time is certainly understandable, Ms. Toscano, but I have to be honest and tell you that—"

"I know what you're going to say," Kate apologetically cut in. "Patience." She looked over at Jimmy and smiled. "It's just that he's lost so much and I want to do whatever I can for him."

Muriel nodded thoughtfully. "He's very lucky to have you." She was now withdrawing some forms from her portfolio. "Just a few more things I'll need you to look over and sign for us as the boy's legal guardian."

It was almost a throwaway line and yet it jumped out at Kate as suddenly as if someone had thrown a neon switch on it. "Excuse me," she spoke up to correct her, "but I'm just Jimmy's aunt." That her sister's death was so recent hadn't allowed enough time for her to plan much beyond the flight back to Las Vegas.

Behind her tortoise shell glasses, there was a significant lifting of Muriel's eyebrows. "But you do have some sort of legal authority granted by the courts to make decisions on his behalf?"

On the surface, Kate depicted ease she didn't necessarily feel. "It's what Cassy would have wanted for him," she said. "The two of us were always close and certainly she knew if anything ever happened to her that our mother—"

"Did she put those specifics in writing?" Muriel sharply interrupted.

Kate couldn't believe what she was hearing. "No one that young ever..." She lowered her voice and measured her words lest Jimmy overhear. "She couldn't have known that something like this would change everything."

Without looking at her, Muriel started to reach for the papers she had taken out only a moment before.

"Listen," Kate said, "this is all new to me but I'm doing the best I can. Just tell me what exactly it is I need to do and what I have to file with the courts and I'll get everything back to you by tomorrow."

"I appreciate your sincerity, Ms. Toscano, but the petition process for guardianship doesn't move quite that fast." The capacity and disposition of the petitioning party, the stability of the home, and the best interests of the child, she explained, all had to be taken into consideration before a decision, even a temporary one, could be rendered.

"At least let me get the ball rolling," Kate insisted, suddenly anxious that if Jimmy had a medical emergency between now and when the ink dried she might not be able to authorize any treatment. "I'm all he has left now."

Muriel was writing down a phone number and handing it to her. "They'll be able to walk you through the hoops. As far as enrolling him in our program at this particular time, however..." Her sentence went unfinished as she glanced over at the subject of their conversation who was now amusing himself by rolling back and forth over Mr. Ollie the speed bump. "By the way," she delicately queried, "I'm assuming that his father not in the picture?"

"Totally lost cause," Kate candidly volunteered. "Wannabe rocker."

Muriel frowned. "He's still alive then?"

Kate shrugged. "I assume so."

Muriel pursed her thin lips.

"Something wrong?" Kate asked.

"Very much so, Ms. Toscano. I'm afraid this changes everything."

Chapter Nine

"**D**o I *look* like a restaurant?" John remarked as a cheerful Abby proceeded to rinse off the trio of dishes following their impromptu guest's departure.

"It was only breakfast," she replied. "You don't have to get so huffy about it."

John rolled his eyes. "First it's breakfast, then dinner, then you've got the two of us packed off to an altar."

"She does seem like an awfully nice girl, doesn't she?"

"And you made an awfully fast appearance for someone who didn't want to be seen," he chided her, recounting the super-human speed with which she had raced upstairs, removed all trace of her Dead Sea facial, and made it back down in time to invite Gabrielle to join them in the kitchen before the latter could get off their front porch.

"It was the least I could do to thank her for returning my glasses."

"Which, I'm sure, you left at Helen's on purpose."

Abby stuck her tongue out at him. "Can I help it if I just want to see you happy?"

"I *am* happy."

"You could be happier," she insisted. "Look at your brother. He's finally settling down."

John dumped out the coffee grounds into the garbage can with a defiant flick of his wrist. "When I decide to follow "settle down", I promise you'll be the first to know."

"Well, it's not going to happen if you don't start putting yourself out there."

"'Out there?'"

"Haven't I always told you that you'd make a wonderful catch?"

John let her praise go unanswered, having had more than enough reminders in the past twenty-four hours that the only girl he had ever wanted to be caught by had thrown him back in the pond without a second glance.

He recalled that he had first really noticed Kate Toscano on a Tuesday afternoon. That wasn't to say, of course, that he hadn't seen her around Avalon Bay for most of his life or that he had a particularly phenomenal memory to remember the exact day of the week.

Like many of his peers, he had tried to squeeze the very last ounce out of a blissful summer vacation over a decade ago; its symbolic ending on Labor Day was no exception that year. When he had grudgingly dragged himself out of bed the next morning, it was with the realization that he was a junior in high school and he hadn't saved quite as much money as he had hoped from part-time yard work to put toward the purchase of his first car.

As always, his best friend Lenny Molino had come up with 'The Plan'.

One of the seniors, Lenny told him, wanted to offload his old car in time for the graduation promise of a coveted new one from his parents. Even without the benefit of a name, John had known exactly who it was.

Brad Leister, in John's view, represented everything that could be potentially bad about Avalon Bay. Out-of-towners from Manhattan, the Leisters had bulldozed their way into the community when John was around twelve and made it immediately clear that they knew more than anything about anybody. Brad's father was a new VP at the bank which, if one were to believe Brad's boasting, meant that their family pockets were virtually bottomless. Neither the smartest student nor the most athletic, Brad nonetheless had a following who'd do anything he wanted.

John, obviously, was not one of them.

"We can't afford to buy his stupid car," he told Lenny.

Lenny countered with the argument they couldn't afford not to. Relying on the generosity and whim of parents to loan them the family car for a date just wasn't going to cut it.

John reminded him that neither of them exactly had the ladies knocking down their doors.

"Because we don't have a car!" Lenny shot back.

The "we" part of his plan was that they'd pool their money and make Brad an offer he couldn't refuse.

"What are we, the Mafia?" John said, certain that Brad would laugh them off no matter what they offered.

Lenny, however, was undaunted. He had already talked to Brad, it turned out, and the latter agreed to meet them in the parking lot when classes were over on the first day back to school.

The first wrinkle was that Lenny forgot he was supposed to run an errand for his grandmother and was going to be late.

The second was that when John reached the perimeter of the parking lot at the appointed hour, Brad was engaged in conversation with a girl who had silky blond hair that fell past her shoulders. From the back, he didn't realize it was Kate, a girl he knew only casually from around the neighborhood and school but never had more than two words with.

Even from a distance, he could see that there was some kind of argument going on. Probably haggling about the price of the car, he assumed. He nearly walked away at that moment, concurrently annoyed by the smug look of triumph on Brad's face and the fact that Lenny had bailed on him. Curiosity, however, prompted him to stay where he was, a decision that put him right in the path of an unexpected destiny.

She had suddenly turned away from Brad and, with head down, was moving quickly in John's direction. A few feet short of him, she looked up and it was only then he saw that her face was glistening with fresh tears. She gave him an embarrassed, almost apologetic smile and was about to continue on her way past him when he found the voice to ask her if something was wrong.

She seemed surprised at first that he should ask and as she quickly brushed her fingertips across a moist cheek, she informed him that she was okay but that she thought all guys were jerks.

How did a member of the accused sex respond to such a statement, John wondered. A hundred things raced through his head at the same time, the majority of them being a derogatory assessment of the jerk who had obviously just made her cry. Across the parking lot, he noticed that Brad was watching them and, for an instant, John was curious about whether he and Kate might be an item; it was a thought that disturbed him, to say the least. Around school, Brad Leister made no secret of the chauvinistic belief inherited from his father that females existed for only one reason.

Kate turned and noticed that they were being watched, too. As she started to move away, John reached out and lightly touched her arm. "I don't suppose," he started to say, faltering as her luminous green eyes met his.

"Suppose what?" she asked with a tilt of her head, presumably unaware of the captivating picture she made with even the faintest return of a smile.

John began his sentence again and steeled himself to finish it this time. "I don't suppose a great pizza would change your mind about all the world's guys being jerks?" he proposed.

She considered his suggestion just long enough for John to assume she was probably going to decline.

"I guess there's only one way to find out," she replied.

C.J. Foster

'Capparelli's' was a typical mom-and-pop pizza shop on the Jersey shore that was frequented by anyone and everyone who wanted good Italian food at a cheap price. Antonio 'Tony' Capparelli, the heavy-set owner, prided himself on being a full-fledged immigrant from Sicily who'd "done good" in his new homeland and never let any of his patrons forget it. Above the bar, the Trinacria flag of Sicily shared wall space with the Stars and Stripes and on every 4th of July, miniature versions of both were proudly stuck into the candle-wax remains of the eatery's tabletop Chianti bottles.

At 51, Tony also prided himself on a full head of black hair that he kept greased back with an excess of Vitalis. Though "Mama", his wife, was rumored to only be in her late thirties, the combination of helping Antonio run the restaurant and bearing a succession of Capparelli children made her look far older than her years. Even as she set down two water glasses and handed John and Kate their menus, the toll of keeping up with Little Tony, the latest Capparelli progeny to start public school, was evidenced in her eyes.

"I can't believe you've never been here," John remarked when Kate asked him what he thought they should order.

"My mom and dad aren't all that much for going out," she said with a shrug and continued her perusal.

To John's ears, it was a response that meant maybe they weren't in favor of her dating as well. Then again, he reflected, when he'd overheard her call home to say she was having pizza with a 'friend', she'd been vague enough that perhaps her parents were as clueless as anyone else when it came to what their teenagers were doing.

"The pepperoni and sausage combo looks good," she remarked.

"My favorite," he said, though in truth she probably could have said anything and he would have agreed with her.

"Although the ham and pineapple could be pretty good, too," she mused. "Sounds like Hawaii."

"Have you ever been there?" he wanted to know. He suddenly wanted to know everything about her but Hawaii, he thought, was a nice enough invitation to start.

"Hawaii?" She shook her head. "No, but someday, I think." In the next breath, she told him that she was going to be a writer and travel the world. She took a sip of water and started to open her mouth to ask him something – perhaps what he was going to do with his life – when the ebullient Antonio appeared at their table.

True to his fashion, he wasted no time in kissing Kate's hand and asking John who his pretty date was. That her last name was revealed to be Italian endeared the restaurateur even more. "My chest, it burst with pride Signor Neal bring you here," he declared. The buttons of his shirt, already straining from his girth, threatened to pop completely and expose the rest of his hairy chest. With a dramatic flourish, he whisked away both of their menus and announced that he was going to make them something special.

"So, you started to tell me about your writing," John said when they were alone again. "You must be pretty good."

Again, the casual shrug. "I've won a couple of essay contests," she replied. "Mostly, though, I write for the yearbook staff."

A fact which John was unaware but wasn't about to admit it.

She told him that she and a friend were thinking of going to Amherst. "It seems like it's a long way off," she said, "but you can never start planning too early."

Big Tony appeared again, this time to ask them if they wanted some garlic bread.

"That'd be great," John told him.

"So, what are your plans?" Kate asked a moment later.

"My plan for right now," he answered in complete honesty, "is to wonder how I got so lucky to be sitting across a table from you..."

Back in the present, John could easily have replayed that evening a hundred times in his head. Instead, the sound of a shriek sent him running up the stairs two at a time with a barking Shelby close behind.

"I told you to call me if you needed help," he heard his mother say as he reached the bedroom store and saw her kneeling on the floor over a crumpled Sean. She looked up in relief as John rushed in. "Damn fool tried to get out of bed by himself," she explained, trying to control the panic in her voice.

"Are you okay, Dad?"

Sean looked from one to the other, blinking in bewilderment. Only when he saw the whimpering Shelby trying to push her way into the middle of things did a lopsided smile come to his thin lips. "Sel-ba," he murmured, trying to reach out with his good hand to touch her. "Dog."

"Plenty of time for dog kisses later, Dad," John promised. "Let's get you up, okay?"

"Thank goodness he didn't make it to the stairs," a fretful Abby said. "If I hadn't come out of the bathroom when I did, who knows what would've happened."

"Better give the doc a call just in case," John recommended. "I can handle things at this end."

With Abby now out of the room, John helped his father back into bed, relieved that the older man hadn't seriously injured himself when he made contact with the floor. "You gotta stop scaring us like that, Dad," he gently reminded him. "When you want something, you need to call one of us first and we'll take care of it, okay?"

Sean was staring off into space but his good hand suddenly tightened on John's thigh. "Can't...leave," he muttered. "Bad."

John leaned forward. "Come again?" he asked. "*What's* bad?"

With difficulty, Sean turned his head on the pillow so that he was now facing him. "Tell...her. Can't."

"You want me to tell Mom you can't do something?"

Sean's expression perceptibly darkened and he tried to shake his head.

"Just take your time, Dad. It's okay."

The older man's lips trembled as he took a deep breath and swallowed hard. "Lid...die," he said. "Can't...leave."

Chapter Ten

"We have a problem," Kate said as soon as Lydia picked up the phone. In the background, she could hear the sound of women screaming at each other. *Another installment of the most current trashy daytime talk show*, she surmised, long cognizant of her mother's twisted fondness for watching strangers pull each other's hair and throw furniture.

"What has the boy gone and done this time?" Lydia wanted to know.

All right, I should have seen that one coming from a mile away, Kate thought. "Jimmy hasn't done anything, Mom. It's Luke."

"Luke?" Lydia shrieked. "What's *he* got to do with...hold on a sec. Let me turn this thing down." She returned a moment later to finish her question.

"Not interrupting your program, am I?" Kate asked. "I can call back." Heaven forbid that real-life problems involving her grandson should keep her mother from learning the outcome of scenarios that

Kate was pretty certain were scripted by writers with a sick sense of humor.

"No, that's okay, I can watch with the sound off," Lydia replied, remarking in disgust that she couldn't understand why these stupid women debased themselves on national television by airing their dirty secrets and then acted so blubbering and devastated when they got rejected for it by their husbands and boyfriends.

"I think the operative word is 'act', Mom. You've gotta know those stories they tell can't all be true."

Lydia wasn't convinced. "So, what's this about your sister's dirtbag of an ex?"

"Well, unfortunately, the individual in question has some legal rights in our, uh, current situation."

"Why are you talking in code?" Lydia snapped. "It's not as if the boy understands."

"We don't know that for sure," Kate said, feeling her anger level start to rise.

Across the room, Jimmy and Mr. Ollie were quietly engaged in a game of their own making, a game in which Jimmy laid playing cards, one at a time, in perfect rows on top of the bear until it was completely covered, then yanked him out and started all over again.

"I had a consultation today with a caseworker," she continued. "The school I want to get him into looks like it'll be something really good. The problem, though, is that they can't move any of the paperwork forward for me and get him enrolled until I've got a legal green-light to do it."

"What's that supposed to mean?"

"It means that he's still got a parent in the picture, Mom. Without Luke's involvement in—"

"Involvement?" Lydia repeated in shock. "Did I just hear that right? Since when was that loser ever involved in anything responsible in his life?"

"I'm not going to argue with you about that," Kate agreed, trying to remain calm, "but as a father, the court's going to insist he still has rights and a say-so in things."

"For *doing* nothing? You told them he and your sister were divorced, didn't you?"

Kate affirmed that she had indeed done so but that it apparently didn't make a difference to the State of Nevada.

"Well, did you tell them that he hasn't even seen the boy in, how many years has it been now?"

Kate was impatient and cut to the chase. "The bottom line, Mom, is that Child Protective Services can take him away if there's not a legal guardian appointed by the courts."

"But what about you? Can't those idiots see that you've assumed total responsibility for the boy?"

"Yeah, they can see that but it doesn't exactly mean they're blessing the arrangement with pixie dust."

She stopped just short of divulging that taking her nephew across multiple state lines hadn't been an advisable move, either. For the time being, she was banking on Muriel Moran, if asked, to say that Jimmy was only with her in Las Vegas on a short vacation. Inviting a charge of kidnapping on top of her existing stress was the last thing she needed right now.

"So, what are you supposed to do?" Lydia wanted to know.

"Well, for one thing, I need your help." Even through the phone line she could feel her mother tensing up in dread. Lydia's next words only confirmed it.

"You don't expect me to take the boy, do you?"

I'd sooner leave him to be raised in the woods by wolves, Kate thought. "No, Mom, but I do need you to go through the boxes of Cassy's stuff. Have they gotten there yet?"

"No, her idiot neighbor's probably been too busy."

"Well, could you call her and see if they're on their way? I really need you to look for a couple of things for me."

"Like what?"

"First off, I need a copy of Cass and Luke's divorce decree."

"Why? I thought you said it didn't make any difference."

"I'm not sure yet." She did know from conversations with her sister that the latter had gotten used to Luke routinely shirking his obligations of sending money. If support payments were specified in the decree, though, and she could prove that he'd been a deadbeat dad.

"What else?" Lydia asked. "I'm writing this down."

"I also need you to see if you can find his last mailing address."

"Why on earth would she have that? It's not as if she had any reason to write to him."

How little you knew your own daughter, Kate reflected. Cassy, a romantic at heart, had often stayed in touch with old boyfriends long past the expiration date of their relationships. The father of her son would have been no exception. "We need to get in touch with him and let him know what's going on," Kate continued.

"Well, what if we can't find him? Does that mean you're off the hook?"

"Not really. We've got to prove that we exhausted every possibility." In a nutshell, she explained, it meant doing public notices in city newspapers as well as trying to track down anyone they could think of who might have known him. She vaguely recalled a sibling of Luke's who not only had been a witness to the nuptials but had also been in some of the pictures.

"You mean the one who looked like Alice Cooper?" Lydia said with undisguised disdain.

Kate smiled. For someone who so rigorously eschewed pop culture as much as her mother, it never ceased to amaze her whenever she'd toss out names in a surprisingly accurate context. Must be all the daytime TV she watched, Kate realized. "What I'm thinking is that it could at least be a name and address to go by."

Lydia wasn't convinced the effort would yield anything. "You can't get blood from a turnip," she scoffed. "Isn't that what I've always said?"

"I don't need the turnip's blood," Kate replied. "All I need is his signature on a couple of pieces of paper." Across the room, Jimmy had abandoned the card-stack game and was now tossing Mr. Ollie high over the back of a chair and running around to the other side to retrieve him.

The "beep" of call-waiting gave Kate just the welcome excuse she needed to extricate herself from further explanation of a game plan.

"Gotta go, Mom. Another call. Let me know what you find out."

"Hey, stranger," said Dee.

"Hi."

"Keeping yourself scarce or what?"

"Never a dull moment," Kate replied, hoping Dee wouldn't ask her to explain.

"You sound mega-frazzled."

"Pretty much, yeah."

"I don't suppose the piece you're doing on the circus is done yet, is it?"

Kate cringed. "It's still on a front burner," she lied to Dee. "Honest."

"I know that tone," Dee softly chided. "You haven't even started working on it, right?"

"Well..."

"Listen, it's no prob," Dee assured her. "They don't call me the Queen of Finesse for nothin'."

"Meaning?"

"Meaning I'm hoping you call my bluff and have something spectacular on my desk by tomorrow."

The length of awkward silence on Kate's end of the conversation was all Dee needed to figure out that the answer was otherwise. "Talk to me, Kate," Dee said. "It's not like you to go clammin' up on me."

Where do I even start, Kate wondered. "It's just all so...I don't know, I'm still feeling my way through the whole parenting thing, I guess."

To her surprise, Dee was uncharacteristically sympathetic. "Listen, it sounds like what you need is a tall, cool one at The Club."

For a moment, Kate wasn't sure whether her boss was referring to a drink or a member of the opposite sex. With Dee, of course, one usually led to the other.

"I can meet you there at six," Dee continued, sweetening the offer with the promise that she'd buy. "If you even want to stretch it out to dinner, we can do that."

Kate glanced at Jimmy. "I'm sorta housebound," she replied. "Why don't you come by my—" She caught herself just as she started to say the word "place". To invite her boss to the same address where she was already the landlord sounded ridiculous. Dee, however, paid the slip of tongue no notice.

"Actually, that's a great idea," Dee agreed. "There's something I've been needing to talk to you about anyway."

Only one...really, Kate noticed. *It can't be that important.*

Whatever it was, Dee let the thought go unfinished.

When did life get so complicated, Kate mused as she hung up.

Across the room, one of the least complicated personas in the world was taking an impromptu nap, his trusted Mr. Ollie splayed unceremoniously on top of his forehead.

Back when she was in high school, everything had been so easy. She'd been smart, she'd been popular, and she knew exactly what she wanted to do with the rest of her life. Okay, so maybe she was still smart and popular and woke up every morning with the realization that she was doing exactly what she'd set out to do: be a writer.

The only thing missing was the fourth part of her high school wish list: to have someone to share everything with.

Had it been left up to her mother, of course, the someone in question would have been Brad Leister. "The boy's family has more money than God," Lydia had declared on more than one occasion, usually in the preface to the suggestion that they invite him over to Sunday supper sometime. Kate always corrected her with the fact that it was Brad's father's bank that laid claim to all those dollar signs and that personally, she'd rather eat alone than break bread with such a conceited classmate. Her beloved father would always come to her rescue, deflecting his wife's attacks on his little girl. "You find the one that's right for you," he would tell her, holding her in his strong arms, protecting her from the world. And from *mom*, Kate would often remember later in life. She always felt safe with him.

When word got back to Lydia through her network of beauty parlor friends that Brad's father was buying Brad a new car as a graduation present, she immediately seized upon the idea that maybe Kate should buy his old one. "Your father and I can put up part of the money for it," she said.

In her mother's eager eyes, Kate could see that she deemed buying Brad's car as just a hop, skip and a jump from bearing his children. The combined argument that she really preferred walking and that she'd rather not get a car until she went off to college fell on deaf ears.

"You should at least talk to him about it before you make a decision," Lydia insisted. "Besides," she added, "I already called his mother and said you'd have time to meet him and take a look at the car after school tomorrow."

Kate's mouth had dropped open in surprise. "But it's the first day of school!" she protested, furious that her mother had gone behind her back. "What if I had plans with my friends?"

"There's nothing wrong with having a friend who's rich," Lydia matter of factly informed her.

Throughout the next day, her first day as a junior, Kate had quietly seethed. Her plan, or so she hoped, was simply to catch Brad at his locker between classes or at lunch and tell him she wasn't going to show at the appointed hour. Each time, though, he was always surrounded by his stupid possie. She tried to catch his eye but he'd just acknowledge her with a nod and go on talking.

By the time her last class was over that afternoon, there was no choice but to go meet him and explain that she just wasn't interested.

"Not from what I've seen," Brad said, flashing his award-winning grin and winking at her. "I'd say you were very interested."

It took her a moment to realize that he wasn't talking about a car sale. Initially irked by his arrogant behavior, she started to explain that the whole thing about meeting him in the parking lot had been her mother's idea.

Brad's gaze was traveling from her sandals to her neckline. "That's what they all say," he teased. "I saw the way you've been looking at me…"

Kate's indignation only gave him more fuel to tease her. "Obviously," he insinuated, "you don't know what the guys in the locker room are saying about you."

Though she knew she had nothing to hide, Kate was furious that he'd even hint she was the object of sleazy rumors.

"Of course, I'd be happy to set 'em straight," he continued, reaching out to trail his fingers down the length of her arm. "I've always wanted to try an Italian."

Kate angrily swatted his hand away, a maneuver that only made Brad chuckle and tease her about pretending to be hard to get.

How dare he!

She turned on her heel and strode back toward the school, her only thought of putting as much distance between herself and Brad as possible. Intent on her escape, she looked up just in time to keep from colliding with John Neal. "Is something wrong?" he asked her with such concern and tenderness that she wasn't sure at first how to react.

Before she knew it, they were sharing a pizza across a table from one another at Capparelli's and talking as if they had known each other all their lives. A couple of times during the meal, she'd wondered whether he was going to ask her about Brad. A part of her recoiled at the thought, especially in remembrance of the veiled threat to spread lies and ruin her reputation. Instead, John made no mention of Brad at all.

When she arrived at school the next morning, her stomach was churning with dread. To her surprise, though, no whispers or looks floated her way that Brad had done anything.

Nor would he ever, she later realized. Of all the guys in school, John Neal was the one person Brad Leister secretly feared.

Chapter Eleven

"Nothing to worry about," Doctor Diaz assured Abby and John after he had examined Sean for any signs of injury. "Why, I've done a lot worse to myself just putting the cat out for the night."

"Somehow the idea of our family physician falling off his porch doesn't exactly fill me with confidence," Abby remarked.

Diaz chuckled. "Yes, but I'm the last of a breed that still makes house calls," he reminded her.

In fact, José Diaz, Avalon Bay's premier physician, was too busy to make housecalls, Abby knew. But he lived just down the street from the Neals and had grown up with Sean. She knew José would have been livid if he found out that Sean had fallen and Abby hadn't called on him to check on his oldest and dearest friend.

Abby asked him if he wanted a cup of coffee to go.

"Don't mind if I do," replied José as he snapped his medical bag shut and issued a good-natured warning to his patient not to go causing them all any more panic.

Sean, comfortably propped up against the pillows, managed a lopsided smile but said nothing as his wife and close friend started to leave the room.

"Oh, by the way," José said, turning to John. "Mind running by the house one day next week? The wife needs you to look at a couple of her elms."

"Are they sick?" John asked in concern.

The doctor shook his head. "Nope. She just wants 'em moved."

"Moved or removed? There's a big difference."

José informed him they were in the process of enlarging their back deck and his spouse had determined that the two trees closest to it would look better if they were transplanted to the other side of the yard.

"Always iffy," John cautioned. "Sure you guys want to do that?" Even immature trees, he explained, have a hard time handling the physical stress of a relocation. Whenever it was strictly for cosmetic purposes, of course, it rankled him even more.

"You're the tree doc," José replied. "I get five feet from 'em and they tell me to "leaf' 'em alone." He punctuated it with a hearty laugh and made his exit with the panache of a stand-up comedian on improv night. Abby groaned and rolled her eyes as she followed him out.

"The doc's a pretty funny guy, isn't he?" John remarked, hoping to nudge his father into a conversation. "Remember how you always used to ask him if he'd take us back if we didn't turn out okay when we grew up?"

With the exception of Mitch, all three of the Neal boys had been brought into the world by José Diaz, a second-generation Cuban immigrant. The impatient Mitch, who still refused to follow any timeline other than his own, had debuted two weeks early on the front seat of Sean's truck, an incident that prompted Sean to keep reminding him for the next 18 years what it had cost to clean the upholstery.

Abby, as the story had been related to them, remained remarkably calm during the frantic drive to the hospital after her water broke. Six blocks short of their destination, her firstborn decided not to wait any longer. In his realization of what was happening in the seat next to him, Sean had slammed on the brakes, narrowly missing a collision with a police car. Yet another story that got retold at family gatherings.

John couldn't tell if any of these reminiscences were registering with his father but for the moment he was in no hurry to leave the older man's side. "So earlier you started to tell me something," he continued. "Do you remember what it was?"

Sean's brow had relaxed and he was gazing off into space, seemingly oblivious to his son's presence or voice.

The reference to "Lid...die" had struck John as strange but he assumed that his father was only parroting a piece of their earlier conversation about him taking Kate to the airport. He'd thought about mentioning it to his mother to see if maybe she could decipher what it meant but then decided it probably wasn't anything for either of them to be concerned about.

If *Lid...die* was something important, John wondered, he'd no doubt bring it up again when the spirit moved him.

"Well, aren't you just the cutest little bundle of yumminess!" Dee declared in delight when she first caught sight of Jimmy. The latter had followed Kate to the front door but quickly ducked out of sight behind Kate's legs as soon as he saw the stranger who had dramatically arrived with a bottle of wine in one hand and a Trader Joe's bag in the other. Dee promptly set down the bag to reach out and tousle his mop of hair but Jimmy was too quick for her.

"Zippy little fellow, isn't he?" she fondly observed, now using her free arm to give Kate a hug.

"Looks like you bought enough snacks for an army," Kate commented as Dee handed the bag over to her. Gourmet cheeses, cold cuts, and a box of designer crackers comprised the top layer alone.

"Well, I don't know about you but I for one am really, really ravenous. You wouldn't believe the kind of day I've had."

As she followed Kate into the kitchen, she slipped off her four-inch pink stiletto heels, a maneuver that still left her a couple of inches taller than Kate. Willowy thin and fashion model gorgeous, Dee had the looks for 1920's haute couture and all the baubles, bangles and beads that went with it. Her only concessions to the 21 century were her hair and makeup which she routinely varied from week to week depending on her mood. "There are some cookies in there, too," Dee pointed out. "Does your little man like cookies?"

"I've yet to meet a child who didn't," Kate replied, even though she didn't think giving sugary snacks to one who already had boundless energy was such good an idea. "That was nice of you," she said in thanks to Dee nonetheless.

"Hey, sweetie," Dee cooed. "Come see what your Auntie Dee brought you."

"'Auntie Dee'?" Kate echoed.

Dee shrugged. "Kids always feel more comfortable when they think they're related to you," she said. "I read that somewhere."

And Mom thinks my ideas of child-rearing are weird, Kate thought.

To Dee's disappointment, Jimmy had run off to a far corner of the living room and, by the look on his face, had no intention of rejoining them any time soon. "He's just a little shy when he meets new people," Kate told her boss, not wanting to digress into details that Dee clearly hadn't dropped by to hear.

"Soooooo," Dee mysteriously said as she withdrew a corkscrew from the drawer and began opening the wine. "You'll never guess who Ashley told me asked her to go out clubbing with him."

Gossip first, business later. In a way, Kate was relieved that Dee hadn't started the evening with a long list of assignments that she really, really, really needed to get done.

"Who?" Kate absently inquired, trying to remember whether Ashley was the newest marketing associate to join the staff or one of the prior ones who had just been promoted to corporate sales. The growth of the magazine in recent months had brought such a wave of fresh faces that, working offsite on features as often as she did, Kate had troubling keeping them straight.

Dee drew out the excitement until she had wriggled the cork free and given it a deep whiff of approval. "DJ," she announced.

Certainly didn't waste any time moving on, Kate thought. "That's nice," she replied, indifferently.

Dee shook her head. "I just can't see it. I'd have thought you two would be the next 'It' couple."

'It' couple? "*It* couple?" Kate repeated.

"Well, I mean 'cuz you've got so much in common."

Kate tilted her head and arched a brow.

"You could've had a lot in common if you'd given him a chance," Dee continued. "You've got to admit he's really, really cute."

Kate was quick to counter that she had no time right now to embark on a new relationship.

Her listener was skeptical. "Oh, come on! You're saying that if some handsome, eligible bachelor walked through that door and wanted to take you out on the town, you'd tell him 'no'?"

"And then I'd introduce him to you and you could go out with him and then I'd have all this great salami and cheese to myself."

With the lithe grace of an athlete, Dee hoisted herself up on the counter and, with slender legs crossed at the knees, sipped the glass of wine she had just poured. "Still not over the cutie homeboy, are you?" she teased.

Why do I ever tell her anything? Kate silently chided herself. "Water under the bridge," she said, handing Dee a generous slice of Cotswold to quiet her.

"Methinks thou doth protest too much," Dee replied.

That her boss could quote Shakespeare was surprising enough, Kate marveled. "Look, it was a long time ago."

"So how come you two didn't make it work?" Dee asked bluntly.

"Bad timing, I guess. I don't know." That wasn't entirely true, of course. In retrospect, John Neal had swept her off her feet fairly fast without even seeming to try. Nor had he pushed her into telling her parents when they first started spending time together.

Dee wanted to know how long they had dated.

Kate corrected her that sharing pizzas and hanging out with mutual friends at the Boardwalk on weekends didn't exactly fit the "dating" definition. It wasn't until the afternoon John asked her if she'd like to go to the homecoming dance with him that she realized it was finally time to broach the subject at home. Lydia had gone ballistic. Kate's father, in contrast, had seen nothing wrong with the idea and even commented that he'd worked with Sean at the factory when they were both younger.

"Well, at least you had an ally in your dad," Dee reflected as she plucked a piece of salami off the platter. "That's cool."

A lump of sadness always came into Kate's throat whenever she thought of her father, dead from a sudden heart attack less than a week after he had championed her choice of a date for the dance. The last thing she wanted or needed right now was to dredge up all the memories again of what the Toscano household had been like in the months that followed his funeral. "I guess some relationships just aren't meant to work out," she opined, a preemptive strike to turn the conversation away from the family sorrow that still lingered. "John and I just went our separate ways. End of story."

Dee wasn't buying an explanation that simplistic. "Yeah, but, don't you think it's just the teensiest bit strange that you just happen to go back home and that he just happens to be driving the cab."

"What's your point?" Kate asked, cutting her off.

"My point," Dee continued, "is that it is karma. You've obviously got some majorly unresolved stuff with this guy and the universe is throwing you together to, well, to get it all resolved."

"You didn't come over here just to lecture me, did you?" Kate said.

"Actually," Dee said, "there's something really, really—" She took a deep breath and raked a beautifully manicured hand through her hair. "Oh, I probably should have just told you on the phone and been done with it."

Kate's relief in finally welcoming a change of subject that didn't involve her love life altered instantly into a state of panic. *She's going to fire me,* she thought. *I've been dilly-dallying around so much on getting those assignments done and not coming into the office since I got back that.*

She took a deep breath and tried to stay calm.

"I realize this is probably the very worst timing in the world," Dee was apologizing, "and, believe me, hon, if there were any other possible way around it."

I should have known it was going to come to this, Kate chided herself, conscious that the blood was now beginning to furiously pound in her temples. *When you try to juggle too many balls in the air, it shouldn't be that big a surprise when they start falling and smacking you in the middle of the forehead.* A part of her wondered whether she should plead her case that she was trying to function under extenuating circumstances and hope that Dee had a change of heart. Then again, the likelihood was pretty high that her go-getter boss had already hired her replacement.

"It may not be as bad as it sounds," Dee was saying. "I know I always feel different after a change of scenery."

Not exactly my choice of words for the interior of an unemployment office, Kate thought. *At least I've got some money in reserve,* she remembered. *Not quite as much as I'd like but at least until I get another.*

Alarm bells were suddenly ringing in her head. Up until a week ago, the unbidden prospect of dusting off her resume and making the rounds for new employment would have been labor-intensive and annoying but not impossible. Goodness knew that she'd had plenty of practice at polished interviews during her climb up the career ladder. The realization that she couldn't go anywhere now — much less land a comparable work-at-home scenario - unless she arranged child care for her nephew made Dee's news a bombshell she wasn't prepared to deal with.

Across the room, she noticed that Jimmy had appropriated one of Dee's stilettos and was scrutinizing it intently as if it had just landed from another planet. Her first impulse was to rush over and retrieve it. Her second impulse was to just leave him be. *When someone is in the middle of telling you that you're fired,* she decided, *there's not a lot of motivation to do them the favor of rescuing their footwear from an inquisitive and possibly destructive five-year-old.*

There was no point in postponing the inevitable question that hovered in her brain. "So how much time do I have?" she asked.

Dee laughed. "You make it sound like you've got a terminal disease or something," she said. "Honestly, it's only for two weeks, maybe three weeks max."

She doesn't have to sound so cheerful about it, Kate thought.

"And you don't have to lift a finger to pack," Dee assured her. "I've already arranged for someone to do it for you."

Kate forced a smile that she didn't feel. "Can't wait to get rid of me, huh?" The uncertainty of the immediate future made her remark come out more sarcastic than was perhaps sensible.

"Listen, I promise to make it up to you just as soon as he's gone."

He? "He?" she echoed.

Dee gave her a puzzled look. "My father," she replied. "Haven't you been paying attention to anything I've been saying?"

"Apparently, I must have missed something. What does your father have to do with my being fired?"

It was Dee's turn to look baffled. "I said he was coming out to visit me for a couple of weeks and I needed to stay here in the condo while he's visiting. What did you think I was talking about?"

Kate's deflated ego suddenly became buoyant again. "Sorry," she stammered, "I guess I must've zoned out a sec."

Dee quickly recapped that she needed to temporarily move back in during his stay so as to deflect any suspicion about her actual living arrangements with Anton. "I suppose you missed what I said about The Grand Suites too?"

The Grand Suites? "What about it?"

"Well, since I'm putting you out 'n' all I've already booked you a penthouse to use 'til he leaves. Really, really posh. All the amenities. Anything you need, just put it on my tab."

While she couldn't fault Dee's generosity, the judgment behind it wasn't particularly sound. "Aren't you forgetting someone?" Kate asked.

Dee shrugged. "Who?"

"I can't take a five-year-old to a casino, Dee."

"I'm talking about the *hotel,* honey."

"I know," Kate said. "I'm not sure it's best for Jeremy right now."

"So, stay in the suite the whole time," Dee countered, deeming this a perfectly reasonable solution. "It's big enough to have its own zip code."

"It's not the hotel, Dee. I need to think about the long term for Jeremy."

"Look, it's only for a couple of weeks, maybe a month at the total worst."

"A minute ago it was three weeks max," a skeptical Kate reminded her.

"At the moment," Dee reluctantly confessed, "it's open-ended. He's got some political wing-ding stuff going with the upcoming election."

"In other words, you don't know?"

Dee sighed in resignation. "I really don't. Hey, I don't know what to tell you, hon. I can't very well call and tell him not to come 'cuz if I make too big a deal of it."

"No, no, it's your place," Kate said, taking solace in the fact that at least she hadn't been fired in addition to being sent packing on short notice. "It'll all work out." *Just don't ask me how.*

The solution, when it finally came to her in the wee hours of the following morning, was the last one she would have expected herself to make. Was this how her sister felt, she wondered, every time a door closed and there were no immediate signs of a new one opening? The difference, of course, was that the one choice Cassy could have made in the best interests of her son's emotional stability was the only one she repeatedly ran away from.

Lydia answered on the third ring and immediately wanted to know why Kate was calling her so early.

"I need your help, Mom," Kate declared. "I'm coming home."

C.J. Foster

Chapter Twelve

Three days had passed since Sean's tumble out of bed and, to Abby and John's relief, he was not only willing to start asking for their help when he needed it but also eager to start talking again at every opportunity. As John popped his head in the bedroom door to leave for work, he was surprised to hear his dad chatting away about umbrellas to the ever-attentive Shelby.

"From the looks of it, I don't think we're going to need 'em any time soon," John interjected.

"Need...what?" Sean asked.

"Umbrellas."

A puzzled Sean returned his attention to rubbing Shelby's tummy with his good hand. "Summer," he murmured. "Sun's...out. No umbrella to...day."

"Silly me," John said, quietly grateful that the older man was cognizant of what season was going on outside his bedroom window. "Just stopped in to see if you needed anything before I go."

Sean turned his head on the pillows to look at him. "Go to school," he said after a moment of sluggish contemplation. The intonation hovered halfway between a statement and a question. It was the earnestness in his eyes, though, that seemed to slant his words toward the latter.

John gently corrected him that he was off to his job to save some neighborhood trees from their owners' misplaced intentions. "Trees and then taxis," he said, explaining that the late afternoon runs to the airport for his friend were not only a good source of tips but also allowed him to stay in a cool cab during the muggiest part of the day.

It wasn't until Sean insistently repeated the reference to school that John realized what he was really asking. "Still thinking about it," he replied, though in truth the college brochures hadn't advanced beyond the borders of the coffee table since their arrival in the mail.

"Still thinking about what?" Abby wanted to know, her slippered feet effectively muffling her approach with an armload of freshly laundered towels.

John teased her about whether she was practicing to become a ninja.

"Actually, it's my Harry Potter cloak of invisibility," she shot back, deftly plucking a warm washcloth off the top of the stack and plopping it on her head.

John rolled his eyes and gave her his usual retort whenever she reverted to silliness. "Are you sure I'm not adopted?"

She held up her hand in the three-fingered scout salute. "I swear I was awake for the entire thing and it was no picnic."

Behind John's back, the sight of Abby sporting a square of turquoise terrycloth dipped above her stenciled eyebrows now sent Sean into his first set of chuckles in over a week. It was all the affirmation she needed that at least one person in the family still appreciated her sense of whimsy. "So, what were you boys talking about?" she asked, snapping her fingers as a signal to Shelby to hop down.

The last thing John needed at the moment was for both of his parents to get on his case about going back to school after he'd already made it clear that he liked his life just the way it was. "Umbrellas," he replied.

"In this weather?" she exclaimed. "You've got to be crazy."

He kissed her on the forehead. "Runs in the family. See yah."

"You won't forget about the lasagna, will you?" she called out before he was even halfway down the stairs.

John assured her that he hadn't forgotten and that he was going to make it before his run to the airport.

"And be sure to make extra," she instructed him. "You know how I like to have enough to freeze for later."

Dee had quickly surpassed all of her prior records for saying the word "really" in the short passage of time since Kate had announced her intentions. "I can't help but think it was something I said or did," she kept apologetically pressing despite Kate's insistence that the sudden decision to spend summer on the Jersey shore had absolutely nothing to do with the magazine.

"I need to focus my energy right now on getting all my ducks in order," she explained. As helpful as Dee had offered to make things in terms of her workload, and even recommending names of lawyers who had been former boyfriends, the fact remained that Kate needed to show the semblance of a more traditional home life if Luke emerged from under his latest rock and chose to challenge custody. Difficult as Lydia could be, a grandmother's presence might hold more sway with the courts than a young, unmarried aunt.

"You don't really think this dude's going to show up now and try to take the kid away, do you?" Dee asked as she watched her star writer finish the last of her packing. "I mean if he's been out of the picture for this long?"

"Unfortunately, the law requires us to give him every chance to prove that he's a jerk."

Dee issued a deep sigh. "Well, it's too bad you don't know any guys in the mob who could just *whack* him for you," she declared, betraying her limited impression of "Joisey" as being a place where swarthy men in black pinstripe suits walked around smoking fat cigars and carrying suspicious violin cases.

"I do know guys in the mob," Kate said, "but they're all too busy working in pizza parlors."

Lydia had made no secret of her objections to Kate's stopgap plan. "I can't have the boy getting into things and messing them up," she told her on the phone, "not when I've spent so much time getting it all just the way I want."

Kate tactfully refrained from pointing out that the plethora of organizing she was referring to had taken place in the three weeks after her husband died and that little if any, improvements had been made to the decor ever since. "I know it's an imposition, Mom, and I swear I wouldn't even be asking if there was any other option."

Lydia had sharply interrupted to ask how long an imposition she'd be forced to endure under her own roof. "In my day," she added, "we wouldn't dream of moving back home and inconveniencing our parents."

And yet Gramps and Nana would have taken you in a heartbeat if you ever asked them to. In Kate's view, it just went to show how little a woman like her mother understood the depth of her own family's loyalties. "In the first place, it's only until I find out where things stand with Luke," she said. As reasonably confident as she was that someone as footloose and flaky as her former brother-in-law wouldn't want to be burdened with a child of any age, a part of her also knew that if he thought he could make their lives hell for awhile he probably wouldn't hesitate to do so. "I can't move forward on anything," she continued, "until he agrees to give up his rights to Jimmy."

"I'm not letting him move in, too," Lydia snapped.

"That never even entered my mind, Mom."

Lydia had asked her again how long she and 'the boy' were expecting to stay with her. It was a question she impatiently repeated two days later when Kate called to tell her that she and

Jimmy were on their way to the airport in a black car courtesy of Dee.

"Hopefully we won't be around long enough to drive you crazy," Kate attempted to quip. "Trust me, I was already there from the last time."

Kate had signed off the conversation in the same way as their previous one - with the optimistic notion that their stay might give her mother the chance to get to know her only grandson a little better.

Lydia Toscano was not convinced in the slightest.

"Your son's quite the little flyer," one of the flight attendants remarked as the two of them were disembarking. Kate smiled, relieved that the unsettling mid-trip incident of Jimmy knocking over his food tray and proceeding to bark like a seal had been excused as nothing more than a cranky child on a long airplane ride. The combination of Fruit Loops and a Thomas the Train picture book had eventually managed to calm him down, though his outburst had given Kate second thoughts about even trying to doze for the remainder of the trip.

As before, the sight of the miniature-sized landscape growing larger as the plane began its descent seemed to mesmerize her young companion. Even after she unbuckled his seat belt and started to collect their overhead belongings, his cherubic face was intently pressed against the glass and she had to remind him that it was time to get off.

When he finally scrambled out of the seat and reached for her free hand with both of his, she felt acute and loving anxiety. *Nobody's going to take you away*, she silently vowed. *Not if I have anything to say about it.*

The airport was teeming with arrivals and departures and as she and Jimmy made their way to the baggage carousel Kate couldn't help but notice that his sticky little grip had tightened. "Now we get to watch for our suitcases to come out," she said, imbuing her announcement with a level of excitement akin to going on a treasure hunt. *Every experience is a chance for learning*, she remembered reading in one of the articles on autism. Colors, numbers, names, the article had related that even some of the most simple associations if repeated often enough, could help a child make progress in recognizing patterns and processing information.

She crouched down to Jimmy's eye level and asked him if he knew what color bags they were looking for. "Are they blue?" she quizzed him. "Are they red?"

His brief flicker of interest in looking at her shiny earrings was diverted by the sound of a high-pitched "yip" a few feet away. They both turned in time to see a young blond woman who was cooing baby-talk to a frazzled Yorkie vigorously trying at that moment to climb out of her oversized purse. Jimmy was completely transfixed.

"Ooooh! What's that in the lady's purse?" Kate quizzed him, hoping to elicit the words "dog" or "puppy". Instead, Jimmy responded as any inquisitive child would and started to bolt toward it.

Only quick thinking on Kate's part, and a quicker grab, kept him from gleefully barreling straight into the young woman's kneecaps. After murmuring a hasty apology to her, Kate took Jimmy's face in both of her hands. "You mustn't do that, honey," she said firmly, trying in the simplest of terms possible to explain to him that he should never run up to people he didn't know, nor should he try to pet strange animals.

"Remember that bad scratch you got from the kitty?" she said. Among her sister's many experiences with roommates, Kate was recalling one particular instance in which Jimmy, at age 3, had tried to befriend a calico cat by chasing it around the room and finally cornering it. The cat, annoyed by his perseverance, had reacted by hissing and taking an angry swipe at his forearm.

Jimmy, however, had either forgotten the incident or was too caught up in the moment to pay any attention to Kate's gentle warning, his neck now craned to watch the blond girl teetering away on impossibly high platform shoes.

"Let's watch for our luggage now, okay?" Kate said, amused by his insistent tugging on her hand as a plea to give chase before they got away. A dog in a sequined purse was a pretty funny sight, she reflected, and certainly one that would make any child curious about what it was doing there. *If only you knew how to put your curiosity into words*, she thought as she tucked his shirt back in for the umpteenth time.

The flashing lights and accompanying shrill beep of the baggage carousel starting up seemed to make Jimmy forget about the dog. Kate pointed to the top of the chute as the first bag, poised like a plump celebrity about to make a staircase entrance, wobbled into view and slid down the ramp. Jimmy clapped his hands in glee as it hit the retaining wall and began its first orbit.

An older man in a business suit to Kate's left chuckled at Jimmy's display of enthusiasm. "I feel the same way whenever my bags make it, too," he remarked. Nearby passengers, Kate noticed, had overheard this and were nodding in agreement, a show of solidarity among those who spent a large part of their lives in airport terminals.

With Jimmy happily entertained by the sliding and colliding luggage, Kate welcomed the brief respite of chatting with another adult. Her fellow passenger, it turned out, was not only a long-time resident of Las Vegas but was also familiar with the magazine.

"And your name again?" he inquired.

"Kate Toscano."

He grinned. "Toscano! Yes, yes, didn't you do that piece a few months ago on the Mayor?"

"Guilty as charged," she replied with a smile, conscious of the fact that those standing closest were subtly eavesdropping. *Ah, celebrity!* Her interview with the city's mayor had garnered a broad share of compliments and she now related to her listener that what had been calendared for a 20-minute session to accommodate the Mayor's schedule had leisurely stretched into two hours.

"Looks like your son's a little man on a mission," the man observed.

Kate started to tell him that Jimmy was her nephew when she realized what he was doing. Squatting on the floor, he had been quietly and methodically removing the contents of her bucket tote while she was talking, half of it now splayed all around him. Her wallet, her keys, facial tissues, pens, an open lipstick tube, all now on the airport ground.

"No!" Kat shrieked, as she bent down and grabbed away a turquoise plastic tampon case that he was trying at that moment to figure out how to open. Humiliatingly conscious of being an unbidden center of attention, Kate scrambled to retrieve her scattered items. As fast as she could redeposit them in her bag, however, Jimmy was reaching in to yank them back out.

"No, honey," she said firmly. "These aren't yours to play with."

He stared at her, his lower lip thrust into a defiant pout as she wrested a pen from his tight little grasp. "Dawggggg!" he blurted out.

It took her a second to realize what he was saying. And when she did, she nearly laughed out loud at the association he had made between the blond girl's purse and her own. "No sweetheart," she said gently. "There's no dog in Aunt Kate's bag."

He peered inside again just to make sure. "No dawggggg?" he said, tugging on the strap.

Whether he was simply parroting the words he had just heard or was attempting to ask a question, Kate only knew that, to her, at least, it felt like a tiny step toward progress.

She scooped him into a hug. "No, sweetheart. No dog today."

As she straightened up to swing her bag over her shoulder, and safe from further exploration, the end of it grazed the upper arm of a passing traveler.

"Sorry," she murmured and returned her attention to what finally looked like one of her bags at the top of the chute.

"Kate? Kate Toscano?" a male voice inquired.

She turned at the sound of her name, her initial reaction of surprise quickly chilling to one of mild disdain. Though the passage of years since high school had engendered a mature physique and more expensive wardrobe, there was no mistaking the cocky smirk and swaggering posture.

"Hello, Brad," she said.

Chapter Thirteen

"I go by Bradley now," he informed her, cavalierly withdrawing a gold-embossed business card from his breast pocket. "As you can see, I've done rather well for myself."

No shortage of ego here, she thought, glancing at the card only long enough to notice that he was now president of the same banking institution where his father had once been a V.P. Noticing, too, that his middle initial was "C", something that she hadn't known before. *Probably stands for "cretin"*, she decided as she smiled politely and handed it back to him. "Lucky you," she remarked.

"Plenty more where that came from," he said as he urged her to keep it. He glanced down at Jimmy as if he hadn't realized until now that the two of them were together. "So," he continued with an eyebrow raised in amazement, "looks like you went the mommy route. Who'd have thought?"

With a firm grip on Jimmy's hand, Kate tried to cut off further chatter with the fact that they really needed to retrieve their bags and get going.

C.J. Foster

"Which ones are they?" Bradley asked, casually snapping his fingers just above his shoulder, an action that brought forth an anemic looking young man in a single-breasted gray suit who had been standing almost invisibly behind him. "Dwayne can get yours just as easily as mine."

"Thanks," she declined, "but I think we can manage."

But Bradley wouldn't hear of it, insisting that being a gopher was exactly what he paid Dwayne to do.

Poor Dwayne, she thought. His hamster eyes, slumped shoulders and projection of meek subservience reminded her of the gaggle of losers who used to blindly follow Brad around throughout high school in the hopes that some of his popularity, and money, might rub off on them. For all she knew, maybe Dwayne was even one of them.

"Oh, come on," Bradley pressed, playfully daring her to voice objection to his offer. "You kinda got your hands full with Junior, right?"

Kate bristled despite the reality that what he said made sense. Having an extra bag more than what she had toted on her last trip from Las Vegas could make things a bit cumbersome. She reluctantly pointed to the suitcase that was already starting its second orbit and Dwayne dutifully trotted off to fetch it. Too late, Kate realized that Bradley's offer was part of a larger agenda; specifically, it now allowed him to snake his way into a longer conversation with her.

"Grabbin' a little R and R away from the hubby?" he asked, making no secret of a downward glance at her left hand.

The words "I'm not married" slipped through her lips before she could think to stop theem.

"Ah," Bradley responded with an insincere, all-knowing wink that sent her thoughts immediately tumbling back to the horrible day in the school parking lot when he had cast aspersions on her virtue.

She quelled her anger under the appearance of casual indifference to his innuendo. "I'm on vacation with my nephew," she informed him. "He's never really been to the Jersey shore in summer."

"Yeah, well, can't say he's missed that much," Bradley opined with an obnoxious snort. "Same-o, same-o."

The reprieve of his cell phone beeping was short-lived.

"So how long are you staying?" he asked her after deciding that the caller ID wasn't one that merited his consideration.

"Not sure yet."

Bradley eyed her with a calculating expression that hinted he thought she was just being coy with him. "Maybe I can do something to change that?"

"Honestly, Brad," she replied. "I can't imagine what."

When it came to his taste in music, John Neal always felt that he'd been born at the wrong time. Sentiment versus earsplitting noise was what governed his selections at home and on the road. He made no secret to anyone that music that touted love lost, love found, and love of life in general held more appeal to him than any discordant histrionics that touted hatred, abuse or violence. He had seen enough of the later during his short stint as a cop in NYC to appreciate the difference. His two years of service in some of the most crime-ridden areas of the City ended with a citation for bravery and a medical retirement from the Police Department.

It was a topic that he and his father had shared no shortage of conversations about before the latter's stroke. The senior Neal had served the public in a different war. He had retired from the Army at Fort Monmouth on the twelfth anniversary of first meeting Abby while stationed at Fork Polk, Louisiana.

Sean's military retirement pay, though, hadn't been enough to live on, much less give three sons the opportunities he felt he'd missed out on in his own childhood. After a brief stint at the factory, he had become a security guard, not only to gain some supplemental income but also to give him some flexibility to be there for his growing boys.

His stroke had come less than a year away from what he and Abby were anticipating would be his Second Official Retirement. A countdown of big red "X's" on the kitchen calendar emphasized its significance. Abby, of course, hadn't wasted a moment giving out plenty of signals that grandchildren would be a welcome diversion once her husband no longer had to leave the house and go off somewhere to work. Temporarily shelved in the early months of Sean's recovery, her campaign to extend the family tree was resuming its original force of late, a tactic that John secretly believed would find as little success with his older brother as it had with him.

"Do the math, Mom," he wanted to tell her. Certainly, for as long as it had taken Mindy to nudge Mitch into an agreement of matrimony, it would take her even longer to convince him that fatherhood, and the crucial investment of time that went with it, should be part of the long-term plan.

John couldn't help but feel a wave of melancholy that a man who loved kids as much as his dad did and who had once orchestrated a toy drive for an orphanage he helped to save in 'Nam wasn't likely to be called "Grandpa" anytime soon. Shelby, it seemed, wouldn't have to relinquish her dibs on the older man's undivided attention.

As he now maneuvered the car into the already existing queue of taxicabs at the airport, it was to the radio accompaniment of Dan Fogelberg singing *Same Old Lang Syne*. John smirked. The lyrics about running into an old lover at the grocery store on a snowy Christmas Eve probably weren't the best thing he could be listening to lately, especially since memories of Kate Toscano kept inviting themselves into his head at the oddest times and stubbornly refusing to be dislodged.

At least half a dozen times since he had seen her, he had found himself driving down the street where she once lived without even thinking about how he got there. Was he wishfully anticipating that she'd suddenly step out on the front porch and wave to him? He had also gone on online when he couldn't get to sleep and searched her name. The extensive body of publishing credits that she had accumulated probably shouldn't have astounded him and yet it did. At the same time, he realized that all of the glamorous celebrities and places she'd been writing about on the other side of the country were just about as far removed from Avalon Bay as they could possibly be.

Life in a small seaport town worked out fine for some people. Kate Toscano, however, clearly wasn't one of them.

Just for a moment, I was back at school, Fogelberg was singing, and felt that old familiar pain.

"Yep, I can relate," John said out loud.

And as he casually glanced over at the terminal sidewalk where newly arriving passengers were impatiently waiting for their rides and rental car shuttles, the unexpected sight of Kate engaged in a conversation with Brad Leister was a major punch of déjà vu that went straight to his heart.

Bradley was insistent that he had plenty of room in his car to give her a lift to her mother's house. No less than twice since Dwayne brought her remaining piece of luggage he had also made a point of emphasizing what kind of car he drove, how much he had paid for it, and that he was already looking to get next year's model because he wasn't entirely sure that he liked the quality of the sound system in this year.

Oh yes, we should all be cursed with such problems, Kate thought, thanking him again for his invitation but remaining firm in her decision to take a cab.

Bradley wrinkled his nose as if he were smelling something unpleasant. "Are you sure you want to do that?" he playfully chided her. "After all, you don't really know where they've been?

Funny, Kate was tempted to tell him, *but the same thing could probably be said about you.*

"Besides," Bradley continued, contradicting her refusal with a smile that set her teeth on edge, "maybe after we drop Junior off, you 'n' I could go somewhere and catch up on old times. What do you say?"

The implication they had any shared history beyond the same zip code and a few high school pep rallies was an insult that had no relationship to reality and she felt her temper rising in response. That Dwayne was observing this exchange and seeming amused by it infuriated her even more.

"Thanks, but it would be a very short conversation," she informed him, wondering how many times she'd have to hit him over the head until the message sank in that she didn't want to have anything to do with him.

Bradley laughed and started to reach out to touch her arm. Suddenly, he emitted an expletive instead and looked down at where a giggling Jimmy had just kicked him in the ankle. "What's with your damned kid?" he snapped, angrily inspecting his pants cuff for signs of irreparable damage to the fabric.

She knew she probably should have scolded the small boy for his act of aggression but a part of her couldn't help but want to tell him "good job".

"We've had a long day and really need to get going," she said to Bradley, wondering whether he'd pick up on the fact that she didn't bother to include an apology with it for Jimmy's behavior.

"Yeah well, somebody should teach that little brat some..."

Bradley let his threatening sentence go unfinished as he straightened up, his expression now that of someone who had just glimpsed a ghost as he looked over Kate's right shoulder.

"Need a cab, ma'am?" offered a familiar male voice.

Chapter Fourteen

S
he had never been happier to see anyone in her life. Nor could she stop repeating her gratitude as John loaded their bags into the back of the cab.

"Threw me for a loop, too," John good-naturedly confessed. "Did you miss us that much you just couldn't stay away?"

"Still trying to get things settled after all that's happened," she replied, not wanting to admit she was homeless.

Did you miss us that much you just couldn't stay away?

She knew that he probably meant "us" in a generic sense and yet it nonetheless made her blush that she was so transparent in her delight to be rescued from the advances of the annoying Brad. She knew he preferred *Bradley* now, but to her, he would always be just Brad, the same old jerk from high school. In truth, she had nearly thrown both arms around his neck like a giddy schoolgirl. *Wouldn't that have torqued Brad*, she thought in wicked amusement. Instead, she had kept her spontaneity in check and pretended as if John Neal's arrival at that moment was perfectly normal. The harder part, of course, was resisting the urge not to turn around as they walked away. Brad's jaw, she was pretty sure, was hanging down to his knees.

That John remembered Jimmy's name earned him extra points in her book, too. All right, so it really hadn't been that long since the one and only time he met her nephew, but his friendliness and affection toward Jimmy were so genuine that it made her heart melt. For the briefest instant as the three of them walked to the cab, Kate caught herself fantasizing that this was what happy families looked like. She noticed several people smiling at them as well and, as an extension of her mini-daydream, wondered whether they were thinking that Jimmy looked more like John or like her. Silly, of course, being the child of neither one but it didn't escape her observation that he looked more like a Neal than the despicable loser whose name was on his birth certificate.

Next to her in the backseat, Jimmy was happily singing a made-up song in which "Dawg", the only distinguishable sound, was every third word.

"What's he singing about?" John wanted to know.

Kate explained that he had seen a dog in a lady's purse at the airport.

"He likes dogs, huh?" John asked.

"Well, he's never really had one," Kate replied. "I think it just got his attention because it was something different."

In the rear-view mirror, John was smiling. "He'd probably like Shelby," he told her.

"Shelby?"

"Our German Shepherd," he answered. "Very sweet, really great with kids. Sort of a bed-hog, though. All things considered, I guess it's our fault for encouraging her."

She didn't miss the fact that he said the word "our". Twice. Nor the disclosure that Shelby liked being around children. John's children. John and a mysterious someone who clearly wasn't her, and never would be.

"So, you haven't told me yet what brought you back," he reminded her. "Or am I being too nosey?"

Where to begin, where to begin.

"Things didn't quite work out the way that I'd hoped," she vaguely replied. *Without question, the understatement of the year.* "Jimmy and I decided to come back for awhile to...uh, regroup."

"Well, you couldn't have picked a better time of year," he said.

She smiled. Most anyone who had grown up on Avalon Bay would probably vote summer to be their favorite season. It came with a long stretch of shoreline where kids could shovel to their hearts' content, sunbathers could bask and flirt, and dreamers could entertain lazy thoughts about buying a boat and blissfully sailing off into the deep blue sea.

She glanced over at Jimmy and wondered if he and her sister had ever built sandcastles like the ones she remembered from their childhood. She added it to her mental list of things she wanted to show him, steadfast in her belief that no matter how vexatious their current situation it wasn't going to interfere with creating happy memories for him.

John was now asking her how long this latest visit was going to be.

"Well, we'll be staying at my mom's until..." *Until what? Until it drives her crazy and she throws us out?* She stumbled over the rest of her reply and felt completely stupid about it. "What I meant to say," she said, "is that we've got some things we need to work out and coming back here for a little while. I guess it's sort of a stopgap 'til I know where we are." *No points for brilliance there*, she chided herself, wishing she could just unload the whole story on his broad shoulders and then soak it with her tears of frustration.

John nodded thoughtfully. "You're lucky that you and your mom are so close," he remarked.

Huh? Of all the adjectives that might have described their relationship, Kate wouldn't have thought that "close" was even close to nailing it. She resisted the urge to correct him, knowing that it would only complicate any further explanation of what they were doing there. Instead, she mentioned that Lydia hadn't spent much time with her grandson since his birth and that summer would give the three of them a nice chance to spend time together outdoors.

- 111 -

"You oughta take him to see Lucy if you get a chance," he recommended.

"Lucy?"

John laughed at her puzzled response. "I can't believe you could forget something as big as an elephant."

Kate's anxious mood suddenly turned buoyant in her remembrance of a senior year field trip to Atlantic City that—thanks to John and some of his enterprising buddies—ended in an unexpected detour to Margate, home of the world's largest wooden elephant. "She's still there?" she said in surprise. An icon at the South Jersey shore, Lucy's odd presence on the sea-swept dunes at the turn of the 19 century had probably made more than one sailor swear off rum.

John assured her that after over a century of popularity, she wasn't likely to be leaving her coastal post any time soon.

Given Jimmy's earlier reaction to a tiny dog in a sparkly purse, Kate couldn't begin to fathom what her nephew would think of a colorful pachyderm with stairs and cubbyholes that people could climb around in and take silly pictures.

"And, of course, you'll have to take him digging for buried treasure, too," John continued, winking at her in the rear-view mirror.

Local legends abounded that the region's outer islands had been a frequent hiding place for cutthroat pirates and other illegal privateers. The marriage of reality and romance when it came to swashbuckling adventures and mutinous ghosts persisted in the 21st century. Kate could remember that even around a place as tame as Avalon Bay she had often encountered no small number of tourists enthusiastically toting metal detectors.

"Do you think anyone's ever found anything of real value?" she mused out loud.

John contemplated her question a moment. "I guess it all depends on what they label as valuable."

As the cab drew up to Lydia's house, a delivery truck from Connor's Florist was just pulling away from the curb.

"Looks like someone got flowers," John observed. "Is it your mom's birthday or something?"

Kate shook her head. "Not 'til October."

"Maybe she got them for you as a welcome home, then."

She didn't think that that was a likely scenario, either, especially given her mother's cool reception to the idea that she and Jimmy would be staying with her at all. "Probably just for a neighbor who's not home from work yet," she decided. As John turned off the ignition, she turned to Jimmy. "Hey, sweetie, recognize this place? It's Grandma's house, remember? Can you say 'Grandma'?"

Jimmy, however, was more interested in pointing at a plump squirrel that had just run across the driveway and up the nearest tree.

"So, what do I owe you for the ride?" she leaned forward to ask John, raising a playful finger in warning as she added, "And don't tell me it's free."

"Let's get your bags out of the trunk first and then we'll settle up."

He was already out of the driver's seat and opening her door.

"I'm paying for that ticket you got, too," she insisted but John wouldn't hear of it.

"It's no big deal," he said. "Really."

"We'll see," she replied, trying to figure out how she could slip him the money without him realizing it.

"I know what you're thinking," he said as he lifted the first bag out of the trunk. "It's not going to work."

"Ah, so now you're a mind-reader?"

"Nope." He grinned. "Long memory."

It took her a few seconds for his comment's significance to register. And when it did, she realized that pressing the matter any further might court the same threat to his pride that it had when they were still in high school. Instead, she opened the other door to the backseat and told Jimmy it was time to get out. Jimmy responded by sliding over to the opposite side and defiantly folding his arms.

"Come on, honey," she said. "We're going to see Grandma now."

She reached in and held out her hand but it only seemed to make him squirm closer to the left door.

"Do you want to get out on that side instead?' she asked. "Okay, we can do that."

She walked around the back of the cab but a giggling Jimmy had scrambled back to the right by the time she got there. She heard John chuckle under his breath.

"I suppose you could do better?" she challenged him.

A mischievous look came into his eyes. "I don't know. Does he like to have piggyback rides?"

"Piggyback rides?" In the first place, she wasn't sure that Jimmy even knew what a piggyback ride was. In the second place, which she voiced out loud to John, "Isn't he kind of big for that?"

"Oh, I seem to recall a certain high schooler who made me carry her down the boardwalk just because she threw a shoe."

Kate felt an instant electric sparkle at his casual reminiscence. "'Threw a shoe'?" she mimicked him. "You make it sound like I'm a horse!" She reminded him it had only been a broken sandal she got from running from ride to ride on the pier at Wildwood.

"So technically it was my fault?" John teased.

"If the shoe fits…"

"Maybe we should show him how it's done," John's voice abruptly cut into her thoughts. He turned around and leaned over. "Hop on."

Kate's mouth dropped open in astonishment at his invitation. "Are you completely crazy?" she said, acutely conscious of his athletic physique and how the rich outlines of his shoulders strained against the fabric in the crouched position he had assumed.

"Certifiably. Come on," he urged her. "If he doesn't get out of the car, I'll just have to take him home with me."

She took a quick glance around, certain that their silly spontaneity would have everyone on the street looking out their windows.

With a nasal twang, John started to sing the chorus of "Save a Horse, Ride a Cowboy". Loudly.

"Oh, all right, fine," she acquiesced, "but only up to the porch and only if you stop singing."

"Yes, ma'am," he replied.

As she straddled his lower back and put her arms around his neck, the warmth of his strong hands radiated through her jeans where he grabbed hold of the back of her thighs. She felt her heart skip in response as he lifted her off the ground, her last vestiges of common sense and decorum skittering off into the bushes that lined either side of the driveway.

John was laughing. Kate was laughing, too, and for a second she completely forgot that it was Jimmy they were supposed to be putting on a show for.

"Is this what you call being a responsible role model?" Lydia's voice rang out from the porch. Neither of them had noticed the precise moment she emerged from the house to witness their juvenile behavior. Nor, they now discovered, had either of them looked back to see that Jimmy had hopped out of the taxi on his own and was intently watching a crow pecking away at the grass.

"So much for performance art," John mumbled under his breath. Kate suppressed a giggle as she ungracefully dismounted and smoothed the front of her shirt.

"Hi, Mom," she said. "Can you believe who met us at the airport? Amazing odds, huh?"

"*Odd*," Lydia unpleasantly remarked, "is certainly one word for it." She looked out at Jimmy. "The boy's not going to keep trampling all over my grass, is he?"

How did Cass and I ever survive childhood, Kate wondered.

"I'll go get him," John offered, and then bring the bags."

In what seemed only a few strides, he closed the distance between himself and Jimmy and scooped the latter up into a wide swing that made the youngster squeal with delight and grin from ear to ear

"He has as little sense about how to handle children as you do," Lydia cynically observed.

Through Kate's eyes, though, a different story was very much in evidence. *This is someone who loves kids and isn't afraid to show it,* she thought.

Lydia waited until John was within earshot to announce that Kate had just received a spectacular bouquet of roses.

"Who'd be sending me flowers?" Kate asked. "Nobody even knows I'm here."

"Obviously Bradley Leister does," her mother replied, adding a snide postscript that Kate knew was entirely for John's benefit. "He's such a successful young man, don't you think?"

Chapter Fifteen

E ver since high school, John and his friends had come up
with a long list of nicknames for Bradley Leister, the
majority of which were unprintable and/or unsuitable for
mixed company. As he drove away from the Toscano house, he
realized he now had a couple of new ones he could add.

In Lydia and Kate's presence, he had suppressed his annoyance
under the guise of indifference. "Nice flowers," he had even
remarked when Kate's mother made a point of saying that she'd
read an article in the newspaper only the other morning about how
terribly expensive roses were getting these days and that these must
have cost Bradley a pretty penny.

"Well then he must have robbed his bank to pay for them," Kate
suggested.

Though her light attempt at sarcasm was lost on her mother, the
inference hadn't been lost on John. He knew she'd said it just to let
him know that she thought Brad was as big a show-off and a jerk as
he thought he was. At least that's what he hoped she was doing.
She certainly hadn't made nearly the fuss one usually associated

with women who got surprised with a vase of expensive roses. Against his better judgment, he caught himself wondering how she would react if his own name had been signed on the card that Lydia so flagrantly waved in his face.

Truth be told, of course, as modestly well as things were going of late in the tree business, the luxury of springing for pricey flowers just to impress someone wasn't something that fit John's budget. Not that he had to compete with Brad in the first place, he harshly reminded himself. No doubt there was someone in Las Vegas who had already bested both of them when it came to winning, and holding, Kate's affections.

Why then, had she dropped the obscure reference to things not working out quite the way she had planned? Did it mean that whomever she shared her life with was reluctant to open his heart to include a small child or, specifically, a child who would require an extra dose of patience? That someone, anyone, could disappoint her when she was only trying to make the best of a sad situation made him angry.

Not as angry, however, as Brad Leister's pompous presumptions that anything in a skirt was his for the taking. John glowered at the realization that Brad had to have called up the florist shortly after he and Kate parted company at the airport. "Kate can take care of herself," a warning voice whispered in his head. A louder voice countered that she also had no idea what a sneaky snake Brad could be when it came to marking his territory. Like father, like son, he reflected.

John's expression clouded with anger in remembrance of how many times Brad had used his influence at the bank to mess up the lives of anyone he perceived to be a threat to his ego. Like the nasty control freak Mr. Potter in "It's a Wonderful Life", the tactics he had inherited from his father, including a penchant for womanizing, were manifested in "lost" loan documents, inexplicable delays in the processing of payments and "accidental" accounting errors.

None of these supposed mistakes, of course, could ever be traced directly to Brad who continued to expand his lofty empire by serving on various prestigious boards, making sizable donations to local charities, and basking in newspaper articles that touted him as one of the community's most eligible bachelors.

Whatever difficulties Kate was currently facing in her life, John thought, the last thing that she needed was a wolf-like Brad stalking her.

Lydia's only digression from her praise of Brad's generosity and thoughtfulness was to ask Kate what she was doing with John.

"It's no big deal, Mom. He was at the airport. So were we."

"And his was the only cab at the entire terminal, I suppose?"

"No, but he was the only one to step up and rescue me from Brad being a pest." She recounted how Brad was apparently reliving his life as an extension of high school and assuming that every female would swoon in his presence. "If I hadn't thought he'd sue me," she added, "I would have kicked him myself, and in a much more vulnerable spot."

It was the wrong thing to bring up, of course. "Well, if the boy's going to turn into a little monster—"

"I think he just thought he was protecting me," Kate interrupted, vexed that her mother was looking for any excuse to withdraw the welcome mat.

"You have no idea what he's thinking."

"And neither do you."

It was a rebuttal that bought her at least 30 seconds of blissful silence.

"You could do a lot worse for yourself," Lydia reminded her when she found the voice to talk again.

Kate rolled her eyes as she flung the strap of one of the bags over her shoulder. "Didn't we have this same conversation when I was in high school?"

"And look where you'd be if you'd only listened to me."

Probably divorced, without a career, and completely broke, Kate thought.

"Did you know Bradley was voted the most eligible bachelor in Avalon Bay?" Lydia continued. "He even had his picture right on the front page of the paper."

And you've probably even pasted it in the family album, haven't you, Mom? "Obviously, he stuffed the ballot box," Kate replied. It also went without saying that, like his father, Brad probably took out lots of bank advertising in Cliff Harwood's daily rag. That Cliff was no stranger to the art of sucking up to anyone he thought was rich and popular no doubt accounted for the landslide tally her mother was raving about.

"Shall I take the flowers up to your room for you?" she was now offering. "They're very pretty, aren't they? I counted two dozen of them."

"All the more reason for them to stay downstairs so you can enjoy them." Clearly, it was time for a change of subject. "I was thinking maybe we could bring down one of the cots from the attic and set it up for Jimmy in my room for the first couple of nights."

"Why on earth should we do that?" Lydia asked as she started to follow her up the stairs. "The spare room in front should be just fine for the boy."

"Not if he wakes up in the middle of the night and gets scared," Kate explained. "He's been through a lot of confusing changes lately."

"Well, no wonder, the ridiculous way your sister always moved around so much."

"Maybe if she'd just been able to come home," Kate quickly rose to Cassy's defense. "Look, Mom, I know she had her faults and that things didn't turn out the way you would have wanted them to. You probably feel the same about me as well. But I need your help right now. Cassy trusted me, and I think she also trusted you, to make sure we do everything for Jimmy that we can." She took a deep breath. "If there'd been any way that I could've just stayed in Vegas and straightened this whole custody mess out on my own—"

Though she let the sentence go unfinished, it was clear from her mother's stiffened reaction that she knew her older daughter hadn't come back to Avalon Bay just because she liked the older woman's company.

"If your father were still alive," Lydia declared, "he would have had something to say about this."

Kate's voice softened. "Jimmy's his grandson, too, Mom. I like to think he'd say 'let's work this out for Jimmy.'"

A crash followed by a squeal coming from the direction of the foyer brought both women rushing back downstairs. Jimmy, wide-eyed with fear and the front of his pants splashed with water was standing a few feet away from where the broken vase had splayed its contents all over the floor. The ecru lace cloth on which the vase had been sitting lay in an unceremonious heap, the trajectory of which betrayed that the dangling temptation of one corner had been tugged off the table by a pair of little hands.

Kate immediately ran over to Jimmy to make sure that he wasn't hurt.

"Oh no!" she heard her mother exclaim. "Just look what he's done to Bradley's beautiful flowers!"

By the time John had returned the cab to his friend's house and walked the rest of the way home, a rosy dusk already settling on the seaport community. For contemplative purposes, it was probably John Neal's favorite part of the day. Much of that, of course, stemmed from the walks he'd taken as a kid with his dad, especially when the latter worked evening security shifts and didn't have to put on his uniform until after dinnertime.

Mitch had never expressed any interest in joining them on these strolls, nor had Jeremy wanted to tear himself away from his favorite TV shows in deference to conversations that were beyond his age level, interest, or juvenile attention span. And so, for those chunks of time that now in retrospect seemed short, John had his dad all to himself and couldn't have been happier. Besides his time with Kate, of course, those were the best moments of his childhood.

C.J. Foster

It was Sean, not Abby, to whom he had always confided his worries and his dreams and his opinions about what was wrong with the world and how he wanted to fix it. His father, too, had been the one to whom he first floated the idea of going to the local community college a few years after he started his landscaping business.

None of them, however, could have foreseen the devastating circumstances that prompted John to forgo transferring to a four-year university after getting his Associate's Degree to don the uniform of a New York City Police Officer. Even Mitch, whose anger level at the time rivaled his own, had tried to talk him out of quitting school and joining the police force. "You're not going to change a damn thing by doing this!" Mitch had told him.

Abby, deep in her own wrenching grief, had also begged him to reconsider what she thought was a knee-jerk reaction he'd live to regret. "I've already lost one son," she said. "I can't lose another."

Only his father had seemed to understand what he was doing and why he was doing it. Only his father had known what it was like to not let an enemy gain the upper hand. "Do us proud, son," he said on the day he left for the Police Academy.

The worry he'd caused both of his parents while he was recovering in the hospital a year later after a shootout with a vicious drug gang was something he still felt guilty about. Mitch, in the true fashion of obnoxious older brothers, couldn't resist saying, "I told you so" at the first opportunity after they all learned he was going to be okay.

The irony is that one of the things John had most looked forward to, leisurely walks around the neighborhood with his dad, had never resumed. Though the latter had switched to a day shift when John finally recovered from his gunshot wounds, he was subsequently too tired when he got home to want to do much of anything other than have his dinner and retreat to the TV. John, having taken an apartment a mile away, was equally exhausted as a result of trying to get his tree business up and running after learning his injuries precluded him from returning to full duty with the police department.

Since his dad's stroke and his move back home to help out with the heavy lifting, John often found himself wondering, just as he did now if they'd ever pick up where they left off. Just an older man and his son, solving all of the world's problems by the time they came full circle and were greeted by the welcoming amber lights of the front porch.

The lights were already on as he stepped into the driveway, a driveway that was occupied at that moment by a car he didn't recognize. Probably a friend of his mother's, he assumed, since his dad's pals tended to drop by during daylight hours.

"Hey, girl," he said, greeting Shelby with a scratch behind her ears as he let himself in the back door. The aroma of the lasagna he'd prepped earlier that day was prevalent, reminding him of how little he'd eaten that day.

"Is that you, John?" Abby's voice called out from the living room.

"No, it's a burglar who's going to empty your refrigerator," he shouted back.

Two sets of female laughter responded to his joke, only one of which he recognized.

Curious, he went to investigate, Shelby close at his heels.

"I was worried you'd be late for dinner," his mother said. "You remember Gabrielle, don't you?"

Chapter Sixteen

S he was wearing her long hair loose this time, her warm-up outfit replaced by a white silk blouse, suit skirt, and heels. "It was so nice of you and your mom to invite me to dinner," she said. "I hear you're quite the cook."

Before he could rally a reply, Abby explained that their guest had spent all day talking to bankers about her plans for the school she wanted to open in Avalon Bay.

John could think of at least one banker she hadn't talked to that day and felt it was his duty to warn her.

"Leister?" she repeated, shaking her head. "The name doesn't ring a bell."

"Not one of my son's favorite people," Abby informed her. "The two of them went to high school together and some of the terrible things that man has done."

"Uh, excuse me, Mom, but haven't you got something burning in the kitchen?" he interrupted her.

Abby sniffed the air. "I don't think so," she replied, turning to ask Gabrielle for her opinion on the subject.

"Maybe we should go check just the same," John said, his intonation leaving no mystery as to why he wanted to take his mother aside.

Abby excused herself as she got out of her chair. "Just make yourself at home, dear. This should only take a minute."

"It's a good thing you made so much lasagna," Abby happily chirped as soon as she and John were out of earshot of their guest. "Do you think we should have some garlic bread, too, or would that be too much?"

John, with arms folded as he leaned against the counter, regarded her with a steely squint that spoke volumes.

"Oh, don't get all Clint Eastwood on me," Abby playfully chided him. "You have to admit she's a lovely girl."

"No question," John replied. "But what's she doing in our living room?" He raised a warning finger. "And don't tell me she just happened to be walking by."

"Maybe it was the lasagna," Abby suggested, taking a deep whiff for emphasis. "I think it's the best batch you've ever made."

"Mind telling me what kind of matchmaker mischief you're up to?"

"Actually, Mr. Smarty Pants, she's here on business," Abby corrected him.

"What kind of business?" he asked in suspicion.

"Well, you know how I mentioned she's thinking of opening up a school for children with special needs?"

"Several times, yeah. So, she needs some trees planted around it or what?"

"What she needs," Abby continued, "is someone who can give her some good advice about Avalon Bay."

"Isn't that what she has a mother for? Why doesn't she just ask Helen?"

"Pffftt! Helen's a dear but she sometimes has the sense of a radish when it comes to knowing what's going on. Anyway, I was just thinking that with everything you know about the town."

"Mom?"

"What?"

"She can stay for dinner but I don't want you to start picking out china patterns."

"Don't be silly," Abby retorted, adding a whimsical postscript, "I hardly even know her."

John smirked. "Funny, I could have sworn she was your new best friend."

Abby shooed him out of the kitchen with the suggestion that he should offer Gabrielle a glass of wine while the lasagna finished cooking. "Besides, I need to go upstairs and see how your dad's doing."

John queried whether his father had followed the doctor's orders and behaved himself that day.

"Not without being a grump," she said. "I asked him a couple of times if he wanted to join us for dinner but he didn't seem all that interested."

John nodded thoughtfully, sensitive to the fact that the Neal sense of pride ran deep. Even if he couldn't articulate it, it was as if the older man didn't want strangers to see him, and possibly form a poor opinion, unless he was at his best. Certainly, John himself had initially embraced that attitude when he was recovering from his injuries, allowing only his immediate family and friends like Lenny to come and see him. Pride, he had quickly discovered, came at the price of loneliness.

"Well, if he changes his mind," John told his mother, "let him know I'm home and can come up and help him."

When he returned to the living room with two glasses of vino, Gabrielle was at the fireplace and admiring the collection of framed photographs that paraded across the mantle, crowding one another for visibility.

"I hope my being here isn't an imposition on your family," she apologized as she accepted a glass from him.

He faltered a moment, wondering how much she had overheard of the conversation in the kitchen. Hoping that maybe she hadn't heard any of it. "No, no problem at all," he insisted. "Italian food always goes better with a crowd."

A Seaside Story

She cheerfully clinked her glass against his. *"Amore! Fortuna! Salute!"* she said.

John shook his head. "I'm sorry?"

"Love, luck, health," she translated. "I spent six months in Italy while I was working on my Master's. Beautiful country! Have you ever been there?"

"Nope. Basically a hometown boy. Someday, though. Maybe."

"Well, you don't know what you're missing," she continued. "In fact, when things went south with my marriage, I was torn between whether I wanted to open a school in Jersey or just hop the next plane back to Italy," she stopped and smiled. "Stop me if I'm being boring."

"Not at all."

"But I'm a guest in your home," she said. "I should be asking you about, well, all these pictures, for instance." She pointed at the closest one in a frame decorated with stars and glued-on seashells. "Where was this one taken?"

"Cape May," he replied. "I swear I don't know what my father was thinking when he bought those scary shorts."

Gabrielle laughed. "And this one?"

"That's my Aunt Patty when she took us to Popcorn Park Zoo. She had this thing for homeless tigers."

"Homeless tigers?"

John explained how the zoo had been set up as a haven for animals—mostly exotic—that had been victimized by humans. "Even after her health started failing and she couldn't go there anymore," he explained, "she loved those tigers so much that she used to send a check every month to keep them in steaks."

"We should all be so lucky," Gabrielle remarked. She picked up a high school graduation photo at the end of the mantle. "This can't be you," she said, holding it up to his face for critical comparison.

"It's not," John quietly replied. "It's my younger brother Jeremy. He was killed several years back."

***

Jimmy had gone to sleep with nary a whimper of protest, the faithful Mr. Ollie tucked under one arm. Kate sat and watched him for a long time, as mystified as ever by where his dreams took him. She had watched him closely since their arrival for signs of recognition. A part of her, in fact, half-hoped that he'd head straight for his grandmother's closet and start pulling out her shoes for an impromptu parade. Just before he went to bed, she showed him a framed picture of Cassy.

"She's always looking over you, you know," she told him, tapping the glass lightly with her index finger. "She loved you more than anything in the world, honey." She searched his face for the faintest flicker of recognition. Although his face remained stoic, he quickly snatched the picture from Kate's hand and pushed it under his pillow. Kate realized he must be going through an emotional rollercoaster since Cassie's death and the cross country moves. He needed some stability.

There was finally no postponing the inevitable. As she left the bedroom and started down the stairs, she mentally rehearsed all the things she wanted to say. All the things she needed to say. And yet when she stepped into the living room and saw the back of her mother's head, the latter engrossed in a crime investigation show, all of the words failed her.

"Mom?"

Lydia picked up the remote and switched it to mute. "What?"

"I think we need to talk and come up with some sort of a plan."

"We could have talked while you were still in Las Vegas." She set down the remote and folded her arms. "I seem to recall the last time you were here you couldn't get back to it fast enough."

Kate mentally flinched and retreated a cautious step before confessing, at the risk of an 'I told you so', that what she needed was more than just a voice on the phone from over two thousand miles away. "I guess it gets down to you being right when you said I was biting off more than I could chew. Even if things with Jimmy weren't as challenging as they are, I swear I don't know how Cassy did it all on her own without running herself ragged. I mean at least I have a high-paying job and the resources to help him, but she always seemed to keep it together."

"A job you just walked away from," Lydia reminded her, along with the curt observation that her younger daughter was hardly a poster child for quality motherhood. "How long do you think you can last if you're unemployed?"

"I'm only taking a breather, Mom. The job will still be there when I get back."

"*I* singular?"

"*We*, plural," Kate emphasized, offended that her mother should even think otherwise. "Dee was great about my taking time off to deal with all this."

Her listener wasn't convinced. "Once people find out they can live without you, they usually find a way to do exactly that." Her face closed as if guarding an unpleasant secret.

It would be futile, Kate realized, to offer assurances that her boss wasn't anything like the norm. Instead, she played to the flattery of reminiscing how well her mother had kept things together for the three of them after her father died. "I guess I never appreciated at the time how many hats you had to wear for us until I became an overnight parent myself."

There was a long and prickly silence.

"So now that you're back here," Lydia said, "what, exactly, do you intend to do with him?"

Kate came around in front of her, obstructing the view of the television. "It's what I intend to do *for* him, Mom. That's the only thing that matters. And frankly, I just don't have all the answers."

Lydia's expression held a note of mockery. "Wasn't that what your fancy school was supposed to teach you? All the answers?"

It was a throwaway accusation but it hit home.

"Okay, I'm confused," Kate challenged her, "but you used to tell people you were proud to have a daughter at Amherst. Ever since we got here, though, you keep telling me I should have stayed in town and settled for Brad. Which is it?"

"'Settled' is hardly the right word. Anyone can see that he's done very well for himself."

Kate kept her tone civil despite her anger. "So have I, Mom, in case you haven't noticed."

"Then all the more reason not to throw it away on something that's not meant to be."

"You're getting ahead of me," Kate said. "What are you talking about?" *As if I don't already know.*

"You're not a teenager anymore, Kate, but twice in a row now I've noticed how you go all gaga whenever that Neal boy is around."

"Oh, come on, now. John and I haven't even seen each other in years."

"Even if he were available, I wouldn't encourage you to go chasing after him."

The words froze in Kate's brain. The dreaded disclosure that she didn't realize until this moment she'd been obsessing about ever since she saw him. *And this surprises you why exactly*, a little voice in her head chimed in. *Did you really think that a handsome, sweet and chivalrous hunk like John Neal would sit around and wait for you forever?* "So," she managed to nonchalantly inquire, "who did he marry?"

"How should I know?" Lydia retorted. "It's not as if I stay up on their lives. The point here is that—"

So maybe the point is that you don't know at all, Kate thought. *Maybe he's just been biding his time, building up his business and—*

"Are you even listening to a single thing I'm saying?" Lydia said. "You just can't count on a Neal man to ever keep his word or be your knight in shining armor."

That she suddenly leaped from condemning John specifically to all the Neal males, in general, struck Kate as a bit strange but she chose not to call her on it. "Believe whatever you want, Mom, but I didn't come back to Avalon Bay to catch myself a husband. I came back to see if maybe just once you and I could be on the same page and do the right thing for your grandson who doesn't have anybody else to depend on." She drew a deep breath that burned in her throat. "If you honestly don't think that's possible, then you may as well come out and tell me now and I'll start making other arrangements for us in the morning."

Neither a "yes" nor a "no" came forth from Lydia's pale lips, preempted instead by the muffled scuffle of small feet entering the room.

"Jimmy, honey, what's wrong?" an anxious Kate asked as she hurried toward him. He was hugging the picture of Cassy to his chest and when she gently tried to take it from him, he resisted with a high-pitched squeal of dissent. "No, no, it's okay," she cooed. "I just don't want you to fall with it and hurt yourself."

His head and his whole body were shaking back and forth in defiance and he squeezed the frame even tighter, the top edge of it now dangerously close to his neck. *Oh God*, she thought in panic, desperate to get it away from him before the glass cracked.

"He'll never come if you keep doing that," she heard her mother remark. Before Kate could respond that it wasn't a good time for a lecture, Lydia suggested she come back to the sofa instead.

"But, Mom, he's—"

"Trust me," Lydia said calmly. "It worked with you and your sister all the time."

Reluctantly, Kate moved away from her young charge, backing up until she had reached the sofa.

"Sit down," Lydia murmured, whereupon she began to casually chat about the weather, the price of mushrooms and the latest book she had finished reading.

To Kate's amazement, a wide-eyed Jimmy drew closer to the two women, culminating in his thrusting the picture toward Lydia's lap.

"Oh my," she said in feigned amazement as if she had never seen it before. "And who is this?"

Jimmy stared at her for the longest time before reaching out to splay the fingers of one hand across the heavily smudged surface. His eyes locked in fierce communion with those of his grandmother, he blurted out a single, unmistakable word: "Mama."

Chapter Seventeen

Being alone wasn't as easy as he was always telling himself it was.

As he slid behind the wheel of his pickup truck the next morning, John couldn't help but tell himself that the previous evening had only exacerbated some of the cracks in the self-imposed wall he had built around his heart. Most noticeably, it had been during the moments his mother kept excusing herself from the table, leaving him to carry on whatever conversation happened to be in progress with their guest. Topics, he later realized, were unsubtly built around his mother's observations of all the things she thought the two of them might have in common.

There were of course worse fates than looking across a lasagna plate and a glass of wine at an attractive, intelligent woman in his age range. Any of his friends, to be sure, would have leaped at the chance to trade places with him and, at the end of the evening, would not have been able to recall a single thing she said.

Admittedly, John's mind had wandered a few times as well, though not for the reasons his peers might assume. Hers was a chair that should have been occupied by Kate, a long-ago fantasy he had conjured about bringing her home to have boisterous holiday dinners with his family. Though Mitch eschewed such Norman Rockwell tableaus as much too sappy for his taste and would likely have fashioned excuses to be absent, John caught himself musing about the dialogues Kate might have had with Jeremy about his homework or whether his mother would have asked for her help clearing the dishes.

"So, have the two of you made any plans?" he liked to imagine Abby taking him aside to ask and he would have told her without any hesitation that he planned to make time stand still so that he and Kate would always be together.

Twice during these musings, Gabrielle had diplomatically tugged him back to the present by asking if she was talking too much about her work. John assured her that she wasn't. Her sincerity and her knowledge about children who had special needs impressed him, especially when she pointed out that the symptoms of autism were often mistaken for something else by parents who didn't have access to quality pediatric care.

Kate had alluded only briefly to her sister's bohemian lifestyle but the comments quickly came back to him during Gabrielle's recitation of statistics. "A friend of mine has a nephew," he said. "He's about five years old or so. A really cute kid. His mom moved around a lot. Maybe now that he's going to be in a more stable environment, he'll be able to interact more with his environment."

Was it just wishful thinking on his part to suggest out loud that maybe Kate was moving back to Avalon Bay for good?

"By all means, she should get him into a clinic for a full set of tests then into a good program of therapy," he heard Gabrielle suggest. "If she's interested, I could get her the names of a couple of doctors I know who are really great."

Even as he thanked her, John felt a twinge of guilt that he'd not only been talking about Kate's personal situation with a total stranger but that he was also soliciting medical advice she hadn't even asked for. Would she appreciate his concern, he wondered, or see it, instead, through the eyes of a liberated woman who preferred to handle everything herself?

Abby had walked in on the end of Gabrielle's offer and wanted to know who they were talking about. When John mentioned it was Kate, his mother shot him a reproving look in the preface to telling Gabrielle that Kate was an "old" girlfriend from high school. "Would you mind running up and checking on your father?" she asked him in her next breath.

"Weren't you just up there?"

"Yes, and I think he was trying to say your name."

John had excused himself, knowing full well she was only orchestrating an opportunity to reiterate to their guest there was nothing going on between her son and the girl whose name he'd brought up.

"Listen," he said afterward when he walked Gabrielle out to her car, "I need to apologize for my mother. Dinner tonight had to be pretty awkward."

She dismissed it with a light laugh. "I think we have the same mother," she replied, confessing that she'd no sooner told her mom she was getting a divorce than the latter endeavored to start filling up her dance card. "It almost affected my decision to move back here," she continued, "but since I'm already seeing someone..."

She dropped it so casually that John nearly missed it.

"We're taking it slow and keeping it very low key," she said, relating that it was her partner in the school she was starting up. "The whole idea of being around someone 24/7, well, we're just going to see how it goes."

A part of him was relieved that she was already taken. Another part of him was reminded of the void in his own life that, for the time being, looked like it was going to stay that way.

When Kate came down for breakfast that morning, it was to the sight of Lydia sopping up the spills from a carton of milk that Jimmy had knocked over. "I swear nothing's going to be safe in this house anymore," Lydia was muttering.

For a moment, Kate wondered whether she had dreamt the scene from the night before when her mother had tenderly rocked her grandson back and forth and even offered to carry him upstairs after he fell asleep. This morning he was back to being "the boy" - the pint-sized bane of her existence.

As she helped herself to some coffee, Kate decided to broach the subject of whether her mother had had any luck finding a recent address for Luke.

"It's not as if you've given me much time to look," Lydia replied. "I barely had time to get the house ready for the two of you swooping in on me the way you did."

A vision of broad-winged pterodactyls sporting backpacks and circling the Toscano chimney caused Kate to suppress a smirk.

"Besides," Lydia continued, "it seems to me that if he's been out of the picture for this long."

"My boss said exactly the same thing."

"Ex-boss, you mean."

Kate let it slide. "We still have to make the effort to find him, Mom. The court says he has rights as a parent."

"Well, if you ask me, those rights ended when your sister finally had the wits to divorce him. Do you want some toast?"

"I can fix it."

"You're talking about the toast, I assume?" Lydia asked. "Because as far as fixing this situation with the boy—"

"You know, it'd help if you stop doing that."

"Doing what?"

Kate lowered her voice. "He's your grandson and he needs to know that you know that."

Lydia started to open her mouth but Kate anticipated what the older woman was going to come back with and pre-empted it. "He may not be able to tell us what he's thinking, Mom, but he knows love and he knows if people are paying attention to him. He's also not responsible for being the way he is." She let the words sink in.

"The way he came over to you last night was so, I don't know, he just seemed so content and like he knew that he was finally home."

She turned her head to look at him and gave a small start when she discovered that he was no longer sitting in the chair where he'd earlier been intently watching his grandmother clean up the milk spill.

"He's under the table," Lydia quietly informed her. "I think he thinks it's a tent."

Kate started to lift up a corner of the tablecloth and coax him out.

"Oh leave him be," Lydia said. "He's having fun."

"And you'd know this how exactly?" a mystified Kate inquired.

"Because some things about being a child never change. Now do you want that toast or not?"

If I live to be a hundred, Kate thought, *I swear I'll never figure her out.*

The smudge of morning sun that dappled through the cloud cover was enough to convince Kate it was a good day to introduce her nephew to the timeless tranquility of Avalon Bay. Once dressed in a pair of designer jeans and a tank top, her first order of business on their outing would be to swing by Cliff Harwood's newspaper and see if she could glean some tips about running a public notice.

"I understand he's hired someone you went to school with," Lydia volunteered when she heard where Kate was going. "A Marty somebody-or-other."

The only Marty that Kate could recall offhand had the IQ of a rock and was far too old to be a delivery boy. Lydia informed her that he was the new editor.

Things are slipping in Avalon Bay, she thought.

"Maybe you could ask him for a job," Lydia suggested. "Working for the hometown paper would be right up your alley."

"Not there yet, Mom."

The sound of the doorbell cut short any further discussion.

Jimmy, who had deemed his hideaway beneath the kitchen table his favorite new place, came out to see what was going on.

Lydia's face momentarily fell when she noticed the address on the multiple packing boxes the UPS driver was depositing in the foyer.

"You know I can always go to the newspaper later," Kate offered but her mother was insistent that she could start going through the boxes herself while they were out. She hugged her arms and Kate was reminded of just how frail and vulnerable her mom could look. "Hard to imagine, isn't it," Lydia remarked, "that a person's entire life could be summed up in half a dozen packing boxes?"

As recently as only a few years ago, Kate had envied people like her sister who lived such compact existences that it didn't take them weeks, or even days, to move from one place to another. She caught herself remembering how much stuff she had put into storage when she accepted Dee's hospitality of a fully furnished, fully accessorized condo. At least a quarter of it, she reflected, was the wardrobe of winter clothes that didn't fit the Las Vegas landscape. "The next time you see all of it again," Dee would tell her, "it'll feel just like Christmas."

Christmas, though, was a time of joy, and joy was the very least of emotions she and her mother were feeling right now as they surveyed the pathetic assemblage of boxes that Cassy's neighbor had packed and shipped off to them.

"I'll be fine with it," Lydia reiterated. "Really."

Kate realized a mother had to have closure as well, as she left Lydia with the few boxes that contained the few items her daughter deemed important enough to keep. These boxes, wonderful memories and her grandson were all she had left of Cassy.

A squeal of brakes and a female voice shrieking her name caught Kate off guard about four blocks from the house. She looked across the street to see Maria Rivera, one of her best friends from high school, alighting from a cherry red El Camino that had seen better days. Maria herself had seen better days as well, most of them as a co-captain of the cheerleading squad when they'd both been much younger. The extra weight she had put on in the interim was evident in the exuberant hug she gave Kate.

"Oh my gosh, I can't believe how fantastic you look!" she exclaimed before turning her attention to Kate's perplexed young companion who was staring at her. "And this is, oh my gosh! I had no idea that you even married."

"Jimmy's my sister's little boy."

Maria's mouth dropped open in amazement. "Cassy? Really?" She dropped down to Jimmy's eye level to check out the family resemblance, a sudden move that made him shrink behind Kate.

"He's a little shy around people he doesn't know," Kate explained.

"Well, he's just the sweetest thing, isn't he?" Maria gushed. "How old?"

On the heels of Kate telling her that he was five, Maria's next question was about Cassy and what she was doing with herself these days.

"Oh my gosh, hon, I'm so sorry," she said when Kate delivered the condensed version. She swiftly enveloped her in a second hug. "Is there anything I can do? Anything you guys need?" She was working at the factory, she went on, but had "gobs" of overtime from all the double shifts she had worked during the holidays. "Crazy, huh?" she quipped. "Remember how we used to say you had to be nuts to work in that place and look where I ended up? But anyway, I'm serious. If you guys need anything, just let me know."

Kate assured her that they were just taking things one day at a time.

"So, you're back here with your mom or what?"

"For the time being. I'm not sure how long."

"Well, I hope it's long enough for us to catch up. Oh my gosh, I can't even remember the last time you were here."

Maria's segue into mental math only served to remind Kate of what a bad correspondent she had become once she went off to Amherst. The only thing she could think to ask was whether Maria was still with Vinny, her high school boyfriend. She guiltily remembered getting a wedding invitation from them, an invitation she'd had to decline because it fell right in the middle of finals.

"Vinny? Pfft!" Maria replied, proudly pointing to her ringless left hand. "This gal's a happy camper just playing the field." She and

Vinny had tried, unsuccessfully, to have kids, she explained, but the final straw had come when Vinny refused to entertain the notion of adoption. "'I'm not gonna raise any kid who's not mine,'" she mimicked Vinny's voice. "So how 'bout you?" she wanted to know.

"Work's been keeping me pretty busy," Kate confessed to her single status.

"Funny, I always thought you and John Neal would hook up. You guys were practically joined at the hip in senior year."

Kate listened to her friend ramble with a vague sense of unreality. *How was I able to get away from him for so long*, she thought, *and yet every corner I turn brings him right back again?*

Maria was extolling the virtues of what a cute couple they made. "If you guys had ever had kids," she added.

"So, who did he end up with?" Kate casually inquired, realizing that a golden opportunity had just fallen into her lap and that feigning ignorance was the only way she was going to find out. If anyone knew what John's story was, Maria's penchant for local gossip was probably still as legendary as it was in high school.

"Well, you probably heard about his brother," Maria replied. "Oh my gosh, it was just the most terrible thing!"

In the back of her mind, Kate remembered her mother's curious warning not to bring up the subject of Jeremy. "I'm afraid I'm out of touch," she said. "What happened to him?"

Chapter Eighteen

I t was Christmas Eve, the year after Jeremy and Cassie's graduation. Jeremy, Maria told her, had moved to Manhattan after high school and had totally fallen in love with it. "He was into the art scene, remember?"

Kate nodded, recalling how John's younger brother liked to follow them around and show her the latest pictures he'd drawn.

A friend in Soho had a co-op gallery and, even better, a loft that he was renting out to four or five friends.

"Four or five in a loft?" Kate echoed. "Did they sleep standing up or what?" Having been to New York a few times herself, she eschewed the myth that sitcom apartments on TV were a reflection of reality real estate in the Big Apple.

The beauty of it, Maria continued, was that the roommates, mostly waiters and actors, all worked different shifts and it was rare that even a third of them were around at the same time. Jeremy had begged his parents to let him stay and see if he could get a job that paid enough to allow him to go to art classes and hone his craft. His first offer, it turned out, was at a mom and pop bakery.

"Jeremy," Maria said, "would open up the bakery early in the morning to fire up the ovens and make the preparations for the day's orders. That morning, as he was walking from his home to the bakery in the Lower East Side, they think he came across a drug deal or something as he crossed an alley."

Kate began to shiver as the image of Jeremy in a dark alley on a cold December morning in NYC. "Was Jeremy?" the question tugged at her heart since she could already tell from Maria's face that the younger Neal never made it to the bakery.

"Stabbed. The cops didn't think Jeremy had anything to do with it. But, in an instant, he was gone."

"Did they ever find out who did it?"

"They had a few suspects, but no arrests. He was just in the wrong place at the wrong time. You can't begin to imagine what it did to the family," Maria continued. "I mean, one minute you're seeing somebody or maybe talking to 'em on the phone about nothing and the next," Maria suddenly blanched at the cruelty of the faux pas she had just committed. "Oh my gosh, that sounded awful, didn't it, what with your sister—"

"It's okay," Kate said softly. "Go on."

"Well, John went crazy with rage, they were pretty close, remember? He just had this I-want-to-kill-somebody look whenever you saw him. Especially when there were no arrests. I think the only reason he didn't get himself in bigger trouble is that, well, I mean he's John and he's such a great guy. Between Jeremy getting killed and everything else that happened, you've just gotta feel really bad for them."

Dare I ask what "everything else" means, Kate wondered. Before she could rally fast enough to ask, Maria suddenly realized she was running late for a doctor's appointment. "I swear I'm such a motor-mouth," she said with a hearty laugh to break the tension that had come about during her story. "Anyway, listen, are you doing anything later?"

"Later being?"

"My boyfriend's playing in a baseball game after work. Maybe you and Timmy can come watch and we can go get a pizza when it's over."

"It's Jimmy, and I'm not sure if we can make it."

"Oh come on," Maria insisted. "It'll be like old times when we used to cheer for the home team."

"I don't have to dig out my pompoms, do I?" Kate teased.

Maria insisted that she'd spring for the food. "Besides, I want you to check out the new beau."

Kate assumed it was someone she didn't know but felt it only polite to ask anyway.

Maria's eyes sparkled. "Does the name Capparelli ring a bell?" she mischievously queried.

"What?" Kate flashed on her last remembrance of the portly patriarch with the bushy brows and heavily greased black hair.

"Okay, I know exactly what you're going to say," Maria said.

"Did you know I was going to say that I think he's too—" There was no diplomatic way to finish her thought. Maria finished it for her.

"Young?"

Kate was now thoroughly confused. "'Young' wasn't the word that sprang to mind. And what happened to Mrs. Capparelli?" she felt compelled to ask. Had he become a widower in the years since she had been away or had his spouse finally decided she was tired of being a baby factory?

"Oh my gosh!" Maria exclaimed in to a flood of giggles. "You thought I meant Tony's father?"

Kate wasn't sure whether she should be relieved, especially since the only Tony she could think of was finishing elementary school when she and John had their unofficial first date.

"It's not a 'forever' thing," Maria predicted in response to Kate's observation that she was robbing the cradle, "but, hey, who couldn't use a little summer romance?"

Lenny called John on his cell phone to remind him they had a baseball game after work.

"I don't know," John replied. "I got an appointment at 4:30."

Lenny snorted. "A hot date, right?"

"In this case, a tree."

"Yeah right."

"You know something I don't?" John asked.

Lenny chided him for being so dense. "Man, everyone's talking about it," he replied.

"What are we talking about?"

"The hot babe who came outta your house last night? Fess up, bro. Who is she?"

John laughed to cover his annoyance with Lenny's nosiness. "A friend of my mother's. She came to dinner."

"And?"

"And then she went home. End of story."

"Yeah, right. Does your mom have any more 'friends' we don't know about?"

"So now you're pulling all-nighter stakeouts of my driveway or what?"

Lenny revealed he'd heard about it from a guy at the factory who heard it from his cousin who was giving a ride home to a neighbor on John's street who was working late at the hospital and saw the two of them saying goodbye.

"Am I the only one who has a life in this town?" John retorted.

"So now that everybody knows,"

"Nobody knows anything," John shot back, "because there's nothing to know."

"A smokin' babe leaves your house in the middle of the night 'n' you're sayin' that's that?"

"Right."

Lenny wasted no time jumping into his next question. "So can I have her phone number?"

"She's not your type."

"She's a woman. She's breathing. She's hot. What am I missin' here?"

"A brain. Listen, I gotta go."

Lenny made one last appeal to see if he wanted to come out to the field and slug a few.

"The only thing I feel like slugging right now," John informed him, "is you."

Lydia had made little progress on the boxes during Kate's absence. To the latter's surprise, however, the one containing Jimmy's toys and clothes had seemingly been emptied first, its contents stacked on the front room couch.

She's got a soft spot, after all, Kate mused. Like gold, of course, one had to spend hours panning for it to even see a glimmer.

"From the looks of some of these play shirts and things," Lydia remarked in dismay, "he's probably outgrown them just since he's been here. And don't even get me started on the kind of flimsy little shoes she bought him."

Probably, Kate thought, *because it was the only thing she could afford*. She made a mental note to go online and order some stuff to fill in the gaps. Funny, she reflected, how her Internet surfing habits had changed so radically in such a short time from *Victoria's Secret* lingerie sales to toy stores and websites related to autism. "Look what Grandma found for you today," she now announced to Jimmy, kneeling and pointing him in the direction of his toys.

If she had been expecting a glimmer of recognition, her hopes went unanswered. Jimmy looked at her, looked at the couch and, then, with a squeal, hurled himself at one of the empty boxes that were laying open on its side.

"Jimmy, don't you want to play with some of these?" she tried to coax him but, for the moment, her nephew was much more interested in investigating the mysterious carton headfirst.

"Your sister was the same way," Lydia remarked, recalling aloud the time Cassy had emptied an entire box of Styrofoam peanuts all over the floor and then jumped into them as if they were snow.

"What about me?" Kate asked, quietly pleased by the neutrality that such reminiscence accorded both of them.

"With you, it was ribbons and bows, especially the stick-on kind you could put all over your head."

Kate sat down and tugged one of the half-full cartons over within reach. "Finding anything helpful yet?"

Lydia shook her head. "I swear I don't know what possessed her to keep some of this junk," she declared, leafing through old crossword puzzles and magazines. Her hand hesitated over the wastebasket she'd brought down from upstairs. Kate noticed for the first time that it was still empty. "I suppose we should go through all of these thoroughly just in case she wrote something down in a margin," the older woman murmured, setting the latest handful on top of the growing stack next to her chair.

Kate thoughtfully palmed a Statue of Liberty magnet that had been nestled in what looked to be the makings of an abandoned macramé project. She remembered her sister's quirky penchant for crafts, most of which were throwbacks to the era that preceded her birth. "I ran into Maria today," she said. "We had a lot of catching up to do."

"So what's she doing these days?" Lydia absently inquired as she added two paperback romances and a handwritten recipe for thumbprint cookies to the pile.

"Well, she works at the factory and makes pretty good money." Kate wisely omitted mention that her former cheerleading cohort was also dating an Italian boy-toy who was many years her junior. "She invited us to a ballgame later today. Not sure yet if we'll go, though." She tried to remember if Cassy had ever mentioned taking Jimmy to watch baseball or, for that matter, if they had ever watched it on TV.

Lydia was refolding a street map. "Why does someone have tourist maps of cities they've never gone to?" she said with a scowl. "And do they even make paper maps anymore?"

"She always said she wanted to go places," Kate offered in reply, reminding her mother of how Cassy had liked to play spin-the-globe and jab her finger at the surface to make it stop where she wanted.

"And instead," Lydia said, "she married someone who was going nowhere."

Kate glanced over at Jimmy who had now turned the box completely on top of himself and was happily alternating between grunts and humming. *Ah, the joys of childhood*, she thought, wishing recently of late that life could be simple enough to just put a box over oneself and be rendered invisible. She cleared her throat and nudged the conversation back to her encounter with Maria. "She told me about what happened to Jeremy. Such a terrible thing."

Lydia said something under her breath that Kate didn't quite catch. "Sean's favorite," she tightly disclosed when Kate asked her to repeat it.

"Oh, I don't know that Mr. Neal had favorites," Kate countered.

"Jeremy was the one who saved their marriage," Lydia cut her off. "If Abby hadn't gotten herself pregnant when she did," she let her critical assessment go unfinished. "Things might have been a lot different, that's all I'm saying."

Chapter Nineteen

The informality of rules observed by the neighborhood baseball teams was such that John felt no rush to show up promptly for the first inning or, for that matter, even the bottom of the third. Players were frequently dropping out, trading positions, and even recruiting runners from the bleachers for those who moaned about bum knees.

It was all in the spirit of having fun, of course, and bringing families out to watch. If their interests ever turned to intellectual pursuits like *Scrabble*, John thought, there was no telling what kind of foreign words, abbreviations and misspellings they'd allow just to rack up outlandishly high scores for themselves.

Though he'd made quicker work of his late afternoon job than he had anticipated, the annoyance of Lenny's comments and subsequent pestering phone calls still lingered even after he had gone home and changed his clothes. Certainly, the last thing he wanted or needed was to be under a magnifying glass at the park when his only objective was just to come and score a few runs. If he arrived well after the game was already in progress, he rationalized, his buddies would either be so glad to see him step up to bat or too buzzed on beers to start giving him the third degree about his supposed love life.

As Fate would have it, John wasn't the only one who saw the wisdom in making a delayed entrance.

They were just coming around the corner as he stepped out of his truck and was reaching in to grab his cap and catcher's mitt off the passenger seat. Jimmy, holding tight to Kate's hand with both of his, was doing a hopping dance of his invention. John caught himself grinning at the carefree picture the pair made, and when Kate looked up and saw him watching their approach, he could have sworn that she incorporated a spring in her step.

"Are you stalking us or what?" she affectionately teased when she had closed enough distance between them to not turn any nearby heads with a shout-out.

"Almost looks that way, doesn't it?" He bent down to say hi to Jimmy. "You guys just out for a walk?"

"Actually, we came to catch part of the baseball game," she replied, explaining that Maria had invited them but that she wasn't sure how Jimmy would handle the noise and excitement. "I thought we'd watch a little from outside the gate first and then maybe go in for a while."

"Then I'll have to make sure I hit a couple out of the park especially for you," he promised Jimmy.

He noticed that Kate's young charge hadn't taken his eyes off of the worn leather mitt he was carrying and now held it out for his inspection. "Want to hold on to my lucky mitt for me?"

Jimmy looked at John, looked at the mitt, and then folded his arms with the stubborn defiance of someone about to be force-fed a plateful of Brussel sprouts.

"That's okay," John said, bending down to set it on the sidewalk so that Jimmy could approach it on his own without any pressure.

Kate tilted her head in amused curiosity. "So, if the game's already started, what are you doing out here?"

"We play by pretty loose rules," he told her. "I had a job to finish for a client and I figured it'd still be going on by the time I showed up." Out of the corner of his eye, he noticed that Jimmy had unfolded his arms and was intently peering at John's offering. "So are you settling in okay with your mom?" he asked, hoping to glean a clue about how permanent a plan she might be making insofar as her current arrangements.

"Oh, about as much as she's going to let me," she replied. "Mom never did take well to changes that she wasn't totally in charge of."

"I think it's a standard default button of parenthood," he said, pleased that his quip made her laugh with a carefree innocence that belied the seriousness of the situation with her sister's nephew.

The light toss of her head dislodged a few wisps of hair from where she had casually pinned it up with a tortoiseshell clip, and it was only with tremendous self-discipline he resisted the urge to reach over and brush the loose strands off her slender neck. She was the kind of woman, he reflected, who could wear little makeup, or even none at all, and yet still be more gorgeous than women who spent all day trying to perfect themselves.

Mentally, he caressed the rest of her qualities. Her flawless skin, her smart green eyes, her graceful, athletic carriage. How, he wondered, had she come to be a thousand times more desirable in only a handful of recent chance encounters than in the culmination of all his dreams put together? It wasn't sensible, his conscience chided him, to respond so heatedly to a woman whose life clearly didn't have any room for him. If she sensed him pulling back, retreating from his fragile introspection about what might have been, she was doing nothing to betray it.

Only vaguely and from a fuzzy distance did he hear her say the name of his younger brother and express her condolences. "I only just found out about it today," she was apologizing. "If I had known earlier..."

Amongst a short bout of disconnected thoughts about the past and present there flashed a brief image of Kate being with him, being with his family when the news had come. Until this moment, he had been conscious only of cessation, of a dark emptiness in his life that wasn't even loneliness. Would she have left her glamorous life in another city, he wondered, and hopped a plane at a moment's notice to be by his side during the agonizing days that followed the senseless tragedy that took his baby brother's young life.

Or did the fantasy of her love and support all get down to being predicated on her never having left his side, never having left Avalon Bay, to begin with? The unbidden level of cynicism he had come to embrace after Jeremy's death and his brush with death and subsequent rehabilitation from his injuries made it too easy for him to assume that most people, even Kate, would probably say anything if it was already too late to act on the sentiments expressed.

He forced a smile and thanked her for her concern. "I should get on into the game," he announced to cut short any further discussion.

Her shoulders drew back slightly as if in reaction to some kind of realization she had just trespassed where she wasn't welcome. "Yeah, I suppose so," she replied, reaching for Jimmy's hand.

Jimmy by this time had picked up the mitt, tilted his head back and was balancing it on top of his face. He squealed and flailed his arms when Kate tried to take it from him.

"Come on, Jimmy, give it back," Kate coaxed him. "You can't keep something that doesn't belong to you."

The warning voice that whispered in John's head reminded him that the same thing applied to the heart he had once loved and lost.

On the one hand, Kate was surprised by the number of faces that looked faintly familiar to her as the three of them came within view of the bleachers. On the other hand, John Neal was enough of a popular fixture at the ballpark that the unexpected sight of him with a woman and a small child was bound to start a buzz before he even got up to bat.

True to her word, Maria had saved her a place. True to her character, she also wasted nary a second after a string of three effusive oh-my-goshes trying to find out if Kate had been holding out on her with what hinted to be some truly primo gossip.

"We just walked in together, that's all," Kate said. "No big deal."

"Yeah, right. So, what did he say? What did you say?"

"I said hi, he said hi…"

"Seriously," Maria insisted. "Doesn't it strike you as just a little too coincidental that you just happen to run into him like that after all these years?"

Had Kate deigned to tell her about the coincidence of two taxi rides, she was certain Maria would declare it downright karmic and start asking her if they had set a wedding date.

"Not so strange, really," she said instead. "It's not that big a town." She braced herself for the inevitable question of whether they were going to start seeing each other again. After the curiously brusque way he had shut down after she told him how sorry she was about Jeremy, she found herself wondering whether she had seen an earlier sparkle of interest in his eyes or whether it was just wishful thinking on her part. Across the field, she saw that he had donned his cap and was talking to a couple of the players. *Is he getting the same third-degree I am*, she mused.

"It's so funny we were just talking about him this morning, huh?" Maria was rabbiting on, pausing only long enough to reach into the mini-cooler at her feet and pull out a beer for Kate and a juice box for Jimmy. "Do you think he'd like this?" she asked.

Kate opened it for him but Jimmy was more interested in trying to reach over her lap and get a better look at the cooler.

"He's quite the little wiggle worm, isn't he?" Maria observed with a laugh. "How old did you say he was again?"

Kate was quietly thankful her friend was ascribing his behavior to age-appropriate excitement and not as yet looking any closer. "He 's five," she said a split second before he smacked the open beer can straight out of her hand and sent a splash of suds down the front of Maria's tee-shirt. Jimmy giggled and tried to grasp at the juice box for a repeat performance.

Kate was helpless to halt her embarrassment, a state intensified by the scrutiny of the spectators seated closest to them.

"Nothin' to see here, folks!" Maria good-naturedly quipped to them, assuring Kate in her next breath that kids were kids and that it was just an accident. "I'll probably spill more on myself when Tony hits a homer," she confessed with a giggle. "Oh look, he's next up at-bat."

Kate was only marginally aware of the lanky, black-haired Italian who was waving in response to whistles, at least a few of which were coming from Maria. Jimmy clamped both his hands over his ears and was now rocking back and forth. *I knew it was a mistake to come here*, Kate told herself, worried that her nephew's erratic behavior at the loud noise was just the tip of the iceberg if they tried to stay around for the entire game. She racked her brain for an excuse that would appease Maria but not require a whole lot of detail.

The sudden crack of the bat not only brought an outburst of cheers but several spectators to their feet as the ball quickly ascended into the sky. Jimmy suddenly stopped rocking and, for a moment, Kate caught the transfixed look of wide-eyed wonder on his face as the ball seemed to hover indefinitely against a backdrop of cornflower blue.

And then it began to come down.

In her brief fascination with watching Jimmy's reaction, Kate nearly missed what was happening on the field. Little Tony had just reached first base and was going to try to take second as well. Try, but not succeed, for there, standing almost directly beneath the descending ball, was John Neal wearing the cocky expression of someone who had found his grail. In a seamless move that appeared almost effortless, he held up his right hand as the ball sailed into his waiting mitt.

"Out!" the ump shouted.

Kate glanced at Jimmy, hoping he had seen it. Jimmy, however, had already lost interest and was trying to peer through the metal gaps between the bleacher seats.

"For an old guy, he's still got it, that's for sure," she heard Maria say.

Kate immediately contested the remark about old. "He's the same age we are," she pointed out.

"Yeah, but I mean compared to my honey," Maria waved and blew a kiss to him as he loped back to the bench. "You gotta admit he turned out pretty cute."

"John?" Kate asked, taking a sip of the orange drink that Jimmy was showing no interest in.

Maria playfully slugged her in the arm. "Tony."

"Oh." She still had her doubts about the age difference but knew better than to criticize her for it.

Maria took a deep chug of beer. "So anyway," she said as if the recent play had been little more than a commercial break in their conversation, "I think he's started seeing someone."

"Tony?" Kate said, perplexed that Maria was handling her new beau's possible infidelity with such detachment.

"John," Maria matter of factly replied. "I mean I don't know for sure but remember Kim Sherzer? She goes by Kimberly Henning now. Anyway, she was at the drugstore this afternoon and she was talking to this new girl in Pharmacy who said that her boyfriend's sister was going to start doing daycare out of her home and she had to go pick up some stuff last night from a friend who got home late and by the time she left she took a shortcut past John's street and she saw a gorgeous brunette leaving his house."

Kate only half-listened as she struggled with her conscience. *Just because a woman was leaving his house*, she tried to convince herself, *doesn't mean he's in a relationship with her*. A louder voice in her head chimed in. *And just because you left him 14 years ago doesn't mean he was going to wait forever for you to come back*.

She nearly missed Maria's next words. "Of course, it sounds like John's not the only one with a hot secret in this town," she said.

"Huh?"

Maria donned a Cheshire cat grin. "I hear a certain somebody got an expensive bouquet of roses from a certain somebody else."

Chapter Twenty

John wasn't aware of the precise moment that she disappeared, only that when he hit the promised homer out of the field for Jimmy and looked into the stands for the gratification of their approval, neither of them was there. A heavyset woman he didn't know had taken Kate's place next to Maria and was messily chowing down on a hotdog. His eyes quickly scanned the bleachers in the hope that maybe she had simply found someone else she recognized from the old days and relocated to another seat to say 'hello'.

He glanced toward the makeshift snack bar but they weren't there, either.

One of his fellow players yelled out his name as he started to lope toward the entrance to the park. "Just gotta check something!" he yelled back, hoping that maybe he had missed their departure by only a minute or two and that they hadn't gotten very far.

A look of despair, however, soon spread over his face. Save for a teenage guy on a bicycle and an older couple walking a scrappy Jack Russell terrier, the street was empty.

Neither the transient triumph of scoring runs for his team nor the anticipation of the losers springing for pizza and bottomless pitchers of beer at Capparelli's could change his mood and by the time he got home that night he had talked himself into the belief that the entire reason she'd left was because of something stupid he'd said or done. When he really narrowed it down, of course, he even knew what "it" was. It was the "none of your damn business" vibe he knew he put out whenever someone wanted to talk to him about what had happened to Jeremy.

People could always say that they knew exactly how he felt or what his family must have gone through during that horrific episode of American tragedy. At the end of the day, though, he couldn't even define that particular level of grief himself. Much as his heart tried to tell him that they were only being nice and were genuinely concerned in expressing their condolences, there still bubbled within him a sense of resentment that they presumed to know something, to feel something so devastating that they couldn't possibly grasp.

That Kate had come so close to being a part of their family had brought him to speculate outcomes of strength and emotional support that, if he got right down to it, maybe had no bearing on reality. The uncertainty and the inherent frustration were the reactions she had probably read on his face and, the more he thought about it, the more sense it seemed to make that he had pushed her away without even realizing it. Kate, of all people, would certainly know what it was like to lose a sibling to a senseless act of fate.

He found himself standing in front of the fireplace and contemplating the photos on the mantle that Gabrielle had been so interested in. And as his glance fell on the kooky snapshot of Jeremy at his high school prom, proudly sandwiched between two grinning female classmates, it occurred to him that at least Cassy had been able to leave behind a living, breathing part of herself who would one day grow up and remember the ever-so-brief time that she had treasured him more than anything in the world.

He closed his eyes, his heart aching with a pain that no amount of time would ever heal.

"I thought I heard you come in," he heard Abby say. "How'd the game go?"

Without turning toward the direction of her voice, he replied that they'd beat the pants off the opposition. "They may as well have just phoned it in for as bad as they were playing."

"So how come you and Lenny aren't out drinking their next week's paychecks?" she teased.

It was the kind of joke that only Abby could get away with, knowing full well that he had drunk himself into enough fistfights and hangovers immediately following Jeremy's death that he had learned his lesson about moderation and rarely drank more than one beer.

"Just bein' sensible, I guess," he said.

"Sensible's a good thing," she agreed in preface to an invitation to join her for some coffee in the kitchen.

"Nah, I think I'll just turn in. It's been a long day."

"John?"

"Huh?"

"Is everything all right?"

Confident that his eyes weren't misty enough to betray him, John turned to flash her a grin and tell her he was fine.

Abby, however, wasn't buying it.

"Until your dad's back on his feet again," she gently offered, "I don't mind being a good listener for the both of us and giving you my two cents."

John quipped that her advice was worth at least double the going rate and that she was selling herself short.

"Discount for family members," she countered. "Come on, the cup I poured for myself is probably getting cold already. Are you joining me or not?"

"I suppose I could go for half a cup," he acquiesced.

"And the advice?"

"Quit while you're ahead, Mom."

"We'll see."

Lydia registered neither surprise nor disappointment that Kate and Jimmy were home much earlier than she expected. "Did you have anything to eat?" she wanted to know.

Kate knew her mother well enough that it wasn't a declaration to cook something for them or, for that matter, to even heat a plate of leftovers. The years she had spent living alone had turned Lydia Toscano into a minimalist when it came to keeping herself fed. The fact she now had two guests sharing her roof was, in her own words, no excuse to suddenly become "Mother Bountiful".

"I bought us a couple of ice creams on the way home," Kate told her, omitting that Jimmy had dropped most of his on the sidewalk when he got distracted by two cats chasing each other and that she had given him the rest of hers rather than walk back to purchase a replacement.

"Ice cream is no substitute for a healthy meal," Lydia informed her, stopping just short of offering to fix him one.

"This from the woman who eats like a bird?" Kate said.

"Well, you can't just give him ice cream and leave it at that. And look at yourself. Have you lost weight since you got here?"

"If I did, it's all because of stress." To which, she thought, she could now add the toll of a broken heart that, suffice it to say, was probably her fault for either leaving Avalon Bay too soon or not coming back to it fast enough. "Do you have any stuff for a salad?" she asked. "I thought I'd just throw something quick together."

Lydia was up from the TV, on her feet, and headed toward the kitchen. "You don't know where I keep anything," she informed her daughter. "Oh, by the way," she added a breath later, "that girl from Las Vegas called you. I left her number next to the phone."

"Dee? I wonder what she wants." She had meant to murmur it only to herself but it was just loud enough for her mother to overhear.

"I'm not a personal secretary," Lydia was quick to remind her. "It's enough that I had to go hunt down a pen to write down where you were supposed to call her back."

Hunt down a pen. Kate smirked in reminiscence of all the times she and Cassy had heard that phrase growing up even though their mother always had no less than half a dozen pens sticking out of decorated aluminum cans right next to every phone in the house. She glanced at her watch, then glanced back at Jimmy who was happily laying on top of a throw pillow, rhythmically scissor-kicking his legs and staring at the woodworking on the side of the coffee table as if it were the most fascinating thing in the universe.

Given the time difference, she could call Dee on her cell phone but still be mobile enough to keep an eye on her young charge in the event he found a new diversion. Dee answered on the second ring.

"Hey you! What's happening?" were the first words out of Dee's mouth.

"Modest insanity. How about you?"

"I wasn't sure if you'd get my message. When I talked to your mom..."

"Yeah, I know," Kate said, dropping her voice a little lower. "She has that effect on people."

"Poor you," Dee replied in sympathy.

"Tell me about it. So why didn't you just try me on my cell?" Even as the words left her mouth, Kate realized that the last time she'd had it turned on was when she'd left the airport. Since settling in at her mother's, the phone and its charger were currently upstairs on the dresser.

"Well, I tried a couple of times, sweetie," Dee explained, "and when you didn't pick up, I remembered your mom's phone number was listed in your personnel file for emergencies."

"You should moonlight as a private eye," Kate complimented her. "So, what's up?"

There was a slight pause before Dee continued, a pause that Kate wouldn't realize until later was a moment of stumbling hesitation prior to delivering disconcerting news. "Well, you know how I said my dad was coming out here for a couple of days?"

Kate refrained from reminding her that the timeframe had still been indefinite when the subject first came up, thus necessitating her vacating the condo. "How's he doing?" she asked instead. "You guys having a nice visit?"

"Well, that's kinda what I needed to talk to you about."

"Oh?"

"You see there's this deal, and I mean a mega major deal he's putting together with some venture capitalists in London who want to launch this really upscale fashion magazine that's going to be translated into God knows how many different languages including, get this, Swahili! Can you believe it?"

"Which part?" Kate asked, "The magazine or the Swahili?"

Dee laughed. "You are too, too funny. It's one of the things I've always loved about you."

"But back to your point," Kate reminded her.

"Well, did I tell you that this is really, really major and they want to get it going right away?"

"And?"

"And I mean this is really and totally the chance of a lifetime to make a huge splash, you know what I'm saying?"

Does a "really and a totally" trump two or more really's? Kate mused. "I'm hearing it but I'm not sure what it means in terms of—"

Dee plunged on in excitement. "The ink's not dry yet but somebody's gotta get over there right away and start things smokin' like schmoozing it up, dealing with advertisers, planning the launch party. Did I mention we're talking to some major A-Listers for the cover issue?"

Kate was only half listening. *London. Fashion. Glamour. Being in charge of what sounded like a mega-bucks global enterprise. A dream job from every angle.*

Across the room, Jimmy had rolled off the pillow and, with a giggle, flung it toward the couch, narrowly missing a ceramic figurine on the end table. As she rushed over to make sure he didn't try to retrieve the pillow for a second throw, a disheartening realization replaced her brief flirtation with fantasy.

A dream job for someone else. Someone who isn't responsible for a high maintenance five-year-old.

C.J. Foster

She interrupted Dee in the middle of a sentence that included Sting and the name of at least one famous designer. "I'm going to hate myself for saying this,"

"Saying what?" a puzzled Dee asked.

Kate took a deep breath. "My priority right now has to be Jimmy. With everything that's going on – plus everything he's going to be needing in terms of school and doctor visits and medications..." *I can't believe I'm hearing myself say this*, she thought. "The whole thing sounds really, really fabulous and—" *Really, really? Have I spent so much time under Dee's influence that even the really's have become part of my vocabulary?* As she struggled for the right words to complete her declinature, Dee was already talking again.

"Well you've got to admit the timing for all this couldn't be better," Dee pointed out. "I was afraid you'd be upset."

Kate laughed. "Upset that you've just offered me the dream of a lifetime? I've never been more flattered! It's just that, well, I hope you can understand why taking care of Jimmy is just something I can't walk away from."

There was a beat.

"Huh?" Dee said.

"The job in London setting up shop. It sounds incredible but,"

"Oh my God."

"What?"

"Uh...did you think I was asking if...oh my God this is really, really nothing like what I expected."

Kate impatiently waited for her to collect her wits and start over.

"The thing of it is," Dee awkwardly continued, "is that Daddy wants me to go to London. The end of the week, actually. That's why I had to get hold of you, to let you know what was going on."

Kate's fair complexion flushed with embarrassment and she was thankful that over two thousand miles separated her from her caller so the latter couldn't see the look on her face. "Boy, do I feel like an idiot," she said, mollified at least by the knowledge that Dee probably didn't know what to say at that moment, either. The only question hovering between them, of course, was why Dee had thought she'd be upset about the announcement.

She didn't have to wait long to learn the answer.

"Much as I hate to close down the mag out here," Dee said, "well, I just can't be two places at once and,"

"You're shutting down *Vegas Essential*?" an astonished Kate responded with a gasp.

"It kills me to do it, sweetie. I mean we've had a tremendous run and you guys are the best." She went on to explain that she'd been busy all day writing recommendation letters and making calls to help find new jobs for the staff before she hopped a plane to the U.K. "I was kinda hoping you'd be the easiest on account of you're not even in town and, well, I mean you're so stellar at what you do, a person would have to be really, really, really stupid not to grab you up in a heartbeat."

Chapter Twenty-One

K ate waited until the following morning to tell her mother that she was officially unemployed.

Lydia, true to form, didn't even seem surprised. "This is the same friend who was going to hold your job open for you indefinitely while you worked things out?" she coolly remarked in her I-told-you-so tone. "So much for keeping her word."

"It wasn't an iron-clad promise," Kate felt compelled to point out in Dee's defense. "We both knew that if something came up, things could change."

"Yanking the rug out from under people doesn't sound like very professional behavior. What are they supposed to do for jobs?"

"Well, a couple of them will be helping her with the start-up in London," Kate explained with carefree defiance that belied her vacillating pangs of envy. In her mind's eye, she could imagine herself eating lunch in Hyde Park, checking the accuracy of her watch against Big Ben, meeting friends for tea at Fortnum and Mason, and marveling at the lavishly decorated displays of gourmet goodies at Harrod's Food Hall.

The excitement of an overseas assignment was something she'd thought about pretty often while she was working on her degree at Amherst. Part of that dream, of course, always included a scenario of John missing her desperately and flying over to surprise her. Instead, it was now going to be somebody else living in a trendy London flat and having an inside track on where to find all the best Indian restaurants and Chinese takeaways.

"And she didn't even think to ask you if you wanted to go?" Lydia cut into her thoughts. She proceeded to remind her daughter of all the work and overtime she had poured into making the magazine a success. "It doesn't sound to me like that so-called friend of yours puts much stock in company loyalty."

"Oh, come on, Mom, you know that I'd have to have turned her down even if she did ask me."

A long pause hung in the air between them and Kate wondered whether her mother was contemplating a criticism that would include the words "the boy".

Instead, Lydia simply went on perusing the archive box she had set on the nearest kitchen chair and murmuring that she couldn't fathom why her younger daughter had been such a packrat.

"It was probably about time for me to polish up my resume anyway," Kate continued, not yet ready to relinquish the topic at hand.

Money, she realized, had been only a minor factor in her most recent decisions, largely owing to the combination of good judgment with credit cards and the discipline not to succumb to excess in a city that defined it 24/7. The luxury of her being able to take as much as two months off, however, had been predicated on returning to the status quo once she'd gotten into the rhythm of motherhood. With Dee now off to London and the magazine taking an unexpected bow, the financial picture had radically changed overnight.

"So, what do you think you're going to do for work?" Lydia asked. Unspoken was the dismal reality that there probably wasn't a lot of call at Avalon Bay for savvy wordsmiths of her daughter's caliber.

"I suppose I could check out what the temp agency has," Kate mused. Despite the cushion of her accumulated vacation pay and a severance check from Dee, it wasn't too soon to start putting her name in circulation. An even more sobering thought, of course, was how her current employment status would be evaluated by the courts. *Is it worse to be a bachelorette in Vegas*, she wondered, *or an out-of-work writer living with her mother on the Jersey shore?*

Lydia was dubious that the local employment franchise would be of much help unless someone was looking to be a waitress, a secretary, or, heaven forbid, work an assembly line at the factory. "The problem," she pointed out, "is that you're way overqualified for the kinds of jobs they're trying to fill these days and with the economy the way it is."

"Can't argue with that," Kate agreed, "but whatever it is would only be a stopgap for some stability until the right opportunity comes along."

Stopgap. She'd lost track of the number of times she'd heard Cassy use that same word to explain why she was washing dishes in crummy diners, stuffing envelopes for fund drives, being a barista, and working the popcorn machine at movie theaters.

Lydia suddenly brightened. "You know who you really should talk to?"

"Who?"

"Bradley."

Kate laughed to cover her annoyance. "Brad? Oh, give me a break."

"I don't see why not. He knows all kinds of people."

"None of whom I'd want to go to based on a recommendation from him."

"And what's wrong with him putting in a good word for a friend?"

"In the first place, Brad and I aren't friends. In the second place, he'd do anything in the book to try to change that."

Lydia clucked her tongue. "Beggars can't be choosers."

"I'm not exactly at the 'beggar' stage, Mom. There's plenty I can do to keep the wolves from the door."

The doorbell rang at that moment.

Kate couldn't resist quipping that the wolves had just gotten the memo about her plight.

"I'll get it," Lydia said.

Kate insisted she stay put. "Heaven forbid they should tear you to bits instead."

If he'd had his wits about him, John thought, he would simply have left his offering at the Toscanos' front door without even ringing the bell. Wasn't that what surprises were all about? The effort he had put into it, however, could so easily be deflated if the intended recipient had absolutely no clue who it came from. Worse, perhaps, if the intended recipient's mother discovered it first and—

"Uh...hi," said Kate.

Distracted as he always was by her natural beauty, John nearly tripped over his tongue saying 'hi' back.

There was no mistaking the puzzlement in her eyes, especially when they gravitated to the small terracotta pot he was holding as if it were the crown jewels.

"I brought something for Jimmy," he announced.

Though her smile hovered on an edge of uncertainty, it was a smile nonetheless. "A stick?"

"It may look like just a stick now," he agreed, "but once we get it in the ground, I think you'll be surprised what it can do."

She contemplated it a moment. "I'm not sure what to say."

John shrugged. "Oh, I don't know. I suppose you could say, 'Gosh! Wow! A tree! Who'd have thought?"

Her face softened with a laugh. "No, what I meant was, what's the occasion? Arbor Day?"

"Arbor Day's the last Friday in April."

"So you're either a couple of months late," she calculated, "or you just wanted to beat the rush for next year?"

"Arbor Day's got nothing to do with it," he said.

"No?"

"Does a guy need a special occasion to give his ex-girlfriend's favorite nephew a tree? You never know, Hallmark could be missing a whole untapped market." In the background, he heard Lydia asking Kate who was at the door.

"It's John Neal," she shot back over her shoulder.

Silence.

Kate returned her attention to John's present. "I'm really the worst person in the world when it comes to trees," she confessed. "Are you sure you want to subject this to potential, uh, stickicide?"

"Stickicide?"

"Yeah, whatever you call it when you kill off baby oak trees."

"At least you knew it was an oak," he complimented her.

Kate smiled. "I surprise myself sometimes."

"Come back here, young man!" they heard Lydia call out.

Jimmy, minus a sock and clutching the life out of a box of raisins, hurled into the foyer with the energy of a squealing tornado and, crashing into the back of Kate's legs, nearly caused her to pitch forward.

"Hey, hey, no running in the house," she reminded him. "And what did you do with your sock?"

Jimmy, however, only had eyes for their morning visitor and what he was carrying. John crouched down so his young recipient could get a better look.

"It's a Northern Red Oak," he explained. "This is what all those big trees out on the street looked like when they were just little guys like you."

Still clutching the box of raisins, Jimmy eagerly reached out with his free hand to try to grab it out of the pot. John's hand, gentle but firm, closed over the smaller one before he could inflict any permanent damage. "We need to be gentle with trees," he said, "or they won't be able to grow up big and strong."

If he'd been expecting Jimmy to yank his hand away and lunge for it again, he was pleasantly mistaken. Jimmy instead was grinning, rocking his head from side to side and making no effort to extricate his fingers.

John looked up at Kate. "You think maybe you've got a place in the backyard we could put this in the ground?"

She hesitated. "Seeing as how it's Mom's yard."

"A new tree back there, she probably won't even notice."

Kate skeptically tilted her head. "Are we talking about the same person? She notices everything." In the next breath, she asked him how tall it was going to get.

"Two feet a year," he replied. "They're pretty hardy."

"Two feet a year," she echoed, "and she couldn't *not* notice."

John was insistent. "Every kid should have their own tree," he informed her.

"Oh?"

"I'm pretty sure it's on the law books somewhere. Besides," he said, noticing that Jimmy still hadn't let go, "it would be good for him to do something with his hands."

"Meaning?"

"Meaning that I'd like to show him how to plant one of these and take care of it." He felt proud of himself for remembering some of the things Gabrielle had told him about her work in engaging young children who had special needs. "I've even got a mini trowel in my truck that's just his size," he added. He left out the fact he had picked it out and bought it not twenty minutes before at Pieczynski's Hardware.

Again, he saw a fragile hesitation in Kate's eyes. A hesitation that he knew had nothing to do with her mother's approval.

"You never know what someone's capable of," he said gently, "unless you're willing to give 'em a try."

"Why's that Neal boy digging up my backyard?" Lydia wanted to know, peering out through the kitchen blinds in the gap she created with her thumb and index finger.

"Something about finding a new route to China," Kate teased her. Smiling in remembrance of the way Jimmy had run alongside John and how the latter had started telling him the story of Jack and the magic seeds that grew into a beanstalk.

Lydia was neither amused by the attention John was giving her grandson nor pleased by the prospect of how much dirt would inevitably be trudged into her house when they were through.

"Honestly, Mom, he's just planting a tree for Jimmy. It's not like they're breaking ground for the next Big Dig." She pulled over another of the archive boxes. "Been through this one yet?"

Lydia opined that after a while they all started to look alike. "I swear I don't know where she got those tendencies from."

"What tendencies?"

"Saving everything little thing. I found an entire shoebox of store coupons that were three years old." She was still peering out the blinds. "What does Jimmy need a tree for?"

"Every kid should have his own tree," Kate absently parroted John as she withdrew a manila folder with the words "To Do" scribbled on the front. The phrase "an unfinished life" came to mind as she found herself gazing at various clippings for yard sales, magazine photos of kicky hairstyles, a supermarket list, and a pastel brochure for a children's beginning swim class in Oakland. *A compendium of goals and dreams*, Kate sadly mused, *that the dreamer didn't live long enough to see fulfilled.*

"And who's supposed to take care of this so-called tree of his?" Lydia asked. "I don't have enough to look after around this place?"

"It's not like you have to take it for a walk or pick up after it" Okay, so maybe the latter half of that statement wasn't quite true, Kate told herself. It would, after all, grow into a gigantic oak and litter its surroundings every fall with no shortage of leaves and acorns.

"The way he runs around like a little hellion," her mother continued, "he'll probably have it knocked down by lunchtime."

Kate started to pull a sheaf of papers out of an envelope that bore the name and return address of an attorney's office in San Francisco. "I'm sure John will teach him to be careful, Mom."

"Yes, but how do you know he'll even understand? If you want my opinion," She stopped at the sight of shock and disbelief now registering on her daughter's face. "What's wrong?" she asked, moving around the side of the table to see what had caused Kate's reaction.

Kate held the document out to her. "I'm afraid this could change everything."

Chapter Twenty-Two

"Who 'forgets' to file her own divorce papers?" Lydia sputtered in raw disbelief.

Kate was only half-listening, intent on combing through the rest of the folder's contents in the hope that the unsigned document was simply a file copy her sister had tucked away.

"It's bad enough that he couldn't even keep a roof over her head," Lydia continued, "but now the little weasel's probably going to come back and want half her estate!"

'Estate', of course, was defining fairly loosely what Cassy had left behind in terms of tangible property stored in the few boxes strewn around Lydia's kitchen. "What we should be more worried about," Kate said, "is that he's going to want all of Jimmy." If Luke's finances were still as spotty as Cassy had always told her, a dependent child under his roof, would make him eligible for government aid, an angle that someone of his character wouldn't hesitate to play.

Lydia snorted her disdain for her former, or rather, current, son-in-law's woeful lack of accountability. "No court's going to even allow him visitation rights," she insisted, "especially considering that hippie lifestyle of his."

"He wasn't born in the right decade to be a hippie," Kate gently corrected her.

"Well whatever you want to call people like that, your sister should have seen the writing on the wall when she first met him. All that anyone has to do is just look at him and know he's incapable of taking care of anything."

"Yeah, but whether we like it or not, a judge is still going to take into—"

A sudden boisterous banging at the back door caught both women off guard.

Kate opened the door to see John holding a squirming Jimmy in his arms.

"We obviously need to work on our knocking skills," he said with an apologetic grin, stepping back just far enough so that Jimmy, a dirty fist outstretched, couldn't repeat his exuberant performance.

Seeing her nephew being carried sent Kate into instant panic mode. "Is he hurt?" she asked, reaching out to touch him.

"No, but I think maybe he's carrying half the backyard in his pockets and on his feet." John delivered his next smile to Lydia who had just come up behind Kate. "Wouldn't want to mess up your mom's clean house."

His thoughtfulness about not wanting to make extra work for her went un-thanked. Lydia, in fact, couldn't wait to relieve him of his wriggling burden so he could be on his way that much faster.

"How can someone so small get dirty so fast?" she declared as she marched Jimmy over to the kitchen sink and began running water for a preliminary clean-up.

"He was quite the little helper," John remarked. "All the makings of a natural arboriculturist."

"That's a bigger word than he is," Kate pointed out in amusement.

"Not to worry, I bet he'll grow into it. You know, you've got some great trees back there, Mrs. Toscano," he complimented Lydia.

"All the more reason I didn't need another one," she tartly replied without turning around.

Kate started to say something but John was too quick.

"I'm worried, though, about the one closest to the house. From the looks of it, it's getting hit with too much water."

"Trees are supposed to have water," Lydia informed him as if he were dense. "It has to get down to the roots."

John chuckled. "Oddly enough, that's what a lot of people think," he replied. "Truth is that tree roots grow horizontally, not vertically. Most of 'em are only about 6-18 inches beneath the surface."

"And that means what to me?" Lydia asked.

"Well, unless I'm mistaken, ma'am, the trunk's in the line of fire with your sprinkler. All that exposure's started a fungi problem."

"So I'll point the sprinkler somewhere else," she cut him off.

"I'm afraid you've already got some decay kickin' in." John shook his head. "Sooner or later, it'll have to come out. Preferably sooner."

He glanced at Kate as he said it and she was struck by the tenderness with which he was conveying to them that the tree had already started to die.

Lydia, however, was more concerned about what it was going to cost her, not to mention the disruption of having her backyard torn up.

"Oh, I think I could make you a pretty good deal," John offered. "How 'bout a date with your daughter?"

"'A date with your daughter'?" Kate echoed a few moments later as she walked him out to his truck. "I can't believe you said that."

John winked. "And did you notice how fast she told me she'd rather call around town and get other quotes?"

"Subtlety isn't her strong suit."

John pushed his lower lip forward in thought. "Well, unless someone comes back to her with a better offer, I'm not that worried."

"Yeah, but you were just joking with her, right?" A part of her hoped that he'd tell her he was totally serious and then ask her what night she was free.

"Was I?"

Was that a yes or a no? She paused for a second, hesitant to remind him that, according to Maria, he was already seeing someone. Hesitant as well to hear it confirmed from his own lips. *Like it hasn't been a bad enough day already to begin with.* Instead, she apologized for her mother's rude attitude toward him, returning his easy grin with as much nonchalance as she could muster. "I know there's no excuse for some of the things she does," she said.

"No need to explain. Some people just get rubbed the wrong way and there's nothing you can do about it." Being nice to them, though, he added in quip, generally drove them crazy.

"For my mother, that would be a pretty short trip," Kate candidly replied.

"Well, listen, I probably shouldn't take any more of your time."

"Uh—"

"Yeah?"

She pushed back a lock of hair that had fallen across her forehead. "It was sweet of you to bring Jimmy a tree."

"He's a sweet kid."

Kate nodded in agreement. "I just wasn't sure if I, uh, remembered to thank you. This morning's been kinda difficult."

"I could use some help in here!" Lydia called out.

Humor was Kate's best defense against the latest rush of embarrassment. "Making me feel like I'm still twelve is what she lives for."

"You and everyone else, I'm sure," John replied. "So what were you about to say?"

Kate shook her head. "Just some things that caught me off-guard."

"Anything I can help with?"

"Wouldn't happen to know a good lawyer, would you?"

"Well, there's my brother Mitch," he replied. "Although I don't know that I'd use his name and the word 'good' in the same sentence."

It was an attempt to make her laugh but, for the moment, Kate's nerves were much too raw to manage much more than a half-smile.

"Something serious?" he asked in concern when she didn't elaborate on what was distracting her.

The last thing she wanted right now, Kate realized, was to divulge the latest details of the escalating mess that was her sister's life. Especially if she ended up crying and the nearest pair of comforting arms belonged to John Neal. She felt his steady gaze on her lowered face and allowed the silence to continue until she realized it was only making them both more uncomfortable with one another. She looked up. "If I'm attacked by a killer tree," she told him, "you'll be the first person I call."

"The tree," John gallantly promised her in turn, "won't have a chance."

After what seemed an eternity, the paralegal finally returned to the line. "I'm sorry," she apologized to Kate, "but we don't have anything in our files that shows the final documents were ever executed."

Kate asked her if there'd been any follow-up on their part to find out why.

"With the volume of paperwork that we have to process on any given day…"

"I realize that," Kate said, "but I'm just trying to understand how this could have fallen through the cracks, especially since there's a young child involved."

The paralegal's voice was definitely a few degrees cooler than when their conversation had first begun. "Whether there are children in the marriage or not," she informed Kate, "we have no way of knowing if a couple has changed their minds unless they tell us they want to withdraw the petition."

"Yes, but if my sister had hired your firm to handle the paperwork."

"Your sister was a one-time client, Ms. Toscano. We served the papers on her husband and did everything we were supposed to do to put the process in motion. According to our records, we attempted to follow up with her several times but her telephone had been disconnected."

"Forgive my ignorance on this," Kate said, "but they had already been separated for years."

"Not legally."

"Excuse me?"

"They may have decided to live apart as husband and wife but neither one of them filed for a legal separation."

Kate gently protested that friends and family had been aware they split up and weren't under the same roof. "Shouldn't that count for something?"

"A legal separation would have an impact on respective earnings, custodial terms, property. This would also have spelled out support payments for the care and welfare of the child." She pointed out that while these things had been addressed in the divorce papers, there was no evidence of any formal agreements between Cassy and Luke before that.

"Well, he sent money for my nephew whenever he could but it wasn't exactly a model father."

The paralegal cut her off. "I wish I could help you, Ms. Toscano, but under the laws of the State of California, your sister and Mr. Finch were still legally married to one another at the time of her death."

"If I could bother you with just one more question?"

"I really do need to go." The sound of a ringing phone in the background seemed to emphasize her impatience with Kate's queries.

"I promise I'll keep it short. The thing of it is, my nephew is now living with my mother and me in New Jersey," she began.

The paralegal expressed surprise that Kate wasn't calling from San Francisco. "How did he get to New Jersey?" she wanted to know.

"Well, I brought him here myself when we heard what had happened to my sister."

"And Mr. Finch was aware of this?"

For the second time since their conversation had first begun, Kate reminded her that she had no idea of Luke's whereabouts.

There was a dull silence at the other end of the line.

"If I were you, Ms. Toscano," she finally advised, "I'd hire an attorney as soon as possible."

Chapter Twenty-Three

"**I** know that look," said Sandy as she removed John's empty lunch plate with one hand and refilled his coffee cup with the other.

"So now I have a 'look', do I?" John teased her.

The morning tree job after he'd left the Toscanos had taken him until a little after two. The regulars at Gull's Galley had long since departed by the time he got there and slid into a window booth. John as yet wasn't sure whether he welcomed the silence to contemplate his latest encounter with Kate or dreaded that the lack of ambient distractions allowed him to think about her too much.

"Sam used to get that look when he was confused," Sandy blithely continued.

"Confused about what?"

"Confused about what his next move should be."

"I don't follow," John lied, pretty sure that he knew exactly where her current chain of chatter was taking them.

"Oh, come on, hon, sure you do," she insisted. "Lenny told me all about it."

"All about what?" He made a mental note to kill Lenny the next time he saw him.

Sandy laughed. "Aren't you the sly one," she teased, "thinking you can keep that kind of thing a secret?"

"It must be pretty well kept then," he told her, "if I don't even know what it is myself."

Sandy proceeded to cheerfully replay the rumor making the rounds that John had a new girlfriend. To no great surprise, the details had been embellished since he'd last heard it. On the one hand, he thought, it was deflecting attention off of Kate and her return to Avalon Bay. On the other hand, of course, was the bittersweet reminder of times past when he'd wanted the entire world to know that they were a couple. For more times in the past few days than he wanted to admit he had caught himself wondering whether Kate had any idea of the electrifying power she still held over him. A part of him suspected she was completely clueless, a product of his reluctance to pull her into his arms and let his body language spell out the obvious.

He interrupted Sandy's hearsay account from Lenny to ask her if she'd ever played the whisper game in school.

She looked puzzled. "What does that have to do with anything?" she asked.

"Everything, actually," he replied. "Because when people start repeating things to each other, it usually ends up far from the original story."

It was Sandy's turn to interrupt him as a customer stepped through the front screen door of Gull's Galley and was greeted with, "Take a seat anywhere. I'll be right with you."

Thankful for the respite to enjoy the remainder of his coffee in peace, John could only hope that the presence of someone else in the café would curtail Sandy's incessant curiosity about his non-existent love life.

"Can I do a take-out order?" he heard a woman's voice inquire. A voice that sounded vaguely familiar to him.

"Sure thing, hon, what'll it be?" Sandy asked.

John glanced over his shoulder to steal a glance at the precise moment the new arrival turned to rummage in her shoulder bag for a pair of glasses and noticed him looking at her.

"Oh, hi!" said Gabrielle with a smile of sweet recognition. "Small world."

"I'm going to run out and pick up a couple of things," Kate announced. "Do you want me to take Jimmy or leave him here with you?"

Even though Lydia was off in the next room, it was still close enough for Kate to catch the words "bull in a china shop". Whether she was referring to the havoc she thought he'd inflict on an innocent store owner's wares or just on the Toscano household's possessions, Kate wasn't sure. Ever since the singularly unhelpful phone conversation with the paralegal and Kate's failed attempts to locate a current address for Luke on Google, tempers between both women were starting to reach a flashpoint. Getting away from one another for a little while, even on an errand to the drugstore, was essential if they hoped to weather the rest of the day and start making a plan of action.

To her surprise, Lydia offered to keep Jimmy at home while she tended the garden. "I have to clean up that terrible mess in the backyard," she added. "Being out in the fresh air with me will do the boy some good."

Kate knew better than to point out that the fresh air in the backyard wasn't any different from the air the two of them would encounter on a walk. Maybe, in her quirky way, her mother was simply recognizing that Kate hadn't had any "alone" time to recharge her batteries ever since she'd first assumed parental responsibility for Jimmy. As she let herself out the front door, a quick mental tally affirmed that Lydia was probably right.

What was it like to be single and carefree? Oddly, the only image that came floating back was walking hand in hand with John Neal on the Boardwalk at dusk and feeling on top of the world. She gave herself a sharp mental shake that was meant to dislodge the scent of his aftershave and the smoky look that always seemed to smolder in his eyes. *You had your chance*, the voice in her head reminded her. *Lightning's not going to strike twice.*

It would have been rude of him to bolt out of the booth and leap into his truck and yet that's exactly what John felt like doing as Gabrielle casually started to stroll toward him. Sandy, of course, was looking like a cat that had just swallowed a cage full of canaries. Further, she made no secret of her intent to inject herself into whatever conversation was about to transpire between them.

"Looks like I'm not the only one who lost track of lunchtime," Gabrielle observed.

"Busy day?" he asked.

"Mostly paperwork for school," she replied, punctuating it with a shrug. "I'd much rather be spending it with the kids."

"Oooh, you've got kids?" Sandy exclaimed in approval as she hovered with her order pad. "How many?"

If Gabrielle was put off by Sandy's nosiness, her face didn't convey it. "Six at the moment," she replied, "although I'm hoping to have a lot more."

Sandy's mouth dropped open in amazement. "Just like the movie stars!" she said. "Are they all from different countries?"

An amused Gabrielle was clearly in no hurry to burst her listener's effusive bubble. "No," she answered, "just the Jersey shore."

Sandy eagerly pointed out that John had always adored children and asked if he had met all of them yet.

"Gabrielle's starting a new school," John felt compelled to explain before Sandy got carried away with her misconceptions.

Sandy, in response, was more interested in the fact her first name was Gabrielle than anything having to do with education. "It's French, isn't it?" she pressed. "Sam, that's my boyfriend, and I have always wanted to go there."

"In the meantime," John suggested, "Would you mind going to the counter and getting my check? I've gotta get back to work."

"You haven't even finished your coffee, hon. Is it getting cold? I'll just give it a warm-up."

John put his hand over the top of the cup. "Just the check."

Sandy remembered she hadn't asked Gabrielle what she wanted to order yet.

"I've heard the subs here are pretty good," Gabrielle remarked. "I'll take an Italian."

Sandy informed her that Italian subs just happened to be John's absolute favorite, too.

"Well, then I can see I'm in stellar company," Gabrielle amicably replied. "Make it two of them, please, and maybe some homemade potato salad as a side."

"Hungry little thing, aren't you?" Sandy opined. "Not that there's anything wrong with a girl having a healthy appetite. Nowadays, everybody wants to look like a stick. It's the Hollywood thing, you know? I swear some of these girls turn sideways and you'd think they'd left the room."

"Speaking of leaving the room," John interrupted her.

Sandy giggled. "Oh, I get it. You two kids want some 'alone' time." She turned to go but not without a mischievous warning. "Now don't go saying anything important until I come back."

John leaned forward and recommended to Gabrielle that the next thing she might want to think about Chinese takeout from Ming's down the street. "You can get out with a lot fewer questions."

She laughed. "I'd forgotten what it was like in a small town," she confessed.

"If she had a camera," John speculated, "our picture would be on the front of this week's gazette."

"Think I should tell her I'm already spoken for?'

He smiled. "I would enjoy freaking her out with that, but it's probably better to leave well enough alone. With any luck, she'll find new gossip before the week's even out."

His mention of Cliff's paper prompted Gabrielle to share the news that she was going to see if the local press would be interested in doing a story about the school, maybe even interview her.

"Well, for what it's worth," he candidly replied, "I've never known Cliff to turn down the chance to talk to an attractive woman."

"Long as it can bring some good attention to what we're trying to do for special needs children and their parents."

"Worth a shot."

"By the way," she asked, "how's your friend doing? The one with the little boy?"

John revealed that not only had he seen both of them that morning but that he had also helped Jimmy plant his first tree. With a half-smile, he admitted that it reminded him of when he and his younger brother had tried, unsuccessfully, to build a treehouse together. "I guess I wasn't working fast enough for him because I remember he kept asking me over and over if I was done yet."

As it turned out, he continued, Jeremy had invited all his friends over to play in it after lunch which was only an hour and a half after the brothers had lugged everything they needed into the backyard. "Try to imagine," he said, "a semi-circle of angry little boys with their arms folded and wanting to know where their fort was."

"So, what did you do?'

"I told 'em my mother had just made a big batch of cookies and to run inside and eat as many as they wanted."

"Pretty wicked."

"Probably. Especially since I told her it was all Jeremy's idea." John shook his head. "Funny how being with Jimmy this morning brought back a memory I hadn't thought about for years."

In a spontaneous gesture more nurturing than romantic, Gabrielle reached across the table to touch his hand. "And I bet you created some great memories today for that little boy."

He nodded in thoughtful appreciation of her praise, completely unaware that Kate Toscano was on the other side of the street and happened to glance in their direction at that very moment.

Sittin' on the dock of the bay...

If there was one thing Kate hated, it was getting a song stuck in her head that refused to go away.   Especially a dismal and depressing song.   Especially since she had been doing exactly what the lyrics said for goodness knows how long in an attempt to dispel what she had seen in the window of Gull's Galley.   The voice in her head reminded her it was a clear affirmation of the question that had been driving her crazy.   It was her heart, though, that was still reluctant to concede defeat.

I'll be sittin' when the evenin' come...

It had to be getting pretty close to five, she realized, though it would still be a long time before dusk rolled in.   Mothers who had brought their toddlers to build sandcastles that afternoon were already starting to gather up beach blankets, shoes, and playthings and getting ready to trek home.   Along the water's edge, a father was dangling a teddy bear above the head of a gleefully shrieking little girl who was jumping up and down, trying to grab it away from him.   Kate caught herself smiling when he dropped down to the wet sand in mock surrender and held the bear out to his daughter with both hands, a gesture she rewarded with a hug that toppled him onto his back.

'Cause I've had nothin' to live for...

An older couple in matching Hawaiian shirts and visors were methodically combing the sand with a metal detector.   The man suddenly stopped and pointed at the ground.   His companion, the more lithesome of the two, squatted down to brush away some sand and, with an audible whoop of delight, retrieved something small and shiny.   He rewarded her with a chaste peck on the cheek and their judicious scavenging continued.

Look like nothin's gonna come my way...

If she put her life to a vote amongst the people she'd been watching, Kate was pretty sure none of them would deem her worthy of their sympathy.   Maybe even their own lives didn't merit all the wistful envy she was feeling.   Were the young moms going home to husbands, or even mothers-in-law, who'd berate them for a messy house or a badly cooked meal?   Was the father squeezing as much fun as he could into a visitation day before he had to return his giggling little girl to his ex-wife? Even the older couple who seemed so content to troll for treasures that others had lost, she rationalized, might be doing it more for economic necessity than mindless fun.

And this loneliness won't leave me alone...

Seeing John with someone else had opened a floodgate of woulda, coulda, shoulda's in Kate's mind. As hard as she had tried to push the image away, she flashed back on a breathless, younger version of herself knocking on his front door 14 years ago.

"If I'd known you were coming, I'd have baked a cake," he said with a grin. Even in high school, his reputation for not being shy around a kitchen hovered near legend status with their hungry gaggle of friends. Her unexpected arrival, too late for lunch but too early for dinner, didn't stop him from asking if he could throw something together.

Food, however, was the farthest thing from her mind at that moment. "I got accepted!" she squealed, hurling herself into his arms. "I'm going to Amherst!"

Only when she had peeled herself away did she sense that John wasn't nearly as ecstatic about her good news as she was.

"So where does that leave 'us?'" he asked her.

She remembered her initial reaction was to laugh at what she thought was just his goofy way of joking with her. "Don't be silly," she said. "This doesn't change anything."

Except that it did.

Hard as she tried in the awkward days that followed to bridge the terrible gulf of misunderstanding, it all kept coming back to the same thing: Kate was moving forward. John was staying behind.

Two thousand miles I roamed...

She sighed, clasped her slender hands together and stared at the ringless left one. She had moved forward once before, she firmly reminded herself. She could do it again. For the sake of Jimmy, she had to.

Chapter Twenty-Four

A black Mercedes was parked in the driveway when Kate got home. If she'd had enough wits about her to recall where she had seen it before, she would have turned around and gone back to her perch on the boardwalk. Her guilt about leaving Jimmy with her mother for far longer than she'd planned to, however, was overriding everything else at the moment.

"Oh, there she is," she heard Lydia exclaim.

It was followed a second later by a male voice that instantly made Kate cringe.

"Looks like we won't have to call the cops and report a missing mommy," joked Brad.

They were both holding glasses of lemonade. From the looks of the full one in Brad's hand, he had either arrived only a short time before Kate got there or was being indulged in Lydia's effusive hospitality with a refill just to ensure that he was still on the premises when Kate got home. Nor did Kate miss the fact that the lemonade was in the crystal water glasses that her mother only brought out for holidays and "special" company.

"Look who just happened to drop by," Lydia said with all the satisfaction of a Southern matron overseeing a successful cotillion.

"Where's Jimmy?" Kate wanted to know.

It was Brad who casually answered that they had put him out in the backyard.

"He's not a dog, Brad," Kate snapped, outraged by his insensitivity. She strode past both of them en route to the back door.

Lydia instantly rose to Brad's defense by explaining that it wasn't what it sounded like. "He kept wanting to go out," she said, "so we thought the fresh air would do him good."

We? So now you're making collective decisions with Brad? "He's a five-year-old boy," she reminded her mother, annoyed that the possibility of Jimmy hurting himself or wandering out an unlatched back gate hadn't even occurred to her. "I can't believe you'd leave him unsupervised."

"You and your sister played out there plenty of times by yourself," Lydia countered but Kate was already out of earshot.

A motionless Jimmy was seated cross-legged in front of the fledgling tree that he and John had planted that morning. The faithful, and discernibly dirtier, Mr. Ollie kept vigil on the ground next to him.

"Whatcha doin', honey?" Kate asked as she knelt beside him.

Without looking over at her, Jimmy pointed at the anemic, leafless little stick and proclaimed, "Shoes!"

Kate suppressed a smile, wondering how "shoes" had come to represent Jimmy's association with John. "Tree," she gently corrected him. "Can you say 'tree'?"

Jimmy responded by laughing and rocking back and forth.

She repeated her question but the giggling Jimmy had now scooped up Mr. Ollie and plopped him on top of his head.

Kate pointed to the tree. "Were you out here watching it grow?"

For a fond instant, she was reminded of the time Cassy had saved her allowance to send away for a pair of genuine seahorses. Her plan, she confided to her big sister, was to toss them in a full bathtub and watch them magically come to life as creatures that would be big enough for her to ride to school. That same watchful intensity was now on the face of her little boy.

Jimmy suddenly stopped rocking and looked from Kate to the tree and back again. "Beemstuck," he happily blurted out.

"'Beemstuck'?" She shook her head. "What does that mean?"

Before he could repeat it, Lydia stepped outside to tell her that Brad had offered to buy dinner. "Wasn't that nice of him?" she added. "Such a gentleman."

Kate doubted that the invitation included her nephew and voiced it aloud.

"What he meant," Lydia said, "was that he thought maybe you'd like to treat yourself to a night off. Besides, it will give the two of you a chance to talk about your little employment problem."

Kate's expression darkened with the realization her own mother had betrayed her current circumstances. "You told Brad what was going on with my job?"

"Former job," Lydia corrected her. "Honestly, Kate, can I help it if he asked where you were working these days?"

"Was this before or after you invited him to 'drop-in'?"

Lydia archly reminded her that Brad Leister was extremely well connected in the community and socialized with the heads of every major business. "I'm sure he has plenty of ideas."

"None of which," Kate predicted, "have anything to do with how I'm going to support Jimmy or keep him from being taken away by Luke." *Oh God*, she thought in dread, *you didn't tell him about Luke, too?*

"So. Fine," Lydia retorted. "What's wrong with just having a nice dinner with someone who still cares for you?" She glanced back toward the house. "It's rude, you know, to keep him waiting for an answer."

"I gave him an answer over fourteen years ago, Mom. And no amount of time will ever change it."

Lydia's eyes narrowed "You're not taking up with that Neal boy again, are you?"

Kate informed her that she wasn't 'taking up' with anyone and that her priority was Jimmy.

C.J. Foster

"I'm only thinking of what's best," Lydia insisted. "You have no idea what it's like to try to raise a child on your own."

Kate was about to point out that she and Cassy had spent the majority of their upbringing in a two-parent household, a scenario that rendered Lydia's argument moot when she noticed that the cocky Brad had just emerged from the house.

"So do I hear a 'yes' on that dinner?" he asked.

"Looks like you and Mom are on your own," she informed him. "Jimmy and I have already made other plans."

As she walked over to retrieve her nephew from his attentive tree-staring, it was to the sound of Brad sarcastically asking what kind of person made plans that revolved around a five-year-old.

"Obviously, you know nothing about parenting," she calmly replied, scooping up Mr. Ollie with one hand and extending her free one to Jimmy.

"So is Blue Man Group holding local auditions?' John asked when he saw his mother's latest beauty experiment.

Abby insisted that her friend Margaret swore by it.

"If you find a third," John quipped, "you could start your own act and give 'em some competition." He helped himself to a beer from the fridge and grabbed a treat from the ceramic canister for Shelby. "How's Dad doing?"

In the background, the sounds of a TV game show were in boisterous progress. From the sound of applause, another contestant has just hit the jackpot.

Abby related that Sean had spent part of the afternoon outside with her and seemed to like it. A wistful smile found its way to her lips. "Sitting with him," she said, "reminded me of what it used to be like before." She laughed. "Not that we ever sat around that much doing nothing but, well, you know what I mean."

Beneath their feet, Shelby was earnestly crunching on a dog treat.

"I'll need you to take him to his therapy appointment tomorrow," Abby continued. "We've got an audit coming up and I promised Joe I'd come in early."

"Sure." He proceeded to tell her about his day, holding off until the last to mention that he had helped Jimmy plant a tree.

Abby's memory needed refreshing on who, exactly, Jimmy was. "You know that's the funniest thing," she said on the heels of his reply, "but Lydia Toscano called just before you got home. I can't believe it completely slipped my mind."

"Lydia called here? Why?"

"Well, that's what was strange. She wanted to know if her daughter was here."

"This is getting stranger by the minute," John remarked. "Did she give any clue why she thought Kate was here?"

"If she did, I missed it," Abby said, reminding him that the last time they'd talked was back before Jeremy was born. "Oh, and I remember your father and I saw her at the funeral for her husband but there was such a crowd." Lydia, she recalled, had made a point of keeping her distance from all but her closest friends.

"Lydia Toscano has friends?" John quipped.

The kitchen timer went off, a signal that it was time for Abby to go upstairs and engage in the next step of her latest treatment.

"You know I'm thinking a pizza from Capparelli's might be good tonight," she opined.

John offered to run out and pick one up.

"Oh, and you know what would also be nice?" she said.

John thought she was referring to a side order and started naming them from memory.

Abby interrupted to ask if he'd mind taking his father along when he picked up their dinner. "Not to go inside with you or anything," she hastily clarified, "but you know how he loves riding in the truck. I think a change of scenery would be good. Not to mention it would also get him away from that silly TV."

John agreed, feeling only slightly guilty that her request would also give him a chance to cruise by the Toscano house just to make sure everything was okay. In the event Lydia spotted his truck, he rationalized, the sight of his dad in the passenger seat would help allay whatever dark suspicions were already building in her mind.

There was something oddly comforting, John reflected, about having the presence of another person without feeling the pressure to keep up a conversation. It had been easier than he thought to help his father maneuver into the passenger seat and as they pulled out of the driveway, he was pretty sure he even detected a smile on the older man's face.

"Wrong...way," Sean told his son as they turned down Chelsea Lane.

"I know, Dad, just taking the scenic route. No rush, we got a few minutes before the pizza's ready, anyway. Besides, don't you like the drive?"

"Good to be...out."

His fond recollection of time spent with his father was quickly replaced by a twinge in his gut as he drove by Lydia's house. As the only Mercedes in Avalon Bay, Brad's car was instantly recognizable parked on the quiet street in front of the house.

"What's wrong?" Sean asked his son, noticing the change in his demeanor.

"Nothing. Nothing's wrong, Dad," John lied. "Let's go pick up dinner."

Kate wasn't looking for a conversation that evening beyond talking to Jimmy and placing her order for pizza and soft drinks. Unfortunately, the best place in town for satisfying her current hunger level was Capparelli's. Whatever plan she might have had for them to unobtrusively slip into a back booth was squelched as soon as she heard Maria call out her name.

"Moonlighting, are you?" a puzzled Kate asked, taking note of the apron that was tied around her friend's waist.

Maria laughed it off in preface to confiding that helping out the short-handed Antonio and Mama by waiting tables was a way to hang out with her hunky honey. "Big Tony likes anybody he can get who's cheap."

"That probably didn't come out the way you meant it," Kate said but Maria had already bent down to say hi to Jimmy.

"How's my little juice box man?" she greeted him. She looked up at Kate. "So, you guys doin' some takeout tonight or you want a table?"

"I was thinking a booth."

"You got it, hon."

The back-corner obscurity Kate was hoping for didn't materialize. Instead, Maria parked them in plain sight of the entire room. "This way, you and the little man won't miss anything," she said.

Even after Kate told her what they wanted to order, Maria was clearly in no hurry to leave their company.

"Aren't you going to get in trouble?" Kate asked, especially when her friend settled hip-shot against the corner of the table and was rambling into her latest bit of town gossip about Cliff firing his latest editor for being a certifiable idiot.

"Believe me, hon," Maria replied, "Big Tony would rather have me schmoozing with the clientele out here than smooching with his son back in the kitchen."

"He does know about the two of you, doesn't he?" Kate cautiously inquired.

"Let's just say we're leaking it to him in stages."

Maria had peeled herself away from Kate and Jimmy's table only long enough to place their pizza order but was back again regaling Kate with the latest she had heard via the Avalon Bay grapevine.

"She's gorgeous and she's French and she wants to have a bazillion kids," she was saying with a mischievous giggle.

Kate was reticent to echo Maria's laughter even if it would have masked the turmoil she was feeling. A part of her was hoping Jimmy would knock over his soft drink just to send Maria scurrying for a wad of napkins to clean up the puddle it would make. Jimmy, however, was being surprisingly well behaved and offering no diversions from what was proving to be a painful conversation.

Even the brief, enthusiastic appearance of Antonio who fussed about "the bambino" failed to derail Maria's train of gossip. No sooner did he table-hop to greet his other customers than she immediately started in again, this time nudging the conversation toward the past. "Funny," she said, "but I always thought you 'n' John would have a full house by now."

"So, tell me more about Little Tony," Kate interrupted, even though hearing about Maria's Italian stallion ranked high on the list of vacuous topics.

Maria started to reply when Jimmy suddenly sprang to life and excitedly pointed toward the door.

"John!" he squealed in delight.

Chapter Twenty-Five

Kate pressed her lips together, flummoxed that what should have been welcomed as a sign of Jimmy's cognitive progress was abruptly overridden by her discomfort that John Neal had once more slipped into their lives without an invitation.

"Well, speak of the devil!" Maria exclaimed as he strolled toward them, thumbs casually hooked into the pockets of his jeans.

His first greeting was to Jimmy who shouted John's name twice more and smacked the red and white plastic tablecloth with both palms. As Kate turned to tell her young charge to settle down, she was surprised to hear John ask her if everything was all right.

"I guess he's just excited to be out in a new place," she murmured, trying not to make eye contact and allow herself to succumb to his steady blue gaze.

"I meant with you," he said.

"Uh…sure. Why?" Her mind raced over their last conversation, trying to remember what she might have conveyed to him to suggest that maybe she wasn't all right.

John shrugged. "Just kinda strange that your mom called," he replied.

Kate's mouth dropped open. "What? My mother called?"

His warm smile melted into concern. "You didn't know she was looking for you?"

Even them leaving the house in a huff about Brad, Kate thought, wouldn't have prompted her mother to assume she'd run straight to John. *Or would she?* Kate threw the ball back into his court by asking what, exactly, Lydia had said to him.

"Actually," he said, "she called my mom to see if you were at the house. I only heard it secondhand."

"Am I the only one who thinks this sounds totally weird?" Maria cut in, perceptibly annoyed that neither of them was counting her in on their cryptic conversation. She now wiggled her unmanicured index finger back and forth between them. "Is something goin' on between you two guys?"

I'm obviously the last to know if there is, Kate thought. Aloud she voiced mild skepticism. "Maybe she dialed the number by accident. Or maybe your mom just got the name wrong."

"Or maybe," John countered, "everybody got everything right and your mom was calling to remind you that you were supposed to be somewhere."

"Such as?"

"I don't know. Maybe she thought you had a date?"

"Who's your date with?" Maria asked.

Kate bristled at the realization he had to have driven by the house, seen Brad's car, and jumped to an stupid and irrational conclusion. "Since when is my personal life everybody else's business?" she shot back. It was intended more for Maria than John but it was the latter who responded.

"Hey, don't shoot the messenger," he said, putting his hands up in mock surrender. "I was just worried something happened. I was wrong."

Jimmy giggled.

"So why don't you park your butt and join us?" Maria invited him before asking Kate what time her date was supposed to get there. "Or are you meeting Mr. Mystery somewhere else?"

"I don't have a date," Kate corrected her, conscious of the heat stealing into her face and neck. "I'm just here with Jimmy."

Maria seized her friend's reply as a chance to reiterate her invitation for John to stay and catch up on old times.

He shook his head. "I've got someone waiting for me out in the truck."

Probably her, Kate assumed, cringing at the prospect of an introduction to the dark-haired beauty who wanted to bear his future children.

Maria's eyes widened. "Oh really?" she mischievously responded. "And who would that be?"

"My dad," he answered. "We've just picked up a pizza."

The glance Maria exchanged with Kate conveyed that she wasn't buying his excuse for even a nanosecond.

"Well then, we shouldn't keep you," Kate said. The declaration was out of her mouth before she realized how much it sounded as if she were dismissing him from her sight. *Your Queen has spoken. Be gone!*

"No," he agreed with her comment. "I suppose not." He waved to Jimmy. "Catch ya later, J."

His leave was pre-empted by Antonio who promptly enveloped him in an Italian bear hug. "Justa like ol' times, eh?" the portly proprietor exclaimed, vocally recounting his remembrance of when John and Kate used to come there after school and hold hands until the candles in the Chianti bottles had dribbled into blobby, alien-looking stubs.

That his voice was loud enough to carry across the room made several of the nearest diners turn their heads and smile. Though minor, it was a level of attention that made Kate want to sink beneath the floorboards. "Why you two not a-holdin' hands now?" he now joked, oblivious to the tension that hovered over the table like a rusty ax. "That Kate, she's one smart cannoli, eh?"

Kate's chest tightened and she bit her lip in an attempt to put her mind on something other than her remembrance of their early days of dating. Before she could fumble her way into a reply to Antonio's question, it was John who bluntly set the record straight.

"Water under the bridge," he said. "We both grew up and moved on."

Abby wanted to know how Sean had enjoyed the drive.

"Seemed to do okay," John said, commenting that his father had balanced the pizza on his lap and clutched the stack of napkins with his good hand the whole ride home.

"And didn't even try to sneak a bite of pizza in the car?" Abby teased, kissing her husband's forehead. "Who are you, Handsome, and what have you done with my husband?"

John waited until she had settled his father back in front of the TV to tell her that he'd run into Kate and Jimmy.

"And everything was okay? No need to file a Missing Persons report?"

"Guess not," he replied. "In fact, she seemed kinda upset that I even asked her about it."

"Oh?"

"It's almost as if..."

Abby glanced over her shoulder as she pulled down a couple of dinner plates from the cupboard. "Almost as if what?"

"I don't know. Like she couldn't get rid of me fast enough." On the short drive home, he'd replayed every word she said and every nuance she hadn't said and still couldn't shake the feeling that somewhere between the tree-planting and the pizza encounter Kate Toscano had made up her mind to suddenly hate his guts.

"Maybe you just caught her at a bad time," Abby softly suggested.

John quickly countered that the death of Kate's sister and having to live with Lydia would constitute a bad time on any level.

"Well then maybe she was just trying to avoid an awkward moment."

"An awkward moment for whom?" John asked, averse to mention how much the sight of Brad's car had rankled him.

"Maybe she was expecting someone," Abby matter of factly replied. "A date."

"Not from what she said. It was just her and Jimmy and her friend the motor-mouth."

"Well, this may come as a bolt out of the blue," Abby continued, "but women don't always say exactly what they mean." She smiled as if enjoying a private joke. "Of course, for that matter, neither do most men."

"Meaning what?"

"Meaning she either didn't want to hurt your feelings or..."

"Or what?" John pounced on the bait.

"Maybe she was hoping you'd call her bluff."

"Kate and I are history, Mom. There's no bluff to be called."

Abby wasn't convinced. "So, I suppose that's why her name doesn't keep coming up in conversations?"

"Coincidence."

"Of course it is, dear. Whatever you say."

John smirked. "Why are you trying to play matchmaker?"

Abby laughed and maintained that some matches were beyond her control.

"Didn't seem to stop you from trying to set me up with Gabrielle."

"Can I help it if her mother and I thought it would give her something new to think about?"

"I'm pretty sure it doesn't work that way," he replied.

Abby suddenly scowled. "Did you remember to tell them to give us parmesan cheese packets?"

"Didn't have to. They know it by heart."

"Well, somebody was asleep at the switch and left 'em out," she observed. "Looks like you'll have to go back."

"Why's it such a big deal? We've got plenty of cheese in the fridge."

He started to move toward the refrigerator to prove his point but she blocked his path. "You know you're going to agonize about it all night."

"The cheese?'

"Wondering if she was trying to tell you something instead of coming out and telling you. If she's there with someone else, then you'll know it's time to move on."

"And if she's not?"

Abby smiled. "Then have a nice evening and it'll be all the more pizza for your dad 'n' me."

"I don't buy it," Maria opined. "He's trying to have his cake and eat it, too."

Why, Kate wondered, *was everyone suddenly referring to her as a dessert?* Out loud, she heard herself defend John's character. "He wouldn't have any reason to lie about his father waiting for him."

Maria shrugged. "He doesn't have any reason to hide his new girlfriend, either. As he said, you guys are water under the bridge."

Water under the bridge. That's what had stung the most even though she knew it was the truth. "You know I think we'll just take our pizza to go," she announced.

Which was why, for the second time in one day, she was now sitting on the boardwalk with Otis Redding lyrics playing in her head. Sitting next to her with a messy mouthful of pizza and his legs happily swinging in contentment was Jimmy, clearly oblivious to everything. Oblivious even to the first sprinkles of rain.

"Come on, Jimmy," she urged him. "Let's finish this up and get home."

Home. The last place she wanted to be at this moment. With a rising sense of dread, she wondered whether Brad was still there. It would be just like her mother, Kate thought, to have invited him to stay for dinner and spend the whole time making plans for her future.

The patter of the rain began to pick up its pace and Kate reached over to close the pizza box. With a squeal, Jimmy flung out his arm, dislodging the three remaining pieces inside and sending them flying into the sand below. Only quick thinking on Kate's part kept the box itself from becoming airborne.

"Okay, I guess we're all finished," she said. A lone seagull had already noticed the arrival of a free meal and, indifferent to Mother Nature's change of mood, was hopping over to investigate.

The rain began to fall harder. Jimmy laughed and gleefully held both hands upward as if to entreat the sky to send down even more.

At least the pizza box could serve as a makeshift umbrella, Kate rationalized. She reached for Jimmy's hand. "Stay close to me," she instructed, hoping that if they scurried fast enough they'd be able to make it back to the house before the storm escalated.

By the time she glimpsed the welcome sight of a bus shelter, their respective clothes were soaked and the pizza box was getting dangerously soggy. The covered bench, she noted in dismay, was also currently occupied by two unkempt men whom she guessed had a lot of familiarity with availing themselves of free public refuge.

"Just a little farther," she told Jimmy in her cheeriest voice. Jimmy, however, was in no need of her plucky cheerleading and seemed to thrive on this unrehearsed new adventure.

As she distractedly stepped off the curb, a screech of brakes and the blast of a horn sounded. Startled, Kate looked over just as the pizza box collapsed and deposited wet cardboard shrapnel down the front of her blouse.

The anger she felt toward herself for nearly jeopardizing both of them was quickly displaced by something a hundred times worse.

The driver was John.

Chapter Twenty-Six

He'd felt like a total idiot driving back to Capparelli's. In truth, a part of him hoped Kate wouldn't still be there. If she saw him walk back in, she'd probably deem him some kind of a stalker. If he walked back in, though, and she was happily sitting across the table from someone else.

He pushed the idea aside, conscious that he could still be as bothered by her presence as he was by her absence. Up until seeing her again the day he had driven her and Jimmy to the airport, he hadn't paid a lot of thought to being lonely during the past fourteen years. Lonely was different from being alone, from making a conscientious decision to do everything on his own terms and in his own time. What was this power she held to mess with his sense of objectivity and to make something as simple as silence, usually such a welcome refuge, feel as suffocating as the inside of a tomb?

He circled Capparelli's twice without stopping. Why was it, he thought, patrolling the dark streets of NYC, knowing bad guys were lurking around every corner, was easier to deal with than the agonizing uncertainty of whether Kate Toscano was sitting inside eating a pizza?

To his relief, the one person who hadn't seen him the first time was just stepping outside for a smoke as John pulled into an empty parking space on the street.

"Tony!" he called out.

"Hey, man!" Little Tony greeted him. "What's up?"

"Supposed to hook up with a friend," John lied, hoping he sounded indifferently casual. "

"You mean Kate?" Tony interrupted.

If he said 'yes' and she was still there, it would look weird if he didn't go in. "Just a guy I work with," he lied. "Wouldn't be surprised if he forgot." He bit his tongue to keep from asking why Tony had assumed he was meeting Kate.

"Oh," a puzzled Tony responded. "Maria says your old girlfriend was here."

Was, not is. That could mean anything. Strange, he also thought, that Maria hadn't told him he'd been there, too. "Small world, I guess."

The front door of Capparelli's opened at that moment and the world as he knew it shrank even further.

"Forget something?" Maria asked when she saw him standing there like a dolt.

"Cheese," he said. "Extra cheese."

If the packets of grated Parmesan riding on the dashboard of his truck had human voices, John was pretty sure they'd be giggling at him. All right, so maybe it hadn't been one of his smarter moves.

"You came all the way back just for cheap cheese?" Maria teased him. "Sure, you did."

He had only made it worse by saying it was the kind his father liked. It wasn't exactly a lie, just a carefully framed omission of the real reason that had brought him back.

"And he didn't notice this when he was with you?" she quizzed with an inexplicable wink.

"Your ol' man was with you?" the clueless Tony chimed in. "How's he doing?"

It was a longer conversation than he'd cared to spend, made longer by Maria's immature insistence on asking him some of the same questions twice. Almost, he thought, as if to trip him up. Goodness knows what kind of stupid rumors would be spun by daybreak if she gave full vent to her hyperactive imagination. The best he could hope for was that none of them wafted in Kate's direction and made her think he was either a jerk or an apologetic fugitive.

The addition of unexpected rain to the mix did little to restore his spirits, especially since he'd just washed the truck that afternoon. "Story of my life," he muttered as he'd pulled away from the curb. The triggered memory of it having also rained like the dickens the day Kate left for Amherst convinced him all the more that the universe was still trying to pound him with a message his heart hadn't wanted to hear the first time.

The rain began to fall harder.

Not until he made a third pass by the Exxon did he realize that he was orbiting in aimless circles again, a subconscious delaying tactic to keep from going home and being asked questions he didn't want to answer. Nor did he want to drive by the Toscano's again, still not convinced that Kate's plans for the evening didn't include the very last person he felt like seeing right now.

"I don't have a date," she'd said. "I'm just here with Jimmy."

He kept replaying the words in his head and remembering how emphatic she'd been about it. That Kate Toscano had never been one to lie, especially not to him, should have been a quiet reassurance instead of the noisy mental ping-pong game that was starting to make his head hurt.

One thing for certain, he wasn't going to accomplish anything if he kept driving around until he ran out of gas. Just as he was approaching the intersection, a woman and a small child on the other side of her stepped off the curb and he hit the brakes and his horn in plenty of time to warn them that they weren't in a crosswalk.

"Kate!" he gasped in shock, stealing a quick look in the rear-view mirror before he threw the gearshift into "park" and jumped out of the truck and into the rain to run over to them. "Are you all right?" It was no wonder, of course, that he hadn't recognized her from a distance, her face previously obscured by an upraised arm and a red and white tent of cardboard.

"Don't even say it," she warned as the faint beginnings of a smile played at the corner of his mouth. In annoyance, she began to flick off the soggy particles from her blouse, unaware of the larger ones that were defiantly clinging to her hair.

"Say what?" he feigned innocence so as not to embarrass her even further. "I'm just glad you're both okay."

Jimmy, his face wet and grinning, was having the time of his life trying to cup a handful of raindrops without spilling any.

"I look stupid!" she angrily sputtered. "That's what you're thinking, isn't it?"

It was a challenge worthy of triggering his sarcastic wit but John resisted. The downpour, he thought, emphasized even more than usual her natural beauty and fresh radiance. It also made her appear something unusual. For the first time since he knew her, she looked vulnerable. He wanted to be her rescuer, to hear her say that she needed him, that he alone could give her something she couldn't get from anyone else in the universe: a quiet haven of simplicity in a world she was always so intent on making far too complex.

At the moment, however, that scenario didn't seem terribly likely. A sense of awkwardness was engulfing both of them; John because he was distracted, and Kate because she was well aware of it and not particularly pleased. She challenged him a second time about whether he was going to laugh at her appearance.

"Wet cardboard's not a look for everyone," he replied, "but the bigger question's whether you need a lift home."

"We're soaking wet!" she snapped at him.

John hesitated, unsure of whether she meant it as mind-numbingly obvious that they needed a ride or that she didn't want to get his seats all soppy.

"Yeah well, I'm pretty much getting there myself," he pointed out as he raked a hand through his wet hair. "So, you want a ride or not?"

Before she could answer, a sheriff's patrol car rounded the corner.

It would be a long twenty minutes before anyone went anywhere.

"The least you can do," Kate insisted as he pulled into the driveway, "is let me pay the ticket."

John wouldn't hear of it.

"I'm the one who was causing a hazard," he reminded her. In his panic and haste to jump out of the truck and rush to their aid, putting on his emergency lights had slipped his mind.

"But I'm the one who stepped into a non-crosswalk," she argued. "Why didn't he write me up, too?"

"Obviously," John countered, "he'd already made his quota today for ticketing beautiful women with cute kids."

If his unabashed compliment registered at all with her, she wasn't letting so much as a blush betray her. Instead, she put forth a compromise of letting her pay half. "It's only fair," she informed him, tossing her wet head in a way that could either be construed as snooty or just an attempt to maintain dignity.

He looked at her as he shifted his body and propped his right elbow on top of the seatback. "Why is winning an argument always so important to you?" he asked.

She shot back that he was the one being stubborn. "As always," she added. "And what's with your arguing about who should drive us home after he gave you a ticket? He was a cop for Christ's sakes!" She glanced down and noticed that Jimmy had grabbed one of the cellophane packets of Parmesan cheese and was earnestly trying to figure out how to open it.

John nodded. "A cop in a cop car. No telling who his last ride might have been."

"Y' know, you're starting to sound freakishly like my mother."

"Speaking of whom," He tilted his head toward the front window where Lydia was peering out at them at that moment. "Besides," he facetiously continued, "can you imagine how people in this town would talk if you came home in the back of a patrol car on a dark and stormy night?"

She smirked. "So you're saying you were just looking out for me?" She succeeded in prying the packet of cheese out of Jimmy's fingers and tossed it back on the dashboard with the others.

"To quote someone I know from Amherst, 'As always'."

Her green eyes flashed in a familiar display of impatience. "Look, I appreciate you coming along when you did."

"But what?"

"What do you mean?"

'It sounded," he remarked, "as if you were about to tack something onto the end of that."

"No, not really. Just thanks, that's all."

She was reaching for the door handle, a signal that he probably couldn't delay her leaving any longer.

"Well, it's not the first time that you've let me rescue you," he pointed out. It was the sort of hopeful statement, he realized, that stopped just short of being a question seeking affirmation. He watched the play of emotions of her face, conscious of the instinctive flutter of distance that his reminiscence about their past always seemed to keep conjuring whenever they were together. Independent woman that she was, he was already braced for her to issue a snappy argument that logistical coincidence didn't really count.

Unexpectedly, she returned his smile, imbuing him with a sense of numbed comfort that his comment had seemingly met with an accord. He now caught himself hoping she'd lean forward and tell him it wouldn't be the last time his services as a knight in shining armor would be needed.

Instead, she only wished him a nice evening.

C.J. Foster

Chapter Twenty-Seven

I f there was a bright spot to the way things had ended, John reflected, it was that Brad hadn't been waiting around for her to come home. The downside, of course, was that he was no closer to figuring out what her feelings were, especially insofar as they involved whatever the two of them were supposed to mean to one another after 14 years of meaning nothing.

Why was it, he wondered, that his defenses enthusiastically surrendered every time she smiled at him? Why did he silently run down a list of verbal blunders whenever she seemed the tiniest bit displeased?   And why did his brow always wrinkle with contemptuous thoughts whenever he imagined that she might be stolen out from under him by someone who wasn't worthy of how special she was? Unbidden, the image returned of how she had looked the day in the taxi when she told him about Cassy's death. The catch in her voice. The way her eyes had looked with tears in them. The way she felt when he'd pulled her close. With vivid clarity, he remembered the split second when he'd been torn between being the rational, sympathetic listener and the red-blooded warrior who wanted to hug her tight and ask her if she needed him to go bash any heads for her because it was a crime for anyone that sweet and beautiful to ever have to cry about anything.

Any fool, of course, would simply tell him he was in love and to do something about it. Easily enough said but clearly running the risk of rejection. The sudden longing for some steady companionship in his life, and specifically with a woman who had already left him once, not only defied rational explanation but threatened as well to contest the belief he was too set in his routine to start compromising it. Even moving back home to help out until his father was more stable had imposed certain parameters on his freedom that put his patience to the test.

The further irony that neither he nor Kate currently lived alone wasn't lost on him, either. With a smirk, he realized that even on the off-chance she was amenable to picking up where they left off, they really would have to "get a room" if the relationship were to segue to the kind of romantic intimacy he'd been daydreaming about more often than he should.

He gave himself a mental shake, annoyed that he was allowing her occasional displays of gratitude to be mistaken by his heart for something else, something deeper, something possibly lasting. Whatever lay behind her enigmatic exterior these days would take more time for him to decipher than the amount of time she was even likely to remain in town. Nonetheless, the idea of her returning to her bright lights of Vegas once the custody issues were resolved with her sister's ex-husband brought a pang of regret that went beyond the wistfulness of rekindling the happiness and optimism they'd once known.

It would also mean losing the closest he had come thus far to feeling what it was like to be a dad.

Jimmy made no protest about being packed off to bed. *At least one thing went right today*, Kate mused as she tucked him in. There was also the useful tidbit Maria had dropped about Cliff firing his short-lived nitwit editor. Unless he'd done so with the idea of bringing in someone who was already waiting in the wings, she thought, maybe it was worth a shot to drop off her resume at the newspaper office in the morning.

Local girl makes good.

She grimaced when she remembered the weekly's headline about her acceptance at Amherst and how many armloads of copies her mother had hungrily grabbed up to send off to all the relatives. *Local girl returns with unemployment woes and has moved back home* could likely be the next one, she told herself, especially given the publisher's quirky new belief that negativity not only enabled him to keep up with "the big boys" but also sold more papers. She'd have to make sure she was guarded enough to keep her inquiry to Cliff breezy, casual and by no means desperate.

For the remainder of this rainy evening, however, there was no forestalling yet another conversation with her mother about Brad. The boldness of the older woman's latest attempt at matchmaking had set Kate's temperature to boiling. If she didn't put an end to it before she went to bed, it would still be there in the morning and, knowing how feverishly her mother's brain worked when she wanted something, would only gain dangerous momentum.

"We need to talk, Mom," she announced without preamble.

"We certainly do," Lydia replied as she set aside her gin and tonic and defiantly folded her arms. "And we can start with the shameful way you're treating the one person in this town who's in a position to help."

"The only thing Brad wants is to help himself into my pants," Kate shot back, "and he's been getting no shortage of encouragement from my mother."

"Bradley Leister is a very powerful man."

"A legend in his own mind. He probably has it printed on his business cards."

"A lot of people in this town owe their lives, and their jobs, to the Leister family."

Kate sharply reminded her that the Toscano household had never been one of them. "And there's certainly no reason," she added, "to join that list any time soon."

Lydia raised a brow. "You're unemployed."

"Temporarily."

"Unemployed," she began again, a little harsher. "You don't know the first thing about being a parent, and you're dealing with a child whose problems are going to cost you more money than you have."

"Brad isn't the answer," Kate cut her off, "and I resent your trying to push him off on me."

"And I suppose you think you could better with that Neal boy?"

"You mean the 'boy' who's in his 30's and runs his own company?" She couldn't resist pointing out that the Neals had probably never done business with the Leisters either.

"Trimming trees and raking leaves," Lydia archly informed her, "is not the same as being at the helm of public trust."

"Look, Mom, I don't have time to be involved with anyone right now. My priority is Jimmy and, frankly, I think he should be your priority, too. He's your grandson and I'm not going to let anyone take him away."

Lydia was silent for a long, brittle moment. When she finally spoke again, it was to suggest that perhaps a two-parent household could provide Jimmy with more stability and attention than Kate could deliver herself.

"I'm not putting him in foster care if that's what you're trying to say."

"What I'm trying to say is that you may not have any say in the matter. It's not as if the same thing wouldn't happen if that loser of a father got custody and couldn't take care of him. The man doesn't even have a job!"

Kate fumed. "You're putting us in the same category now?"

Lydia tried to temper her remarks with the observation that her remaining daughter still had her whole life ahead of her. "What kind of marriage prospects can you expect to attract if you're trying to raise a child all by yourself?"

"This isn't the 1950's, Mom."

"No, but that still doesn't change what it's like to try to make it on your own."

For an instant, Kate flashed back on something odd her mother had said earlier, something she hadn't made the time to pursue with a question that might have clarified its meaning. This time, she wasn't going to let it slide. "How would you even know what it's like?" she challenged her. "You and Dad raised Cass and me together 'till he died."

A sudden, icy contempt flashed in her mother's eyes and Kate noticed that she'd been absently twisting the gold wedding band she had never removed.

"Relationships," Lydia ruefully murmured, "aren't always what they seem."

Save for the occasional lone jogger braving the elements, the combination of heavy rain and wind had rendered both the shoreline and the boardwalk empty. When he finally looked at his watch, John was surprised by how much time had elapsed since he dropped Kate and Jimmy off. Snatches of long-forgotten lyrics wafted in and out of his head, songs that he'd never make any conscious effort to memorize and yet which now seemed to form a solid soundtrack of his existence.

Look like nothin's gonna come my way...

He was hovering in the odd "tweener" stage of inertia, he realized. If he had gone home immediately afterward instead of driving around aimlessly, his mother would have assumed that he saw Kate with another guy and endeavor to cheer him up with one of her other-fish-in-the-sea speeches. If, on the other hand, he stayed out for another hour or so, she'd mistakenly assume the two of them were on a date together and want to hear all about it.

On top of that, he was also starting to get hungry.

And this loneliness won't leave me alone...

He pulled out his cell phone, hesitating a moment before taking a deep breath and punching in a number that his brain was already trying to warn him he was probably going to regret before the evening was over.

"Hey, it's me," he said as soon as the phone picked up. "Doing anything tonight?"

Lydia's sudden need to unburden herself caught Kate completely by surprise. *Is it one too many gin and tonics doing the talking*, she wryly wondered, *or is this all part of a more elaborate plan that will somehow circle back to her annoying belief that I shouldn't let Brad Leister get away?*

"Your sister hadn't been born yet," she began her story, "but your father wanted us to have more children. A lot more children."

"And you didn't?"

Lydia confessed that having one was quite enough. "It's not that you were that difficult," she continued, "but once you started preschool, I was looking forward to going back to work, being around people I could talk to." Her husband, she said, hadn't liked the idea at all. "It was that damn stubborn pride of his that he thought people would think he couldn't support his own family and had made me get a job to bring in more money."

He had finally conceded, she explained, to letting her work part-time on the condition that as soon as she got pregnant again, she'd have to quit.

It was a side of her father that Kate had never seen when she was growing up but, in hearing about it, she could empathize with her mother's determination to stay in the workforce for as long as she could.

"They liked me there," Lydia went on. "I felt like I had a purpose and was able to be my own person."

"You've always been your own person, Mom." *Not a person I've always agreed with but nonetheless.*

"I didn't want to just be a wife and a mother," Lydia insisted. "When I was at work, people started noticing me and asking me what I was thinking about and it made me feel happy." One person in particular, she said, had started making her wonder if maybe her marriage was a big mistake.

Kate's jaw dropped. "This other person was?"

"A man," she bluntly replied. "A man I'd met who made me feel different from how your father treated me."

"No offense, Mom, but I never saw Dad treat you badly or take you for granted. Maybe you were getting a little bored?" *If she tells me she had sex with this guy, it's going to be way more information than I want to know.*

"I don't know what I was feeling when it started, only that he became the most important thing in my life."

Apparently even more important to you than I was, Kate thought but didn't say it out loud. "And this, uh," *Affair? Flirtation? Casual confiding in a member of the opposite sex over coffee?* " went on for how long?"

"Not as long as I wanted it to," Lydia confessed with a sad smile. Her moist eyes met Kate's. "I just wasn't happy with your father anymore and I started hating having to come home."

Though the floodgates had now opened and a long-repressed torment was finally finding its way to the surface, Kate refused to condone her mother's transgression with a show of sympathy. "It shouldn't have taken someone else for you to realize that," she chided. "If you weren't happy, you should've done you and Dad a favor and gotten out." In the back of her mind as she said it, she couldn't help but wonder which parent she would have ended up with in the event of a divorce.

"And how was I supposed to support myself? And you along with it?"

The question hung between them. The larger shadow, though, was cast by the implication that the onus of single parenting gave them something in common. Such a curious form of double-think angered Kate all the more for the way her mother was trying to push the agenda that a woman without a man to support her was some kind of loser. "And what would you have done if your mystery man asked you to run off with him?" she pressed. *Oh Lord*, she thought in mounting dread, *it wasn't Brad's father, was it*?

"It never came to that," Lydia grimly replied. "His wife went and got herself pregnant."

"He was married?" Kate blurted out. *This is all getting just too weird.* She forced herself to listen with a vague sense of unreality to her mother's explanation that he and his wife had grown apart.

"Obviously, not so far apart that they were sleeping in separate beds," Kate cynically remarked, mindful of how many men had tried to use that same kind of pick-up line on her to justify a fling at infidelity. "So, what happened then?" she asked. That her mother could carry on a dalliance for more than a nanosecond with a married man under the noses of a town as snoopy as Avalon Bay was nothing short of bizarre.

Lydia issued a deep sigh of resignation. "He told me he had to stay with her, and I, well, I didn't have any choice except to try to make things work out with your father. I suppose if there's any satisfaction I can take it's in knowing he probably never forgot me and that I'd always be the love of his life."

Just not the one he wanted to spend it with. "To save me the mental math," Kate started to say but Lydia had already anticipated her next question.

"Cassy was definitely your father's," she confirmed. "We'd already broken things off between us and your sister didn't come along until more than a year later."

"And, so, they moved out of town or what?" She stopped short of asking whether her father and the man's wife had ever suspected what was going on.

The effect of Lydia's reply was likened to a graveyard. "They're still here," she said. "It was Sean Neal."

Chapter Twenty-Eight

L ydia's confession, dredged from a place beyond logic and reason, refused to grant Kate any semblance of sleep that night. As if the REPLAY button was sitting in a permanently stuck position, the unbidden details of her decades-old infidelity had accomplished only one thing as far as the listener was concerned. *At least now I know why she's always tried to discourage a lasting relationship between John and me.*

Had they ever progressed to the altar, Kate could easily envision the discomfiture of half the new in-laws over cake and punch. The awkward glances. The forced gaiety. The head-splitting pressure not to accidentally slip up by saying something he or she would supposedly have no way of knowing.

It also explained, she realized, why her mother eschewed mention of Jeremy. Had the third Neal son not been conceived, an entirely different future might have unfolded, a future that clearly would not have included Cassy. Or Jimmy. It seems *we're all painful reminders of the happily-ever-after Mom thought she was supposed to get.*

Though her mother had insisted that neither her husband nor Abby had ever gotten wind of the affair, Kate couldn't help but wonder whether it was more a case of wishful thinking than actual reality. Certainly in her own limited experience of dating, there was telepathy that kicked into gear when one's current love-interest was starting to get bored and wandering off. How, she mused, could two people like her parents live under the same roof and sleep in the same bed every night and yet be so out of touch with each other's feelings that a third party's presence wasn't felt?

The bigger mystery, of course, was how they had eluded detection, and censure, within the confines of Avalon Bay. Even the passage of years wouldn't have dulled the acid tongues of those who lived for a good scandal. She was suddenly remembering the first time John picked her up in the cab and was talking about Ed the barber and his third bride. Funny that she and John hadn't even been born yet when Ed left his first wife for a comely librarian from Cape May, overnight, generated more conversation than a steamy episode of *Peyton Place*. Though the fling hadn't resulted in matrimony, there were still wicked snickers to this day whenever someone in Avalon Bay talked about "checking out a new book".

The uncertainty which had been aroused by her mother's disclosure brought with it another unsettling thought. *Does John know, too?*

She tried to push it from her mind. Mothers, she rationalized, would be more inclined to share their feelings with a daughter as a cautionary tale than to confide in a son. On the other hand, she'd had no way of knowing how John's parents reacted when she and John broke up. Human nature being what it was, it wasn't uncommon for families and friends to immediately start dissing whoever was no longer in the picture. Had Abby told him to count his blessings that she was gone or, domestically oblivious to her husband's connection to the Toscano household, simply told John he'd meet someone else someday?

Though the new day was less than five hours old, she could already hear movement starting up downstairs in the kitchen. Whatever awkwardness she'd felt the previous evening in listening to her mother's story was nothing compared to the impending prospect of both women facing each other over coffee. At least, she reflected, most of her anger had dissipated during the night and been replaced with something that bore a closer kinship to pity. She couldn't begin to guess what this awkward turn of events had done to her mother's already mercurial nervous system but she did know the impact it was having on her own.

Just get through it, she told herself as she started down the stairs. *Water under the bridge.*

John awoke with a splitting headache, his first conscious thought being the realization that it was early morning and he was lying face down in the lumpy cushions of a strange couch. To move from his curiously splayed position would have taken more effort than his fuzzy brain was telling him he could muster any time soon. He licked his lips, wondering why the inside of his mouth felt like he'd been chewing on socks soaked in Jack Daniels. If memory served, and that was certainly more than debatable in his numbed state, the last time he'd felt this rotten was when his first and only hangover was experienced in a jail cell along with a charge of disturbing the peace.

He shuddered, disturbed that he could suddenly remember with such fierce clarity what he'd been doing that long-ago night but was loopy on what he was doing in a strange apartment. Without shifting his body, he turned his head on the cushion to try and get his bearings at the precise moment the kitchen light snapped on across the room.

"Oh good," said a voice in response to John's knee-jerk reaction to the sudden brightness. "For a minute, I thought you were dead."

"About last night," Kate and Lydia stopped simultaneously when they realized they'd both picked the same three words to start their conversation. Kate broke the tension first by laughing about their

A Seaside Story

stereophonic opener. "I guess great minds run in the same circles," she said.

"I was going to say 'like mother, like daughter,'" Lydia murmured, "but maybe under the circumstances."

"Listen, Mom, I'm the last person in the world to judge you. I'd be lying if I said your affair,"

Lydia's interruption was prefaced with an embarrassed cringe. "Affair sounds so cheap," she said. "Isn't it bad enough?"

Bad enough that you cheated on Dad or bad enough that you weren't your paramour's first and final choice? Kate resisted the sarcastic urge to label them as friends-with-benefits. "Whatever you want to call it," she continued, "it kinda blew me away but I supposed people looked at survival differently in your generation than mine. Women today don't have to stay in a relationship if it's not making 'em happy, and they sure don't have to find a relationship just to keep their head above water."

Though she hadn't meant it to be a segue to the present, her mother nevertheless pounced on it. "I've already seen one of my daughters try to struggle with being a single parent," Lydia said. "If it turns out that you're going to have to do all of this on your own, it's going to be next to impossible for you to ever, well, to have anything else."

"Anything or anyone?" Despite her resolve to stay calm, there was a tinge of exasperation in her voice that she couldn't dislodge her mother's sexist views.

"A man these days isn't going to want a ready-made family."

Not so, Kate's heart faintly whispered back, though aloud she declared, "Then he's not going to be the right one. And he's certainly not going to be the likes of Brad." She let the remark sink in a little deeper. "Promise me we've seen the last of him."

"You know I can't promise you won't run into him," Lydia countered. "It's not like we live in New York."

"I meant in our living room."

"Can I say just one thing?"

Have you ever said 'just one thing'? "What?"

"He was very concerned about everything that's going on and asked me if he could do anything to help."

"'Everything being?'"

Lydia shrugged. "We had a long time to chat. I may have mentioned a little more than I should have."

"Why am I not surprised?" *Especially if Brad was also doing the pouring.*

"Oh, I wouldn't worry," Lydia insisted. "I'm sure nothing will come of it."

A groggy John tried to focus on the stout ceramic mug of black coffee that had mysteriously been thrust into his hands, coffee that he was fairly sure was probably strong enough to dissolve a spoon.

"Uh, did I say anything weird last night?" he asked. "Something that maybe I shouldn't have?"

His listener, however, was out of earshot at the moment.

John drew a deep breath as he hazily tried to reconstruct the past evening.

Pizza.

Something to do with a pizza.

Capparelli's pizza.

Pizza and cheese.

Pizza and rain.

Pizza and?

His mind suddenly locked on the blurry image of Kate and Jimmy and Kate being mad at him about something. But what? He took a big gulp of coffee and nearly spit it out. Bleah! It tasted, and looked, like tar. Hot tar. Disgusting tar and nary a trace of sugar.

He conjured Kate's beautiful face again.

Kate angry.

Kate soaking wet.

Kate looking as if she wanted to lean in and kiss him and then?

And then emptiness.

Blackness.

Blackness that was blacker than the disgusting cup of coffee in his hands.

"You okay?" he heard a hollow voice inquire.

"Did I say anything weird last night?" he asked, wondering why his question felt like déjà vu.

"Define *weird*," the voice replied.

Kate's first order of business was to drop off a check at John's to cover the traffic ticket she had cost him.

"Why so early?" her mother asked when Kate told her that she'd need to watch Jimmy for her. Already hovering in the wings was an inevitable second question about why her daughter had donned a linen skirt and heels since their previous conversation.

"Just a lot of stuff to do this morning," Kate quickly lied, seeing no need to explain that she'd just as soon not run into John after the awkwardness of their last encounter. If she simply slipped a note in an envelope under the mat at the Neals' front door and left, he'd have no choice but to accept it.

Or bring it back, the voice in her head played Devil's advocate. *Is that what you're really thinking? Wanting? Wishing?*

"I'll also need to borrow the car," she added. Although it certainly looked as if the day would be rain-free, the last thing she needed was any more surprises.

True to form, Lydia asked her where she was taking it.

"If I tell you, it could jinx it," Kate teased.

Her mother's face brightened. "A job interview?"

"Just dropping off my resume at the Gazette," Kate replied. "I doubt Cliff's even there this early but at least he'll know I'm interested."

"What if he is?"

Kate shrugged. "Then I guess I'll see if he has time to pencil me in." *Or if he even remembers me.* Although the summer she had volunteered between her sophomore and junior year to proofread copy stood out as a favorite memory, she also knew that Cliff rarely recollected anyone who didn't bring value-added to his sense of prestige.

"Hmm," Lydia murmured with a hint of disapproval.

"Hmm, what?"

"Do you think linen's a good idea if he keeps you waiting?" she queried, critically eying Kate's skirt.

"Since when is linen a bad idea?"

"Lap wrinkles," Lydia replied without missing a beat. "I'd go with a nice jersey knit instead..."

Kate could whimsically imagine what Dee's reaction would have been to her going upstairs to change her clothes. It even made her smile despite the apprehension she felt as she pulled up to the Neal house.

"Don't take this as a sign I'm going to start doing everything you say," she had felt compelled to inform her mother.

Lydia, in kind, had responded that at least it was a start.

She absently smoothed the navy jersey print before she stepped out of the car. *Nary a lap wrinkle. So far, so good.*

The morning newspaper was still laying on the doormat, a sign it seemed, that no one was up and about yet. The front curtains were closed as well, a modest assurance that her stealthy approach to the front door wouldn't be noticed.

She bent down to tuck the envelope under the rubber band but before she could straighten up, the door suddenly opened and she was knocked to the ground by the German Shepherd that came bounding out. From her undignified sprawl, Kate caught a brief flash of fluffy bunny slippers and a bathrobe before the black and tan beast hovering over her began excitedly licking her face.

"Shelby! No!" a woman's voice sharply called out, followed by, "Are you all right?"

Kate wasn't sure who was more startled as she made eye contact with the woman who was helping her to her feet, a woman whose face was completely slathered with a light green paste except for the two circles around her eyes.

They both started to talk at once, Kate with an apology for scaring her and the woman saying she'd just stepped out to get the paper. "My son's the one who usually brings it in," she said, grabbing the dog's collar. "Shelby! Stop that!"

"Mrs. Neal?" The words were out of her mouth before Kate realized how stupid, and possibly insulting, it sounded to preface it with a gasp.

"Yes?"

Before Kate could scramble fast enough to say something clever about not recognizing her at first under the layers of facial, Abby. Neal looked out toward the street and started laughing in mild embarrassment. "You're not with one of those reality shows, are you?" she asked.

"Excuse me?"

"Hidden cameras? Publisher's Clearing House? Ed McMahon jumping out of the bushes to give me a check?" She touched a hand to her cheekbone before reaching up to adjust the towel turban on her head. "Goodness! And today of all days!"

The cavalier way in which she responded to the prospect of a televised intrusion despite her comical appearance almost made Kate wish her pending explanation wasn't so pedestrian.

"I'm just a friend of John's," Kate cut in, "and wanted to drop off something for him."

"The girl from school!" Abby declared with a broad smile. "It's, uh, Kate, isn't it?"

So at least he's mentioned my name recently to his mother, Kate thought, unsure of what exactly that was supposed to mean. She refrained from supplying John's mother with a surname. *Just in case she decides to call the dog back to eat me.*

In the next breath, Abby asked her if she'd like to come in for some coffee. "I just made a pot of regular but we've got decaf if that's better?"

Kate politely declined, explaining that she'd only stopped by to leave something for John and hoping that his mother, under the auspices of innocent helpfulness, wouldn't call him to the front door to collect it in person.

A look of puzzlement crossed Abby's face. "You mean he wasn't with you?" She asked. "Well, I'll be sure to give it to him."

Could this moment get any more awkward, Kate thought.

"Well, speak of the devil!" Abby proclaimed in delight as John's truck suddenly pulled into the driveway. "Looks like you didn't have to miss him after all."

Chapter Twenty-Nine

That he was wearing the very same clothes she'd seen him in the evening before wasn't lost on Kate. Nor was he doing a very good job at hiding a decidedly guilty expression as soon as their eyes met. With a shudder that she hoped neither John nor his mother caught, she realized his disheveled appearance could only mean one thing.

Enough already, she silently chided the *universe. I get the picture, okay?*

"Is this a new look?" Abby teased him.

"I was about to say the same," he replied but his eyes were on Kate. "What are you doing here?" he asked.

Annoyance drew her brow as she ignored his question and informed him instead that she had to go. She bade his mother goodbye. "It was nice talking to you, Mrs. Neal."

"Feel free to stop by any time," Abby cheerfully encouraged her. "And I promise not to be such a fright next time."

He allowed Kate to get halfway to the car before padding after her and telling her to wait up.

"I'm running late as it is," she said, conscious of the scent of alcohol that clung to his shirt. Conscious, too, of how the beginning hint of five o'clock shadow gave him an even more manly aura while his bed-mussed hair concurrently made the years melt away.

"Late for what?" he wanted to know. He made no secret of taking in the way she was dressed and letting his eyes communicate curiosity.

"Not everything I do in my life is about you," she retorted, hoping he wasn't coherent enough to realize that what she just said had no bearing on anything he'd said. Out of the corner of her vision, she could see his mother slip inside and discreetly close the front door to give them some privacy.

His mouth slid into a lopsided grin that was either the product of his previous night's imbibing or amusement with putting her on the defensive. "So how come you're here at the crack of dawn?" he asked.

"The crack of dawn was a few hours ago," she coolly replied. "You must have been, uh, busy and missed it."

He shrugged. "Still doesn't answer the question," he said, repeating it for her.

She kept her features deceptively composed, knowing that an on-spot admission would cause what had seemed like a fairly good plan to backfire on her. "Just to say thank you for the ride last night," she answered. "Now will you please take your hand off the car door so I can be on my way?"

"Okay but just answer me one thing first."

"Fine. What?" She folded her arms and gazed off into space as if bored. In truth, of course, it was way too easy to get lost in the way he kept looking at her if she continued facing him.

He took his hand off the door handle and gently reached up to turn her chin back toward him. "How come everything I do seems to annoy you?"

She cleared her throat, pretending not to be affected, and as the words slowly came forth, she realized it was as close to an honest response as she dared to make. "Maybe because I never know what it is you want."

If his fuzzy brain cells had been able to rally fast enough with a reply, he would have told her that he wanted the same thing he had always wanted but that she was the one who kept moving the goalposts on him. Instead, he watched her drive away and realized he was more confused than ever.

"Kate seems nice," Abby remarked as he wandered back into the house and slouched without preamble into the nearest kitchen chair.

"Yeah." He took the wet chew toy that Shelby deposited in his lap and half-heartedly began to engage her in a game of tug.

"I was kinda surprised to see her," she continued.

"You 'n' me both."

"That's not exactly what I meant."

John looked up. "Huh?"

"Well, when you didn't come home last night," She shrugged as she set a mug of black coffee down in front of him. "Not that I keep any tabs on you."

"I crashed at Lenny's," he explained.

"Was that before or after you drowned your sorrows?"

"Never gonna live that down, am I?"

"Probably not but we still love you anyway."

"At least we weren't disturbing the peace," he replied. "I know it's no excuse."

"How 'bout your peace of mind?"

John remained silent.

Shelby, sensing John's disinterest in their game, released her end of the toy and trotted over to see if there was anything new in her dog bowl since the last time she had looked.

"I was surprised you didn't at least kiss her goodbye," Abby commented.

"Shelby?"

"Kate. She was looking awfully kissable, don't you think?"

"You know, for someone who claims she's not keeping tabs on my life..."

"No," she said, "just tabs on your heart and a person would have to be blind not to see who it belongs to."

Yvette Brown's mouth dropped open in astonishment when she looked up and saw Kate walk through the front door of Avalon Bay Gazette. "I don't believe it!" she exclaimed with a gasp of delight as she wriggled her corpulent frame out of her chair and ambled toward the half-wall that divided the waiting area from the rest of the office. "Is it really you all pretty and grown-up?"

Though she didn't address Kate by name, there was no question but that the Gazette's grandmotherly receptionist never forgot a single face, even one she hadn't seen in years. She leaned over the wooden barrier to envelope Kate in a bosomy, heavily perfumed hug, then held her at arm's length to offer gushing praise of how well she'd turned out.

If there was a single ally Kate had learned to have in her corner during her semester stint at the paper, it was Yvette. Dubbed "The Warden" by everyone who knew her, it was Yvette who controlled what phone calls got through, which visitors got buzzed into Cliff's inner sanctum, and which ads mysteriously got priority placement in the classified section. Make an enemy of Yvette, as so many had found out the hard way, and you made an enemy for life.

Given the circumstances that were bringing Kate back to these familiar haunts this morning, she was more than a little grateful for the long-ago time she had contributed to Yvette's candy dish, given her a card for her birthday, and offered the use of her umbrella one afternoon when the older woman had forgotten hers at home.

"I don't suppose Mr. White is in yet?" Kate inquired after giving her listener an abbreviated version of what had brought her back to town. Even though she'd become a certifiable adult since the last time she'd seen him, she decided it was better to err on the side of formality than to refer to him outright as Cliff.

To her surprise, Yvette informed her that he'd been in for the past hour and was meeting with someone in his office even as the two of them spoke. In the next breath, she asked Kate if she'd heard about him firing their most recent editor.

"And not a moment too soon, either, if you ask me," she continued. "The man couldn't take a good picture to save himself!" His shaggy ponytail and disregard for any kind of business dress code had rankled Cliff as well. "And," Yvette continued under her breath. "between you and me, he wasn't the sharpest tool in the shed, either." Yvette always had a way with words. "So what can we do for you?"

Kate withdrew an envelope from her purse. "Well, it's sort of funny you should ask," she replied. "I was hoping to talk to him about my doing some writing for you guys." She quickly added that if it looked like he was going to be a while, she could just leave her resume and come back at a better time.

Yvette's voice rose in surprise. "You're applying for editor?"

"Nothing quite that grand," Kate candidly replied. "But thanks for the vote of confidence."

"Oh, you'd be a natural! Just what this ol' place needs to shake things up." Yvette, as Kate recalled, had never kept secret her views that Cliff wasn't the planet's most progressive persona.

"I was thinking maybe some freelance pieces, local interviews, city council meetings." As she continued laying out her ideas and watching Yvette 's glowing reaction to them, it suddenly struck Kate that she was starting to get excited about the prospect of writing and creating again.

It was a rush of euphoria that lasted exactly 10 more seconds, the amount of time it took for Cliff's office door to open and his visitor to step out.

"No, no, the pleasure's entirely mine," Cliff was saying as he followed in the young woman's wake, a scene mildly comical for the fact she was at least 6 inches taller than he was. He was now enthusiastically shaking her hand with both of his. "We'll look forward to seeing quite a lot more of you, Miss Delvaggio."

"No, please," she graciously insisted, "call me Gabrielle."

Oh great, Kate thought with a sudden queasy feeling in her stomach. *She's not only got the guy, but she's probably also just got whatever job I was hoping for.*

Cliff leaped forward to gallantly hold the swinging gate open for her. As if to add further insult to injury, she pleasantly smiled at Kate on her way out. Cliff watched her entire exit, seemingly oblivious that there was anyone else in the room.

Had Yvette's cheery "Look who came to see us!" not stopped him in his tracks, Kate was fairly sure he would have gone back into his office without even acknowledging her.

"Well, what do you know!" Cliff responded with the voice and face that conveyed he had nary a clue.

To spare Kate the embarrassment of having to jog his memory, Yvette jogged it for him. "Why I was just saying it seems like only yesterday that Katie Toscano was a student interning with us!"

A light bulb seemed to snap on in Cliff's bald little head and though he didn't step forward to shake her hand, he made the obligatory gesture of asking what she'd been doing with herself since graduation.

Before Kate could react, Yvette grabbed the envelope out of her hand. "You should take a look at this," she informed Cliff as she passed it over to him.

Not exactly the "ta-da" I would have gone for, Kate thought, nonetheless heartened by the receptionist's declaration that the newspaper paper could use someone like her. "If you have some time this week..." Kate started to say to him.

"Why not right now?" Yvette suggested, reminding Cliff in the next breath that he wasn't doing a damn thing until lunch.

How does she keep her job, Kate wondered. Given Cliff's pomposity, of course, maybe it was as simple as a shortage of takers if he ever decided to replace her. Besides, it was no secret that Yvette kept Cliff in line and he would be utterly lost without her.

He shot his receptionist a look. "I'm running a newspaper that's competing with the internet," he retorted. "It's a losing battle. I need someone full-time to help me turn this paper around."

"All the more reason, then, to hear what Katie has to say."

Rather than continue an argument he wasn't likely to win, Cliff informed her that he did indeed have a few minutes. Yvette flashed her a double thumbs-up as Kate followed him into his office.

"Let's take a look," he said upon settling into his desk chair and sliding a letter opener under the sealed flap.

"You'll be happy to know I made good on my journalism background and degree," she said, suddenly feeling anxious that this wasn't going at all as smoothly she had envisioned it on the short drive over.

Was it her imagination or had she just seen a small piece of paper flutter to the top of Cliff's desk when he unfolded her resume?

He had lowered his head and was now sternly regarding her over the top rim of his wire-framed glasses.

"What's this about?" he sharply inquired.

Caught off guard, Kate started to reply that she was hoping to be able to do some freelance writing.

He turned the page around so that it dangled in front of her, "What I meant," he said, "is who's John?"

Chapter Thirty

A shower and a shave had made John feel almost human again. What he didn't feel, however, was particularly smart, especially after he opened the envelope his mother said Kate had left for him. Did she not know that he already thought she was smart? Giving him a resume replete with all of her past salary information seemed, on the one hand, to reinforce the message that Fate was so aggressively intent on spelling out for him in capital letters: Kate Toscano was out of his league.

On the other hand, he mused, maybe it was a roundabout way of her asking him for some help in finding her a job. Given his line of work, it went without saying that he knew plenty of people in Avalon Bay. Certainly, he'd have no problem talking her up and saying lots of good things.

Kate is smart.

Kate is responsible.

Kate is a hard worker.

Kate is—

He froze a moment in his mental inventory. If Kate was asking for his help in looking for employment, it could only mean one thing. People didn't go looking for jobs that paid her sort of salary unless they were thinking of staying put for a while. Grocery baggers, waiters, clerks, he'd known enough of them who slid through entry-level jobs like a revolving door because their needs and interests were youthfully transitory. Someone like Kate, someone with a child to support, would be looking for something with more permanence and a healthy side-order of benefits.

Trouble was, he realized, the town's biggest employer was the factory. That was pretty much blue-collar, not to mention that he knew from personal experience its benefits package left much to be desired. Local businesses that might better suit Kate's style were a far cry from Madison Avenue slickness in terms of their needs for a savvy wordsmith. PR would be a perfect match, he thought, as he reread her background, dismayed that the only agency he could recall off the top of his head was run by two spinster sisters who would resent the presence of someone young and attractive.

A personal assistant maybe? He'd heard the term before but wasn't entirely sure what all it entailed. Besides, someone like Kate should have an assistant running errands for her and not the other way around. The bottom line that a job carrying any kind of sophistication and glamour would be more likely to lurk in Atlantic City or New York. Neither one of them, however, would be a place Kate would probably want to raise a boy like Jimmy who needed so much in the way of family love and medical attention.

A smile suddenly came to John's face and he wondered why the perfect solution hadn't come to him sooner.

He fingered the resume before carefully folding it and putting it back into the envelope. There'd be no need to make copies, he decided. All he had to do was lock down one "yes" from the right person.

"Well?" Cliff said.

Kate couldn't have felt more uncomfortable if she were eleven and sitting in the principal's office for passing notes.

"There's a perfectly good explanation," she heard herself say and immediately wished she hadn't. *What a cliché!* At least she hadn't said "logical" instead of "good" and implied that there was more purpose behind this stupid mix-up than actually existed. *But why did I go and say "perfectly"?*

"Yes," Cliff was saying. "That's what I'm waiting to hear." There was no humor in his eyes or intonation. He was already clearly perturbed she was there without an appointment; now his time was being further wasted by her hesitation to explain herself.

As if her life were rapidly passing in front of her eyes, she ran through a series of responses. If she told him that she had been in a hurry, he'd think she was sloppy. If she told him she'd been distracted, he'd think that multi-tasking was beyond her capabilities. If she told him that her life was overwhelmed of late, he'd probably tell her to go home and not come back until she got her act together.

"Weren't you supposed to marry some kid named John?" Cliff suddenly cut into her thoughts.

"Uh, excuse me?"

"Pretty sure it was you," he said. "Ran prom pictures on the front cover." He recalled aloud it had been a slow news week and somebody, *maybe it was you*, had talked him into it.

Of all the times to have selective memory, Kate thought. *He can remember I dated someone named John but doesn't remember I'm a kick-ass writer.* For the moment, she realized her best strategy was to compliment him on his flash to the past. "I think I still have a copy somewhere," she said.

"So how'd that go for you?" he interrupted, making a point of peering at her left hand. "I don't see a ring."

"Uh, didn't work out," she replied, hoping he'd move on.

He didn't.

"Divorced?"

A part of her wanted to remind him that it was the 21 century and that such questions about her status were completely inappropriate. Another part of her was still hoping to recover from the resume faux pas and convince him that he needed her.

"Still happily single," she answered. "And about the mix-up on my resume,"

"What resume?"

Remind me again why I want to work for this guy. "The one you're supposed to be looking at," she said. "When we're finished here," – *why do I have the feeling I'm finished already?* "I'll drop another copy off."

Cliff briefly considered this and tapped the page he was holding. "Sounds like this one's got a better story."

"Not really, no."

"If you say so. So why again are you here?"

"I was hoping to talk to you about my background as a writer."

"Oh?"

Kate proceeded to give him the highlights of her career.

"Vegas, huh?" he interrupted midway. "Sin City. Long way from home, aren't you?"

"Avalon Bay is home," she informed him. And for the first time since she had sat down, she saw the faint beginnings of a smile.

"So you've come back to carpe diem?" he remarked, informing her in his next snooty breath that "carpe diem" meant to "seize the day".

He must think I'm a total moron. "Well, today's about as seizable as it gets," she flippantly replied.

By the time he smiled at her again and asked what kind of stories she thought she might be good at writing, Kate realized that things were slowly but surely starting to look better.

Yvette looked up from her crossword puzzle at the sound of the door opening. "Can I help you?" she asked. Her voice was always a bit sharp when she was in the middle of something important.

The man on the other side of the gate inquired whether the publisher was in.

"Do you have an appointment with him?"

"Not really," he confessed with a grin as he removed his dark glasses. "Is that all right?"

Yvette's demeanor instantly brightened when she recognized who he was. "I don't believe it!" she declared as she hurried around the desk to hug him. "I swear you're getting to look more and more like that handsome father of yours every day!"

"Guess there's no getting away from those darn Neal genes," John quipped.

"And why would you want to? So, how's he doing these days? And Abby? Lordy, I haven't seen either of them in ages."

"Still taking it a day at a time. I'll let 'em know you asked."

Yvette wanted to know how the tree business was going. "I can give you a special on an ad this month," she offered. "It'll only take me a minute to write it up."

John thanked her, explaining that word of mouth publicity from happy customers was already keeping him busier than ever. "Actually, I stopped by to see if you guys are doing any hiring."

Yvette mistook his query as a personal interest in working for the Gazette. "No offense, dear, but you're so outdoorsy you've never really struck me as someone who'd be happy to be cooped up inside all day."

"Oh, it's not for me," he said. "It's a friend I kinda want to do a favor for."

Yvette stiffened. "It's not that dreadful Molino boy, is it?" she asked in suspicion.

John realized she'd never forgotten some of the goofy pranks Lenny had pulled when he was younger. "Lenny's pretty happy where he is," he assured her.

"That's because the boy never had as much ambition as you," she opined. "So, what kind of work are we talking about?"

"Well, I was hoping maybe you could use a good writer."

Yvette bit her lip.

"Something wrong?" John asked.

"We don't usually have that much call," she said. "I mean we have the regulars 'n' all on staff and a lot of people who like to send in their own press releases and so when something opens up."

He could see that she was on the defensive and now felt sorry for putting her on the spot. "Hey, I understand," he interrupted, "but I was thinking if maybe you were short-handed." He held out the envelope to her. "My friend's got a pretty good background. If you could just give this to him? You never know."

"The thing of it is," Yvette confided, "we do have something right now but," she tilted her head toward the closed office door. "I'm pretty sure he's already making an offer."

John followed her glance. "So I don't suppose it would be cool if I burst in and told him he was making the biggest mistake of his life?"

Yvette laughed as she took the envelope from him. "I suppose we can keep this on file just in case. Like you said, you never know."

Though there was a definite spring in John's step when he left the Gazette, there was still something that bothered him. For Kate to accept that he really did have her best interests at heart, he still had to recruit as an ally the one person who was bound and determined to keep him away from her.

"Nothing ventured, nothing gained," he murmured under his breath, oblivious to the car that was parked only a few spaces away from him.

C.J. Foster

Chapter Thirty-One

C liff was beginning to warm to the notion of a female's fresh perspective. "Not so much all that women's libber bra-burner crap, though," he emphasized. "That may work for some rags out West but not for our readers."

And when was the last time you did a poll on what your readers want, she would like to have challenged him. Instead, she bit her tongue and let him rabbit on about what an idiot his last editor, Marty, had been. "About your age, too," he realized. "By the way, how old are you?"

Clearly, Kate thought, Cliff had never bothered to brush up on what constituted inappropriate questions. She opted to make him do the math himself and replied with the year she had graduated.

"Yeah, that'd be about right," he said. "So, you must've known him then?"

"Not that well." She hoped it would be to her benefit, given Cliff's reputation to judge everyone by the company they kept.

"Well, he used to show up in shorts and those cheap Hawaiian shirts to take Garden Club pictures and then brag about what a great spread of free food they had. And, of course, he couldn't take an in-focus shot to save himself."

And the reason you even put this idiot on your payroll was what?

"I assume you're pretty good with a camera?' he continued. "You didn't mention it in your 'Dear John' letter."

I'm never going to hear the end of that, am I? "I'd be happy to bring you some of the samples in my portfolio," she offered. "Would tomorrow be all right?" Twenty–four hours, she thought, should be enough time to put something together that would meet his persnickety taste. "I covered quite a few celebrity events for Vegas Essential."

To her surprise, Cliff interrupted to tell her that it wasn't necessary. "I'm having a thought," he announced. "Fluffy piece that's right up your alley."

Now he thinks I'm 'fluffy'?

In the next breath, he explained that there was a woman who was starting up a school. "The kids who go to it are kinda slow if you know what I mean," he joked, "but if their check clears for advertising, we'll owe 'em some ink. Maybe above the fold if your work's any good. Think you can handle it?"

Kate did a quick tally of the past 20 seconds. *He thinks I'm a lightweight, he refers to special needs kids as 'slow', he's questioning my ability to put a story together, and he's offering me a front-page slot.* A part of her wanted to stand up at that moment, thank him for his time, and leave. On the other hand, she was intrigued enough about his mention of the new school that she could justify her acceptance of the assignment as a way to help Jimmy. "How soon would you like it done?" she asked.

"Soon as I give you a green light." There was no sense in giving her any of their contact info, he explained, until the ad itself was a done deal.

In the awkward silence that descended, Kate realized there'd been no talk as yet about pay nor whether he was open to her pitching a few freelance ideas she wanted to develop.

"Was there anything else you'd like for me to work on?" she ventured to inquire.

C.J. Foster

"Nope, not off the top of my head. I'll get back to you." He made a dramatic point of looking at his watch, a sign to Kate that their meeting was over. His gaze fell on the letter to John and the check that had fallen out of it. "You'll probably be wanting these back," he said in a good ol' boy voice that rankled her even more.

Kate rose to thank him for his time even though she still wasn't sure how exactly any of it bode for the future.

"You can tell Yvette to put in an order for cards on your way out," he curtly instructed. His private line rang before she could ask him to explain what he meant by that and she found herself being shooed off in the same manner one would bat away a flying insect at a picnic.

The good news was that she could count on Yvette to decipher it for her. The bad news, though, was that Yvette was on the phone and in the arduous midst of taking a complicated classified ad from someone whose first language obviously wasn't English or Spanish. Rather than wait around for her to finish, Kate scribbled a Post-It note. *Cliff said to order cards.* Yvette grinned, gave her another thumbs-up, and went back to her phone call.

I guess that's a good sign, Kate mused as she let herself out, conscious that there was now a slight spring in her step that hadn't been there when she arrived. It vanished just as fast when she glanced at the letter and check in her hand and realized she still had to deliver them. With any luck, John would already have left for work.

"I'm probably the last person you expected to see," John said when Lydia opened the door.

"No, that would probably be Robert DeNiro," she replied with an uncharacteristic show of humor.

John wished he could have countered with a clever impersonation of either one of them but the only line he could remember on such short notice was, 'You talkin' to me?' Unfortunately, he realized, it probably would advance the cause of trying to win Kate's mother to his side. Instead, he apologized for disappointing her.

"Kate's not home," she informed him, turning away for a moment to catch the squealing Jimmy before he barreled out the door and straight into John's legs. "Looks like one of us is pleased you're here," she remarked.

John let her snub slide and replied that Kate wasn't the one he'd come to see. "I think you and I have some things to talk about."

"Oh? I can't imagine what."

"The truth is, Mrs. Toscano, we've all made choices in the past that probably felt right at the time we made them. My being here's gotta be pretty awkward for you 'n' all but you may as well know that I know what's going on and, between you and me, I don't mind how many people I have to slip a word to."

Lydia stiffened. "Do you think that's such a good idea?"

"If it would help Kate, I'd do anything."

"And how would you...telling what you know possibly 'help' her?"

"Word travels fast in a small town but, in this case, there's no harm in giving it an extra nudge. I was hoping you'd be pleased." He studied her face. "From the looks of it, though, I don't seem to be accomplishing that."

"I can't believe you'd stoop to something that...that low," she said coldly.

"Uh, how is helping your daughter and Jimmy stay in Avalon Bay a bad thing?"

"What?"

John scratched his head. "Are we on the same wavelength here?"

"I'm not sure," she cautiously replied. "What are you talking about?"

He grinned. "Ladies first."

"No, you," Lydia said. "I insist."

To Kate's relief, John's truck was nowhere in sight at his parents' house. The plan was that she'd simply tell his mother about the mix-up in envelopes and ask her to please see that John got the right one this time. Then she'd be on her way.

The sound of Shelby vigorously barking on the other side of the door seemed to suggest that Mrs. Neal was on her way to answer it. When a longer time passed than she would have expected, however, she determined that maybe the dog was home alone. She started to bend down to put the letter and check under the doormat when she heard a thump from the other side and a tentative jiggle of the doorknob.

Rather than get knocked silly a second time by the household's black and tan canine bullet, Kate stepped to the side as the door slowly opened. When she saw the difficulty with which the older man in the wheelchair was maneuvering to look out at her, she felt even worse for having come back. Two unsettling thoughts raced through her mind simultaneously. *This is John's father. This is the man my mother was going to leave us for.*

"I'm so sorry," she apologized. "I didn't mean to bother you."

Shelby, surprisingly docile this time, only gave Kate a cursory sniff, wagged her tail, and then loyally circled back to her master's side.

"Cookies," the man murmured, half of his mouth drawn into a smile.

He thinks I'm selling cookies? She couldn't begin to imagine what part of her outfit, much less her age, made him think she was a Girl Scout. "No, sir," she cheerfully replied, "I don't have any cookies."

"Cookies," he repeated a little louder. He lifted his hand over to stroke Shelby's back. "Shelby...likes...cookies."

"Oh, well then, I'm doubly sorry I didn't bring her any. Maybe next time."

He thoughtfully nodded at this and the sincerity of the gesture suddenly overwhelmed her with sadness. He looked back up at her. Whether his squint was part of an attempt to focus or simply because the morning sun was directly behind her, Kate couldn't be sure. She moved slightly to the left to put his questioning face in shade.

"I brought something for John," she continued. She started to hold out the envelope to him, then hesitated, sensitive to the possibility that he might not be physically strong enough to hold on to it.

He nodded. "You know...John," he asked.

"Yes, I know him. We went to school together a long time ago." *Another lifetime.*

He continued petting Shelby. "John," he mumbled, "should...go."

"Go where?" Kate gently asked. *Out of my life? Out of your house? Out of this town?*

Sean Neal took a deep breath. "School," he replied. "Tell...him."

I have no idea what that means. "All right, sure. Next time I see him, I'll mention that."

This seemed to please him. His rheumy eyes now gravitated to the envelope in her hands and she saw a brief flicker of something that looked like fear in them. "Money...doesn't bring...him back."

It was Kate's turn to look confused. *What has John told you about me?* "I just wanted to pay his traffic ticket," she explained, a little defensively, but the older man's attention had wandered off to the sounds of a woman pushing a stroller across the street. For a fragile moment, Kate was reminded that she was experiencing the same kind of frustration level she sometimes had in communicating with Jimmy. *I wish I knew what it was you were trying to tell me.* She cleared her throat and announced that she needed to be on her way.

She bent down to prop the envelope against the wall just inside the front door. "I'm just going to leave this right here," she said, "so John can get it next time he's here." She felt compelled out of courtesy to ask him if that was okay.

"Okay," he murmured. "John."

It wasn't until she slid behind the wheel that Kate realized whatever resemblance she had to her mother, once supposedly the great love of Sean Neal's life, had failed to register on him at all. And, for that quiet quirk of irony, she breathed a sigh of relief.

Chapter Thirty-Two

The sight of John's truck defiantly parked outside her mother's house when she got home made her contemplative mood immediately veer to one of anger. Happy as Jimmy always seemed to be whenever he was around, there was no discounting the potential for confusion if he continued to foist himself upon their lives. Girded with resolve to inform John Neal once and for all that it was best if they had a parting of the ways, Kate strode into the house.

The sound of laughter, John's, Jimmy's and, oddly, her own mother's, drew her to the back porch where they were engaged in a game of three-way catch with Mr. Ollie. It was Jimmy who noticed her first and, flailing Mr. Ollie over his head and into the nearest planter, came running toward her.

"Oh hi, dear," said Lydia. "I didn't hear you. There's lemonade in the fridge," Lydia announced instead. "Shall I get you some?"

"I can get it," John offered.

"Okay, refresh my memory here," Kate said, "why are you two suddenly getting along?" *And why am I so annoyed about it for all the times I kept telling you to be nice to him?*

"Well, I realize he's probably the last person you expected to see in the backyard," Lydia began.

"Unless you count Robert DeNiro," John added.

Lydia exchanged a glance with him and laughed.

"All right, this is getting too weird," Kate said, baffled by what seemed to be an insider joke she was clearly standing on the outside of.

John shrugged. "Maybe we just realized we have a lot in common."

"Although it's only one thing in common," Lydia said.

"Two, though, if you count Jimmy," John countered.

"Oh always, yes," she agreed, then turned to look at her daughter. "You see, John and I have been talking..."

Kate could feel her face clouding with uneasiness. *Oh no, you're not confessing your past to everyone.*

"The thing of it is, you've got enough to think about with Jimmy and your worrying about what you're going to do for a job shouldn't be one of them," Lydia resumed her explanation.

Kate arched a brow. "So what? So you're going to team up and go rob a bank for me?"

"Much as I'd love to do that to Brad," John replied, "our options would probably be better if we picked one out of town."

"But seriously," Lydia cut in, "I think because of John you're going to be hearing some good news very soon."

"Yeah well, I still have no idea what you're talking about but I do happen to have good news and furthermore, I got it all on my own."

"Oh?" her listeners said, nearly in unison.

"For your information, Cliff's just asked me to write for The Gazette."

Lydia looked at John who was now grinning in satisfaction. "Do I know how to deliver or what?" he remarked. He held up his right palm to Lydia.

"Why are you giving him a high-5?" an exasperated Kate wanted to know.

"Because he took your resume to The Gazette and said he put in a good word for you."

"And when was that exactly?" she asked, reminding her mother that she knew very well she was going to The Gazette herself that morning for the express purpose of finding out if Cliff had any openings. She further reminded John that, given his condition the last time she'd seen him, it seemed unlikely he'd have gotten to the newspaper before she did. In the flash of a dumbstruck moment, Kate wasn't sure whether she should be grateful for his initiative or thoroughly peeved that it would only give Cliff more to rib her about.

"Well, I didn't talk to Cliff personally," he clarified. "He had someone in his office at the time and so, oh, wait a minute, was that you?"

"I didn't ask for your help," she informed him.

"Then why did you give my mother a copy of your resume?"

Kate fumed. "She got the wrong envelope, okay?"

"So what was in the 'right' envelope?" he teased.

"You know, I think I'll just take Jimmy inside," Lydia said. "You two obviously have a lot to work out."

"Mom..."

"Oh, stop being so stubborn, Kate. Does it really matter how you got the job?"

If I got the job at all, Kate thought, hoping that neither one of them would ask when she was supposed to start and how much it paid.

"By the way," Lydia said, "when do you start and what does it pay?"

"We're, uh, negotiating the details." She felt compelled to point out that her first assignment was still in the works.

They both spoke at once to ask her what it was about.

"Well, apparently there's going to be a new school for kids like Jimmy," she replied, her tone softening in remembrance that if nothing else came of having to endure the pompous Cliff, she might at least come away with something that could benefit her nephew.

The comment jogged something in her mother's head and the latter now turned to John. "Tell her about Gabrielle."

What? The amusement in her mother's expression instantly incensed her. "Oh, that's it!" Kate blurted out. Three pairs of startled eyes, including Jimmy, reacted to her outburst. With hands on her hips, she fired her next question at John. "Is there anyone in town who doesn't know about your girlfriend?" she demanded to know.

John looked puzzled. "Which girlfriend?" he asked.

Oh great, there's more than one and I didn't know that, either? With as much poise as she could muster under everyone's scrutiny, she delivered the name that was apparently on the lips of everyone in Avalon Bay. "Gabrielle."

John exchanged a look with Lydia but didn't say anything at first.

So, Kate thought, *it's really true. End of story. Happily ever after...for someone else. At least I have a job. I think. Unless Gabrielle's the new editor and Cliff tells me I have to work for her.* Life, as she knew it, could not get much worse.

"Well, that explains a lot," John finally remarked.

What's that supposed to mean? "What's that supposed to mean?" she challenged him.

"I'll just take Jimmy inside and get him ready to go," Lydia announced.

"Go where?"

"Oh, you'll see," she cryptically replied, steering her young grandson toward the door.

John stayed behind to deliver his answer to Kate's question. "Three things," he said. "The first is that Gabrielle never is, never was, and never will be my 'girlfriend'. Secondly—"

Kate interrupted. "Wait a minute. How come everyone thinks you're seeing someone?"

He shrugged. "Small town, small minds, too much time on their hands. Who knows why people think anything? Can I continue?"

"Be my guest."

"Secondly, I didn't just come over to tell your mom I was trying to help you out with a job—"

"Which it turns out I didn't need."

His eyes narrowed. "You know this story's going to take a lot longer to finish if you don't stop interrupting every other word."

"Fine. Go on."

"As I was saying, it wasn't just about the job. It was to ask her if she and Jimmy wanted to go with me to visit a school for other kids he could relate to."

A light came on in Kate's head. A disturbing, illuminating, magnificent light that made Kate feel like a total dolt. "You mean the school that—"

"Yes," John said, "the school you're going to be writing about. The one that's run by my new *friend* —"

She heard it in her head before he said it out loud. *Gabrielle*. "So what's the third thing you were going to tell me?" she said.

A smart-ass little grin preceded his reply. "Y' know, I think I'm going to make you wait."

The sound of laughter in a backyard play area reached their ears as they approached a modest facility that temporarily housed the school. An older woman with sparkling blue eyes and short-cropped grey hair pleasantly greeted them, introducing herself as Dr. Susan Mitchell. Her enthusiasm was undisguised as soon as John told her why they were there.

"Oh yes, of course!" she exclaimed. "Brie's told me so much about you." She squatted down to put herself at eye level with Jimmy. "And this handsome young man must be Jimmy."

He regarded the stranger with caution but did not dart behind Kate in hiding as was his usual fashion around people he didn't know; to the contrary, he was now looking past her at the oversized color cubes, toys and child-size modular furniture in the waiting area. A freckle-faced little redheaded girl who looked to be around Jimmy's age was sitting in one of the chairs, rhythmically swinging her legs and possessively hugging a large picture book to her chest.

"Brie's out back," Susan told them, "but I can show you around and tell you about what kind of programs we have to offer." As they passed the little girl, Susan held out her hand to her. "Do you want to come with us, Annie?"

Annie stopped her leg-swinging, guardedly dividing her glance between Susan and the young newcomer who was staring back at her. She looked down at the book she was clutching and bit her lower lip, looking back at Susan with a hesitant, unspoken question.

"You can bring your book with you," Susan gently told her, adding that maybe Jimmy might like to see it, too.

Annie looked at Jimmy again and, seemingly satisfied that it was okay for him to be there, hugged the book to her chest again and wriggled out of the chair to come and join them.

Annie, Susan explained, had recently celebrated the milestone of saying her first word – 'juice'. "Her mom was here that day and I don't know which one of us was crying the most from total joy."

Kate divulged that Jimmy knew quite a few words. "Just not always what they mean or the right order to put them in."

Susan smiled. "Every child is unique, which is why we individually tailor our curriculum and therapy sessions so they can each move at their own pace and comfort level." She reached down to tap the spine of Annie's book, then pointed to Jimmy. "Can you show Jimmy your new book?"

Annie looked up at her, shook her curly head in defiance and hugged it even closer.

"All right then. Maybe later." Susan continued her explanation to Kate and John that it was critical not to rush things. "It's always a delight when we see amazing breakthroughs that come about as a result of the children learning new skills from one another."

"Is everyone around Jimmy's age?" Kate asked.

"Well, they currently range from four to twelve but their level of functionality is often much lower. We've got one young man, for instance, who knows his A-B-C's but can only recite them backward. We also have a little girl who's a year older than Annie and loves all kinds of music. She can mimic any song in perfect pitch but it's always in her made-up language."

The back door opened at that moment and a laughing Gabrielle poked her head in to ask for some paper towels. "Oh hey!" she said with a big smile when she saw John. "I see you're getting the tour." Her second smile went to Kate. "Hi," she said. "I'm Gabrielle."

It was John who made the introduction, adding the news that Kate was going to be doing a story about the school as a feature for The Gazette.

And hopefully, all this talk's not jinxing it. She cast John a quick look she hoped he'd interpret as a request to zip his lip.

Gabrielle's face brightened an extra notch. "The newspaper office! I thought you looked familiar. So you're a writer?"

"One of the best," John proudly answered for her. "I told you, didn't I, that Kate wrote for a magazine in Las Vegas?"

Does he think I've lost all power of speech, Kate thought. Still, it was hard to be too mad at him for only trying to put her at ease.

Annie dropped her book on the floor with a thud and eagerly ran toward Gabrielle.

"Ah, Vegas," Susan said with a fond smile. "Quite a change of pace from our sleepy seaside town, isn't it?"

A high-pitched squeal from the backyard pre-empted Kate's reply.

"Listen, I'll catch up with you guys after the tour," Gabrielle excused herself. "I think my troops are digging their way to China." She deftly caught the roll of paper towels that Susan now tossed her. "Think Jimmy would like to come out and join us for a few minutes?" A curious Annie was already following the sounds of fun coming from outside.

Kate hesitated. "I'm not sure. When he's in new situations, he doesn't always..."

Her sentence went unfinished as she watched Jimmy pick up the fallen book, walk confidently toward Gabrielle, and follow the little redhead who had already made her exit.

"I think we can take that as a 'yes'," John remarked.

Across the desk of the office she and Gabrielle shared, Susan had just finished explaining the school's evaluation process. "And, of course, when we're able to expand to a larger facility, we'll be bringing on more staff." She smiled as she tilted her head toward John. "Thanks to the help from our friends, we're hoping it could be as early as this fall."

He shrugged off her praise of his assistance. "You never know unless you ask," he said. "And one thing I'm certainly not shy about is asking."

Nor, Kate realized, had he been shy about sitting in on the meeting and asking a million questions about what kind of activities Susan thought would be the best fit for Jimmy's capabilities. *You think you really know a person*, she caught herself thinking, reluctant to admit how wrong she'd been to listen to town gossip and jump to false conclusions.

Gabrielle had popped her head in twice, both times adding in a postscript that Jimmy seemed to be having fun and fitting in well with his new pals. *Two hours ago I hated the very thought of her*, Kate reminded herself, *and now she's growing on me.* Much of it, she realized, was how much Gabrielle genuinely loved her job and believed in what she and Susan were trying to accomplish. *All right, all right, that and the fact her interest in John is obviously platonic.*

"I think you'll find," Susan was now explaining, "that we're pretty flexible in accommodating the schedules of working parents." She paused to smile at Kate, then John. "And, of course, we encourage your participation so that what we teach here at school can be reinforced at home."

Yikes! She thinks we're a couple, Kate thought. Before she could scramble together an explanation of their actual relationship, John was suddenly scooting his chair back and announcing he was going to go check on Jimmy.

"Such a nice man," Susan remarked in pleasant admiration as soon as she and Kate were alone. "Brie said the two of you went to school together..."

"We're, uh, not a couple," Kate said, anxious to clarify that she alone would be responsible for whatever arrangements were necessary to enroll her nephew in school and get him properly tested by the pediatric specialists with whom Susan and Gabrielle worked.

Her listener raised a brow in amused surprise and offered the observation that if she had seen the three of them on the street together, she would have assumed otherwise. "It's so clear you both have Jimmy's best interests at heart," she candidly continued, "that I have to admit I completely forgot he's not your own son."

'Your' plural? The irony wasn't lost on her.

Susan was now pulling out a clipboard of paperwork. "Let's get you started on some background information," she announced. "And, of course, if you've brought copies of his medical records."

Kate's hesitation in taking the clipboard was just enough to prompt Susan to ask her if something was wrong.

There was no getting around the inevitable entry on the proffered questionnaire. "I tried to get Jimmy into a school in Las Vegas," she confessed, "but I hit some snags."

"Oh?"

"Jimmy's father has been out of the picture for most of his life," she replied, certain that her disclosures about his marriage to Cassy would erase whatever enthusiasm had been in place up until this moment. "I'm taking the steps to track him down and to become Jimmy's legal guardian but I don't know how long it's all going to take." She felt her throat start to close up in response to reliving the same frustration she had endured in Vegas. "I suppose you're going to tell me to come back when it's all straightened out," she said with an underscore of resignation.

Susan shook her head. "Actually, I was going to ask if he could start tomorrow."

Kate couldn't believe her ears. "But what about all the paperwork?"

"I think you'll find Brie and I do things a little differently here," Susan replied. "A child's future shouldn't have to be put on hold while adults work out all their issues. Between what John's told us about your particular circumstances plus what I've heard from you myself, I'm hard-pressed to think a biological father would oppose what you and John, or rather, just you, want to do in Jimmy's best interests."

"You don't know Luke," Kate warned.

"True," Susan agreed. "But then again, he doesn't know us."

Chapter Thirty-Three

I t wasn't until John had dropped them both off back at the house that Kate remembered he still hadn't told her what the third "thing" was.

"Well, unless you're still mad at me," he playfully replied, "I was hoping maybe I could talk you into a picnic dinner and a walk on the bay tonight."

A rush of feeling that was both elemental and alien at the same time swept over her. "Uh,"

His blue eyes shot her an irresistible look. "I'm sensing some hesitation here."

"It's just that, oh, I don't know, you don't think it's moving too fast?"

John chuckled. "You mean because I just broke up with a woman I was never dating in the first place and now you think I'm on the rebound?"

He was playing his game with a purpose, daring her to admit that she was relieved the rumors about him and Gabrielle had all been false. "You're never going to let me forget this, are you?" she said.

The staggering challenge of his nearness as he took a step closer made Kate feel even more off-balance. "In 14 years," he remarked, "I haven't forgotten anything else about you. Why should this be the exception?"

The unbidden pressure of awareness, invitation, and acceptance became a swirling blur punctuated only by giggles from Jimmy who was now running circles around them.

"It's all kind of short notice," she heard herself murmur, conscious of how lame it came out. She could feel the giveaway heat in her face and welcomed the diversion of pretending to watch what her nephew was doing.

John, however, was not so easily distracted and seemed to relish putting her on the spot.

"Hmm," he replied. "So does this mean that you're one of those girls who want someone to ask her out three days in advance in case she already has major plans like washing her hair?"

Kate smirked. "There's nothing wrong with giving someone time to organize their calendar."

"There's nothing wrong with spontaneity, either," he countered. "Although technically I suppose it probably shouldn't count as off-the-cuff if I've been thinking about it since last week."

"Last week?"

"Maybe longer. So are you free tonight or what? Rumor has it that I throw together pretty good grub."

She tried to explain that it wasn't fair to ask her mom to watch Jimmy while she went out for the evening but John already had an answer to that one, too.

"I meant the both of you," he said. "That way, it doesn't really count as a 'date' if that's your only hang-up."

"I don't have hang-ups," she shot back, embarrassed that it sounded more defensive than she intended.

"Good," he replied, "because unless you've got someone who's been flying under the Avalon Bay radar the whole time you've been back here, I'm going to guess you don't have a boyfriend."

"And what if I do?" she teased, determined to engage in this sweet banter of warfare for as long as he did.

John shrugged. "Then I suppose I'll just have to chase him up a tree and never let him come back down."

Lydia wanted to know what they'd been talking about on the porch. "It looked important so I didn't want to interrupt," she said.

Kate laughed. "Who are you and what have you done with my mother?" In the next breath, she explained that John was treating her and Jimmy to a bay picnic that night and would be by to pick them up when he got off work.

"So the two of you are a couple, now?"

"I have no idea, Mom. I really don't. On the one hand, it feels like we're falling back into old times."

"And?"

"And, on the other hand, I remember how the old times ended and I just don't want to go through it again."

"Understandable," Lydia agreed, "but that's still not a very good reason to turn down a picnic."

"This from the woman who's been chasing him away?"

"No, this from the woman who finally looked at him and saw something I think you should appreciate."

Kate listened with a vague sense of unreality as her mother reminded her of all the nice things he'd done to show her that he cared. "Okay, is this reverse psychology?" she interrupted. "That if John Neal's suddenly the greatest thing since sliced bread I'm going to run screaming in the opposite direction?"

"Oh, I hope not," Lydia casually replied, "because I forgot to tell you that he's having dinner with us on Sunday."

As if the day hadn't already packed enough walloping surprises, an afternoon call from her friend Maria delivered yet another.

"Aren't you the sneaky one?" she exclaimed when Kate picked up the phone. "I had no idea you were gonna go for it!"

"Go for what?"

Maria laughed in response. "And to think you have me to thank! You should buy me a beer. Maybe two."

"Which I'm sure I'll gladly do if I had any idea what you're talking about."

"Honestly, girl, did you really think you could keep it a secret?"

A confusing rush of dread swirled to the surface. *Is the whole neighborhood bugged or what?* Kate glanced at the kitchen clock, noting that barely four hours had passed since she'd agreed to go out with John. *There's no way anyone could have found out about us that fast. Not even Maria.*

"So," Maria playfully pressed.

If she feigned ignorance, it would only make her high school pal even more aggressive and, further, make it look as if there were more to the story than just a picnic with an old friend. An old friend who coincidentally happened to be her ex-boyfriend and who, with very little encouragement, was making it clear he wanted to change his status from past-tense to present. Kate decided to take the offensive and ask Maria, "How did you find out?"

"Well, it's the funniest thing but I went by the newspaper office on my lunch break to place an ad for this yard sale I'm having next week,"

Oh great, it's worse than I thought. It was humiliating enough that Cliff had teased her about the mix-up in envelopes but now he was apparently using it in his repertoire of stupid anecdotes.

"and Yvette was just blown away and told me she couldn't be happier for you," Maria was babbling on.

"What was that again?"

"Yvette," Maria said. "I mean it's not like the whole town won't be talking about it by tomorrow!"

"I'm actually surprised anyone's even talking about it today." *Have we replaced Reality TV as everyone's favorite entertainment?*

"Oh, don't be so modest! I think it's great. Anyway, Yvette said they're going to run your old yearbook picture 'cause they don't have a current one but I think it's a cool idea."

"What?"

C.J. Foster

"What part are you saying 'what' to?" Maria asked, startled by the sudden volume of Kate's interruption.

"All of it, actually. What's this about yearbook pictures?"

"For the front page of the Gazette." Maria giggled. "Oops! You mean you didn't know they were going to do that?"

Kate was fuming. "I hardly think it's front-page news," she informed her, "much less anybody else's business."

Maria was silent for a moment. "I'd have thought you'd be happy about it. I mean you've gotta admit it's the most perfect thing that could have happened to you."

"I don't know that yet, Maria. And until I do, I'd rather not have everyone second-guessing it like they did the last time."

It was now Maria's turn to sound confused. "I thought you loved it," she said. "Isn't that why you majored in Journalism?"

"What does my majoring in Journalism have to do with my going out with John?"

"Oh my God!" a squealing Maria blurted out. "When did that happen?"

The shock of realization that she'd jumped to entirely the wrong conclusion about Maria's latest gossip hit Kate full force. "Maybe we should just start this conversation over," she awkwardly proposed amidst Maria's new barrage of questions about her love life. "What exactly have we been talking about?"

An impatient Maria was happy to accommodate her if it meant they could move on to an obviously juicier story. "Cliff's putting a thing in tomorrow's paper that you're going to be his new editor," she replied.

Okay, so I guess that settles the question of whether I got the job.

"Your turn," Maria said. Even over the phone, Kate could tell that her friend was smiling in anticipation of her answer.

"I'll tell you over a beer," Kate promised.

"Tonight?"

"Tomorrow."

Chapter Thirty-Four

J ohn had spared no expense in putting together a deliciously moveable feast that included an Italian quiche, salad, pita bread, spicy hummus, a variety of finger-food appetizers, and some fresh baked cookies for dessert. There was even, she noted, chicken tenders and a small box of Fruit Loops. "Did I get that right?" he asked. "I remember he was really scarfing 'em up when I took you to the airport."

The only thing more amazing than his thoughtfulness, Kate remarked out loud as he withdrew three plates from the picnic hamper was that he'd been able to pull it all together on such short notice. "Weren't you working up until the time you came to get us?" she asked.

"Just goes to show how easily it all comes to me," he replied, holding out a nugget for Jimmy.

The latter studied it for a moment before reaching out to close his entire hand over it and shove it into his mouth.

With the practiced eye of someone who made his living on quick estimates, he pointed out that he'd also staked out the very best spot on the beach for watching another day fold to a close.

"And what a day it's been," she murmured, not yet having mentioned her conversation with Maria who, by now, was probably already spreading her version of their relationship.

"I thought champagne would be a nice way to celebrate," he said. "It's pretty exciting they're going to be able to get him in so fast."

"A lot faster than Vegas," she agreed.

"But?"

"But what?"

"I don't know. You've got a worried look."

Jimmy was excitedly reaching for another handful of chicken nuggets.

"I'm afraid we're still working on table manners," Kate apologized for him as she reached for his wrist. A squirming Jimmy tried to pull away, sending the remaining pieces of chicken airborne.

"Hey, Jimmy, check this out!" John said, producing a chilled spear of asparagus as deftly as a magician and waving it back and forth. As Jimmy reached out for it, John held it higher, a maneuver that made his young audience want it that much more. "Oh, okay, I guess you can have it," John conceded and surrendered it to him with a heavy sigh.

"That's unbelievable," Kate remarked. "Mom and I have been trying to get him to eat vegetables all week and he hates them."

"Maybe you just need to make it more of a game," he suggested. "As soon as the veggies start playing hard-to-get, they're going to be the only thing he can think of."

"Is that so?"

"Well, isn't it?" He recalled with a chuckle how he used to tell Jeremy that the chocolate he got in his trick-or-treat bag was poisonous.

"That's pretty cruel," Kate said.

"Neh, just payback for all the stuff Mitch used to tell me." He handed her a glass of champagne and clinked it lightly with his own. "But back to you," he said. "What's got you worried?"

"What?" she said in surprise as she watched him take his first sip. "Not even a toast?"

"Sorry. What shall we toast to?"

Kate frowned. Almost anything she could come up with on short notice. "To us", for instance, might be construed as—

As what? the little voice in her head cut in. *As the possibility of more dates on the beach and a happily ever after with someone you've never stopped loving?*

"How about a toast to Jimmy and his new school?" she proposed.

"Done," he said and clinked her glass again. "And how about that new job of yours? That's probably worth a toast, too."

"Yeah, there's kind of a funny thing about that."

"Funny 'ha ha' or funny strange?"

"No, just funny weird but altogether in keeping with the way Cliff does stuff."

John look concerned as he handed Jimmy another asparagus spear. "He didn't change his mind, did he?"

"No, he just made up his mind without telling me what-all it encompassed." Her eyes met his. "Apparently, I'm his new editor."

"Hey, that's great!"

Though she didn't respond at first to his praise, her face spoke volumes. "He doesn't know about my situation with Jimmy," she explained. "He's going to expect me to jump in and be there every day and put in overtime to get the paper out and with everything else I've got going on right now," she broke off, conscious that the whole thing had started to make her hyperventilate.

"It's not like you're not used to pressure," John quietly remarked. "It's also not like you have to do everything yourself."

"I'm responsible for him, John. I can't take him to work with me and it's for darned sure Cliff's not going to let me write at home."

"Would you just stop and listen to yourself for a second? Jimmy's got his own agenda going on right now. He's going to be going to school, he's going to be making new friends." He reminded her of how Jimmy had taken to the new surroundings so quickly and that he'd been in good hands with Gabrielle and Susan. "A big part of what they do is teaching these kids how to be more self-sufficient and confident." He glanced at Jimmy who was earnestly trying to fold a piece of pita bread into eighths and giggling at the way it fell apart. "And you heard what they said about working around schedules. If you're not able to drop him off or pick him up, you can always ask me or your mom or — hey, for that matter, we can probably even recruit my mom to do it."

Kate shook her head. "He's not your responsibility and I can't change that."

John trailed his hand down her left arm to interlace her fingers with his, a touch that was almost unbearable in its genuine tenderness. "If that's the only thing causing you so much stress, honey, maybe I can change that. In fact, maybe I want to change that."

Honey. His smile was disarmingly generous, his courting of her senses both persuasive and chivalrously patient. If Jimmy hadn't been sitting only a few feet away from them at that moment.

"I just don't want anyone to take him away," she said.

"You mean Luke?"

"I mean anyone." It was one thing, she went on, that Gabrielle and Susan had made an exception to put him in their program and initiated arrangements for testing. "What happens after that, though? It's not going to be easy for me to jump through all the legal hoops as long as there's any angstrom of possibility Luke's going to say no to it."

"Well from what you've said, it's not exactly like he's been an active parent. Listen, you want me to talk to Mitch about it? Maybe he's got some ideas. For all his faults, he is an exceptional lawyer."

"I thought you two didn't get along."

"We don't, but nothing says I can't work on him through his future wife."

Kate suppressed a smile. "You make it sound so simple."

"Life should be simple."

***

"If a certain little someone weren't fading out on us," John remarked two hours later, "I'd recommend we hit the boardwalk and spend all our quarters on the Ferris wheel."

"Amazing it still even works," Kate opined, gently stroking Jimmy's hair as he lay curled up asleep on the blanket next to her. "Remember how it used to get stuck when we were at the very top and I was scared they'd never get us down?"

John laughed at her reminiscence. "Yeah, it's amazing how many mechanical breakdowns you can get if you slip the operator a five..."

"You set that up?"

"Of course, the going rate now's probably up to twenty,' he mused.

Kate shook her head. "Just when you think you've really gotten to know someone."

He was starting to gather up the rest of their picnic items. "If you think that's something, wait'll you hear about my boat."

She cast him a sidelong look of disbelief. "What boat?"

"I can't believe nobody's told you," he said in amazement, alluding to all the other gossip about him that had been flying around lately. "Then again, it's a good thing since now you can hear it from me first."

"Since how long have you had a boat?"

"Awhile," he cryptically replied. "Sort of a work-in-progress. I haven't had as much time as I'd like between the tree biz and helping out with Dad, but one of these days." He quietly added that Jeremy had worked on it with him a few months before he'd moved to Manhattan. "And, of course, Lenny's usually good for a half-hour of labor if I bribe him with enough free beer. Mostly, though, it's just me."

Kate confessed that she'd never really pictured him as a boat type. "Outdoorsy, yeah, but a boat?"

"Remember back in school when you used to look at the ocean and say you wished you had a boat so you could sail away from everything?"

C.J. Foster

She couldn't believe what she was hearing. "You...bought a boat...because of me?"

"Actually, I bought it for me," he corrected her. "You'd already left, remember?"

"Well, good for you," she said, still too flummoxed to know what to make of any of it. "So this boat of yours, dare I ask what you named it?"

She was half-expecting him to say "Kate".

"I didn't name it 'Kate', if that's what you're thinking."

"Of course not. Why should you? Like you said, I'd already left."

"I call it 'My Boat'," he announced.

" "My Boat'?"

"Yeah, I can't believe no one ever thought of that one, can you? Makes sense, though. I can say to people, 'Hey, want a ride on My Boat?' or 'Have you checked out My Boat?'"

"I get the picture," Kate said. "So where do you keep it?"

"Where else? Right here at the Bay."

Jimmy was now stirring and issuing a yawn big enough to turn himself inside out.

"Hey, Jimmy, want to go see My Boat?"

"Don't you think it's getting a little late?" Kate cautioned. "He's already had a really long day."

"Then what better way to top it off than seeing a beautiful boat under the stars? Come on, let's go put this stuff in the truck."

He stood up and gallantly offered her his hand.

"You are incorrigible," she teased him.

"Then I guess you won't mind if I do this," he replied.

Kate felt her knees weaken as his arm quickly encircled her waist, his free hand drawing her face toward his and tilting her chin for the kiss that had gone unclaimed for 14 years too long. When at last their embrace came to an end, the whisper of his breath on her cheek made her forget all sense of time and place. "Welcome home," he murmured.

The sound of Jimmy tipping over the picnic basket brought both of them back to the present.

"Looks like somebody wants us to get a move on," John remarked.

To which a suddenly unsleepy Jimmy shouted back at them, "My boat!"

Chapter Thirty-Five

"W hy does Jimmy keep saying 'my boat' over and over?" Lydia asked her the next morning over breakfast as they were getting him ready for his first day of school.

"Obviously, John's boat made a big impression on him," Kate answered. Truth be told, it had made an impression on her, too, with its spotless deck and a snug galley that he'd assured her was more than enough room to cook a gourmet meal.

"So he still has it then?"

"Still? You mean you knew about it?"

Lydia shrugged. "I assumed he sold it when he started his tree business." Boats took a lot of time, she pointed out, time that she couldn't imagine he had a lot of, especially considering everything else he was doing.

To Kate's surprise, her mother had asked very little about how her date the previous evening had gone. *Is it that obvious from my face*, she wondered. The memory of the second soul-drenching kiss when he'd brought them back home still lingered. A kiss that she was pretty sure wouldn't be the last.

Self-conscious that she was probably starting to blush, Kate steered the conversation away from John and started speculating aloud how busy Cliff planned to keep her with her new duties at the paper. "Still weird to me how he just jumped in and made a decision without even telling me," she said.

Lydia opined that it was no stranger than her former boss calling to tell her she no longer had a job.

Kate let the purposeful snub slide and replied instead, "Yeah, but isn't it kind of over-the-top putting the announcement on the front page? Must have been a pretty slow news week that he could move everything around the day before and make a space for it." She tried to remember what her old yearbook photo even looked like and hoped that her dated hairdo and makeup didn't look too ridiculous. *Would it have killed him*, she thought, *to just take a new one*?

Lydia predicted that the phone would probably be ringing off the hook with anyone and everyone in Avalon Bay wanting her to write feature stories about them once they found out who the new editor was. "You'll be lucky to even find the time to breathe."

With a pang of guilt, Kate realized that the rest of Cassy's boxes were still awaiting her attention.

"I think Jimmy could make a great first mate," John remarked as he filled a thermos with coffee.

Abby smiled. "I would have thought you'd want a certain young lady to have that title."

"First things first," he replied. "She's got to get Jimmy situated in school and figure out how busy Cliff's going to keep her. Speaking of which,"

Abby listened thoughtfully while he explained how it might take some juggling of schedules. "Things won't be squared away with her new office until Monday, but I was thinking maybe I could bring

Jimmy by for a little while when I get off work today and he could meet you and Dad."

"And Shelby," Abby added. "Does he like dogs?"

John smiled. "What kid doesn't?" Shelby happily thumped her tale as she gnawed on a rawhide bone under the kitchen table. "And what better dog to be his first than Shelby?"

"I swear you could have knocked me over with a feather," Yvette was gushing.

"You 'n' me both," Kate agreed. She had stopped by the newspaper after dropping Jimmy off at the school in order to fill out forms that would officially put her on the payroll.

"Well, that's our Cliff for you. And wasn't it just the funniest thing about that mix-up with your resume?"

"Hilarious." Kate paused a second as she came to the line about who to notify in case of emergency, realizing she had just been about to write in John's name without even thinking about it. She listed her mother instead.

"I'm so happy for you," Yvette continued. "Who'd have thought you'd come back to us after all this time and rescue a sinking ship!"

"Excuse me?"

"That came out wrong, didn't it? Not that it's really sinking per se, of course, but that chucklehead of an editor we had last time sure didn't do it any favors running it into the ground."

"I'm sure he wasn't that bad," Kate said, though in truth she'd heard very little lately to suggest otherwise about her predecessor.

"Well, I'm just glad you're here to give the ol' place some fresh ideas and a woman's point of view!"

Kate smirked. "To the extent your boss will let me." She glanced at the front page, as perturbed by the sight of her high school graduation picture as she was about the uninspired caption that conjured déjà vu.

"You mean our boss!" Yvette said in chirpy prelude to tripping down memory lane and reminding her of how much she'd always enjoyed the candy Kate used to bring in when she was still a student.

Note to self, Kate told herself. *Bring in candy.*

She returned to filling out forms but was interrupted yet again by the arrival of the last person in the world she wanted to see.

"Well, well," Brad remarked, "if it isn't Wonder Girl". He was holding a copy of the latest edition in his hand and now unfolded it as if to compare her to the black and white headshot. "You don't look a day over seventeen!"

"And you don't act a day over twelve," she glibly countered.

He laughed but his eyes held no humor. "Did I mention I'm one of this rag's biggest advertisers?"

His nasty insinuation of power, Kate thought, couldn't have been bigger if it were in neon and hung on the Ferris wheel. "How nice for you," she said and went back to studying her paperwork.

Sensing building friction between them, Yvette interjected herself into the conversation to exclaim how wonderful it was that Kate was going to be their new editor starting on Monday.

"So, I heard. I don't suppose I could talk you into a celebration dinner?" he offered with a cavalier wink. "My treat?"

"You never give up, do you, Brad?"

"Why should I? It's what's made me a success."

Kate and Yvette exchanged a glance, each mildly daring the other to be the one to point out that he'd only succeeded his father and that the large sums of money he bragged about managing all belonged to the bank.

Cliff chose that moment to open his office door. "Brad! What a surprise! I thought I heard your voice out here."

"You also have a meeting with him," Yvette said, tapping the face of her watch. "It's on your calendar."

"Have you said hello yet to our new editor?" Cliff asked him. As he opened his mouth to make introductions, Brad informed him that they'd gone to school together. "Kate," he arrogantly lied, "is the one who got away."

Kate couldn't resist facetiously quipping, "Can't say that about many girls in our class."

A silken thread of warning rippled through Brad's chuckle as he feigned admiration for Kate's joining the staff. "Threw me for quite a loop, though," he said. "I mean, isn't being a full-timer going to take away from your being on the mommy-track?"

"What mommy-track?" Cliff sputtered.

Yvette gasped in astonishment. "Oh my, Katie! Does that mean that you're…"

Brad's mouth lifted in a sarcastic smile.

"Just when you think you know how low a person can go," Kate told John on the phone, "they always surprise you and dive even lower." She had called him on his cell after giving herself some time to cool down. "Leave it to Brad to try to screw up a good thing."

"Are you talking about the job or about us?" John asked in concern. "'Cause frankly I don't think Brad has that much influence either way."

"Well, he did make things pretty embarrassing for me." She explained that she hadn't said anything earlier to Cliff or Yvette about her situation with Jimmy simply because she didn't think it was any of their business. "Although the way everybody likes to talk around here, I'm kinda surprised they didn't already know."

"It's not like he can fire you," John said. "There are laws against that."

"Technically, though, the ink's not even dry yet on my hiring papers. I suppose he could just say he changed his mind."

"After he already ran the announcement on the front page of his own paper?"

"Yeah, you got a point. Listen, I'm taking you away from work. I was just so mad."

John changed the subject and asked her how Jimmy had fared when she dropped him off that morning.

She asked him if he remembered the red-headed girl with the picture book. "She and her mom were already there when I arrived and he seemed pretty excited to see her. Of course, he panicked a little bit when he saw that I was leaving but I suspect he's doing just fine." Gabrielle and Susan, she added, were very thorough in explaining the various tests they'd be scheduling with the developmental pediatrician that worked with the school. "I don't want to get my hopes up," she said, "but they told me that a lot of times symptoms can get misdiagnosed and turn out to be something like a hearing problem or some kind of chemical imbalance that can be treated."

Cassy would be at peace, Kate thought, to know her son would finally be getting some consistency in his medical care instead of being shuffled through free clinics that dealt in seeing as many people in as little time as possible.

"So here's a thought," John proposed. "What if I pick you guys up after work and we take him over to meet my parents?"

Kate was dubious. "Wouldn't that be an imposition?"

"Nah, my mom's crazy about kids. And my dad, well, it might do my dad good to see a new face."

"I'm not sure," she replied, remembering the awkwardness of communicating with Sean at the front door. "Sometimes Jimmy can be, well, you know, unpredictable."

"Not that much different from my dad, then. I have a feeling they'll get along just fine."

Kate remembered that she'd promised Maria a beer when the latter got off work at the factory. "Mom was going to watch Jimmy."

John insisted that Lydia needed a break just as much as her daughter. "You've both been doing a lot of heavy lifting lately. What do you say we both take him over, you go have some fun and then come back and get him?" He even tossed in the bonus that she could borrow his truck to go meet Maria.

Kate smiled. "That's a lot to ask."

He reminded her that he was the one who had volunteered it. "So is that a 'yes'?"

"In the meantime, what should I do about Brad?"

John chuckled. "Brad is all talk and no action. There's nothing that buffoon can do that you and I can't handle."

Jimmy was exhausted but happy when Kate picked him up.

"He was a little shy at first about participating," Susan said, "but he's very good-natured."

"You haven't seen his stubborn side," Kate warned.

Gabrielle laughed. "And you've seen five-year-olds who aren't from time to time?"

They both asked a few more questions about Jimmy's father. "Naturally," said Susan, "we try to get as complete a health picture about both parents as we can. If, for instance, there's a genetic history in the family or if, and I do have to put this bluntly, any substance abuse issues or addictions that may have contributed to Jimmy's development while your sister was carrying him."

"I never knew much about Luke's family," Kate said, "but I can tell you he was a loose cannon in his lifestyle. In fact, my sister had almost called off the wedding because he was doing drugs."

"And your sister," Gabrielle gently asked, "was she part of that, too?"

"I want to say 'no', but I'm really not sure," Kate replied. "During the time they were together, we just weren't as close as we should have been. After she got pregnant, though, I know she wouldn't have done anything to endanger the baby or herself." She could feel her eyes starting to moisten. "She was the best mom she knew how to be under the circumstances."

"Looks like somebody had a good day," John remarked when he came to collect them.

"He's been Mr. Giggles ever since I brought him home," Kate said, adding in a wistful postscript that she wished he had the words to tell her all about it. "Want to help me look for his other shoe?"

"Comes at a price," he teased. His arms encircled her, one hand in the small of her back, his lips feather-touching hers with a tantalizing persuasion. It was a kiss for her tired soul to melt into and just enough to make her almost forget they were standing in the foyer of her mother's house.

Lydia cleared her throat. "Children and mothers in the room!" she announced, though there was no trace of the censure that had marked her earlier assessment of their relationship. She was also holding up Jimmy's missing shoe. "Looking for this?"

"I think she's warming up to me," John remarked as he helped his two favorite people into the front seat of the truck.

Kate had to ask again whether it wasn't too much trouble to keep Jimmy awhile. "I'm sure Maria would understand if I moved this off until next week."

"By next week," he replied, "she'll have circulated a rumor that I've kidnapped you. As I said, Mom's just fine with it and it'll give Jimmy a chance to play with Shelby. Besides," he added, "I have it on good authority somebody's making tacos tonight."

"Sure that's not a recipe for disaster?" She reminded him of her nephew's uninhibited zeal at their harbor picnic. "He's probably going to be wearing it if you don't watch him."

"Trust me."

I do. I really, really do.

She squeezed his free hand in response, her pulse quickening in the realization that happily-ever-after didn't get much better than this.

"I had Mom put Shelby upstairs with Dad so Jimmy could meet everybody one at a time," John explained as they approached the back door.

"Probably a good idea," Kate agreed, recalling how her encounter with Shelby had sent her ungracefully sprawling. She glanced down at Jimmy who was taking in the surroundings of a new backyard in between huge yawns. A good sign, she thought, that he'd be a manageable guest during the short time she was away. She was also relieved he hadn't grabbed the omnipresent Mr. Ollie to bring with him. As docile as Shelby was, John told her, it had taken him quite a while to train his pooch that not everything was her personal chew toy.

"We're home," John called out as they stepped into the kitchen.

Home. Kate repeated it in her mind, liking the warm sound of it.

Abby didn't see Jimmy at first, his small body hidden by the counter as she emerged from the living room. She had a big smile of greeting for Kate. "Bet you didn't recognize me without all the face goop," she joked.

Kate reached for Jimmy's hand. "Come on, honey. Let's say 'hi' to Mrs. Neal."

Jimmy suddenly decided to be shy and flattened himself out face-first against the wall beneath the counter.

"Oh, that's okay," Abby said, coming around the corner. "Sometimes when children are in a strange place." A look of surprise and a soft gasp escaped her lips when he turned at the sound of her voice, his eyes bright with defiance at a slight that, in his young mind, was either real or imagined.

Chapter Thirty-Six

I t was a reaction Kate was still trying to decipher as she sat in a booth across from Maria at Kelley's Bar. Abby had recovered quickly by saying that John hadn't warned her what a "handsome little heartbreaker" Jimmy was but, to Kate's ears, it didn't quite ring true. Nor was there any chance to ask John about it in private before she left. She had lingered only long enough to see how her nephew was going to cope with the adventure of encountering the boisterous Shelby when John brought the dog downstairs.

"Told you they'd hit it off," he had remarked in satisfaction, gently guiding Jimmy's hand down the length of Shelby's back and showing him how to scratch her behind the ears just the way she liked it. Though the German Shepherd could easily have knocked Jimmy down by virtue of her weight and canine energy, she seemed to sense that there was something special about him that called for patience.

"Are you paying any attention to what I just said?" Maria sharply cut into her thoughts.

C.J. Foster

"Sure," Kate replied, thankful that she'd been tuned in just enough to catch that her friend had something exciting to tell her. "You said you had a surprise."

"Guess."

"Uh - Animal, vegetable or mineral?"

"Oh, definitely animal," Maria replied, "with a potential for some very major mineral if I play my cards right."

"You're making it too easy. Tony proposed and he's giving you a rock?"

Maria tossed back her head and laughed at her friend's reply. "That is so second-grade. You can do better."

"Afraid I can't," Kate confessed. "I'm not exactly focused lately."

Maria decided to cut her some slack in light of all the things Kate had earlier divulged in order to bring her up to speed. "Okay, here's the deal. I'm quitting the factory. My last day's two weeks from tomorrow."

"What?"

"You should see the look on your face," Maria teased. "You thought I'd be there forever or what?'

"No, it's just that," *All right, truth be told, I did think you'd be there forever.* "So what are you going to do?"

Maria excitedly explained that she'd applied for a secretarial job on a lark and got the call that she'd aced the interview. "I'm going to be in real estate at Martinez and Martinez!" she proudly announced.

Of all the career paths Kate might have imagined her high school chum pursuing, real estate probably wasn't one of the ones that would first have sprung to mind. Especially considering that it called for a wardrobe beyond jeans and logo sweatshirts.

"The deal is," Maria continued, "that I'm going to start answering phones and stuff and running searches of neighborhood listings so buyers and sellers can see how a certain house fares in the market compared to others."

"I suppose that could be interesting," Kate remarked, still distracted by thoughts of how Jimmy was doing at Sean and Abby's and whether he was behaving.

"So, anyway, I'm in there on the morning of the interview and I'm leaving the office and this really cute guy named Charles walks in." Maria giggled. "And I guess he thought I already worked there 'cuz he said he was looking to buy a house for himself in Rumson and did I have any ideas." Rumson, Maria reminded her, was the address of choice for musicians, movie stars and absolutely anybody who was anybody worth knowing. "You probably have to make six figures to even walk down the sidewalk," she said. "Anyway, I must've made a hot impression 'cuz they wanted me to start right away."

"Tony must be really proud of you."

"Yeah, but let me tell you more about this Charles guy who's a stockbroker and he's not married, and he wears these cute little glasses that make him look like a grown-up Harry Potter."

The passage of years, Kate realized, clearly hadn't dulled her ability to read Maria like a book and recognize where this breathless story was headed. She waited, however, until Maria had finished extolling the endless virtues of the perfect Mr. Charles Bailey, III to inquire what she and Tony were going to do to celebrate her new career.

"Well, you see the thing of it is," Maria replied, "Tony and me, we've kinda been drifting apart."

"Could've fooled me."

"No, seriously," Maria insisted. "Besides, weren't you the one who told me Tony was way too young for me?"

"And, uh, this Charles person?"

"You wouldn't believe all the things we have in common!"

"All this from just one conversation in an office doorway?"

"It was a meaningful conversation."

"Meaningful enough that he already knows you've got him in your sights?"

Maria laughed. "You make me sound like a big-game huntress or something."

"Let me rephrase it then," Kate said. "Where does this leave Tony, a.k.a., the great love of your life?"

"Oh, come on, Kate. We've always known it wouldn't last forever. Not like you and John. Speaking of which, are you guys gonna be needing a house? I could start looking at listings for you."

Maria's insistence that they get something to eat made it much later than Kate had intended when she finally returned to the Neal house. She walked around to the backyard and was surprised to see John by himself about to take some dishes inside. "Hey, what did you do with everybody?" she asked.

"Mom's calling it an early night," he replied. He was wearing a conspiratorial smile. "Come on in. I want to show you something."

She followed him inside, through the kitchen, and then heeded his finger-to-lips instruction to be quiet before they went into the living room.

Shelby looked up from her spot on the floor and thumped her tail but she, too, obeyed John's signal for silence. Across the room, the TV was on but the two who had been watching it on the couch were sound asleep, Sean Neal with his head tilted back on the top cushion and his good arm draped protectively around the small bundle nestled next to him.

"Looks like somebody was worried for nothing," John softly whispered.

Her mood was suddenly buoyant again, warmed by the sight of the two figures on the couch and wishing she had been there to watch it all unfold. The questions tumbled out of her as soon as she and John were back outside beneath the stars.

"Dad was a little confused at first when I brought him down," John explained. "Kept wanting to call him 'Germy.'"

The name jogged something in Kate's memory. "Same thing you used to call your brother when you thought he was being a pest."

John nodded thoughtfully in reminiscence. "Yeah, Mom noticed it, too."

It was as good a time as any to ask him why Abby had reacted the way she did when she first saw him.

"Well, she's not going to come out and say anything," John candidly replied, "but I know she thought the same thing I did when I first saw him."

"You mean that he sorta looks like you?'

"More so that he looks like Jeremy. Not that you can blame her, I guess. When you lose someone you love, it takes a long time, if ever, for even the smallest reminders of them to fade away." In the weeks and months following his younger brother's death, he related that his mom often found herself running up to strangers who looked like Jeremy from the back.

Kate suddenly felt guilty that as innocent an act as introducing her to her nephew had triggered such tragic memories. "Maybe this wasn't such a good idea," she murmured.

"What are you talking about? It was a great idea. Besides," he said, warmly cupping her face in his hands, "you two are a package deal as far as I'm concerned. I'd like him to spend as much time here as he wants."

"Sure you know what you're getting into?"

His hands slipped down her arms, bringing her closer. "Oh, I bet I've pretty much got it figured out."

Gazing into his eyes sent the universe giddily spinning around her. "I may need some time to think about that, Mr. Neal," she coyly replied, though in truth she knew it was exactly what she wanted as well. *A family. A husband. A future.*

"So tell me what I missed tonight," she said after a moment, enjoying the contentment of being held and feeling as if they truly had all the time in the world.

"Well, he was a little shy right after you left but then he started picking things up and taking them over to Dad's lap. And when it came time to eat, it's the funniest thing but he wanted to be right there next to him." Both of his parents, he went on, seemed to enjoy all the boundless energy he had. "And, of course, he and Shelby are best buds now."

"Just like you said they'd be."

He shrugged. "When I'm right, I'm right. Oh, and by the way, I'm going to build him his own treehouse."

"A treehouse? Do you think that's wise?" A momentary shudder coursed through her body at the thought of Jimmy losing his balance and falling out.

John assured her there'd be nothing about it to put him in danger. "Did I forget to mention it's only going to be six inches off the ground?"

Kate laughed. "Okay, but why a treehouse?"

"Why not?" From what he'd been reading recently about autism, John explained that special needs children liked having cozy cubbies where they could watch the world and not feel threatened.

"He does seem to like hiding under the kitchen table a lot," she recalled. "Of course, now I'm jealous I never had one when I was his age."

"Then I guess I'll just have to make yours my next project."

A fallen oak on one of John's biggest clients' home precluded seeing one another again before dinner on Sunday. Though Kate tried to rationalize that it would give her time to go through more of Cassy's belongings as well as to pick her mother's brain for potential newspaper stories, she'd have been lying to herself to say she didn't miss him. Sunday, she decided, just couldn't come fast enough.

An email from Dee reminded her that she hadn't filled her in yet on what was going on and she made herself a glass of lemonade before sitting down to answer it. Funny, Kate reflected, that the last time they'd talked was when, in Lydia's words, Dee had pulled the rug out from under her. *I'll have to tell her that it actually turned into a flying carpet.*

Dee, of course, was nothing less than ecstatic that she'd found a new job so soon. As for Kate's news about getting back together with John, her former boss didn't seem all that surprised. "I wish I'd bet money on it, girlfriend," she wrote, punctuating it with a trail of smiley faces.

She noted with amusement Dee's postscript that a few celebrities had told her to tell Kate 'hello'.

I'm definitely not in Oz anymore. Kate couldn't help but smile and be thankful for the quirky road that had brought her back home where she belonged.

The doorbell rang a few minutes after five while Kate was still in a tank top, a pair of yellow capris, and barefoot.

What might have been initial panic that John was nearly an hour early was quickly replaced by excitement. With Lydia upstairs helping Jimmy with his bath so he'd be clean and presentable for company, the promise of time alone, however brief, with the man she loved caused Kate to enthusiastically fly to the front door and fling it open.

Except that it wasn't John.

"So I hear you've got my kid," Luke said, drawing a long drag on his cigarette before flippantly dropping it on the porch and grinding it out with the pointed toe of his snakeskin boot.

Chapter Thirty-Seven

By any definition of the word, John could claim it to be a great week, a week that was about to culminate in asking Kate Toscano if she'd do him the honor of becoming his wife. There were those, of course, who'd probably tell him he was rushing things. The truth, though, was exactly the opposite, a reality brought home to him as he withdrew the small black box that had been residing in the drawer of his bedside table for the past fourteen years.

His memory flashed briefly on all the agony he'd put himself through in trying to find just the right ring. There'd been only one jewelry store in Avalon Bay that year and goodness knew that if he had ever paused more than a nanosecond at its window displays, word would have spread like wildfire from one end of the town to the other that he was going to propose. His worst dread was that Kate would hear about his intentions before he got the chance to declare them.

It seemed funny now to remember how he'd hatched the plan to buy her ring out of town where he wouldn't encounter anyone he knew who might blab. At his first choice, Spring Lake, he ran into two of his mother's best friends. At the Mall, he ran into Lenny. The belief that no one would possibly recognize him in the sprawling mecca of Atlantic City backfired when he ran into none other than Kate herself out shopping for bikinis with Maria.

And so in desperation, he had resorted to the one venue left that would assure relative anonymity, an online jewelry site that could express his purchase to him for an extra charge of $19.95. He had even planned his whole schedule around getting to the mailbox first, a feat he might have accomplished if a nauseous Jeremy hadn't come home early from school after lunch that day and beat him to it. At least, John reflected, his younger sib had put it on his bedroom dresser instead of leaving it out in plain sight.

Whether or not Jeremy told anyone about it became a moot point within twenty-four hours. The same mailman who had delivered John's order had also delivered Kate's acceptance letter to college. The part of John that wanted to give her the ring anyway was canceled out by the part that knew it was wrong to force her to make that kind of a choice.

And so there it had sat in the drawer until now.

He opened the box, uncertain of what additional memories it might unleash. Instead, he saw a simple white-gold band with three small diamonds; a ring that almost seemed too ordinary and commonplace for the accomplished and beautiful woman she'd become. He glanced at the bedside lamp, wondering whether there was enough time to rush out and replace it with something more befitting and worthy of her. And this time, unlike before, he didn't care how many people saw him or who knew how much he loved her.

The phone rang.

It was Lenny asking him if he wanted to play some stick and catch a flick.

"Already got plans," John told him. "I'm going to Kate's."

Lenny groaned that if he kept it up he was going to become domesticated and wouldn't be fun to hang out with anymore.

By the time Lenny finally signed off, it was too late for John to go look in any jewelry store windows. With dismay, he realized it was also too early to show up for dinner. If there was one thing he'd learned about being a guest, people always freaked out if they weren't quite ready for you.

Luke's mouth spread into a thin-lipped smile as he tried to look past her into the house. "Aren't you going to invite me in? Sis?"

Time had improved neither his unkempt looks and grunge threads nor the ingrained indifference of his manners. His lanky frame easily topped six feet by several inches and, from just the visible preview of his sinewy arms and neck, was no stranger to tattoo parlors. Kate inwardly shuddered that he'd ever had a physical relationship with Cassy, much less given her a child. *If I slam this door in his pock-marked face, he'll only put his fist through it.*

Determined not to show that his attitude or his scrutiny could intimidate her, she asked him what he was doing there.

"Three guesses," he responded with a sneer, "and the first two don't count. You got something of mine and I'm here to collect."

She firmly informed him that he'd come at a bad time.

Luke snorted in disdain. "Yeah, well I've been havin' a bad year!" he replied, nastily counting off the particulars on his fingers. "My ol' lady buys it, my drummer gets busted for meth, and my kid gets grabbed by his do-gooder aunt!"

Her adrenaline level began to furiously rise, fueled by the sight of an empty car parked on the street. The one he'd come in and, quite possibly, the one he was planning to take Jimmy in. If it came to that, she'd have to do whatever she could to stop him. "There's a time and a place for us to talk about that."

"There's no 'us' in any of this!" he hotly snapped, taking a menacing step closer. "He's me 'n' Cassy's kid and I just dropped two gigs in Frisco to fly the hell back here! Now, are you gonna give 'im to me or not?"

"You're in no position to make those demands, Luke." She could hear that the water had stopped running upstairs and talked louder so that her mom might hear their heated conversation. "And if you don't stop yelling, I'm going to have to ask you to leave."

"You stole my kid!" he accused her with hatred blazing in his bloodshot eyes. "They can lock you up for that!"

"What happens next is for the courts to decide."

He repeated the accusation she'd gone behind his back in Vegas and that there were laws against it.

"There are also laws against deserting your child." She informed him that they'd been trying to locate him since Cassy's death but hadn't had any success owing to his transient lifestyle. "Where did you expect your son to go?" she challenged him. "He doesn't even know you!"

He ignored her question, replying instead that she'd been asking the wrong people. "When you got the right friends," he boasted, "stuff has a way of gettin' done." An oily tone crept into his voice. "And I do mean gettin' done permanent."

Kate's eyes conveyed the rage within that he dared to think he could threaten her. Responding in kind, though, was probably exactly what he wanted and it took every ounce of control for her to tell him they had nothing further to talk about.

"You can't keep me from takin' my own kid," he cut her off. "I'll be back for him."

And with that, he turned, swaggered across the grass, and drove off.

A sheer panic like she'd never known before welled in Kate's throat and whatever residual discipline she'd employed to keep from shaking in Luke's creepy presence was now completely drained as she scrambled to deadbolt the front door.

"Is he gone?" Lydia called down.

"For now, at least." She hurried upstairs and clung to her mother outside the bathroom door. Jimmy, oblivious to the drama that had been just transpired, was happily splashing in the tub with the new bath toys his grandmother had bought him.

C.J. Foster

"If he'd tried to come up here," Lydia said, "I would've locked us in the bathroom and screamed my head off out the window for help."

Kate smiled despite her frazzled nerves. "I really need to get you a cell phone, Mom."

"Well, it was either that or clobbering him good with a lamp." No jury would convict her, she maintained, since it clearly would have been self-defense. "We should call the police," she said in her next breath. "Maybe they can catch him."

"And do what, exactly?" Kate said, infuriated with the compromising position he'd just put them in. "It's going to be my word against his and you know darned well the first thing he's going to tell them is that we kidnapped his child." She glanced at Jimmy and feared for the worst. "We can't let them take him away."

Lydia was appalled that such a thought would even enter the equation. "Just one look at that filthy man and they're going to know he's not even suitable to raise a houseplant!"

"Unless it's weed."

Lydia pounced on her daughter's response to suggest that the police could arrest him for drugs. "Do you think he was on something? Did he look crazy? You know they don't stand for that kind of gang stuff in Avalon Bay."

"He's not in a gang, Mom, and even if he did get busted for possession, it's not going to make him go away." Her mind was racing the entire time her mother was talking.

"I don't see how he even got here in the first place. Did he say he flew?"

"Could've just been an expression. Frankly, I don't know how he could have sprung for a ticket." With fares as pricey as they were, she opined, it'd be more likely he'd use that kind of money to support his sleazy lifestyle.

"You know if you hadn't started looking for him," Lydia cynically pointed out, "he'd never have known."

"Unfortunately," Kate said, "that might have put us in even more trouble. To get a guardianship, you have to show you've done everything you can to find the missing parent."

Unspoken between them was the irony that they should have been rooting for failure instead of success.

Jimmy was now gleefully squealing and tossing his wet toys out of the tub. As Lydia crossed over to calm him down, she reiterated that she still thought that calling the police was a good idea in case Luke came back later that night. "Of course, I'd like to see his face if John is the one to answer the door."

With a start, Kate realized that in the aftermath of her brother-in-law's ugly visit, she had totally forgotten John was even coming.

"Your mom's right about notifying the police," he said after they filled him in on what had transpired. "If they've got a heads-up that this guy could make trouble while he's here, you need to tell them as much as you can remember about what he said to you."

Kate was adamant about the risk that someone from the county's Child Protective Services would want to remove Jimmy to foster care in the interim of a court fight and that he'd be scared and confused.

"Which is exactly what the county folks don't want to have happen," John assured her. "The stability you and your mom are giving him right now is going to count big-time. And don't forget Gabrielle and Susan. You've got them in your corner who'll vouch that taking him away from you could have catastrophic effects."

The mention of Jimmy's school set the alarm bells ringing even louder in Kate's head. "What if he tries to go see him while I'm at work?" An expletive escaped her lips in the remembrance that tomorrow was Monday, her first day at the newspaper. Cliff would be expecting her bright and early. "I'll just have to call and tell him something's come up," she said.

"And what about the next day?" John asked. "And the day after that?" He squeezed her hands tightly in his own. "You can't let this guy scare either one of you into changing your whole routine."

"But what if," Lydia started to say.

"'What if *if* is all he's got," he interrupted her. "You can drive yourselves crazy trying to guess what his next move's going to be but until he actually does something, you can't let it take all your energy."

He asked Kate to repeat what Luke had told her about his having friends. "I didn't think he was even from around here."

"He's not," she said. Nor, she added, could she imagine anyone in their right mind loaning him money for airfare or motel rooms.

"Or a lawyer," Lydia piped up.

"Even if they did," John pointed out, "he's got to be on a tight clock. I think his end game's to scare you into giving him money to make him go out of your lives so he can scurry back to that rock he crawled out from."

Kate reminded him of Luke's demands that she give him his son.

"Only because he knew you wouldn't," John said. "That's why I also don't think he's going to do anything illegal to try to take him." It was further consistent, he noted, that Luke hadn't divulged where he was staying or given her a number to call. "All part of the intimidation to keep the ball in his court and make you wonder when he's going to pop up next."

"Well, it's not like we couldn't call the motels around here and ask if he's registered," Lydia suggested. "Wouldn't it help to know where the little creep is staying?"

"As creepy as he is, he's also got the right not to be followed around. But we'll let the police make that call. Whoever he says his friends are, have probably already told him that."

Lydia wanted to know if they could at least assign someone to keep an eye on the house.

"Only in the movies, I'm afraid. If you're worried, though, there's no problem with Jimmy staying at our place for a couple of days." He winked at Kate. "And I'm sure Shelby wouldn't mind sleeping on the bed and playing guard dog. Besides, he probably already knows about me and that I was a cop. He'll think twice about coming to my house."

Kate reminded him of his own words about not changing their whole routine.

"Then I'll change mine," he gallantly offered, "and lay a sleeping bag on this side of the front door." He smiled.

The oven timer went off, causing both women to jump.

"I'll go see to dinner," Lydia excused herself, though, in truth, none of them except Jimmy felt much like eating.

John pulled Kate into the loving protection of his strong arms. "Whatever it takes, honey, nobody gets to you without having to go through me," he promised.

A hot tear rolled down her cheek. "I don't want to lose him."

"And I don't want to lose either one of you."

It wasn't until he returned home after dinner and felt the ring still in his pocket that he realized the evening had ended quite a bit differently than he originally planned.

Chapter Thirty-Eight

K ate and her mother had taken little comfort in their conversation with the police, save for the exercise of now having their concerns on file. Lydia lamented that she hadn't looked out the window and tried to get a number off the car. "Can't you just call around to the rental places until you find which one rented to him?" she had asked while the report was being taken.

The female officer had been sympathetic but firm in her response that they not only didn't have the manpower but also lacked the justification to do that. "The best I can tell you is to just be cautious and to notify us if he makes any contact that you feel is of a threatening nature." She also dissuaded them from doing anything that could be construed as trying to purposely hide Jimmy from his father. "It will be up to the courts to work out the custody or visitation issues but until that happens you ladies need to play everything as straight and above-board as possible."

It was John who accompanied Lydia to school to drop off Jimmy and explain the situation to Susan and Gabrielle. "Nothing's going to happen to your little man on our watch," Susan assured them.

For Kate, there was at least one bright spot in that Yvette had forgotten to call and tell her that the office was being repainted Monday afternoon and so she'd only be able to work in it for the first part of the day. With Cliff out of town for the morning, she wasn't going to be under as bright a spotlight as she'd anticipated. Girded with resolve to maintain her focus, Kate hunkered down to the task of learning her new responsibilities.

She was on the phone with John just before the painters came when Yvette brought her the mail. "Now are you going to be wanting me to open everything for you and staple the envelopes to the backs of the letters?" she asked. Kate's predecessor, she explained, had always been very secretive and never wanted her to open anything. Yvette voiced her opinion that it only went to prove he was doing something shady. "And, of course, anything addressed directly to Cliff," she said, "I'm not supposed to touch at all."

"Since it doesn't look like very much," Kate observed, "I'll just go ahead and do it for today. We can work out some kind of system later on after I get settled in."

Yvette seemed satisfied with that and ambled back out to her desk.

Kate reached for the plastic letter opener, glancing briefly at her new surroundings. It had been so long since she'd worked in an actual office instead of at home that she'd have to give some thought to decorating it. *Maybe some large framed prints from Pier One*, she mused. *And plants. This place could use some greenery to spiff it up.*

And then there was the matter of her desk. Except for a computer monitor, a phone, and a box of office supplies Yvette had scared up for her, the surface was devoid of personality. *Pictures*, Kate thought. And in her mind's eye, she fondly imagined a happy collection of photographs of Jimmy and John and her mom and—

She stopped just short of thinking the word "wedding". *Day at a time*, she told herself. *It's not as if he's even asked me.*

She reached for the next envelope, noting in surprise that it bore her name. *Word does travel fast in this town*, she thought, amused that everything she'd opened so far had either been addressed to the man who previously occupied her chair or simply said the words "Gazette Editor".

The return address was a local law firm.

The contents, though amicable on the surface, affirmed her worst fears.

She'd been reluctant to call John back and tell him about it, justifying that she was already taking enough of his time. Yet when she got home and showed the correspondence to her mother, the very first thing the latter did was ask whether she'd told him about it.

"What I don't understand," Kate said, "is how Luke could even afford a lawyer."

Though the name of the law firm meant nothing to either of them, what was particularly unsettling was that the correspondence had been sent to the newspaper instead of to the house. Kate quietly thanked her lucky stars that Yvette hadn't opened it first and peppered her with intrusive questions about what it all meant.

Lydia reminded her that Luke had said he'd just flown in from the West coast. "So, he couldn't have known about your job, much less hired somebody last week to mail the letter for it to arrive on a Monday."

The timing was all wrong and it was driving Kate crazy to think he may have been spying on them.

"I suppose I shouldn't have done it," her mother confessed, "but I spent this morning calling around to area motels." She shook her head. "He must have registered under another name because nobody's got any record of him." In response to her daughter's puzzled look, Lydia sheepishly replied that she'd watched enough episodes of *Murder, She Wrote* to know motel clerks would tell you practically anything if you convincingly pretended to be somebody else on the phone. "I told them I was his mother," she said, "and explained he was on a trip and I couldn't remember where he'd told me he was staying." Unfortunately and with regret, she related no one had heard of him.

Kate voiced the alternative that he was sleeping in his car.

"And whoever he hired wouldn't know this about him?" Lydia said in disgust.

"Who knows why people do things sometimes?" Kate replied, reminded of how many times she'd read about lawyers representing dirtbags in high profile murder cases and wondering what possessed them to plead for their freedom. "Maybe it's just another job to this guy. As long as the check clears, he probably doesn't even care."

"You can't put off calling him back," John advised that evening as he read the contents of the attorney's letter. "If nothing else, it'll help you get a feel for what they're planning to go for."

"Shouldn't I get a lawyer first?" Kate asked, overwhelmed by the thought of yet another expense she hadn't seen coming. In the back of her mind, there still hovered what John had said earlier about the possibility of Luke wanting to be paid to go away. Whether it went to court or was settled outside of it, it was a sure bet that resolution wouldn't come cheap.

They were sitting outside watching Jimmy and Mr. Ollie watching the tree. John had brought over a yardstick and a magic marker so that Jimmy could learn to associate his tree's growth with the color marks and the numbers on the ruler. Now and then, Jimmy would suddenly clap his hands, point at the yardstick, and toss Mr. Ollie up in the air.

"What are you thinking?" John quietly asked when he caught Kate in an extended pause of contemplation.

"Kodak moment," she replied. "I want to always remember us just like this." She indicated the letter that John had set down on the patio table. "For the first time in his life, Jimmy's finally got a chance to have everything Cassy wanted for him but could never have given him. If Luke wins and takes this away."

"Which he won't."

"Which he could if we can't afford to fight him."

"Well, for what it's worth," he offered, "I'm going to call Mitch first thing in the morning and see if he has any ideas. Maybe Mindy, too. She used to clerk for a judge who did a lot of divorce cases. Maybe there's something we just haven't thought of."

His smile reached the depths of his eyes and Kate took comfort in his nearness. There was so much more that she wanted from him right now and yet she couldn't allow herself to completely relax until everything with Luke was behind them.

"I've missed you," she murmured. He lightly touched his fingertips to her lips to keep her from saying anything more.

"I know, honey. I've missed you, too."

Sleep was impossible for Kate that night. At least twice she'd gotten up to check on Jimmy, mindful of the pressing need to reassure herself no one had taken him. Down the hall, she thought she heard the faint sounds of a movie playing and realized that her mother was having just as hard a time. She had almost tapped on the door to ask if she should make them some tea, then thought better of it. Any conversation they might have would cover the same frustrating ground they'd been on since Sunday.

And so she turned instead to the two remaining boxes of Cassy's possessions.

Overall, there'd been few clothes to speak of that could be donated to charity. Nor would the shirts and pants that were Jimmy's have much use left in them considering that he was already exhibiting healthy signs of growing. She smiled in remembrance of John's promise to make the three of them his "world-famous" hot Belgian waffles with vanilla ice cream the next time they came over.

She pulled out an envelope full of loose snapshots, noting in dismay that several of them were pictures of Cassy and Luke in happier times. *Happier times. Now there's a misnomer*, she thought, wondering how her sister could have known as little as a single day of bliss with someone as irresponsible and hot-headed as Luke.

There were several of Luke by himself and Luke with his bandmates. Kate's initial impulse was to vent her anger and rip them into a million pieces over the wastebasket. The only thing that stopped her was the unsettling speculation that someday Jimmy might want to have them. Though it seemed unlikely Luke would ever mature and clean up his act, he had nevertheless fathered a child, a child who might be curious about what he looked like or what kind of clothes he'd worn. Certainly, she and Cassy had had no shortage of laughs when they were young girls and thought their parents' hairstyles and prom pictures were the funniest stuff they'd ever seen. *Someday maybe you'll be good for the same thing, Luke. A lot of stupid laughs.*

It was the odd assemblage of knickknacks that Kate had the hardest time trying to decide whether she should toss or keep. However small or silly, they were items that had meaning only to Cassy. Kate's heart broke in silence as she tried to will them into talking to her and telling her their respective stories. *I should keep these for Jimmy*, she rationalized, though it was closer to the truth to say that she wanted to keep them for herself so she'd have something, anything, that her sister had once held dear.

It was nearly 3:30 in the morning as she got to the bottom of the remaining box and found another large envelope containing letters, postcards, and, to Kate's anguished surprise, every birthday and holiday card her sister had probably ever received. She glanced briefly at the backs of several of the postcards. Un-dated cheery greetings from friends who dotted their I's with hearts and told her to come and visit "soooooooon". Had Cassy ever made any of those trips, Kate wondered. Or was she already too absorbed in trying to reform Luke and live the American Dream?

She sifted through some of the birthday cards and recognized her mother's handwriting among them. Two of them specifically mentioned a check that was enclosed. All of them were signed "with love". None of them included Luke's name on either the envelope or in the salutation.

Kate hesitated over the small stack of letters. Whoever had written to her sister had done so with the honest expectation that she would be the only one to ever read the contents. It would be a violation of trust and privacy to open them now, she thought, and yet she couldn't deny her curiosity and desperation to know who had taken the time to put their chatty news down on paper and put a stamp on it. *Did anyone even write letters anymore?* She'd once remarked to Dee that sending emails these days was like writing on air; unless you purposely printed out a hard copy, whatever information was conveyed could evaporate as if it had never existed, leaving a receiver to rely solely on his or own memory.

She looked at the clock again, annoyed that if she stayed up much longer, she'd be totally punchy and functionally useless for the new day ahead. With a sigh, she put the letters on the nightstand. They'd just have to wait until later.

Chapter Thirty-Nine

J ohn called her the next morning before she'd even finished her first cup of coffee.

"Mitch is at a corporate offsite until Thursday," he said, "but I got hold of Mindy."

"By calling her at the crack of dawn?" Kate asked. "That's no way to endear yourself to your future sister-in-law."

"Maybe not, but she was good with it, especially when I told her what was going on. Anyway, she had a great idea that could buy us some time when you call the guy back."

"I'm all ears."

"You're gonna love this," he said. "She said you should tell him that Luke needs to take a paternity test."

"Excuse me? Where does the 'great' part fit into this? We already know he's the father."

"I know we know," John replied, "and that's where he's going to trip up if he's only trying to scare you into getting him to leave and never return."

"I'm not following."

"Paternity tests freak guys out because if they prove someone's a father it means there's going to be a financial responsibility to support that child until it's eighteen. Right now, Luke's probably only thinking about a payout of some sort. He blows into town to make things as ugly as possible for you in the hope that you'll do whatever you have to, pay him whatever it takes, in order to keep things the way they are."

Kate was dubious about defiling her late sister's reputation by raising any suggestion that Jimmy was anyone's other than her husband.

John was silent a moment. "At the end of the day, I think you have to ask yourself what Cassy would have wanted. When you and I were watching Jimmy play last night and you told me how much you wanted the moment to always be that happy and peaceful. It can be, Kate. And I'm going to do everything I can to make sure that it is."

She called the attorney from her cell phone before she entered the newspaper office, not wanting to take any chance of being overheard by Yvette or Cliff. A pleasant female voice on the other end of the line replied that Mr. Graham was going to be in court all day and did she want to leave a voicemail for him. Kate thanked her and said "yes".

As his outgoing message played, Kate glanced heavenward, hoping that Cassy was looking down on her and blessing what she was about to do.

"Mr. Graham, this is Kate Toscano. I'm sorry I didn't get back to you earlier and I understand you're out of the office today. I certainly look forward to discussing this matter at your convenience. Before we proceed, however, I'd like to respectfully ask that you arrange for your client to take a paternity test. Please advise when this can be done."

***

There'd been two chances in as many days to pop the question and yet here he was, still walking around with an engagement ring in his pants pocket. On the one hand, John reminded himself that Kate had too many things going out right now and might turn him down. On the other hand, he didn't want her to say "yes" just because everything else was falling apart and he happened to represent the nearest available port in a storm.

As recently as that morning, he had contemplated leaving it at home in a drawer and just waiting until life returned to a peaceful state of calm. Waiting too long, though, was what had caused him to lose her the first time and he couldn't bear the thought of it happening again. And so he continued to carry it around. The next window of opportunity, when it came, wasn't going to be preempted for lack of preparation.

As he started to unload equipment off his truck at his first appointment of the day, the garage door was opening next door and a charcoal Lexus slowly emerged into the summer sunlight. Was there anyone in Rumson, John mused, who didn't drive a classy car or send their children to the nicest schools?

"Excuse me," a male voice called out to get his attention. The driver was leaning his head out of the window just enough for John to recognize him as someone he'd seen on television. He asked John if he had a business card on him. "I've got a couple of trees in the back that need looking at," he explained. "What do you charge?"

It was typical of how this business worked, John reflected, as well as a testament to how he'd been able to grow it from scratch. People saw him on a job or asked their friends for a referral and, before he knew it, he was getting more work than he'd imagined possible. Maybe even enough, he thought, that someday he just might own a house in Rumson himself.

He smiled.

Rumson would be a good place to raise a family.

Yvette tapped on Kate's door just before lunchtime to tell her she had a visitor. Kate instantly tensed. If it were John, Yvette would simply have said so.

"Did he give a name?" she warily inquired.

"It's a she," Yvette said, calling over her shoulder into the outer office to ask the visitor what her name was.

"Maria," Maria said.

"Maria," Yvette dutifully repeated. "Shall I send her in?"

"My, aren't we the fancy one!" Maria exclaimed as she was admitted to what she quipped was the "inner sanctum". She held out a small potted plant. "I thought you'd like this for the new digs."

"Thanks. I was just thinking about getting some greenery for in here." She noted the time. "Listen, I've got to clear out so some painters can come in. Want to go to lunch?"

"Love to," Maria replied.

"I didn't tell you that Charlie's a Brit? Hey, maybe you could write a story about him!"

"Charlie?"

"Honestly, Kate, don't you remember anything I tell you?" She refreshed Kate's memory that he was the rich guy with the Harry Potter glasses. "Of course, he was only born in London and came here when he was a baby so he doesn't even have an accent."

Tony, Kate determined, had apparently already slipped into the realm of past tense.

"Anyway," Maria excitedly went on, "you were on the way and I wanted to bring you the plant." She was meeting her new beau for coffee just down the street.

"Well at least I can walk with you part way," Kate offered. "There's something I need to ask you."

"Spill."

"Not here," Kate said. "Wait 'til we're outside."

"So why the mystery?" Maria asked when they were half a block away.

Kate prefaced her question by praising that nobody knew Avalon Bay and the people who lived and worked there better than she did. "Ever hear of Frank Graham?"

"You mean the lawyer?" Maria responded. "What do you need a lawyer for?"

"I don't. His name came up and I just wondered what kind of guy he was."

Maria immediately assumed that there was already a problem in the paradise known as John & Kate World and that the latter was thinking about playing the field for a while.

"John and I are fine," Kate assured her. "I only wanted to know if you knew anything about his background."

"Only that he's bad news."

"Oh?"

"Well, what else would you expect from anyone who's a stooge of Brad Leister?"

"Maybe it's just a coincidence," Lydia said when Kate related what Maria had told her. "Someone as prominent in this town as Brad is bound to know lots of lawyers and doctors and business people."

"And how many of them could he coerce into doing whatever he wanted them to do?"

"But why?"

"Because he likes to ruin things, Mom. He always has. What I can't figure out, though, is how he'd make the connection to Luke." She flashed back on her brother-in-law's boast about having friends who could make things happen. "And if you flip it, there's no way someone like Luke would even know to seek him out, much less win him over." Whatever was going on, she continued, had to have all been put in place before Luke ever showed up at their front door.

Lydia suddenly turned pale. "Oh my God," she murmured, turning to look at Kate with eyes that were full of guilt.

"What is it?"

"The evening I invited Brad to dinner," she began, "the evening you got mad and took Jimmy and left, do you remember?"

Kate urged her to go on.

"He seemed so concerned about how you were doing and was asking a lot of questions. I didn't read anything into it at the time because I was still thinking he'd be so perfect for you." She paused. "I think I may have told him that you weren't Jimmy's legal guardian and how afraid you were that Luke might show up and try to take him away."

The enormity of what she'd inadvertently done began to sink in.

"Oh, Kate, I'm so very sorry. I had no idea."

Kate nodded thoughtfully, Brad's motives now becoming clear to her. *Divide. Conquer. Destroy.* It was the only motto a person as arrogant as Brad lived by.

The phone rang and a shaken Lydia went to pick it up. She came back a moment later to tell Kate that it was Frank Graham returning her call.

"I've spoken with my client about your request," he crisply informed her, "and we find it completely unreasonable."

It was all Kate could do to keep from railing at him for his suspected association with Brad. In and of itself, there was nothing illegal about their relationship and, thus, nothing she could do. Even if Brad was willing to underwrite the entire sleazy mess with his own money, no one could stop him from doing that, either. With as much calm as she could project, Kate replied that it was in the best interests of all parties concerned to verify who her nephew's father was.

"My client," Graham informed her, "believes this is nothing more than a delaying tactic on your part and we intend to move forward as quickly as possible to reunite the boy with his father. Unless you have substantive evidence to the contrary, Ms. Toscano, I suggest that you hire an attorney rather than attempt to negotiate these waters on your own as an amateur."

She passed on seeing John after work, offering the truthful excuse that she hadn't gotten any sleep the night before. Even in her voice, though, he could tell that there was something more.

"The paternity test idea backfired," she revealed. "The lawyer called and said Luke refused."

John believed he was playing straight to character and wasn't that surprised. "What else did he say?"

"Besides telling me to get a lawyer?" Her tortured conscience was still fighting whether she should tell him about the connection to Brad. If she did, she feared John would go completely ballistic.

"Then if getting somebody's what we have to do," he matter of factly replied, "I'll start asking around." He switched over to the lighter subject of how Jimmy had done in school that day.

"He drew you a picture of a boat," she said, knowing the news would make John smile. "At least I think it's a picture of a boat. It kind of looks like a banana with a big wing and a bunch of triangles."

"Yeah," John agreed, "that sure sounds like a boat to me." In the next breath, he said he'd look around for a couple of magnets so he could put it on the refrigerator.

"Are you sure your mom won't mind?"

John laughed. "It's been ages since she's had refrigerator art. She'll love it."

He asked her what else was going on and whether she'd had a good day at the newspaper.

"A couple of story ideas cooking," she replied. "And Maria brought me a plant." She touched only briefly on her friend's latest flirtation. "You think she'll ever find the real thing?"

"Left to her own devices and with enough time," he replied, "I suspect she could find the real thing every twenty minutes."

Kate suppressed the start of a yawn. "I feel like a wuss to be crashing so early."

"Well, I'd say you should get your beauty rest but, frankly, I don't see how you could be any more beautiful than you already are."

"John,"

"Hmmm?"

"There's something I have to tell you but you have to promise me something first."

"That's a pretty tall order," he teased her. "What if it's to take you to an operator to learn to knit mittens?"

She told him it was more serious than that. "I need you to promise not to kill someone."

There was a long pause at his end of the line as he tried to discern whether she was joking with him.

"Kate, do you know why I didn't push staying on with the Police Department?"

"I thought it was because of your injuries," she replied.

"I could have fought that. Maybe even taken a desk job. Truth is, I was done with that life. I took two men's lives on the day I was shot. Maybe they deserved it. Maybe not. Who am I to judge. Either way, it didn't bring Jeremy back. I did enough killing, Kate. They even gave me a medal for it. Therefore, you have my solemn word that I'd never take a life unless it was the only way to save one."

Kate took a deep breath and confided her suspicions that Brad was behind Luke's appearance in Avalon Bay. "Mom told him more than she should have and I think he thinks it's some kind of twisted payback for the past."

John considered this for a moment. "Then we just have to make sure he doesn't win."

"And you're not going to rush out and kill him?"

"No," he assured her. "But only because a promise made is a promise kept. Sweet dreams, angel. Tomorrow's another day."

Chapter Forty

L ydia popped her head in to ask Kate if she wanted to watch the late-night show with her and have a glass of wine.

Kate declined, indicating the two boxes she had repacked, one with the items destined for charity and the other with things she couldn't bring herself to part with just yet. "I figure I won't have much time to get to this after—" She let the sentence go unfinished, not wanting to reference any further the impending dread of what the combined nasty forces of Luke and Brad might do to them in the coming days and weeks.

Lydia asked her if she needed any help with whatever was left.

"Just some personal correspondence." Kate shook her head. "I'm still wrestling with whether I feel comfortable going through any of it."

Her mother nodded thoughtfully. "If there are some addresses with them, though," she said, "maybe they don't know yet what happened. Your sister moved around so much."

Kate opined that Cassy's friends seemed to embrace the same wanderlust and that any contact info she came across might long since have become useless. "A couple of postcards from a girl named Rhonda were from three different states in five months," she said.

"Maybe she just traveled a lot," Lydia suggested.

"Not sure. She mostly talked about 'Renn fairs' so I'm guessing she probably went wherever the action was."

She noticed while they'd been talking that her mother's gaze had wandered to the small stack of greeting cards that had been separated from the rest.

"She kept every card you ever sent her," Kate quietly divulged, stopping short of adding that she knew some of them had contained checks and gift certificates.

To her surprise, it was her mother who now acknowledged the content. "I never stopped hoping she'd use the money to come home someday. Do you think she knew that?"

"I know she knew you still loved her, Mom. At the end of the day, though, she was always going to be Cassy and do whatever made her happy. Even if that definition included Luke or trying to raise a baby on her own."

"She could've come home as soon as she found out she was pregnant," Lydia interrupted. "A stable home may have helped him more."

"Jimmy had a loving mom. That was enough," Kate said, quietly amazed that in the relatively short space of time since they'd first come back to Avalon Bay Jimmy had gone from being called "the boy" to being a grandson that her mother would now do anything to ensure he wouldn't be taken away.

Lydia's eyes were moist as she asked again why Cassy had stayed away. "Avalon Bay was where she grew up. Everyone she knew was right here, right where she'd left it."

Kate's reply, spoken from the heart and her own experience, said it all. "Sometimes that's harder than being a stranger in a place where no one knows your name." In the glamorous world of Las Vegas that she'd left behind, she couldn't have named half a dozen tenants who shared her high-rise address if her life had depended on it. Though she had a small circle of friends, mostly associates from the magazine, she had largely moved with anonymity throughout her day. "When I came back here, well, you know what it's like. You can't sneeze without someone saying 'bless you' or buy a diet soda without someone asking if you're trying to lose weight. It's the best and worst of both worlds to have so many people scrutinizing everything you do, can you really blame her for wanting to live anywhere but here?"

Lydia wasn't entirely convinced but was willing to concede for the time being. She purposely changed the subject. "I'm going to close my account at Brad's bank tomorrow," she announced.

"Oh?"

"I'm also thinking of telling my friends Millie and Nora and a couple of other people about what a skunk he's been and before long he's going to be sitting there in an empty bank with nothing to show for it."

Kate laughed. "My mother, the activist."

"Well, don't you think it's a good idea?"

"I don't know that it'll set the banking on its end," Kate candidly replied, "but if enough of you get on board, I imagine it'll irritate him."

"And don't even get me started on what could happen with all the community boards he serves on. Word travels fast in this town."

"Yeah, tell me about it."

"Are you sure you don't want to watch TV with me and have some wine?"

"No on the TV, but you've twisted my arm on the vino."

The oldest letter in the batch was from a teacher Kate and Cassy had both had in high school. The ancient Miss Burris had praised the latter's good grades, congeniality, and enthusiasm and offered to write her a letter of recommendation to Monmouth University if it was on her list of college choices. Like an old wound that ached on a damp day, Kate was reminded of her sister's bright potential and how it had dimmed much too soon.

There was a letter from Rhonda that asked lots of questions about the baby and whether she'd be interested in some hand-me-downs from a girl she used to work the dunking booths with and then a full page about a cute new red-headed guy she'd met named Giant Gerry who swallowed fire and walked on nails. Kate made a mental note to do an Internet search and see if Giant Gerry was still doing the circuit. Rhonda, if she was still involved with him, might have advanced to email by now and would welcome a message, albeit an unhappy one.

There were thank you notes from friends lauding the cleverness of crafts projects Cassy had given them for their birthdays. One of them even went on at length about the karaoke tape she'd made and how much they thought she sounded just like Mariah Carey. *You never told me you sang. Or that you knew how to make scented candles. Or that you were learning to cook organic because it would be better for the baby. Or that your favorite ride was the carousel on the boardwalk.*

How could we have been sisters, Kate sadly reflected, *and there's so much I never knew about you?*

It was the last envelope, though, with a New York City postmark that now had her full attention. She glanced only briefly at the second page of the neatly handwritten letter and was startled to discover that it was from Jeremy.

Kate shifted uneasily, uncertain of how to proceed. It was one thing, she thought, to read correspondence to her sister from friends who were presumably still alive. The knowledge of Jeremy Neal's tragic fate weighed heavily on her and she felt a mix of apprehension and a faint though distant nervous anxiety that she was about to trespass where she shouldn't. She started to refold it. *I'll give it to John*, she decided. *It's something his family might want to have.*

As she started to slide it back into the envelope, she realized she was now shaking. It was the handwriting that brought it home the most, the fact that he'd sat down with pen and paper instead of at a keyboard. Notwithstanding that he might have typed exactly the same content, or even hit a SEND button, there was something so personal, so poignant about the very act that it brought a lump to her throat.

She drew a deep breath. If it was important enough for Cassy to save it among her treasures, she had to have known that one day it might be found and its contents read by a different set of eyes. If it was important enough for her to keep, Kate could do nothing less than read what her sister's best pal from high school had written.

Hey, C.

If my life were a movie, and how many times have I said that? I would have run after your bus this morning and yelled and waved my arms and the passengers on the bus would have said to the driver, "Hey, dude, slow down. There's a guy trying to catch the bus." And he would have stopped the bus and opened the door so I could get on but I would have told him to just wait a minute 'cuz there was something I had to do. And then I would have gotten down on one knee in the aisle and told you it's the craziest thing I've ever done but that I just had the greatest 3 days of my life and I wanted to have 3 million more just like it. What an early Christmas present!

Okay, I know you're rolling your eyes and thinking it's lame to read it in a letter but believe me it would have sounded way better in person. And the people on the bus would have been staring and waiting for you to say something and then you'd jump into my arms just like Forrest Gump and Jenny in the reflecting pool at the Lincoln Memorial and everyone would have cheered. Of course, they probably would have been more impressed, and maybe so would you, if I'd been in an Army uniform instead of an apron that said Bernstein's Bakery but you get the picture.

The Bernsteins really liked you, by the way. I wish I hadn't had to work Saturday morning 'cuz we could've seen more stuff but they said, actually it was just Mrs. Bernstein 'cuz her husband doesn't know yet, that if you wanted a part-time job, you'd be great behind the counter. I think so, too. Remember I said they've been married 43 years and they met in high school just like us? Mrs. Bernstein says she married her best friend.

Ackckckck! I should just tear this up 'cuz it's probably sounding stupid. Remember how Miss Burris used to say I rambled? Okay, let me get to the point. It was so much fun being with you and I thought it was cool that even my roommates who can be real cement heads figured out we needed some privacy and I've already heard that one of them is getting married and moving out so you'd even have a place to stay til we can get a place of our own somewhere. It won't be much at first but, okay, I'm rambling again because even as I write this, you're on a bus and everything I should have said while you were here in person you're now having to read in a letter.

You said you came back here to do some thinking about what's his name and now you say you're going back to L.A. to do some thinking about me. That sounds funny to me 'cuz we've known each other since forever and what's left to know? We use the same toothpaste, we both drink two percent milk, we both think clowns are creepy (their smiles are way scary) and we both think there's life beyond Avalon Bay (but try to tell that to my brother). I want us to be like the Bernsteins and finish each other's sentences and wake up together like we did on Sunday and go "Wow! The world's our oyster! Let's go crack it open and see what we find!"

I know you say you like this musician guy in San Francisco. And that he has good qualities but why does he make you cry so much? I also know you think maybe he's going to change and be somebody else but I don't agree. I don't agree because I know you deserve someone who makes you laugh and who puts you on a pedestal and who would go rent a big white horse (even though I'm terrified about falling off) and ride around and tell everybody in Central Park, "I love Cassy Toscano and I don't care who knows it!"

Okay. I've said everything I can think of. Maybe by the time I come back from putting this in a mailbox, there'll be a message on the machine and you'll say, "Hey, J. I'm in L.A. and I've changed my mind and I'm getting on another bus and can you come and meet me at the station?" And I will. I'd do anything you asked. I'll even pretend to be happy if you say that you and what's his name have worked everything out but deep down I'll always know you could have done better.

You've always been the one. I just wish I hadn't waited so long to let you know. I hope it's not too late. Let me know.

Love, Jeremy

Tears welled within Kate's eyes as she turned back to the first page.

The letter was dated December 23, the day before Jeremy was killed.

Chapter Forty-One

L ydia was watching a show about stupid pet tricks when Kate came into the room.

"Finished already?" Lydia asked.

Kate gravely nodded. "There's something I need you to read." She sat down on the couch next to her and handed her Jeremy's letter. "I think this changes everything."

A few minutes later, her mother's face was streaming with tears. "Oh my God," she murmured. "Oh my God."

The pieces that Kate had mentally been stitching together since she'd read the words herself were all making sense now, including Jimmy's birth date. "Remember when we wondered if his autism had something to do with his being born a few weeks early?" By Kate's calculations, Cassy had to have gotten pregnant the weekend she was visiting Jeremy in Manhattan.

"But if she knew it was Jeremy's, why didn't she just come home? Why get married and pass it off as Luke's?"

How much simpler things would have been if she'd chosen the first option, Kate thought. Then again, it wouldn't have been like her sister to demand anything in terms of support from the Neals if it was only her word that she was carrying their youngest son's child. Door Number 3, of course, was that maybe she'd been seduced by the fantasy of Luke's band hitting it big sometime and resulting in a more glamorous life than sharing a Soho apartment with Jeremy's roomies. For all Kate knew, Cassy might not even have known that Jeremy was killed that Christmas Eve.

"And if she did know," Kate said, "and found out she was pregnant, maybe she was just too scared to think about raising a baby by herself."

"Which she ended up doing anyway," Lydia pointed out. A faraway look suddenly passed over her face. "I just realized something."

"What's that?"

"All those years ago when I was wishing for my life to be different, I realize that if Sean hadn't gone back to Abby, she wouldn't have had Jeremy. And Jeremy wouldn't have given me my grandson."

Kate nodded. "He's given Sean and Abby a grandson, too, Mom. They just don't know it yet."

"You should call John."

"It's getting late."

"Yes, but if he's been losing as much sleep as the two of us worrying about Jimmy, he'll probably answer on the first ring."

"I don't know. This isn't the kind of thing you tell someone over the phone."

"Then tell him to come over. I'll put on a pot of coffee."

Half an hour later, two people were standing at the Toscano's front door.

"I hope you didn't mind," John said. "When I told Mom what it was about."

"There was no way I wanted to wait until morning," Abby declared as she stepped into the entry.

A Seaside Story

Kate tensed a moment as her mother stepped out to meet the woman she had once deemed her rival. Whatever anxiety she might have had quickly dissipated, however, when Abby warmly greeted Lydia like a long lost friend. *Either she never knew*, Kate realized, or *she's a class act who would never let on.*

"I've got some coffee in the kitchen for us," Lydia said.

John slipped an arm around Kate's waist as they followed a short distance behind their mothers. "Are you okay?"

"A little shaken," she confessed, "but I'm much better now that you're here." She hadn't wanted to tell him on the phone but the words had spilled out before she could stop them. "It's funny how I've been thinking how cute they always looked together in high school and wondering why she always used to chase after the guys who were all trauma and drama."

"Maybe she just didn't want to lose her best friend by going out with him."

"Maybe not."

A few moments later, Abby began to read her late son's letter, John standing behind her and leaning in to follow along. Their reaction was not unlike Kate and Lydia's and, through tears of her own, Abby gently inquired whether it would be all right with them if she were allowed to keep it.

"Absolutely," Lydia insisted, reaching across the kitchen table to squeeze her hand. "It's yours."

"Although you'll probably need to borrow it back to show the attorney," John remarked. "As you've said, this changes everything."

Abby quickly added that whatever else they'd need she'd be happy to supply it. "I have a lock of his hair from when he was three," she said. "Can they get DNA from that, do you think?"

"It may not even come to that," John opined, filling his mother in on what they'd found out about the connection between Luke's attorney and Brad.

At the mention of the latter's name, Abby scowled. "That Leister boy was always such a troublemaker." She turned to ask Lydia if she remembered Brad's father. "You can see where he gets it from."

"I'm going to close my account at his bank," Lydia said.

C.J. Foster

Kate and John exchanged a glance of amusement that they were chattering away with a familiarity befitting old friends.

Abby asked Lydia if she could look in on Jimmy while she was there.

"I suppose as long as we're quiet so we don't wake him."

"He's such a little sweetheart," Abby continued as they got up from the table. She shared the story of Sean calling him "Germy" and wistfully speculated aloud whether her husband had somehow sensed something before any of the rest of them. "I think they're going to be very good for each other," she said. "Oh, and we're going to want to help out with anything Jimmy's going to need like school or medications or toys." She confided that they had put the money from the life insurance after Jeremy's death into investments. "Since we could never talk John into using it to go back to college, it should be doing pretty nicely by now."

Kate and John followed them up the stairs but paused on the landing. "Four's a crowd," he said. "That'd wake him up for sure."

They sat down on the steps, knowing their mothers would probably be a while. John asked her again how she was doing.

"Sunday night," she replied, "I felt like everything was falling apart and there was nothing I could do to keep any of it together." She smiled. "And now it's like Cassy's keeping that letter so I could find it all this time later is, I don't know, I just can't imagine it any more perfect than right now."

"I can."

She looked at him in confusion as he reached into his pants pocket. "To take a page from Jeremy, 'you've always been the one'. And you always will be." He held up the ring that in the light of the staircase and the magic of the moment was now the most perfect ring in the world because it was going to be on Kate Toscano's finger. "Would you do me the honor of becoming my wife?"

The joy of surprise bubbled in her laugh and shone in her eyes as she threw both arms around his neck. "Why John Neal, I thought you'd never ask!"

About the Author

C.J. Foster enlisted in the military after graduating high school. After several tours of duty, C.J. went to medical school and became a physician. Returning to the military, C.J. spent the next few decades stationed throughout the world, including serving in both Iraq and Afghanistan, learning foreign languages and experiencing different cultures through medical engagements on multiple continents.

A Seaside Story is his second novel.

More From Foundations Book Publishing

Dempsey's Grill
By Bryan J. Fagan

Gibson Baker had it all. A beautiful house in Seattle, a beautiful girlfriend and a steady teaching job.

But when Gibson's loses his job and his girl on the same day, he's forced to crawl home to Eugene, Oregon.

Dempsey's dreams are always that – dreams. But what starts out as a wild dream, a desperate plan and a dare, soon takes on a life of its own.

Can Dempsey and his friends pull together and grow beyond their previous failures, or will they give up their dreams to do the safe and responsible thing?

One More Sunset
By Jolyse Barnett

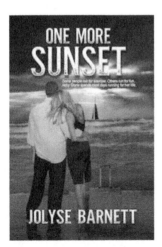

When Abby Stone's politically connected ex shows up at her new hideout and she uses a wine bottle in self-defense, she has nowhere left to turn. Miraculously, a magic suitcase appears, propelling her into an unsettling game involving a sexy, kind stranger while she stays one breath ahead of her stalker.